W0010544

Made in the USA
Middletown, DE
05 December 2023

44760285R00234

ALSO BY JEREMY WALDRON

CHAPTER ONE

HE SWIVELED HIS CHAIR AND MOVED TO THE SIDE, bringing his attention to the second set of computer monitors he had sorting through a difficult set of data. There were four monitors in total and all were operating at max memory capacity. Everything was moving faster than expected—including his fingers racing over the keyboard. He hadn't planned to work at light speed, but he welcomed the challenge as if the universe was testing his resolve, asking him to prove he was worthy of going through with his master plan.

As Loxley worked, he listened to the buzz and clicks gathering speed from his hard drives, remaining confident that he had assembled a machine capable of handling his request. He was impressed, patted himself on the back for creating something as dangerous and powerful as what sat before him. It was a marvelous masterpiece, one that was designed to kill.

Without thought, he reached for his cold drink and sipped from the narrow can of Red Bull. The explosion of taste straightened his spine, opened his veins. His fingers tapped with greater intent as they moved across the keyboard in a steady drum before coming to an abrupt stop.

In that split second of pause, everything went quiet and still and so did the machine as he exhaled a built-up breath of relief.

Sweeping his gaze to the left, he watched the data compile on one of the four monitors. His knee bounced with uncontrolled anxiety as he stared without blinking, hoping it all would come together like the greatest of puzzles he loved working on as a kid. He had the skills—he knew it better than anybody that he could do this—but the jitters of nerves bounced in his stomach as a part of him still couldn't believe he was actually going through with his idea.

He felt the vibration in the floor through the soles of his slippers before hearing the loud rumble from a passing motorcycle that ripped along the street between the buildings outside his window in downtown Denver.

Unflinching, he kept his focus on the task at hand. The curtains were drawn and the only light inside the little rectangular office no bigger than the size of a backyard shed came from his LED monitors which he had dimmed because it was easier on his eyes. He continued to stare at one of the monitors and couldn't stop drumming his fingers on this knee as he waited for his request to gain access into the home security system. It would either be accepted or denied.

A fan in the back kicked on the AC and soon the cool air blew across the back of his neck. He wiped the pellets of sweat from his brow and continued monitoring the data his computers were feeding him, waiting for the portal to open and welcome him inside.

His cat jumped into his lap, nudging, prodding, and purring when the red light suddenly flicked to green. A slow grin spread across his face as he cast his sparkling gaze to his cat and said, "Some things are just meant to be, Little John."

Little John flicked his tail and purred louder.

The upper right computer monitor's black screen flicked

to life and, with it, brought a clear picture into the private life of Richard Thompson. There was no easier way to break inside somebody's house than to do it remotely—watching them without them ever knowing. The ease and transparency of modern society was both a blessing and a curse, Loxley thought as he watched his subject move between frames.

Richard Thompson was alone, being watched through the lenses of his own security cameras. He worked behind the computer inside his private study, just as Loxley wanted. For the past six weeks Loxley had had his eye on Richard. He'd learned Richard's routine, familiarized himself with Richard's life patterns, and even got to know Richard's community as Loxley remotely traveled along with him wherever Richard took him. Loxley knew everything there was to know about Richard, including the secrets that he didn't want anyone else to know about.

Loxley grinned and pulled his headset over his ears and dropped the attached microphone in front of his mouth. It was just after 6PM on a Saturday in May and he had less than an hour to complete his task before Richard's wife would arrive home.

Rolling his chair closer to his desk, he nudged Little John off his lap and got to work. First, he checked that he had full access to Richard's house, including his appliances, and once he was confident he did, he worked his way into the telephone line, taking over full control of it as well. This wasn't Loxley's first time gaining access to Richard's house, but each time was different and with it came unexpected leaps that Loxley had to work through. The difference tonight was Loxley knowing that this would be his last time breaking through Richard's security system.

Richard was still in his study when Loxley called the house.

"Hello?" Richard answered after the second ring.

Loxley didn't respond, only stared at his monitor watching his victim finally give in and hang up, assuming it was a wrong number. Loxley smiled as he thought about how helpless Richard was—how he didn't even see death staring him in the eyes. The irony brought a chuckle to Loxley's lips as he amused himself by locking Richard inside his house in case he tried to run.

Little John jumped on his desk and Loxley turned to him and said, "Now, the rabbit in the hat trick. How to trip the fireplace without having it ignite. Think I can do it, LJ?"

Little John flicked his tail and lifted his head higher.

"I knew you would believe in me, little buddy." Loxley patted his cat's head.

With the poisonous gas spilling into the house, it didn't take long for the smart home system to pick up the dangers already taking effect on Mr. Thompson. Loxley could see the data coming through on his monitors as he kept a watchful eye on Richard who was across the hall blinking through the first of his symptoms.

As the numbers rose, Loxley finally decided to send the alarm and make the call.

The house phone rang and Loxley watched Richard react to the alarm going off in the hall. The line continued ringing as Richard hurried into the kitchen to retrieve the phone off the wall. "Hello."

"Mr. Thompson, this is Rocky Mountain Home Securities," Loxley said. "I'm calling to tell you that we've detected high levels of carbon monoxide in the living room and hall area. Are you in the house now?"

"Yes. I just heard the alarm."

Loxley smiled at the sound of panic cracking Richard's voice. Maintaining an even tone, Loxley continued, "I'm going to ask you to evacuate the premises immediately. The fire department is on their way."

Richard rubbed his brow, stumbled a little as he hurried to the front door. He pulled and tugged at the handle but the door didn't budge. He tried to twist the dead bolt free but it kept springing back in place. "What the—"

"Everything all right, sir?" The corners of Loxley's eyes crinkled with amusement as he watched his victim sprint to the back door. Again, he couldn't open it. Loxley bit his knuckle to stifle the laugh he felt bubbling up inside of him. A tent pitched in his pants and he felt the swell of arousal throb hard and steady as the first signs of climax showed.

"I can't seem to open my doors." Richard's voice raised higher.

Loxley leaned closer to the computer screen and looked his victim directly in his eyes, saying, "That's right, Richard Thompson. I've locked you inside and now you will die for the crimes you've committed against the many innocent and unassuming victims of your fraudulent past."

Loxley leaned back, smiling, as he listened to Richard scream into the air and beg for mercy.

CHAPTER TWO

I was with the girls, and my teenage son Mason, kicking off summer with our first backyard barbeque of the season. Mason and Allison were shooting hoops in the back near the garage while I manned the grill and listened to Erin tell us the funniest story I had heard in quite a while.

"It was the first time with this doctor," Erin paused to give us all a look, "who happened to be a male but I thought was a woman."

"Kind of like how everyone thinks Sam is a man?" I said.

"Right, but his name was Cortney."

"Who names their boy Cortney?" Susan turned her head and looked to Heather. "Don't they know they're just setting their child up for a lifetime of troubles?"

When Susan looked to my sister, Heather said, "Don't ask me, I don't have any kids."

I laughed and sipped from my beer. I loved nights like this where it was just us girls with no outside pressure to act a certain way. May had brought seasonally warm temperatures, flowers, and plenty of sunshine to keep us happy. Here, in my backyard, we could let our hair down and not act all tough when fighting our way through a man's world that seemed determined to keep us feeding at the bottom.

"Anyway," Erin continued, "once I learned Cortney wasn't a woman but a man—and a rather attractive one at that—I went from confident to nervous and uncomfortable in a second flat."

"No kidding. I would have just walked right on out of there," I said laughing.

"Wish I did." Erin nodded. "Instead, I put my feet up in the stirrups and did the most foolish thing ever—I started a conversation with him." Erin slapped a palm against her forehead and shook her head, her cheeks reddening with absolute embarrassment.

"What did you say?" I asked.

"More importantly, why?" Susan couldn't stop laughing. "Was it because he was that attractive?"

"I don't know. I was nervous. But this is what I said." Erin looked me directly in the eye. "So, do you enjoy your job?"

Heather spit out her beer in a fanning spray that coated the backyard privacy fence as we all burst out laughing.

Erin's face was as red as a tomato. "The nurse even couldn't contain her chuckles. I sounded like such a perv!"

"What did he say?" I asked as I listened with one ear as Susan mocked Erin with my sister before her cell phone rang and she took the call inside. "Please tell me you got his number."

"I don't think I can ever go back there again." Erin fell into her chair and wrapped her lips around the beer bottle, draining it until it was empty.

"Dr. Cortney won't forget you, I can assure you that." I laughed, turned to face the grill, and flipped the burgers and portabella mushrooms over. They sizzled and smelled delicious.

"Sam," Erin snuck up behind me and was now whispering in my ear, "have you told Susan about your reporting?"

I stared at the grill, thinking about my story being printed in tomorrow's paper. I'd spent the last six weeks investigating a wealthy business owner who was using his charity foundation as his own piggy bank. The story was certainly going to bring legal troubles to the owner, but that was the least of my worries. Just yesterday I'd received an email that had me doubting everything—including my own safety.

The email came through our website *www.RealCrimeNews.com* and I was certain the subject of my story sent it. I'd thought about it all last night and it still put a chill up my spine.

Be warned, Dearest Bell, you're barking up the wrong tree. If you publish even just a piece of the fabricated story you're investigating, there will be hell to pay.

Someone knew about my highly secretive investigation and I still hadn't figured out who—or how—but this inquiry wasn't an anomaly. I had others I was investigating and now that my secret wasn't so secret anymore, I didn't know how far word had spread.

"When, Sam?" Erin's words were back in my ear. "You know she won't like it if she reads about it first."

"I know," I said, watching Susan step back outside, wondering how I could possibly break the news to her. Something was wrong, I could see it by the way she was hugging herself. She was crying. "What happened?" I asked.

Susan's eyes found their way to me. "A client of mine is dead."

We moved to Susan and took her hands into our own. "Who?"

Her teary eyes landed on mine. "Richard Thompson." *The subject of my investigation.*

CHAPTER THREE

WITH THE LAST OF THE CHARCOAL DYING OUT, I CALLED my editor at the *Colorado Times*, Ryan Dawson. News of Richard Thompson's death may have hit me harder than Susan. The difference between us was simple. I knew the truth of the man he was, including the assumed threat he had sent me. Where Susan allowed her emotions to spill out of her, I was simply shocked into paralysis, wedged between a rock and a hard place thanks to my story I couldn't seem to tell to one of my best friends.

"Sam," Dawson answered his cell phone, "this better be important. Ethan has a game and I don't want to miss it."

I could hear parents screaming and cheering, children calling out in the background against the pinging sounds of metal bats striking baseballs. "This won't take long," I said, "but I just heard Richard Thompson is dead."

The background noises continued but he didn't respond. Then I heard the crackling of what I assumed to be Dawson's facial stubble scratch over the microphone. He lowered his voice and asked how I knew and I told him. I didn't have to vouch for Susan, Dawson knew her to be a credible source.

"Jesus, Sam, do you know how it happened?"

Dawson was one of only three other people who knew what I was working and it was clear by the sound of his voice he couldn't believe the timing of Thompson's death either.

"I don't," I said, "but I would like to be the one to report on his death."

Again, Dawson paused before giving his response. Erin was glaring at me and now I wished I would have told Susan my secret sooner. I felt the blood drain from my face as if somehow it was my fault Richard Thompson died.

"Mom, you want the last bratwurst?" Mason called out to me.

"No. You finish it." I smiled and put on my best poker face to hide the truth from my son before he figured it out himself. Then I turned and faced the house. "So, is that asking too much?" I asked Dawson.

"Garcia should be the one to do it," Dawson said. Joey Garcia was the business correspondent, and under any other circumstances it would make sense. My colleague had covered Thompson's businesses for years, but even Garcia didn't know what I'd uncovered.

"You want me to call him, or will you?"

"I'll give him a buzz," Dawson said. "In the meantime, I'm still waiting on the final version to Thompson's story, which, Sam, I still have planned to go to print tonight."

My eyebrows pinched. "It's there. I dropped it in our shared folder this afternoon."

"I checked before I left the house an hour ago, Sam. It wasn't there."

I knew I had put it in there, but I hurried inside the house regardless, with the intention of making deadline. "Give me a minute," I said, lifting the lid to my laptop computer.

"Sam, thanks again for the barbeque," Allison whispered

as she and Susan gathered their things and headed home for the night.

I covered the microphone on the phone and turned my attention to my friends. "Thanks for coming, and I'm really sorry about your loss," I said to Susan. She nodded and gave me a weak smile. "I'll call you tomorrow."

As soon as they left, I navigated to the *Times* cloud and found my shared folder with Dawson. I felt my breath hitch when seeing he was right. It wasn't there. The file I'd dropped in earlier was gone. Could it be I was simply thinking I'd done something that I hadn't? It didn't matter. I copied the final draft from my external hard drive and dropped it in Dawson's folder.

"There, it's coming through the cloud now."

"Sam, I know you worked hard on this story, but if don't want to publish this story now that—"

"Dawson, don't be ridiculous," I cut him off before he could finish. Like he said before, Thompson's death changed nothing.

"All I'm saying is that it's your call. We can find other stories to fill the gap in the meantime."

It was a nice offer, and it was clear he had given it some thought, but this story was finished and I knew it needed to be told. Now was the time. "Thanks, but I've already made my decision."

"Think on it, Sam. Once it's out, there is no turning back and this one has the potential to explode."

I lifted my gaze and stared straight ahead at nothing in particular. Dawson was right. This story was big, and had already put one threat on my life. Maybe it would serve me well if I hit pause and waited for things to cool down.

"But I need a decision soon," he said.

"Give me until 10 and I'll have my answer."

CHAPTER FOUR

DONNY COUNTS STOOD TALL AND PROUD, TAKING A WIDE confident stance as he listened to the auditorium burst into a round of applause like he had never heard before. He stared out into the crowd of thousands, smiling beneath the stage lights thinking how they'd all come to hear his story.

The *whoops!* came from above and echoed off the walls, mixing with the variety of cheers before everyone started chanting his name, *Counts! Counts! Counts!*

For Donny, this was what it was all about. He swiveled his neck from side to side, taking it all in while asking himself how he could ever top this performance.

He enjoyed his time on stage at the Denver University campus, particularly liked engaging with the crowd and getting them to laugh as he shared his rags to riches journey that began with a simple dream.

But, for Donny, this was the dream.

The vision to be filthy rich—to be seen, to be heard, and have young gorgeous women eyeing him like candy wherever he went. Including the beautiful slender blonde with glimmering blue eyes staring at him from the front row.

Donny locked eyes, smiled, and held her stare as he pretended to undress her with his eyes. It wasn't hard to imagine how she would feel as he raked his fingertips across her soft, porcelain skin, her firm breasts inside his palm.

The vibration from the crowd filled his chest with a sense of invisibility that only money and fame could buy. Finally, after a brief escape into his daydream, he angled his body and bowed to his fans, blowing kisses to the top rows who continued screaming his name. Donny moved smoothly across the stage, waving his hand through the air.

In just twelve short months, his net worth sky-rocketed to numbers beyond his wildest dreams. Now, his name was synonymous with overnight success and Donny Counts seemed to be everywhere. On the TV, in the radio, across the internet, and on people's phones as they used his exchange in pursuit of their own quick riches. It was all part of his strategy to use the media to sell his image, to give him a brand he otherwise wouldn't have.

And it worked like magic.

Not bad for a skinny little kid from the suburbs of Phoenix, Arizona who once was picked on by the high school jocks, he thought as he turned back to the blonde who was still staring in his direction. *God, she was gorgeous.*

"Donny Counts, everyone!" The MC shook Donny's hand.

"It's been a pleasure," Donny said into the mic, watching a dark silhouette move between the aisle and perch himself against the wall near the front. "And remember, if you want to be rich like me, the time to invest in cryptocurrency is now. Thank you."

Everyone in the crowd cheered but one. The lone, dark figure against the wall remained stone-faced and bitter looking. Never once taking his eyes off the keynote speaker, he had the look of someone who knew the truth about

Donny. And it was a secret Donny couldn't afford to have let out.

CHAPTER FIVE

A HALF-HOUR LATER, ERIN AND I ARRIVED AT RICHARD Thompson's six thousand square foot mansion on the south side of Denver. I turned my wheels to the curb and pulled the emergency break. Casting my gaze to the front of the house, I kept thinking how much energy I had spent on this man. The sleepless nights, the runaround that came with fact checking different sources, and the gathering of evidence to know that what I was uncovering went beyond just rumor. Yet, even in death, I had nothing positive to say about him. Not with what I'd learned and what he'd done to con people into giving him their hard earned money under the disguise of a charitable donation.

Bile rose in my throat the more I thought about what Richard Thompson did.

Erin rolled her neck and looked me straight in the eye. "You're the best reporter I know, Sam. The story you wrote about him," she flung her hitchhikers thumb toward Thompson's front door, "was accurate, and just because he died doesn't change what he did."

I smiled, reached for her hand, and squeezed it. I knew

the truth, but that didn't erase the fact that someone—maybe him—threatened to release hell if I went through with putting the story to print. "Let's see if we can't get any answers to what happened."

Together we stepped out of the car and made our way across the green grass, joining the growing crowd of media and spectators there to watch the show. There was a warm evening breeze that kicked up every so often and the fading baby blue skies above did nothing to keep me from feeling creeped out by the strange timing of his death.

"Hey Samantha." Nancy Jordan, a TV news reporter with a local Denver affiliate, was there. I wasn't surprised. Nancy was always looking for an edge to separate herself from the pack. We'd worked together in the past, but I wouldn't say we were friends.

"What did I miss?" I asked her.

"Nothing. Pretty uneventful as they're not letting anyone unauthorized through." Nancy glanced over her shoulder and looked to the road. I knew she was seeing if my boyfriend, detective Alex King, was here with hopes of me passing on the inside scoop. "What about you? Have any insight to what might have happened?" she asked, naturally assuming I'd share whatever secrets I knew myself.

I shook my head no and took in my surroundings, looking through the faces of bystanders and noting anything out of the ordinary or suspicious, which was nothing. It was clear Garcia wasn't here, though I expected to see him soon if he was going to tell this story instead of me. Then again, Garcia probably already knew enough about his subject to skip the party without sacrificing accuracy, so maybe he would sit this one out.

Staying in the thin patch of grass, I moved past Nancy to work another angle. She called after me, "Let me know if you learn anything."

I tossed a hand in the air to acknowledge her without turning to look or promise anything.

"She's only here because Thompson was rich," Erin said, keeping stride with me.

"The coroner is inside," I said, not wanting to get distracted by Nancy's—and every other reporter who was here for the wrong reasons—questionable ethics, "but I don't see King's sedan anywhere."

Erin looked around. "That's a good sign."

I nodded. "Means Thompson's death was probably an accident."

When I turned my gaze near the firetruck parked horizontal to the driveway, I caught Matt Bales, a new recruit with the Denver Fire Department, staring at Erin's backside. It was obvious Matt had a thing for tall blondes, or maybe just Erin, and even from across the way I could see a hint of loneliness in his eyes that made me call him over.

I waved my hands in the air and managed to get his attention.

Matt was surprised to see me, but flashed a friendly smile and didn't hesitate to meet up with us.

"Hey Matt." I smiled. "Samantha Bell with the *Colorado Times*."

"Yeah, I remember," he said as we both recalled our first encounter. It was two weeks ago when I introduced myself to him for the first time. I had traveled with Dawson to the firehouse for the inauguration of the new tanker truck. It was a lovely afternoon and a nice break from my Thompson story, and now I was glad to see my connections coming to fruition.

"What brings you here this evening?" Matt asked as he kept glancing in Erin's direction.

I pointed to the house. "I heard Richard Thompson died."

Matt rubbed the back of his neck and stared at the house.

He lost that smile he'd carried with him on his way over to us. Though I hated doing it, I had to use his weakness for blondes against him.

"This is my friend, Erin."

The spark was back in his eyes when he shook Erin's hand. "Nice to meet you."

"Pleasure." Erin smiled with an extra layer of charm. "Was it a fire that killed him?" Erin was onto my game and already in character.

"Carbon monoxide," Matt said between easy breaths.

Good work, Erin, I said to myself. "Anybody inside the house besides the owner?"

Matt rolled his gaze over to me. "Just him."

"Strange he didn't get out of the house," Erin said. "Was he sleeping at the time of death?"

"Unless he slept in shined shoes and a neck tie, I'd say no." Matt shifted his weight to his opposite leg. "Victim was found unconscious near the back door."

"Was the door locked when you found him?"

"That, I can't say for sure." Matt turned his head and locked eyes with me. "However, the house was outfitted with detectors. Nice new smart home technology. Stuff I couldn't afford but wish I could."

I inhaled a deep breath through my nostrils as I turned my attention back to the house, thinking it strange Thompson didn't just open the door and leave. "He must have had symptoms before he died?"

Matt shrugged. "Hard to say. I'm only telling you what I know, and even that is already probably more than I should be saying."

Erin reached out and put a hand on his muscular shoulder. "Your secret is safe with us."

Matt smiled. I thanked him and told him it was good to

see him again. "Yeah, you too, Samantha," he said as he turned and winked at Erin.

"What are you thinking?" I asked my partner.

"I'm thinking why you didn't introduce me to fireman Matt sooner."

I quirked a single eyebrow.

"He's hot."

"Pun intended?"

Erin chuckled. "Seriously, it seems like Thompson should have had more than enough warning to escape before succumbing to carbon monoxide poisoning."

I thought the same. What Matt told me didn't sit well with me. I knew I needed to get inside the house and draw my own conclusion to why the man whose crimes of fraud I was only hours away from exposing had suddenly been found dead.

CHAPTER SIX

LOXLEY PARKED HIS TOYOTA 4RUNNER A BLOCK FROM where the emergency vehicles and coroner's van remained stationed outside Richard Thompson's residence. He rolled down his window before turning off the engine. Resting his arm on the sill, he breathed in the sweet cool flirtation with summer that opened up his lungs with rejuvenation.

Spring at a mile high, he thought as a smile tugged at his lips.

It was the season of rebirth and high spirits, but also the time when people were waking from their winter slumber. And everyone seemed to have come out tonight to enjoy the show.

Casually watching from afar, Loxley took his time before deciding to show his face. He stared at the media vans, scowling at society's infatuation with people of great wealth. Jealously took hold and Loxley yearned to gain their attention as he stared at the backs of their heads. Was that why he came out tonight? Why he risked getting caught? To seek the attention and notoriety from a TV reporter? He might be desperate for attention but he was no fool. However, the idea of sharing his excitement with those same boring news junky souls waiting to hear what happened to poor Richard Thompson certainly appealed to him.

Loxley stroked his chin, thinking again why he was here if not to begin his game of cat and mouse. Perhaps it was the rush to see what he could get away with, or the hunt when looking for more thrills and spills that made him feel alive. But, above all else, perhaps it was the intense magnetic pull to get closer to his first kill, needing to see it with his own eyes as if seeing it in person instead of through a pixelated computer screen would make it seem more real.

Loxley rubbed his limp crotch, wanting to feel the excitement from before. It was long gone and, with the way he was feeling know, he doubted he'd ever feel that great sense of release ever again.

The light was fading into a dark curtain of disguise and the soft murmurs traveling from the bystanders only had him more curious to hear what was being said. Finally, he opened his door, stepped out, and shut it before making his way down the path and joining the group of civilians by taking a spot in the back.

No one paid attention to him, even with Loxley standing a head taller than most. Everyone remained focused on the front door hoping to get a glimpse of a dead body—including the reporters and news cameras whose attention he desperately craved.

Questions of why and how and who swirled around him as gossip about Richard Thompson and his sometimes questionable character began to take root. There was a lack of urgency that only Loxley could truly appreciate. This wasn't a crime scene, only an unfortunate accident that could have happened to any one of these people. His plan had worked and, suddenly, Loxley felt invisible, like he could do and get away with anything, including giving these people the greatest gift of all—erasing the greed and cleansing the earth of the one person who stole without remorse.

He wondered if they knew how lucky they were to have him. Probably not. Then everything suddenly became clearer when Loxley spotted his favorite journalist only twenty-five yards from where he stood.

She was standing with her thumbs hooked in her jeans pockets. Her hair was pulled back into a ponytail and her t-shirt bunched around her waist showing off a perfect backside. Blood rushed down his spine and suddenly the feeling of power and masculinity was back.

This, Loxley thought, was why he came out tonight.

It was because of her.

To see Samantha Bell.

For if it weren't for her, he would have never even considered killing poor Richard Thompson.

CHAPTER SEVEN

COOPER, MY YELLOW LAB, WAS SNUGGLED UP AGAINST ME on the couch as I nursed a glass of red wine. Mason was at a late movie with his friend, Nolan, taking advantage of not having to work tonight, and the house was quiet as I was still mulling over my options of taking Dawson's advice and delaying the release of my story, or just run it as planned.

I was hoping my visit to Thompson's residence would have given me the answer I sought. Instead, I was beginning to think that Dawson might be right. He messaged me a couple of times and I kept responding that I needed more time to make my decision. He was losing patience and I couldn't blame him. We were coming down to the wire. I needed to make a decision soon.

Erin and I left the scene after seeing Richard Thompson's body get wheeled out and loaded up into the coroner wagon. We left without any further insight to what happened. Matt Bales gave us a good picture of what they found, but I still wanted to see it for myself and learn how and where the gas leak occurred.

I pulled another sip of wine from my glass and found

myself staring at my own windows. Then I rolled my eyes to the front door, asking myself what would prevent me from leaving the house if finding myself in a similar position as the one Thompson found himself in tonight.

I had a dozen different ways of how I might not get out, but my house was much smaller, with dated locks and latches than what I assumed his sprawling mansion had and I just didn't see it ever happening to me.

Dropping my heels to the floor, I set my wine glass on the coffee table and moved through the house, checking my own smoke and CO detectors to make sure the batteries weren't dead. It had been nearly a year since I even thought of checking them. They all beeped loud and were in prime condition—just like what Matt said Thompson had himself.

Thompson's detectors must have gone off, I thought as I joined Cooper back on the couch. Smart home systems also came with outside support networks that called and relayed information directly to the client's cell phone. So what happened and where did the line of defense fail? I scratched Cooper's ears as the thoughts tumbled over, bouncing around inside my head until I heard a soft knock on my front door.

Cooper's wagging tail told me who it was. A second later, King stepped inside and I padded lightly across the floor, meeting him by the door, and greeted him with a kiss. His lips were firm and soft and had a cool minty taste that tingled my tongue.

King's fingers tightened their grip on my hips as he released a deep, guttural groan.

Hanging onto his neck, I dropped my heels to the floor and met his gaze. He looked like he'd had a day. "I opened a bottle of wine, would you like a glass?" I asked.

He said, "I'd love one."

I disappeared into the kitchen—feeling his gaze linger the entire way—and collected a glass from the cabinet, deciding to bring the bottle out to the couch with me. King was already leaned back with his arms spread across the back. His feet were stretched out in front of him and crossed on top of the coffee table.

King sipped his wine, and when he set it next to mine on the table I crawled up his body and planted another sensual kiss on him. He held me in his arms, stroked my back, and played with my hair as I asked him about his day.

"There was another gang-related murder in Five Points," he whispered into the ceiling.

With the warmer weather always came more shootings and crimes. King told me more about his work and, after a brief moment of silence, I asked, "Did you hear about Richard Thompson?"

King had heard bits and pieces as the news developed. "What's it mean for your story?"

I thought about how Thompson's death should have lifted the weight I'd been carrying for so long, but instead, it only seemed to add a couple more pounds. "Dawson's having me decide if we should delay running it or just get it out as planned."

"And what did you decide?" King's deep voice cracked with exhaustion.

"I haven't," I said, wanting to discuss the many questions I couldn't make sense of.

King listened as I shared both my concerns and theories. Then he said, "All I know is that everyone was saying it was carbon monoxide that killed him."

I rolled off his hard chest and reached for my wine glass. Hearing the cause of death again didn't sit well with me. It was too easy—too convenient. King must have felt the tension between my shoulders because it didn't take him long to ask what was eating me up. "I don't know. I guess it's just the timing of it all."

King's touch was soft as he tucked a thick strand of hair behind my ear. "Does Thompson being dead change what he did? Absolve him of his sins?"

I held his gaze and quickly got lost in it. "Not at all."

"Then do right by his victims and publish the story."

CHAPTER EIGHT

LOXLEY SAT NEAR THE WINDOW WITH ONE LEG CROSSED over the other, feeling the morning sunshine warm his back. He was well rested, somewhat surprised by how well he had slept considering the big day he had yesterday. There was no night terror or regret making him doubt his decision to kill Richard Thompson. His mind was only filled with rainbows and butterflies, both of which were mixed with plenty of warm sunshine. It was perfect—he was perfect—and it could only get better from here.

His foot swung like a cradle as he sipped his cappuccino and scrolled through his iPhone. Loxley stopped on his cryptocurrency exchange app, opened it up, and paused when seeing today's valuation of CountsCoins.

"Unbelievable," he whispered. "And certainly too good to be true."

Loxley kept reading, scrolling up and down, navigating to the history of CountsCoins' rise to fame. The digital currency was performing extremely well, considering less than a year ago it was floating in obscurity. But now, thanks in part to a well-orchestrated social media campaign endorsing the digital coins as the next big thing, CountsCoins ranked in the top 20 of all digital currencies currently being traded on the open digital exchange market.

Loxley swept his gaze to the left and stared out the window, lost in thought.

After making a brief appearance to listen to the founder of CountsCoins, Donny Counts, speak yesterday, Loxley spent his night learning more about the man who seemed to have it all. He had lots to catch up on, but, like Thompson, Loxley had begun his research on his subject far in advance to showing his face yesterday at Denver University.

Donny was the driving force behind the exchange's quick rise. Mixed with the fear of missing out and the current cryptocurrency bull market, everyone was suddenly interested in blockchain technologies with hopes of striking it rich. Donny recognized the opportunity early and knew it was the perfect time to orchestrate the con of a lifetime.

Loxley turned his gaze to his phone and stared at the data, feeling the surge of fire ignite inside of him. It was the same feeling he had when he decided Thompson needed to go, and this was no different. The same fire in his belly perked him up and made him anxious to figure out his next plan of attack. Loxley was confident in his assumption that Donny Counts was taking his investors for a ride, and Loxley needed to do something about it before more unassuming victims' life savings were stolen for the benefit of Donny's insatiable greed.

Without giving himself away, he closed out his phone and rolled his gaze lazily across the room, suddenly finding himself staring at today's front page headlines.

A charitable hero who died too early, were the words that caught Loxley's attention below the headline, *Investor and Philanthropist, Richard Thompson, Dead at 62.*

Even from across the café, Loxley could read the deceit of

the man he knew Richard Thompson to be. The only good coming from the article was that they were still calling his death accidental.

Feeling betrayed by the *Colorado Times* and the reporters who worked at the failing paper, a mixed bag of emotions filled Loxley's insides with disgust. He'd have to figure a way to control the narrative of his next victim, he thought as the woman reading the headline news turned the page.

Loxley picked up his head and he felt the corners of his lips curl as the *Times* redeemed itself—or rather, Samantha Bell did. Her story called Thompson what he was— a fraud, a grifter who stole for personal gain—and nothing made Loxley happier than to know that he and Samantha Bell shared the same understanding. He knew she was the one, and together they could do great things.

"Samantha, my dear, I knew you would come through," he said to himself, smiling at the thought of getting away with murder. He wrapped his lips around the rim of his coffee mug and felt his sense of purpose only grow larger.

Loxley never thought it could be this easy—or this enjoyable—to sit freely amongst his peers, the same people he took up arms for and swore to protect, without them suspecting he was their Batman vigilante protecting them from the rise of evil that surrounded them all.

With Thompson out of the picture, he wondered if Samantha also knew about the crimes Donny Counts was committing. He was certain she did. Samantha was as smart as he was—certainly cleverer—but Loxley amused himself in thinking that he would be the one to tell her.

The woman reading the paper caught him staring and scowled. It was an ugly frown and a glare that would push most men away. But not Loxley. Instead, he gave his best smile and even tossed in a friendly wave. She didn't bother reciprocating, only raised her paper higher to keep her face from being seen.

Loxley grinned.

If only she knew he wasn't after her, but had his mind set on one woman in particular—a beautiful woman that filled his dreams with flowers—then maybe she would realize he was only wanting to learn today's news.

The front door jangled as it opened.

Loxley shifted his attention to the front. A well-dressed career woman stepped through the threshold sweeping in the morning sunshine with her. Loxley watched as her eyes traveled to the menu above the counter. He took her in and watched the woman who was just reading the paper pass in front of his field of vision on her way out the door. He turned to where she was sitting and, to his delight, found the *Times* waiting for him to take.

"What a nice thing for you to do," he said, retrieving it. With Thompson gone, the world was already a better place, he thought. *I can only imagine what a great place it will be once Donny Counts is gone, too.*

CHAPTER NINE

DR. BENJAMIN FIRESTONE RETRIEVED HIS LUGGAGE FROM the back of Susan Young's car. Placing it near the curb, he turned and faced his girlfriend of less than a year. "Goodbyes are always the hardest," he said, hooking her chin with his finger and bringing her gaze to meet up with his.

Susan stared up into his chocolatey eyes, cursing herself for feeling so selfish for not wanting him to go. He'd spent the night with her, consoling her as she came to grips with the sudden death of one of her clients, and then the evening inevitably turned into something more.

Their night was filled with passionate intimacy that they had cherished since the inception of their rather short relationship. Yet, to Susan, it still didn't feel like it was nearly enough.

"This isn't goodbye," she murmured. "You'll come home."

Benjamin responded with only a gentle kiss. His lack of words didn't make her feel any better about the situation, but she melted into his kiss, curling her toes deep into the soles of her heels as she felt the electric buzz shoot pleasant waves of heat up her spine.

Taking her by the hips, Benjamin pulled her body into his. Susan wrapped her arms around his tight waist and let her head come to rest over his heart. She listened to it beat, ignoring the hustle of other passengers getting dropped on the curb around them.

Benjamin held on to her, saying, "It's only for two nights."

"And I'll miss you every second that you're gone."

Benjamin pulled back. "I'll call you as soon as I land."

Susan nodded, hugged, and kissed him one last time before letting him go. It was a kiss designed to make him remember who was waiting for him back in Denver; a kiss to tell him how much he meant to her.

Benjamin stepped away, took the luggage handle with his right hand, and blew one last kiss with his left before heading inside. Susan watched him enter the terminal, pushing down the immediate feelings of loneliness as something inside her told her that this was it. She was certain Benjamin would take the job at Dartmouth. She could still hear the sound of excitement fill his voice the day the recruiter called asking him to come to New Hampshire for a visit.

Sliding behind the wheel of her car, she was already late for work. Punching the gas, Susan sped west trying not to worry about the future. It was out of her control what Benjamin decided—or if he would even be offered a position at the teaching hospital he seemed so eager to get.

Tightening her grip on the wheel, Susan found herself doubting she was more important to Benjamin than his career. Again, it was a selfish thought, but one Susan couldn't stop thinking. She tried to put herself in his shoes, reversing the role, and asking herself if she would sacrifice her career for him. She wasn't so sure she could. Not after working so hard to achieve all she had.

They hadn't been together long, but what they shared had been incredible as they seemed to be a perfect fit for each other—both driven and married to their careers—it was a match made in heaven. Susan had initially thought.

Approaching the Colorado Boulevard exit, Susan put a call in to her employee, Carly McKenzie, to say she was running late. Carly assured Susan she had things handled at the office, so Susan pulled off and swung into a nearby coffee shop wanting to bring Carly and the rest of her staff breakfast.

As soon as Susan stepped inside, she heard her name being called.

"Susan, over here." Susan smiled at her friend Maggie Brissay. "What are you doing this side of town?" Maggie asked.

"I was just dropping a friend off at the airport." Susan hugged her friend.

"Hey, I'm sorry about Richard Thompson." Maggie released Susan and took one step back. "He was a client of yours, if I recall."

Susan nodded. "Thanks. It's sad. Richard did lots of good for our community."

Maggie gave her a funny look. "I guess you didn't see?"

This time it was Susan who had the puzzled look. She titled her head to the side, drawing her eyebrows together, at the same time wondering what it was her old friend was referring to.

"Your reporter friend, Samantha Bell," Maggie raised her sharp eyebrows high on her head, "wrote a very eye-opening piece on Richard Thompson in today's paper."

"She did?" Susan sounded surprised.

Maggie blinked and angled her head to the opposite side. "I'm sorry, I thought you knew."

"No. I wasn't aware." Susan spoke with a light touch.

"It's sad indeed," Maggie looked down and to the left, "but the universe has a way of balancing out the world, I suppose." She swept her eyes back to Susan's. "Perhaps it's for the best."

Susan felt like the room was spinning around her, too afraid to ask what Samantha had written and why she hadn't bothered mentioning it at all to Susan.

Maggie gathered her purse, slung it over her shoulder, and turned to the exit. "It was really good seeing you," she said before leaving. "We should plan it next time."

Susan agreed and watched her friend leave when suddenly today's paper was being handed to her. She glanced to the paper that seemed to have come from nowhere and then up to the man holding it out for her to take.

"I'm sorry, I couldn't help but overhear your conversation and thought maybe you'd like to read it yourself."

Susan didn't know what to say to the man whose smile beamed back with a familiar radiant glow.

"Go on. Take it."

Susan forced a smile and muttered, "Thank you." He smiled, held her eyes for a second longer than what was needed, but something about him made Susan feel comfortable, like she might have met him before. "I'm sorry, is there something else I can help you with?" she asked.

His eyes glimmered like he had something important to say. Then, to her surprise, the stranger said, "Can I buy you a cup of coffee?"

CHAPTER TEN

MORNING COULDN'T COME QUICK ENOUGH. I WAS OUT THE door and heading to the newsroom early Sunday morning with the intent of putting my doubts about Thompson to rest.

All last night, sleep escaped me. Thompson haunted my thoughts unlike any other story I'd worked before. King left just before midnight, not long after Mason arrived home from the movies. I still hadn't made the commitment to him sharing a bed with me when my son was home. King understood my hesitation, and I liked that he was patient with my decision. I couldn't have it any other way. I wanted to be a healthy example of what a relationship should look like to my son, even if I knew Mason already understood what was happening when he was gone.

Finally, I had enough tossing and turning and decided to take Cooper for a run. We hit the streets before 6AM and kept at it for a solid hour. The run did little to ease my anxieties and I still doubted my decision to go through with publishing Thompson's story in today's paper, even after King told me it was the right thing to do. But I had to trust that my reporting would speak for itself—just like Erin said it would. By 8 o'clock I was entering the newsroom with the intention of avoiding today's paper at all cost.

Phones rang and keyboards clacked, and it didn't matter that today was Sunday. The newsroom activities were the same as any other day. Nearly everyone was putting in more and more hours just to keep up, proving their worth and dedication to our loyal readership, but mostly to the new faceless owners who recently purchased the rights to our paper and whom we all assumed cared nothing about the current state of journalism or its future.

I swung by Joey Garcia's desk on my way to my own with hopes he would know better than me who might benefit from Thompson's death. I was after closure and, if I could have this one question answered for me, then maybe I could accept the medical examiner's ruling that Thompson's death was in fact an accident. Until then, I wasn't sure I could let this one go.

I took a pen from the jar and scribbled down a quick note asking Garcia to call me as soon as he was in, and stuck it on the side of his computer monitor with hopes of him not missing it. His desk was mostly clean and a quick assessment gave me nothing about what stories he was currently working, but Garcia had covered Thompson before and attended more of the same social and political gatherings than anyone else I knew. If anyone might know Thompson better than me, it was definitely him.

Trisha Christopher caught sight of me as soon as I exited Garcia's pod and I kept walking as she hustled between the work desks, telling me to wait up. I shortened my stride and could only imagine what this could be about. Trisha was the source of all bad news and was the one person everyone in the office sought when needing to catch up on gossip that mostly involved office politics, which I cared little about.

"No. I don't want it," I said, stiff-arming my hand in her direction and brushing past her when catching sight of the paper she was holding out for me to take.

Trisha hooked my arm, spun me around, and slapped the damn thing against my chest, forcing me to read it. "Great work, Sam. No matter what you're doubting, don't. It's stories like these that wake people up."

I heard the paper crinkle in my grasp as I stared into Trisha's big round eyes, silently cursing her for being obtuse and inconsiderate.

"Hopefully after today more scumbags like him will think twice before running a scam."

Trisha smirked, made an *uh-hum* sound with her lips, and hit me on my shoulder with her fist like I had done her a great big favor. Then she spun on a heel and walked away with the same swagger as what she carried with her when she arrived. I hated her for doing it, but now that I had the paper in my hands, I couldn't help but steal a quick peek.

Slowly, I tucked my chin and glanced down to today's headlines. Then my eyelids popped with surprise when seeing that my headline story had been replaced with Garcia's article covering Thompson's death. I quickly turned the page, searching to see where my piece landed, and found my story on page 2.

Suddenly, my feelings of remorse were replaced with fiery anger.

Why had I been bumped to the second page? Was Thompson's death bigger news than the crime he committed? This couldn't have been Dawson's decision. Someone else was behind this and I would like to know who that was and why.

I picked my head up and headed toward my desk, continuing to hug the paper close to my chest. Was it that obvious I was doubting my work? Because I swore that wasn't what this was about. It was only the timing of having to decide when to release it, combined with not accepting Thompson's death as an accident. Maybe Trisha could read through my disguise, but I doubted it. With her, it had to be about my piece getting bumped to the second page and the water cooler gossip that would fill her day.

My feet shuffled across the floor as I stuck my head into Garcia's article. The irony of the conflicting stories seemed larger than what I originally imagined. That surely had to be one reason why I had been bumped from the front page. On one hand, Garcia had told the story of a man who died too young in an unfortunate accident at home, and on the other side of the coin, I was tearing the man down by labeling him a con man who was duping a lot of people into thinking he was something that he wasn't. It couldn't have been a more obvious spar between reporters—even if that wasn't my intention.

I paused and stopped to lift my head in thought. But what did it matter now that Thompson was dead?

I tried to reason with myself that his story went to the grave along with him. Except it did matter, and the foundation he funneled money through would continue on whether he was alive or not. My story was supposed to be the beginning of his end. And that was the exact mindset that got my thoughts to circle back to asking myself, why couldn't he get out of his house and save his own life? Thompson was a fighter, a man of action. In business and in life, so why not also in death?

I turned the corner and was one foot inside my own cubicle when I slammed on the brakes and hit pause. Without looking too closely, I knew immediately something about my work desk was off. It was the angle of where my chair had been left, and how there was trash that I knew wasn't mine left in the bin.

After a quick glance around to see if anyone was near, I

lunged forward taking the mouse into my right hand. Wiggling it until the monitor lit up, suddenly my worst fears became real. My computer's password had been breached.

Everything was exposed. Nothing was secure. I couldn't believe my own eyes.

With a spiking pulse, I quickly went in search of the folder I shared with Dawson. As I clicked around, I thought about how my file wouldn't sync last night and if this was the reason why. None of this made sense. I always logged out and never shared my password with anyone, so how did this happen?

Lowering myself into my chair, a masculine scent lingered in the air. I was disgusted by the trail of evidence that was left behind. A coffee lid was turned over near brown drops of drying liquid splattered next to my wonky keyboard. The mess was only half the problem, the real issue was wanting to know why my computer's password had been breached and, with it, access to all my secret files and works in progress.

Then I clicked the open document on the bottom of the screen, feeling my heart pound in my chest. The tab popped up and I quickly realized that I was in far bigger trouble than anything the Thompson article would bring.

CHAPTER ELEVEN

DETECTIVE ALEX KING WAS DRINKING STALE COFFEE AT HIS desk inside the Denver Police Department near City Hall when his partner, John Alvarez, dropped today's paper onto his desk. It landed with a soft thud next to King's forearm. King was slow to react but rolled his gaze to the right and stared at the paper, asking, "What's this?"

"You're not curious?" Alvarez lifted an eyebrow when he glanced over his shoulder before dropping into his chair.

It was a silly question to ask. King knew damn well what it was and why Alvarez gave it to him. After his conversation with Samantha last night, he knew her story about Thompson's charity fraud was going to ruffle some feathers, and though they both expected some kind of reaction, King hoped it would be well received. That was the best case scenario. Worst, it made Samantha a target.

"Your girlfriend sure knows how to push people's buttons." Alvarez leaned back in his chair, causing it to squeak. Lacing his fingers behind his head, he stared at King with a wrinkled brow, waiting for a response.

"What'd she write this time?" King played dumb.

Alvarez barked out a laugh. "You expect me to believe you knew nothing about this?"

King only stared. After a moment of pause, Alvarez flung forward, leaned over King's shoulder, unfolded the paper and turned to the second page, jabbing his thick index finger into the heart of Samantha's story. "Everyone is talking about this."

King didn't have to read it to know what it said, but he pretended to anyway. "It's a good piece."

"No doubt it is," Alvarez said, falling back into his chair. Still looking at King, he continued, "But that's not why everyone is talking about it."

King arched a single brow.

"Not only does the man die, but then Samantha has to go writing about what a crook the guy was? Seems cold for Samantha." Alvarez shook his head.

"That's why people are talking about it?" King cast his gaze back to the article, wanting to bark out his own feelings of disbelief, but instead restrained himself. "They should be asking themselves how much money this asshole stole from them." When Alvarez didn't respond, King said, "You know she was working this story for the past six weeks, right?"

"And you've been holding out on me all this time?"

King chuckled. "I didn't know until recently."

"But you knew before all of us."

"Perks of the trade."

This time Alvarez chuckled. "Maybe I should sleep with the enemy."

The further King traveled into Samantha's lengthy article, the more he learned Samantha had kept from him. It got him thinking about the strange timing of Thompson's death once again, and Sam's worries that it seemed too coincidental to not be suspicious.

"If you were in her shoes, would you not have published the story?" King asked his partner without looking up.

Alvarez didn't bother taking his eyes off his computer as he worked to enter data into a spreadsheet. "If it were me, I would have given the guy and his family at least of week of peace before reminding everyone what an asshole he was."

King snapped the paper straight and stared into Thompson's image, thinking about Samantha's question of why he didn't get out of the house before it was too late. After a minute of thought, he stood and tapped Alvarez on the shoulder and said, "C'mon."

Alvarez glanced over his shoulder. "Where are we headed, partner?"

King was already halfway to the exit by the time he responded. "To the medical examiner's office."

"What the hell for?" Alvarez called after him.

"To see if we should open up an investigation into the death of Richard Thompson or not."

"Christ," King heard Alvarez grumble as he hurried to catch up. "Why is it that the rich demand the most of our time?"

CHAPTER TWELVE

Susan was relaxed, sitting across the table near the window with the handsome stranger she had just met. He introduced himself as Damien Black, and after an initial hesitation, Susan finally took him up on his offer to buy her a coffee.

With her right leg swung over her left thigh, she casually leaned back, keeping one hand on the warm mocha Damien purchased for her. They sat at a table near the window as Damien charmed Susan with easy small talk and gentle laughs. It was a nice distraction from thoughts drifting to Benjamin or circling back to asking herself why Samantha kept her investigation into Richard Thompson a secret.

The *Times* was on center display between them, and though they both stole glances to the headlines currently rocking the airwaves, they kept their conversation mostly to the good Thompson did for the community of Denver, neither one of them wanting to speak ill about the deceased.

"Just goes to show, you never can tell who a person really is," Damien said, staring at the paper.

"No, I guess you can't," Susan said gently, surprised to find Damien staring at her.

Damien's dark eyes had a playful, almost childlike glimmer that Susan couldn't stop staring into. She liked looking into his magnetic browns and certainly took an immediate attraction to him. Damien was well dressed, casually covering his tall six-foot frame with a dark gray sports coat and white t-shirt above blue jeans and expensive leather shoes that matched his belt.

"I worked with him on several events," Susan said, thinking of Thompson.

Damien titled his head and squinted his eyes.

"I'm an event planner."

Damien smiled. "I know."

"You knew?"

Damien nodded once. "It's why I asked to buy you a coffee."

Susan's lips parted as she stared, suddenly feeling suspicious of his unspoken intention.

"Wait," Damien gave a sideways glance, "you didn't think that I was trying to—"

"No. Of course not." Susan laughed and shook her head. *Of course I didn't think you were trying to pick me up.* Susan pretended to roll her eyes, if not a little disappointed when learning the truth. She knew he was too young for her—and certainly out of her league—but it was still fun to dream. "But how do you know what I do for a living, and what other things do you know about me? I know nothing about you."

"The school shooting several months back." Damien licked his lips after taking a sip from his coffee. "Your face was everywhere."

Susan smiled as she recalled the tragedy of that day and how the governor randomly chose her company to handle the victims fund without first approving it with Susan.

"When I saw you, I knew I had to talk to you."

"Here we are," Susan turned her palms to the ceiling and gave him a cute smile, "talking."

Damien laughed and cast his gaze back to the paper. "What was Richard Thompson like to work with?"

Susan inhaled a sharp breath, giving herself a moment to think over her answer. The sound of grinding coffee echoed off the walls behind her. "At the time, he was a great client and I would have never thought he was a fraud."

"That's why they call them con-men." Damien took a pull from his coffee. "Truth be told, I find it extremely interesting, but can't personally speak on the matter as I've never donated a penny to Thompson's charity. Thank God."

"But a lot of people have."

"Which is why I'm glad your friend, here," he casually pointed to Samantha's byline, "is exposing his lies."

"Yeah." The jab of betrayal hit Susan's gut once again. What was Sam trying to protect her from by keeping this from her?

"What's she like?"

Susan swept her eyes up to his. "Who? Samantha?"

Damien nodded. "She's your friend, right?"

Susan knew Damien had overheard her conversation with Maggie and that was the reason he was asking. Not thinking any more into it, Susan said, "Samantha is not only my best friend, but also a hell of a reporter."

"It takes balls to not only write that story, but then to release it the morning after he was found dead." Damien shook his head and laughed.

"She might not have had a say in the matter." Susan came to her friend's defense. An awkward silence settled between them. "Are you suggesting that Samantha is a cheap shot?"

Damien fell back in his chair and stared. "That's not what I'm saying."

"Because that isn't who Samantha is. She helps people and only wants what is best. Would it have made a difference if he didn't die yesterday? Would that change your opinion?"

"I'm sorry if I said something to offend you." Damien reached for his knees and turned to face the window. He was surprised by Susan's sudden lynching. "That wasn't my intention." He turned back to face her. "I guess what I'm saying is that we should be grateful to have journalists as brave as her."

"I'm sorry," Susan apologized. "I've had a rough morning. I don't know what's gotten into me."

"It's quite all right."

"But you're right, Samantha's job does sometimes sound exciting." Susan forced a smile. "But it can also be dangerous working the crime desk. She often sees the dark side of our city, the city none of us want to admit exists—telling stories many of us aren't courageous enough to speak about ourselves."

Damien grinned. "I know it all too well."

Susan changed direction when asking, "What do you do for a living, Mr. Black?"

"Damien."

Susan fixed her eyes on his cognac gaze, once again feeling her body tip forward, and felt a little breathless when doing so. There was something about this man that made her travel up and down and all around.

"Call me Damien." He paused. "Go on, say it."

"Damien." Susan felt her cheeks blush as she couldn't believe she was falling for his brazen confidence. She would be the first to admit his distraction was a nice way to forget the secret Sam had kept from her, as well as having to imagine Benjamin taking a job in a different state. With Damien, he made her believe she was single and on the market, and that was a refreshing feeling that made it easy to forgive.

"That's right." He winked. "I founded a non-profit computer science lab, Backstage, in East Denver and fill my days keeping it organized."

"And your nights? What do you do with those?" The crown of Susan's head pulled to the ceiling with a sudden surge of confidence. She couldn't believe she'd asked, but the opportunity presented itself and now there was no turning back.

Damien's eyes narrowed with flirtation. "That is a secret of mine that your friend might want to investigate."

Susan laughed and Damien followed her lead. Then she asked, "How do you fundraise? Maybe I could help."

"I was hoping you'd ask." Damien reached inside his sport coat and pulled out a business card. Handing it to Susan, he said, "Why don't you swing by the lab tomorrow and I'll give you the complete tour."

"The *complete* tour?" Susan's eyes sparkled with innuendo.

Damien smiled, stood, and tugged on his coat. "Call me. My number is on the back. I promise to make it worth your time."

CHAPTER THIRTEEN

My surroundings disappeared as I dove into researching why this particular folder was chosen to be opened. I forgot where I was—who might be watching—and spent the next ten minutes clicking through old files, familiarizing myself with the notes I had taken eight months ago on a potential story I had been working on a young entrepreneur who went by the name Donny Counts.

Donny Counts was born Donald H. Wallace and changed his last name to Counts halfway through his junior year while attending University of Texas at Austin where he later dropped out to move to Denver with his roommate, Josh Stetson.

Both men majored in Business with an emphasis in Computer Sciences. Neither of them graduated, having decided they would cut their school short and begin their life in business. They found quick success creating software programs that they eventually sold to schools across the country, becoming millionaires in their early twenties. They partied much of their riches away, but then cryptocurrency came along and changed everything.

Supposedly the two men had a falling out somewhere along the way. Stetson went one direction, Counts another. Then, eight months ago, I had been assigned to cover Stetson's criminal trial. That was where I first met both Counts and Stetson and they were quite the dynamic pairing, though only one of them was facing a ten year sentence.

Stetson had been convicted of running a scam called "SIM swapping" and was being accused of stealing close to $10 million in cryptocurrency from over fifty victims. I spoke to Allison about this one night over margaritas and essentially SIM swapping went something like this.

A computer hacker would convince the target's mobile phone provider to port their phone number over to a SIM card belonging to a hacker. In this case, Josh Stetson. Then, once the swap occurred, the hacker essentially hijacked his target's mobile device, including one-time passwords, verification codes, two-factor authorization codes sent to the hacker's phone, all of it opening up access to email, bank, cryptocurrency accounts, and even social media profiles. It was just a new way for criminals to steal someone's identity and Stetson was hoping he could hit and run before the authorities even had a clue what these new technologies were capable of doing. In the end, Stetson was wrong and he was convicted by a jury of his peers. But on my way out of the courthouse, I was told by a reliable source to keep my eye on Donny Counts, for he would be the next one to be wearing the orange jump suit.

I never did find anything story worthy from the crime angle to launch an investigation into Counts, but I knew Garcia covered him extensively. Counts's cryptocurrency exchange seemed to rise out of oblivion, along with his coins which were currently ranked in the top twenty. It meant nothing to me, and I wondered if that was the problem.

I reeled my hands away from the keyboard and fell back

into my chair, thinking maybe that was the reason someone had dug up Donny's folder. I didn't have any dirt on him, and he certainly wasn't on my radar with all that I had going with the Thompson story, but maybe it was worth revisiting.

Suddenly, I was dizzy with thoughts that Thompson's story was only the beginning.

It was time I talked to Dawson.

Closing out my computer, I made sure to lock the screen before leaving. Gathering my important files and drives, I turned and exited my cubbyhole only to immediately collide into the breastplate of a white t-shirt being worn by a man who was peering down on me.

Bouncing back, I regained my balance and flicked my gaze up into his indifferent eyes, apologizing for not watching where I was going. He shrugged like it was no big deal, side-stepping around me. I watched him enter my workspace as if it was his own.

My brows knitted with a twist of confusion as I studied his face.

I didn't recognize him and it wasn't like we had a lot of new faces around with the way journalists and staff members were being asked to exit their careers faster than leaves falling from trees. But that didn't mean he didn't belong, either. He certainly looked like he did, I thought as he turned his head and stared.

He had the confident gaze of youth, taking what he wanted without asking, and lowered himself down into my chair as if wanting to rub salt into my damaged ego. I watched him swivel around and reach for a pen. He jotted something down that I couldn't read, and then he did something I couldn't believe. He logged into my computer, by passing the protected password with extraordinary ease.

"Whoa. Wait a second." I leaped forward and put my

hands on my keyboard. "What the hell do you think you're doing?"

He'd already logged himself on. It happened so fast, I could barely keep up.

"Working," he casually said as he stared back.

"No. Not here, you're not."

He didn't seem too concerned, leaned back, dropped one set of slender fingers into his lap, and wrapped his lips around the bright red straw sticking out of his soda and slurped his drink while looking at me like I had interrupted him.

"This is my computer and you're trespassing."

"I'm nearly finished." He twisted around and set his soda back on the desktop.

"Finished?" My eyes bounced between him and my computer. "Finished with what?"

"Installing a new security update."

"That's all?"

"That's all."

"I'll handle it from here," I said. "Now, please leave. There are important files on that computer that aren't meant to be shared."

"Samantha." I heard Travis Turner from IT call my name from behind. "Everything all right?"

"No. Everything is not all right. Do you know this man?"

"Brett Gallagher." Travis stopped outside my office and stood with his hands rooted into his sides. "My summer intern."

"You let an intern on my computer? Travis," I gave him my best angry look, "he had a secret folder opened."

"I'm just updating the software like you asked," Brett said to Travis.

I snapped my neck and bore my eyes into the bridge of Brett's large nose. "A folder was opened, and you know as well as I that you opened it."

"I'm sure it was nothing, Samantha," Travis said, hoping to ease my worries. "We've detected malware and believe our private data may have been breached."

"By who?" I asked.

"Can't say for sure, we're still looking into it ourselves, but in the meantime we're going around the building and looking for vulnerabilities."

"When did this happen?"

"Again, tough to say, but one thing is certain, our entire system is dated and I'm not convinced that we have the resources to bring it up to where I believe it should be."

It was a real drag to hear Travis discuss the dilapidated tools we all relied on daily to get our work done as efficiently as possible, but no wonder we were attacked. At least I wasn't making this up. I knew it all too well. It was a living nightmare. There had been so much change around the newsroom in the last year I couldn't make what was heads from tails.

We all turned to face my computer when it chimed.

"There. All finished," Brett said. "Make sure to do the software updates when the notifications arise."

"Yeah, yeah, yeah," I said, rolling my eyes.

"It's the least you can do to protect yourself from hackers." Brett stood and skirted past me, heading to the cubbyhole next to mine. "And don't click on everything for fear of missing out. That's when real trouble begins."

I turned to Travis. "Is he serious?"

Travis pointed to my laptop. "Got good security on that thing?"

I knew I did because of Allison. "The best," I said.

"I'll take a look at it if you want," Brett called out.

Travis grinned and shrugged.

"Not a chance," I said. "And I'll be changing my password as soon as you two are gone."

CHAPTER FOURTEEN

I MARCHED STRAIGHT TO DAWSON'S OFFICE TO ASK HIM what the hell was going on only to find him stuck in a meeting. Circling the fishbowl like a vulture with hopes of drawing him out, Dawson knew he had no choice but to excuse himself and come talk to me.

"Sam, what is it?" he asked in a hushed tone, stepping away from the dozens of eyes watching from behind the window glass.

"You know Travis Turner has a new summer intern?" I felt the fire in my belly still raging hot.

"Yes, Brett." Dawson placed his hand in the center of my back and nudged me into his office where he shut the door. "Did something happen?"

I kept pacing in tiny circles. "They were on my computer going through secret files without my permission."

Dawson told me about the attempted hack and how they were still trying to learn if it was successful and if anything was taken.

"I heard all about it," I said. "Received the same lecture from the Skinny Tree Brett Gallagher." I stopped shuffling my feet and turned to face Dawson. "Is that what your meeting was about?"

"It was part of today's docket." Dawson leaned back in his high-back chair with one hand up close to his mouth. "Don't take it personally, everyone is having their software checked."

"Maybe you didn't hear me when I said they were poking around in files they shouldn't have been looking in."

"I heard you," Dawson said. "It's a serious security breach we're dealing with here, Sam. This place if full of great reporters, but even those great journalists aren't so great at keeping their software up to date."

"Are the police involved?"

"Not yet, but I wouldn't rule it out." Dawson held my eyes. "Travis is certain that it was the reason your Thompson file didn't properly sync last night."

"What else did he say?"

Dawson shook his head. "That he's investigating." A pause in our conversation brought quiet to the office. "You never did say what you found last night when visiting the Thompson residence."

"You promised me the front page."

"I'm sorry, Sam, but I wasn't convinced you were even going to want to run the story."

I folded my arms and stared through the glass into the newsroom. "Have you talked to Garcia today?"

"He'll be in shortly." Dawson leaned forward and brought his elbows to his desk. "It wasn't his decision. Don't take it personally."

"It's not that."

Dawson lifted a brow.

"Intern Brett had Donny Counts's folder opened." Dawson looked confused so I explained who Donny Counts was, the reasons for my concern, and my need to ask Garcia about it.

"Ah, I see," he said. "Look, Sam, don't beat yourself up. Your piece on Thompson is some of the best work I've seen from you."

"But it doesn't make me feel any better about kicking the man after he died."

"That's not what you're doing."

I gave Dawson an arched look. "Matt Bales was one of the fireman called to Thompson's house last night. Remember him?"

"From the tanker truck inauguration?"

I nodded and relayed the message Matt shared with Erin and me. "Thompson was awake, Dawson. He had all the security in place to warn him of the silent danger slowly killing him. Yet he still died. Now tell me, why didn't he open the door and just leave before it was too late?"

Dawson's half-mast eyes stared from beneath a heavy brow. "What are the police saying?"

"Not much. But I know his death is being ruled an accident."

"You've got to let this go, Sam. It isn't your fault that he died."

"Maybe not, but there is something I didn't tell you."

Dawson's head floated up when he perked an ear.

Reaching into my back pocket, I pulled the folded piece of paper I'd kept from the email that was sent to me and showed Dawson the threat I received the night before Thompson died.

Dawson pinched the paper with both his hands and read the text. "Thompson sent this to you?"

"I don't know who did, but I assumed it was him."

"Have you received anything else like this recently?"

I shook my head no. Dawson scrubbed a hand over his face and sighed heavily as he pushed the small rectangular paper back to me. "I'd like to think that Thompson sent it, but what has me worried is that maybe he didn't."

Dawson's brow pinched with concern. He understood what I was saying, and the outlook wasn't pretty. "Any way you can find out?"

"Only if I can get myself into Richard Thompson's house."

Dawson gripped his desk and pushed his shoulder back into the chair. Raising his brows, he said, "Then I suggest you hurry before the window of opportunity closes."

CHAPTER FIFTEEN

DONNY COUNTS WAS OUTSIDE LOUNGING BY HIS POOL, basking in the sun and thinking about Josh Stetson when he received a text message from an unknown number.

You can't ignore me forever. We can do this now, or I'm taking it public. Your choice.

Donny squeezed his phone inside the palm of his hand, willing it to break. The ride he had been on this last year was coming to a close. He could feel it. It was a similar feeling to when Stetson went down for running his SIM swapping scam. The walls were closing in and everyone around Donny seemed to be wanting a piece of the pie. Donny didn't know how many more slices he was willing to give up just to keep them quiet. Even those closest to him he eyed with suspicion, unsure anymore who he could trust.

Closing his eyes, his arm fell lazily over the lawn chair. He uncurled his fist and heard his phone drop to the hot concrete below. Soaking up as much sunshine as possible, he knew he needed to act quickly. There were too many questions being asked, too much speculation into how he managed to grow his company as quickly as he had—and get his early investors' money back in record time. Then there was the man who followed him out the doors after his speech at Denver University yesterday.

Donny rubbed his face and felt his puffy eyes sag. He dove his hand inside his shorts pocket and retrieved a circular white pill of OxyContin. Popping it into his mouth, he felt better almost instantly. But the memory of the look on the stranger's face told Donny everything he needed to know, and it was a problem that needed to be dealt with. Donny didn't know how much he was willing to give to make it go away.

Suddenly, Donny heard the glass doors to his patio open and slam shut. He rolled his head to the side and found his girlfriend, Rose Wild, hurrying over to where he was relaxing. Her silky white robe flared behind her like a cape and she had a look that Donny knew well. Pushing himself up on his elbows, he prepared for the collision heading his way.

"Rose, baby, what's going on?" he asked.

"This." She shoved her cell phone into his face. "This is what's fucking going on."

Donny gripped the phone with one hand and pushed his sunglasses to the roof of his head with the other. He squinted at the small screen, asking, "What the hell is this?"

"Dead, Donny, dead," Rose growled.

Donny scrolled through the news about Richard Thompson—his death and the charity fraud scheme the *Colorado Times* had uncovered. It was the first Donny had heard about it. Remaining calm, he said, "We barely knew him."

"That's not my point, Donny." Rose swiped her hand through the air and stole her phone back. "My point is, how is what you're doing any different than what this guy did?"

"Chill, baby." Donny clamped his hand around her small wrist. "Don't be so dramatic."

"Don't tell me how to feel," she spat.

Donny pulled her into his lap. Cupping her ass with one hand and cradling her with the other, he peppered kisses down her bare arm until he felt her body melt into his. "He died of CO poisoning. You're thinking too much into this."

Rose flicked her angered gaze over to him. "And you expect me to believe that?"

Donny gazed up into her gorgeous eyes full of flames. Running his fingers up her thigh, he murmured, "I love it when you're on fire."

She slapped his hand away and squeezed her thighs together. "I don't have a good feeling about this." She turned and cast her eyes to the depths of the pool. "Our time is running out," she whispered.

"It's not as bad as you're making it out to be," Donny said. But even he knew it was a lie. Rose was right. Donny felt the end coming, too.

"The reporter keeps calling," she said. "I don't know what else to say to get them to stop."

"Stop answering."

"I can't. Not if you want to pick and choose which reporters are friends and which are enemies."

"That's how this works. It's the game we've been playing since the beginning." Donny swept his hand from the house to the pool. "Look how well it's working."

"This reporter is different." Donny could hear the concern in Rose's voice. "I know they know, but I don't know how much they know or who else they've told."

"Did you write down their name?" Donny asked, even though he already knew the reporter's name.

Rose turned to face Donny, shoving her fingers through his hair. "On the kitchen counter next to the phone. But what are you doing to say? And how long will this go on?"

Donny hooked her chin and gazed into her eyes. They were living in an era where the fall was enjoyed more by the public than the rise to the top. It scared the hell out of him, but he would never admit it to Rose. He'd risked everything knowing the consequence of getting caught. Yet the promise of easy riches was too good to pass up, even if he believed he might have pushed the limits a little too far.

Rose pressed her hand against his chest and slid her palm down his washboard abs before stopping on his insulin pump attached to his side. "Promise me you know what you're doing."

Donny smiled and kissed her. "I'll take care of the reporter. You have nothing to worry about."

CHAPTER SIXTEEN

DETECTIVE ALEX KING OPENED HIS CAR DOOR FROM THE driver's side and had one foot on the ground when he heard Alvarez grumble again about this visit to the coroner's office being a complete waste of their time.

"Would you prefer we just go to Thompson's residence and take a look around ourselves?" King looked his partner in the eye and asked.

Alvarez showed King his empty palms. "All I'm wondering is why you can't accept the fact that the man died of CO poisoning."

King stared at his partner. Counting off on five fingers, he listed reasons that kept him suspicious. When he was finished, he asked, "Should I go on?"

"I get it." Alvarez exited the car and rounded the back, meeting up with King on the other side. Together, they entered the coroner's office still discussing King's reasons why they were here. "I just don't understand why a rich man's death should take precedence over the dozen other cases we're working."

King slowed his step. "I want to know why his detectors

didn't go off, and why he didn't just leave when he could have."

"Or maybe there is something you know that I don't."

King glared and kept walking. He pulled the door open, checked himself in at the front, and made his way to the back, Alvarez grudgingly trailing him. The coroner's office was quieter than most days of the week but they found medical examiner, Leslie Griffin, in her lab coat and busy working.

"Why am I not surprised to see you two here on a Sunday?" Leslie greeted King and Alvarez with a warm smile.

"We can't let you work alone." Alvarez had his hands hiding in his pants pockets as he rocked on his heels at the table.

"What can I help you with today?" she asked.

"We're hoping to hear your analysis on Richard Thompson." The scent of formaldehyde and other chemicals hung in the air that went straight to King's head.

Leslie's eyes moved behind protective glasses. "Victim of carbon monoxide." She paused to look at them both. "Unless you have reason for me to take a second look?"

"No, no, no." Alvarez lifted a hand and shook his head. "I trust your conclusion, my partner, on the other hand, can't seem to accept the result, thinking the victim should have simply walked out of the house before succumbing to the poisonous gas."

Leslie looked to King. "It's a great question. One I asked myself."

"And what are your thoughts?" King asked, stepping forward.

"There are many reasons why victims of CO don't just leave."

"Explain."

"The most obvious is that they are sleeping and just don't

know what's happening if the house isn't outfitted with detectors."

"The report says the victim's house had new, working detectors; did they not go off?"

"That's a question you can ask the fire chief. Another reason is that the victim might have been drunk." Leslie moved across the floor and motioned for the detectives to follow. "In both scenarios, the victim may die before they experience any symptoms."

"And is that what happened here?" King asked.

Leslie picked up a chart and flipped a page. "I ran a tox screen as soon as I got him here last night." She handed King the report. "His blood alcohol was high. Probably the reason he didn't realize he was being poisoned."

King handed the report to Alvarez.

"Oh, and I did find this in his pocket." Leslie picked up an evidence bag from the desk and gave it to King.

King held it up to the light. Squinting to see through the plastic liner, he stared at the tiny sliver of paper, reading off the digits—*57b605f014671fc65e931b7d30738d2 551825146c7c-c8d4780a5170507916007.*

"What is it?" he asked.

The corners of Leslie's eyes crinkled. "You're the detective. You tell me."

King handed it off to Alvarez. Both detectives were as clueless as the ME.

"I've never seen anything like it before, but glad you stopped by," Leslie said. "Maybe you could put it in the hands of its rightful owner. I figured it might be important, but who knows, I've been wrong before."

CHAPTER SEVENTEEN

ERIN HAD HER HEADPHONES PULLED AROUND HER NECK when she opened her front door to let me inside. She kissed me on the cheek and I reciprocated the greeting by handing her today's paper. Erin opened it up and I fell into the corner of her couch, kicking my feet up on her coffee table and watching her flip back and forth between Garcia's headline and my article.

"They put it on the second page?"

I shrugged. "Dawson fed me some bullshit about being too late making a decision."

Erin cast her gaze back to the paper, shaking her head. "For what it's worth, Sam, our online forum has never been so busy."

I sat forward and perched my elbows on my kneecaps. "Because of my story?"

Erin gave me a knowing look, tossed the paper on the coffee table in front of me, and said, "Numbers are up. Listeners, subscribers, everything."

"But why? I don't understand." I tucked a loose strand of

hair behind my ear. "The man is dead and I'm still swinging punches at him."

Erin raised a single brow and I watched her eyes glimmer.

I pointed at Garcia's headline. "I didn't even get front page."

Erin skirted around the coffee table and came to sit next to me. Holding my eyes inside of hers, she said, "People were swindled and you exposed the crime. They view you as a hero."

"I'm no hero."

"You did the impossible."

"It's just reporting."

Erin shook her head. "It took courage to tell the story you did. But that's not all, Sam."

I felt my insides tighten with fear of what she knew that I didn't. I wasn't sure I could handle any more surprises. I was all surprised out.

"Come look at this." Erin took my hand and pulled me to my feet as she towed me into her home office where she opened up her computer and navigated to our online forum. "Go on." She turned her chair around for me to sit. "Read what our audience is saying and maybe then you'll understand what I'm telling you."

I swallowed a deep breath and gently lowered myself into the leather chair. I swiveled around to face the computer and took the mouse into my right hand. I scrolled through the comments one-by-one, beginning to understand Erin's excitement. I recognized a couple names who I'd interviewed during my investigation into Thompson's fraud, but the comments kept going as Thompson's victims seemed to have found commonality in a safe place to publicly speak out against the man they all learned to hate.

"People are very angry with the new ruling class," Erin

said over my shoulder. "And they want to know who else is lying to them."

I felt my neck tighten and, though I understood their reaction, I didn't like the energy I felt building. One nudge on the wrong shoulder and this thing could completely change the trajectory of what was otherwise a peaceful movement.

"I was meaning to mention this to you sooner," Erin squeezed my shoulder, "but I assumed you already knew."

I stared at the monitor and shook my head no.

I had been so consumed with Thompson's sudden death, I hadn't bothered to check our forum. The knots of uncertainly slowly unraveled inside my belly as I kept scrolling. "Do they really think we're hiding more names?"

"Why wouldn't they? It's our job to uncover the dirt, isn't it?"

My thoughts immediately turned to Donny Counts and Josh Stetson. A flush of annoyance sent heat waves up my collar as I thought back to how Travis Turner had his summer intern casually browsing through my computer without me knowing.

"We're on to something that clearly resonates with a lot of people, Sam. I don't think we should stop just because Thompson is dead."

I understood Erin's desire to want to ride this wave, as something like this didn't come along very often, but I was hesitant to jump on board and certainly wasn't sharing her confidence. Then my heart stalled in my chest when hovering over one comment in particular. After I read it, a chill zipped up my spine.

"Did you see this?" I asked Erin.

Erin bent at the waist and leaned over my shoulder. Her eyes scanned the text and I listened to her read it aloud. "Thompson is the first of many more to come. If you don't believe me, just ask these two."

Erin glanced to me. "Is it a trap?"

"You have antivirus software installed?"

"Yeah. It's good." I gave her a look and Erin nodded. "Click it. See what happens," she said.

I twisted back to the keyboard and clicked the highlighted link. Immediately, an image popped up and we couldn't believe our eyes.

"Is that us?" Erin asked.

Unfortunately, I knew it was as soon as I saw it. "Yeah. Taken last night, when we were outside the Thompson residence speaking with Matt Bales."

CHAPTER EIGHTEEN

JOHN ALVAREZ PUT HIS HAND ON THE ROOF OF THEIR police sedan when giving Alex King a look. "Now are you satisfied?"

King stared into his partner's eyes, opened his car door, and dropped his tall body behind the wheel, shutting the door behind him. He had looked at the key code Leslie had given them so many times, he practically knew it by heart. But he was no closer to explaining the mystery of what it was or who he should give it to than when they left the coroner's office.

"Just admit it," Alvarez continued, "this was a complete waste of our time."

"The key code means nothing to you?" King gave him an arched look.

"If it was a receipt found in the victim's pocket, would you still be asking me if it meant anything to me?"

"Depends where that receipt came from and what was purchased."

Alvarez stretched the seatbelt over his shoulder, crossed it over his lap, and buckled himself in. "Still, nothing suggests foul play on either the victim's body or at his house. It was a simple accident. Now please, can we just move on?"

King retrieved the key code from his sport coat pocket and handed it to Alvarez. "Have you seen anything like this before?"

Alvarez cast his gaze down into the alphanumerical code and counted off the digits. "No. Can't say I have."

"There are 64 digits."

"I know, I counted."

"It's too long for a bank account or routing number, so what could it possible go to?"

"Maybe nothing."

"No. A man like Thompson just doesn't carry random codes around in his trouser pockets. I bet whatever this is, is real important to somebody."

Alvarez stared through the windscreen glass with a knitted brow. "You think it has anything to do with what Samantha revealed?"

King looked at his partner and slid the key into the ignition. "Maybe," he said just as his cell phone buzzed. He answered. "King."

"Alex, its detective Robbins."

"What can I help you with?"

"You got some free time to swing by Richard Thompson's residence?"

King's brow furrowed, his brain scrambling to understand what in the world Detective Robbins was doing at Richard Thompson's house. Lieutenant Baker hadn't mentioned the Thompson case being investigated as a homicide, but by the sound in Robbins's voice, King was starting to believe something may have changed. "Alvarez and I could head over now. What's this about?"

"I'd rather not say over the phone, but you're going to want to see this."

CHAPTER NINETEEN

THE THOMPSON RESIDENCE WAS A HIVE OF ACTIVITY WHEN King pulled up to the house. Two Rocky Mountain Security vans were parked near the garage along with a single HVAC rig. The crews were working inside and King could only speculate to why Detective Robbins had asked him to come.

"God damn," Alvarez said under his breath. "You don't see this every day."

King heard him mumble something about the rich living in a constant state of fear and how they were some of the planet's most miserable bastards, but instead of engaging in Alvarez's misery, King stepped out of the car and entered the house with renewed interest.

A team of two from Rocky Mountain Security was working on the house's smart home system when King stopped to chat. He introduced himself, flashed his badge, and asked if everything was working as it should be.

"So far so good," the older of the two men said.

"You heard what happened here yesterday?" King asked as Alvarez caught up to him.

The man nodded. "Terrible. Absolutely terrible."

"Yeah." King glanced around the room, listening to the *clicks* and *clangs* coming from somewhere near the kitchen. He motioned with his head for Alvarez to question the HVAC crew on their findings. "I assume the carbon monoxide detector is routed through the same system?" King pointed to the glowing blue screen as Alvarez trudged away.

"It is."

"Any record to confirm whether it was working yesterday?"

"Everything we've checked tells us it was."

The man diverted his eyes and King knew there was something he wasn't sharing. "Is there a record of it kept somewhere?"

The man sighed. "The system records everything and stores the data away in a ledger that then gets transferred to the cloud and can be later accessed by a technician at our company headquarters."

"Okay." King arched a brow.

"Well, I took a look at the ledger, and there wasn't any indication that the CO levels ever rose. Not when the fire department was called, or before it, or ever."

King touched his face and stared at the machine hanging on the wall. "You checked the entire house?"

"Every single detector. They all are doing what they're told."

King caught sight of Alvarez waving him over. "All right. Let us know if you find anything else." King slapped the man on the back of his shoulders and met up with Alvarez. "What did you learn?"

"Nothing. The crews have checked all the appliances in the house for possible malfunctions or any kind of interference that might spark a CO leak."

King's gaze bounced around the house. "Did they check the fireplace?"

Alvarez nodded. "And the stove and furnace. According to them, everything is working efficiently."

None of this was what King thought he would hear. He was certain someone would be able to trace the leak to some kind of failed appliance. Rounding his lips, he exhaled a heavy sigh and was only more perplexed by the story of what happened to Thompson than before they arrived.

"I hate to admit it," Alvarez flicked his gaze to King, "but you might have been right about thinking Thompson's death needed a closer look."

King couldn't help but smile inwardly. As he bounced his gaze from wall to wall, he realized the entire scene had been contaminated. If Thompson had been killed, investigators wouldn't have a fair shot at determining what might have caused his death now that a couple dozen people had been inside the house.

"We need to get the fire chief on the phone. Who was on call last night?"

Alvarez didn't know as they continued on their journey through the back of the house. "How many people do you think live in this gigantic house?" Alvarez asked.

King shrugged as he heard his name being called.

"King, back here." Detective Robbins was standing in the hall. "I thought I heard your voice. Thanks for coming so quickly."

"What brought you here to begin with?" King asked Robbins.

"We were only assigned to do a quick walk-through because of who Thompson was." Robbins looked to both King and Alvarez.

Alvarez slapped King between the shoulders. "See, it's what I've been saying all along. The rich get preferential treatment."

King ignored his partner and asked Robbins, "But you found something to suggest it might be homicide?"

"Not quite." King gave Robbins a questioning look. "Follow me; I'll show you why I called."

Together, the three detectives entered Richard Thompson's study. King took in his surroundings, noting the wood paneled walls housing a marvelous metal photograph of the Maroon Bells near Aspen. Robbins's partner, Detective Mike Zimmerman, was at the mahogany desk glaring at King. King locked eyes and felt his muscles involuntarily flex.

"What's up, Zim?" King greeted his colleague. "Did Thompson leave me in his will?"

Zimmerman didn't even smirk as he lifted up several printed pages and asked, "How did our victim get himself a copy of this before it went to print today?"

King stepped forward and pinched the stapled packet with his right hand. He felt the blood drain from his face when he recognized it as the final draft to Samantha's article on Thompson. Lifting his eyes, he locked his gaze on Zimmerman. "What are you suggesting?"

"We're not suggesting anything," Robbins said. "But it's why I called."

"It doesn't look good for your girlfriend." Zimmerman cocked his head to the side and stared at King. "Especially since the lieutenant has four of his homicide detectives looking further into one dead man's past."

King's heart thundered in his chest as he wondered how in the hell Sam's article found its way to Thompson's desk. He doubted she would have given it to him.

Alvarez moved to the desk and King watched him pick something up.

"That was paper clipped to the article," Zimmerman said, looking to Alvarez.

"Any idea what it is?" Alvarez asked him.

Zimmerman shook his head.

"What is it?" King stepped forward.

Alvarez drew in a breath and released it as he held up a key code similar to the one Leslie had given them. "Look familiar?"

"You two know what that is?" Robbins asked, looking to his partner as if they were both thinking it might have belonged to Samantha.

King took the second key code between his fingers and said, "No. Not quite. But something tells me that we should soon find out."

CHAPTER TWENTY

I THOUGHT THE FIRST MESSAGE I RECEIVED WAS BAD. BUT the public comment that there would be others following Thompson's death kept me on pins and needles. Not only did it bring into question Thompson's cause of death, but it also had me wondering if we'd been put on the clock and were expected to count down the seconds until the next person was murdered.

"LilJon," Erin said, hovering the mouse over the username who claimed Thompson's death was the first of many more to come. "Mean anything to you?"

"Lil Jon is a rapper, but this isn't him."

"No, but maybe someone who likes his music?"

Once again we were working a puzzle with few clues and not enough pieces to know where things fit and in what order, if at all. I didn't care that we had been photographed without our knowing. I always assumed that someone was watching me. It was the life I chose, and I accepted that. But what I refused to accept was a public threat on someone's life.

"Whoever wrote this," I said, pointing at the monitor, "knew we would see it."

"But is it intended *only* for us, or for everyone to see?"

I scratched my head. There was no way to know for sure. "More importantly, does it confirm that Thompson was murdered?"

Erin's eyes were filled with doubt. I certainly thought it did. But I might be overthinking LilJon's response when everyone was lashing out at Thompson.

"I want to know who was watching us and why?" Erin shook her head and I could feel her unease tighten the muscles in her back. "There is nothing more unnerving than thinking that Thompson was murdered and the killer was watching the investigation unfold while using us as his tool to learn what's being said."

I had the same sunken feeling, my body cold with uncertainty. "I should visit Thompson's house again."

Erin spun her head around and looked me in the eye. "To do what?"

"To find out if he threatened me with that first email."

"And what if it *was* him? What would that prove?"

"Then I know that I'm not chasing a ghost and I can let it rest."

Erin's eyebrows raised. "And if he didn't?"

I flicked my gaze to the computer monitor. "Then we find out who this LilJon is and ask him what this comment means." I pointed at the words still glowing back at us.

"We should do that anyway." Erin paused with thought. "Unless you would like company?"

"No." I stood, gathering my things, and headed out of her office. "It's better I do this alone. You try to identify LilJon. Maybe try to engage him in conversation."

Erin agreed, walked me to the door, and I promised to call her as soon as I learned anything that might give us a start into deciphering what exactly we were dealing with. "Sam, be careful."

"I will."

"We're the only ones that seem to be questioning Thompson's death. If we're right, whoever killed him isn't going to like us bringing attention to it."

I squeezed Erin's hand. "Then we won't."

On my drive across town, I thought about the interest my story sparked and the angry people voicing their opinions online. I questioned whether these same people would let this anger pass or actually be motivated to do something far worse than type a comment while hidden behind the anonymity of the internet. It was tough to say what would happen, but one thing was crystal clear—someone wanted to take credit for Thompson's death, and I was determined to learn if the threat was legitimate.

I wasn't sure what I was expecting to find when turning onto Thompson's street, but I hadn't anticipated this. My pulse throbbed in my wrist as my heartrate spiked. I parked on the side of the road, turned off the car, and sat for a minute to gauge the scene.

Despite catching me off guard, the chaos coming in and out of the house played in my favor. I could just walk inside and pretend like I belonged. Then I caught sight of the unmarked cop cars hiding beneath the big cottonwood a half block down from where I sat and realized my plan might not be as easy as just stepping inside.

I drummed the steering wheel, hemming and hawing through my options. I was certain it was King's car I saw and with it came mixed emotions. On one hand I was happy that the police were looking into a death I also thought suspicious. On the other, I knew them being here was going to impede my own investigation.

Knowing I wasn't going to leave without at least

attempting to get some answers, I flung the door open and made my way along the concrete path following the hedges that led me to the front door. Finding the door open, I glanced to the street, then stepped inside with ease.

There was more foot traffic coming and going now than what I saw last night. HVAC and security, all checking the house for flaws into what might have caused CO to be leaked into the house. No one seemed too concerned that I was there, so I wondered what they'd found.

"Is that where the CO was leaked from?" I asked the man working the natural gas fireplace.

"I don't think so." He flicked on the flames and I watched them ignite. Then he took a reading and extinguished the flames before cycling through the same pattern again. "I've conducted a systems check and everything appears to be working just fine."

I moved on and found my next person to question. He was a short chubby man of about fifty who had trouble keeping his pants above his ass crack.

"Who called you to come?" I asked.

He gave me a funny look. "The owner."

"Mrs. Thompson?"

"I assume." He tinkered with the security system. "Wasn't the one who took the call."

"Are you here to fix or install?"

He pushed his glasses further up on his nose. "Conducting a system maintenance check." His brushy brows squished as he fixed his gaze on me. "Who did you say you were again?"

"Oh, I'm nobody." I smiled. "Just trying to figure out what it is you're doing."

"Do you live here?"

"I'm not that lucky."

I heard the whiz of weed whackers and trimmers in the back, wondering how Mrs. Thompson could continue on with her life and have all these people rummaging through her house only hours after her husband died. It was something only she could answer, but I hoped to God she wasn't doing it to keep up an appearance that everything was all right.

"It's the darndest thing," Chubby Man said. "I just can't figure out why this system failed. It doesn't make any sense. Everything seems to be working normally."

I continued on my stroll, moving between rooms and taking note of the smart home technology that Matt Bales mentioned to me last night. I took photos with my cell phone and dictated notes, stating what everyone was working on. They seemed to be finding no flaws in the system to suggest how Thompson might have been exposed to carbon monoxide when my cell phone lit up with an incoming call.

I found a quiet room and answered. "Dawson, now's not a good time."

"Where are you?"

Biting my lip, I muttered, "I'd rather not say."

"Sam, what are you up to?"

"Again, I'd rather not say."

"Christ. Now's not the time to be difficult. Lieutenant Baker just called looking for you."

I plugged my opposite ear and lowered my head. "Did he say what he needed?"

"He did." Dawson's tone dropped and grated like gravel. "He asked me to tell you to go the station."

"Did he say what this was about?"

Dawson swallowed hard enough for me to hear. "There's no easy way for me to say this, Sam." He paused. "He said he has some questions he needs to ask you about the murder of Richard Thompson."

Murder? My head picked up as I blinked away the stars.

Frozen to the floor I glanced around the room, suddenly

thinking that coming here wasn't the best decision I could have made. But I needed to find out if Richard was the one to have threatened me. "I can't do that right now, Dawson."

"And why is that?"

My head pounded as I took small but deliberate steps toward the exit. "Because I'm *inside* Thompson's house."

"Shit. I forgot." I heard Dawson's face fall into his hand and I imagined him pinching the bridge of his nose as he shook his head in disbelief. "You better get yourself out of there before this thing blows back on us."

Suddenly, I caught movement out of the corner of my eye and it was coming at me in a flurry of motion that prevented me from seeing what exactly it was. Reflexes kicked in and I ducked and flinched, feeling each sting of small hands come flying down over my head and neck.

"You did this!" Mrs. Thompson swatted at my face in a rage. "You killed my husband!"

I ducked again and took cover, trying to get away from the freight train barreling after me when I turned the corner and hurried into the hall. Suddenly, my toe caught on the wood flooring and sent me flying through the air. I landed hard on my stomach, smashing my mouth into the hardwood. The dull metallic taste of blood filled my mouth as a sharp ringing filled my ears. My head bobbed on my shoulders as I flattened my palms and pushed myself up. A sharp tug on the back of my head had me screaming for mercy.

Mrs. Thompson kicked me to the ground and growled like a tiger. "Because of you, I'm left with nothing. How dare you come into my house after what you said about my husband."

I kicked and flailed but she had a good pin on me and my body refused to budge. Then, suddenly, the weight of her body disappeared and I knew someone had pulled her off of me.

"Get up." A big hand gripped my elbow and pulled me to my feet.

My gaze traveled up his broad chest. "King?"

Alex peered down into my eyes. He had the biggest look of disappointment I had ever seen. With that look alone, I knew that I was in hot water.

Turning me around, King took my hands behind my back and said, "Christ, Samantha, why the hell did you come here?"

"What's going on? Why are you here?" I danced on my toes as I struggled to keep up with King's pace as he dragged me out of the house. "Was Richard Thompson murdered?"

King's vice grip tightened on my arm, cutting off the circulation as he pushed me closer to the exit. He kept his gaze forward and his voice low. "I suggest you stop talking before you say something I can't erase and you find yourself in bigger trouble than you might already be in."

CHAPTER TWENTY-ONE

WITH ONE HAND ON THE STEERING WHEEL AND HIS FOOT securely on the brake, Loxley wasn't paying attention to anything but the Backstage website. He was busy browsing the page on his smartphone when suddenly the music on the radio stopped for the news update.

He swept his gaze to the radio and stared with intense focus.

"The accidental death of billionaire Richard Thompson has sparked an outcry from many throughout Colorado, who now must ask themselves if they will ever see their money again and who else might be ripping them off."

Loxley turned the volume up and stared out the windshield as sound bites from hard-working middle class Coloradoans poured through his car speakers expressing their anger.

"Again," one man said heatedly, "here is another example of how the One Percent is finding a way to defraud the middle class by stealing more of the money we work hard for to increase their personal net worth. It's maddening," the man growled, "and thank God for journalists like the woman who exposed his scam, because who knows how much more this jerk would have stolen before finally getting caught. I'm glad he's dead."

Loxley smiled, knowing that his killing of Richard Thompson was what brought the conversation to the surface. But it was Samantha Bell's article exposing him as a fraud and hypocrite that made it all possible.

He listened to more soundbites of Thompson's victims speaking out, and the more Loxley heard, the more he felt like he was floating on cloud nine. Sinking into the bucket of his driver's seat, he closed his eyes and let his thoughts drift to Samantha.

Loxley's attraction to her was undeniable. He needed to get close to her without her knowing his true identity. They were a perfect team—perhaps better than he would have ever thought. Now, if he could get her to do it again...

Slowly, he slid his hand down his thigh before moving it between his legs. He felt the urge to kill blossom inside his chest, but even with the excitement budding, the heated pleasure of arousal escaped him.

Squeezing his eyes shut, he dug deeper into his mind trying to relive the moment he orgasmed when killing Richard. It was a feeling like no other and one he wished to experience again. His body craved it—cherished the universal power of his masculinity. But no matter where his thoughts took him, he couldn't do it, couldn't recreate the feeling or the same intense pulsating throb of that day that made him feel like the man he knew he could be.

"Damn you!" he cursed, snapping his eyes open and punching the dash with his right hand. "What kind of man are you if you can't get hard?"

His chest heaved as he breathed heavily. Soon his thoughts drifted back to Samantha. She was absolutely amazing. If there was one woman in the world he thought was made for him, it was her. She did a noble thing by exposing Thompson's fraud, and Loxley planned to one day send her his gratitude—perhaps even do it in person so that he could brush his lips across the backs of her silky soft knuckles and taste her for the first time.

When his cock twitched, he glanced down and smiled.

"He had what was coming to him," another pissed off victim said through the radio. "I'm sorry for his family, but he got what he deserved."

Feeling satisfied, Loxley turned the volume down, removed his hand from his lap, and dove his fingers inside the take-out bag in the seat next to him, eating the last bit of hamburger and washing it down with soda pop when an alert on his phone beeped.

He paused mid-chew and glanced at the relayed message. The system he had in place told him the image he left on Samantha's public forum had been clicked and viewed on the internet IP address he matched to the router belonging to Erin Tate.

"Let the games begin." His lips curled upward as he thought about his next move.

Loxley had hoped his comment would catch the attention of his two favorite investigative reporters and now that they knew they were being watched, it was time Loxley started thinking about preparing himself for the hunt—perhaps even inviting the two of them along with him.

His body tingled with excitement. Games. He loved his games.

By the time he lowered his smartphone onto his lap, he caught sight of the bright yellow Porsche rolling through the front gates he'd been staked out in front of for the past hour.

Loxley gave the Porsche a fifteen second lead before putting his car in gear. He eased his foot off the brake and transferred it over to the gas pedal as he pursued his target.

Following close behind the peacocking asshole, Donny Counts, Loxley tossed the hamburger wrapper into the bag, with plans to further his cause—especially knowing there was more work to be done now that his favorite crime reporter was putting her nose where she shouldn't.

CHAPTER TWENTY-TWO

KING HAD ME OUTSIDE THE THOMPSON HOUSE IN TWO seconds flat. Thank God for it too, because Mrs. Thompson would have happily gouged both my eyes out before I managed to escape her wrath.

Pushing me up against the side of his vehicle, King asked in a low voice, "Sam, what are you doing here?"

His right arm caged me in and a part of me wanted to reach up and stroke those sexy lips of his before reality pulled me back to earth, asking him the same. "Me, what are you doing here?"

King tilted his head to one side and gave a look. "You really shouldn't be here."

"Dawson told me Lieutenant Baker wants to speak to me about the *murder* of Richard Thompson." King's eyes narrowed as he exhaled a heavy breath through his nose. "I was right, wasn't I?"

"There is still a lot that needs to be answered."

"You can start by telling me what you found to make you open a homicide investigation."

King's eyes were sharp and focused. "We're not sure it was murder."

"Are you sure, because I'm only repeating the words Dawson relayed to me over the phone, the words that *your* lieutenant told him." When King didn't respond, I said, "Besides, I asked around inside. No one could point to a possible carbon monoxide leak so you must have found something else."

King gave me a look and glanced behind him. "You know the wealthy get preferential treatment in cases like these."

"Don't feed me any lines, Alex. I'm serious."

King looked me in the eye and asked, "Are you here because of your story?"

"This isn't about the story. It's about the threat I think Richard sent me before it went to print."

King pulled back and cocked his head with a mild look of surprise flashing in his eyes. "What are you talking about?"

I told him about the message I received and how I came here to verify if Richard was the one to have sent it. "This whole thing is just bizarre," I said. "The timing of his death and the release of my story highlighting his crimes."

"How did you expect to verify if Thompson was the one to have sent it, and why am I just hearing about this now?"

"I don't know." I brushed my bangs out of my eyes. "I didn't have a real plan. Search his office, I guess."

"Jesus, Samantha." He ran a hand over his head. "This is bad."

"What's bad? I don't understand."

King's hands were on his hips when he turned his head and glared. "I have to stop while I'm ahead."

"King, what's going on?"

"Stop." He held up a finger and I watched his gaze fall to my lips. "Listen, I'm not sure how much I can help you, but those two men heading our way—" King glanced over his shoulder to see how much longer he had me to himself before continuing. "They're going to ask you politely to come down to the station so they can ask you some questions about the death of Richard Thompson."

I pushed myself up on my toes to look over King's shoulder, finding myself staring at the two detectives—whose names I couldn't remember—encouraging Mrs. Thompson to go back inside and forget she ever saw me in her house.

"Am I a suspect?" My heels hit the street.

"Should you be?"

"Don't mess with me." I shoved one hand into King's chest. He barely budged.

"Just go along with it and do as they say." King took two steps back and lowered his voice. "Got it?"

"At least give me a glimpse into what this is about. You're scaring me."

King rooted his hands into his hips and turned his back. "I can't say."

"You can't or you won't?"

King turned his head and glared over his shoulder, smart enough not to respond.

"I'm calling my attorney," I said, pulling my cell from my back pocket.

King's hand landed on my arm and stopped me from making the call. "Make it easy on yourself and just hold off before you go involving a lawyer."

I kept my thumb hovered over the green call button as I heard Mrs. Thompson still barking my name from the house. The two detectives strode away from the front door, nodding to King as they passed. I made a mental note of the box the second detective was carrying, unsure of what it was. But something told me that might have been the reason I was being summoned downtown.

"Alex, you didn't read me my rights."

King turned his head and said, "You can drive yourself. I'll follow you there. Now, c'mon, let's go before someone decides to write you up for trespassing."

CHAPTER TWENTY-THREE

A HALF-HOUR LATER, I SAT ALONE IN INTERROGATION ROOM 4 waiting to see if I needed to call my attorney or not. King hadn't convinced me I was out of the woods yet, and I kept my fingers crossed that everything would soon shake itself out. But I needed to know what exactly this was about and why I was asked to come here in the first place.

My eyes followed the lines of the concrete bricks on the wall as I turned over the stones in my mind, looking for clues to how I'd found myself here. My nervous reflection stared back from the two-way mirror on the adjacent wall, and I did my best to keep my confidence up.

Time never felt as slow as it did when sitting under the light. I hoped the police wouldn't waste too much of my day without good cause, because I still had important work to do.

In my heart, I knew I had nothing to do with Thompson's death. But I didn't know what the police knew or what they had on me to bring me all the way down here just to talk.

That was what kept my knee bouncing beneath the table with anxious flutters tickling my insides. I was convinced it had something to do with my article. It was the only explanation that made sense. The combination of Thompson dying and my investigation was the perfect storm and I'd managed to stir the waters to a point where it seemed I had everyone's attention.

I tapped my nails on top of the metal table and glanced around, thinking about the way Mrs. Thompson attacked me. I wanted to be sympathetic to her grief—could relate to the intense pressure I assumed was squeezing her chest, strangling her heart. Coming to terms with a spouse's death was never easy. I knew what it was like, having said goodbye to my own husband years ago. But if she was the reason I was here now, I would never forgive her for accusing me of killing her husband.

The heavy metal door creaked open and quickly slammed shut. Homicide Detectives Robbins and Zimmerman—the two detectives from the Thompson house—stared as they entered the small square box. Robbins took the seat across from me as Zimmerman leaned with his back against the wall and glared with arms crossed. Neither of them spoke for the longest time as Robbins shuffled through a half-dozen manila folders to further intimidate me.

I turned to the mirror. Though I couldn't see him, I knew King was listening from somewhere. Maybe Lieutenant Baker, too. My two allies—colleagues left over from when my deceased husband, Gavin Bell, worked on the force. It seemed like a lifetime ago.

I finally broke the ice, asking again, "Was Richard Thompson murdered?"

Robbins swept his gaze above the rim of his reading glasses and glared. Zimmerman didn't react. "Is that what you think happened, Mrs. Bell?" Robbins asked.

"I only know what's being reported, that Mr. Thompson died of CO poisoning."

"And you believe that?"

I gave him a funny look.

"Because you being at the Thompson house suggests that maybe you have some doubts."

"Without knowing the facts, it's impossible to make a conclusive statement."

"What were you doing at the Thompson residence today, Mrs. Bell?"

"Working. Just like you."

"Did you know that we would be there?"

"How could I possibly know that?"

I was smart enough to know their tactics. I trusted my ability to steer their inquiry away from making a false admission of guilt, but I couldn't underestimate them, either. They were good at what they did and had years of experience interrogating Denver's worst.

"Someone has to keep the department in check." I grinned.

They never confirmed whether or not Thompson had been murdered. That left me nervous with what they thought I knew.

Robbins opened up one folder and produced today's newspaper. "Let's talk about this article you wrote for today's paper."

"What do you want to know?"

Zimmerman stepped away from the wall and approached the table. "Let's start by having you tell us who you tried to sell your story to."

"Sell my story to?" I brought my elbows to the table and leaned forward. "Maybe I should remind you that I don't have to sell my story to anybody as I work for the *Colorado Times*."

"At any time throughout your investigation was there any doubt that the *Times* wouldn't publish this story?"

"No."

The detectives stared with a salty look that dried out my

own eyes. For the remainder of the hour, they took turns asking me about my job, if I felt like my career was secure, and if I had ever accepted outside payment to keep my findings quiet. I answered each question to the best of my ability —and always truthfully—and still didn't see how any of this was relevant to learning the truth of how Thompson died.

"You clearly want to steer me in a certain direction, so why don't you just come out and say what it is," I said. The truth was, their dizzying array of questions was working— wearing me down like a tire without tread—and I was quickly loosing traction.

Robbins looked at me from beneath a heavy brow. "It's not uncommon for someone like Richard Thompson to be blackmailed."

I pinched my eyebrows, wondering where Robbins was going with this. "And what, you think I blackmailed him?"

Robbin's eyebrows raised just enough to convince me he did.

I fell back into my seat and folded my arms below my breasts. "Then show me the evidence."

Zimmerman licked his finger and reached for a second folder. I watched him open it and retrieve a stapled printout. He flipped it around and held it up for me to see. "Recognize this?"

My heart stopped beating. "How did you get that?"

"So you do recognize this?"

I didn't answer. We all stared, hoping someone would cave before they were forced to be the first to speak.

"For the record," Zimmerman said, "let us indicate that the interviewee, Samantha Bell, does recognize Exhibit B—"

"Oh this is bullshit." I snapped forward and stared at the date printed in the top left corner of what was clearly the final draft of my Thompson story. How the hell did someone get their hands on it, and where did they find it?

"I want my lawyer," I said, and just like that everything stopped.

Zimmerman stepped forward. "We thought you might say that."

My heart was knocking so fast I didn't know who to blame for this debacle. King, or the asshole who stole my work and clearly gave it to Thompson as a heads up to what was coming. Now I was convinced Thompson was the one who threatened me to try to silence me before the story broke.

There was a knock on the metal door and a second passed before Detective John Alvarez entered the room. He nodded to Zimmerman and motioned for both detectives to leave. As soon as it was just Alvarez and me, he looked to the mirror and said, "Turn off the cameras."

I glanced to the video camera in the ceiling corner and watched the red light flick off. Alvarez checked too before turning his attention to me.

I remained seated when I asked, "You don't actually believe I had anything to do with his death do you?"

"Of course not, Sam." He lowered himself down in the chair opposite me and gave me a sympathetic look.

"Then what's this all about? I wrote an article. The man died. It doesn't make me an accomplice to murder."

Alvarez was nodding as he listened to what I had to say. Then I watched him open the same manila folder and finger through the documents before finding the page he was looking for. As if knowing where my story was found wasn't enough, I couldn't wait to see this next piece of evidence.

"This was found with your article inside Richard Thompson's home office." He spun the image around and I made note of the long string of alphanumeric digits, wishing I had a photographic memory. A single glance wasn't going to be enough for me to commit it to memory. "Maybe you can tell me what it is."

"Well, since I don't know how my story got into the hands of your victim before it went to print, how in the hell can I identify that?" I kept my eyes trained on the image as long as possible but he finally put it back in the folder.

Alvarez locked his eyes on mine and sighed. "The question the department wants an answer to, Samantha, is who gave this to Thompson, if not you?"

CHAPTER TWENTY-FOUR

Escaping the afternoon sun, Susan entered the redbrick Tudor north of downtown that was home to Allison's digital marketing business. Scents of hot lunches and afternoon tea filled the halls as Susan made her way to the back where she found Allison clicking away on her computer. The door was open but Susan knocked regardless. Allison picked her head up and smiled.

"Sugar, c'mon in." Allison waved for Susan to come inside. "I'm just finishing up my last client review before I head out and take my afternoon jaunt around the block."

"I'll let you finish up." Susan pointed to the breakroom.

"It shouldn't be long," Allison said, waving. "Give me five minutes."

After several hours in the office, Susan needed a break. All morning, since meeting Damien Black, Susan couldn't wait to tell Allison more about her potential new client and the nonprofit he ran. Patty O'Neil, Allison's Chief of Operations, was at the table eating lunch when Susan joined her.

"Hey, Susan, you here to join Allison on her afternoon walk?"

"Anything to have her take a break."

Patty smiled. "In case you're curious, I have been keeping track of her schedule and I'm happy to report that Allison is taking breaks more often than before."

"That's great." Susan smiled.

"Eating healthier, too."

After Allison had been diagnosed with Huntington's disease, Susan and their group of friends asked Patty to make sure Allison followed through with her new commitments and what she promised them and her doctor. They didn't need a repeat of what happened, and certainly didn't need any one of them to have an extended hospital stay like the one Allison had endured. To make the change easier for Allison, they all vowed to live a healthier life.

"I'm sorry to hear about your client," Patty said. "Allison told me the news."

"Thanks." Susan wondered if Patty had read Samantha's article or not. She didn't ask.

"You still seeing that doctor?" Patty asked when she was at the sink, washing her plate. "He was cute."

"Took him to the airport this morning." Susan turned in her chair to face Patty.

"Visiting anywhere exciting?"

"He's traveling for work. Received an invitation from a job recruiter to visit Dartmouth."

Patty gave Susan a questioning look. "He's not going to take it, is he?"

Susan sighed. "I don't know."

She glanced to her cell phone, expecting Benjamin to call soon. She had been so distracted by Damien that she'd stopped thinking about Benjamin's future and where she fit in it—if at all. She felt awful for it, but also knew there was no harm in enjoying a friendly conversation with the opposite sex. And that was all it was with Damien—a potential client who just happened to be extremely good looking.

"Hope you got your jogging shoes on," Allison said happily when she stepped into the kitchen. "I'm getting fast."

Susan laughed, stood, and said to Patty, "It was great seeing you."

The women headed out the door, turned up the sidewalk, and began moving at a brisk pace. "Have you seen today's paper?" Allison asked.

Susan rolled her head to Allison. "And Sam's article. Couldn't believe it when I saw it."

Allison cast her gaze to the ground. "Me neither."

"How could she keep this from me?"

"She probably didn't want you to tip him off."

"Sam knows I can keep a secret."

Allison pumped her arms quicker and glanced up at Susan. "You're telling me that Sam's article wouldn't have put a strain on your relationship with Thompson?"

Susan knew it would have and decided to change the subject. "I didn't come here to talk about the article, and I'm not going to hold a grudge against Sam."

"No?"

Susan shook her head. "I came here to ask if you would like to visit a new computer lab with me."

Allison stopped, turned to Susan. "A new computer lab, huh?"

"Yeah. I met this guy this morning—"

"Does Benjamin know about this?"

"Benjamin is on his way to New England." Susan gave a knowing look. "And, no, he does not know about this potential new client."

"What's his name? This *potential* new client," Allison teased.

Susan started walking, passing through the shade of the trees, as she summed up her morning talk with Damien.

"Never heard of Backstage," Allison said with a pinched brow.

"Neither had I."

"And you're skeptical because you haven't heard of it or his non-profit?"

"I'm skeptical because he approached me like a hawk who had his eye on me."

Allison raked her eyes over Susan's attire. She was wearing a single-button pantsuit and looked like a million dollar executive. "You look great. What's the problem? I'd kill for a man to pick me up at a coffee shop."

Susan kept her gaze cast toward the ground. She couldn't admit to what she was really thinking, but when Allison suddenly stopped and pointed at Susan, she knew her friend had already figured it out.

"So you are here because of Sam's article."

Susan rolled her eyes and continued walking. Allison quickly caught up and kept stride. "I just thought maybe you had heard about Backstage," Susan said. "Since you're in a similar industry."

"And you want to know if I think this guy is legit?"

"Sure. Why not?" Susan shrugged her shoulders.

The corners of Allison's eyes crinkled when she flashed a knowing smirk. "Because Sam's article got you thinking there could be more scammers out there than we think."

"Yes," Susan admitted. "Of course it got me thinking. The last thing I need is to be caught up doing business with someone else running a scam."

"You didn't know about Thompson—"

"No," Susan snapped as if feeling offended. "If I would have known he was a con-man, I would have never done business with him."

"I know that, honey. None of this is your fault."

Susan locked eyes with Allison. "But I could have done a background check before signing him on."

"We learn from our mistakes." Allison looped her arm through Susan's and continued on with their walk. "You want to do your background check on this new man of yours? Let's start by having you tell me more about this mysterious Mr. Black."

"Well, for starters, he's young, rich, and completely enthusiastic about what he does." Susan leaned her shoulder into Allison's.

Allison held her chin high as she grinned. Staring straight ahead, she asked, "And is he single?"

"Does that mean you'll come with me?"

Allison gave Susan a playful look and they both burst out laughing.

CHAPTER TWENTY-FIVE

Loxley parked three spots behind Donny Counts on West 32nd street in the Denver Highlands. Stepping out of his vehicle, he followed Donny on foot. Weaving through small knots of people, Loxley kept pace with his target without drawing attention to himself.

Sensing he was being followed, Donny glanced over his shoulder and picked up his pace. The look on Donny's face almost made Loxley laugh. It was clear Donny was feeling paranoid. His eyes bloodshot red and his pace erratic and jumpy as a squirrel being hunted by a fox. But it wasn't Loxley that had Donny nervous. No, it was something else that had him scrambling for cover.

Loxley didn't worry about Donny recognizing him. He could operate in plain sight, blend in with the regular civilians and go undetected. And even if Donny managed to get away from Loxley, he had his target's phone traced, making it impossible to disappear for long before being tracked down once again.

Donny angled his body to the side and locked eyes with Loxley.

Loxley didn't flinch, knowing there was always a chance his target might spot him coming. But Loxley's research into his target almost certainly gave him an advantage to anticipating his next move far before he himself knew what that was.

Loxley picked up speed when Donny turned around the next corner, vanishing down a side street.

Donny's paranoia didn't surprise Loxley. He'd been watching Donny for nearly a year now, and each month that passed without someone learning of his secret only worsened Donny's anxiety. He was living a lie and he knew he would soon be caught if he didn't do something to stop the inevitable from knocking on his door.

Loxley hit the corner and turned just as Donny disappeared through a storefront.

He slowed and shortened his stride, looking around to see who else might be watching—if anyone else was following. When Loxley was certain he was alone, her read the sign above the door for an IV bar.

He smiled at the irony of stalking his prey while his target was coming to a rehydration IV bar with hopes of discovering the fountain of youth. Tech millionaires like Donny would do anything to extend their life, Loxley thought as he debated whether or not to enter himself.

Shuffling through his choices, and knowing the setting was small and intimate, there was always the risk of Donny knowing who he was. But Loxley liked games, liked subtle intimidation, and that's was all this was to him, a game—this one called, Chameleon.

Loxley pulled his cap down over his eyes, reached for the door handle, and entered.

He was immediately greeted by reception and Loxley made note of Donny's whereabouts. His target was seated in a leather recliner between two large snake plants not more than twenty feet from where Loxley stood. He was getting set up with his IV treatment.

"And what can we do for you today?"

The receptionist was a brunette with small breasts and flaring hips. "Not sure," Loxley said, looking up at the menu.

"First time?" Her eyes glimmered in the soft light.

"Is it that obvious?" Loxley charmed her.

Brunette laughed and was kind when explaining to Loxley the different options on the menu. "Really, your choice depends on what your goals are. We have jet-lag for those who just arrived to the Mile High City. Altitude sickness who can't handle the thin air." She giggled. "Hangover is self-explanatory; our athletic blend for those who push their daily limits physically; or simply health and wellness for those who want to feel their best."

"The thin air doesn't bother me, I'm not hung over, and I want to feel my best so, I guess I'll choose the health and wellness option."

"Excellent choice." Brunette wagged her head. "Let's get you set up."

Loxley was well aware of where Donny's eyes were pointed and what his hands were doing. He kept his spine straight and his pulse even as he followed Brunette to an empty chair, two down from where Donny was leaning back with his eyes half-closed.

"This should only take an hour." Brunette connected Loxley to the hydrating IV drip. She was wearing a perfume that warmed the base of his spine. "You should feel a boost in hydration almost immediately, and the energy kick will follow shortly after."

Loxley thanked the young woman and settled in with a magazine, preparing himself mentally to stay for the next hour. He paid no particular attention to Donny, and he was certain Donny hadn't recognized him—though a close look would certainly give him away.

Five minutes passed before the doorbell jangled at the entrance.

Loxley flicked his gaze to the man who'd just arrived and listened to Brunette speak to him as if he was a regular customer. He was tall, lean, with short cropped dark hair and a clean five o'clock shadow. Loxley knew who he was immediately—had seen him around with Sam—and when Brunette led him to the chair next to Donny, Loxley wasn't at all surprised to see the man tap Donny's knee.

Donny opened his eyes and sat up in his chair. Loxley knew by the way the two men were talking that they had planned to meet here. Did Samantha also know their secret? Loxley doubted it as he pretended to read his magazine, appearing to ignore what they were saying, and watched the man hand Donny the yellow envelop he had tucked under one arm when he had arrived.

"She has a file on you," the tall man told Donny. "According to her notes, has been investigating you and your business since Josh Stetson's trial."

Loxley stared into his magazine but kept an ear on the conversation, making notes of new information he could use to his own benefit—a justification to kill, if he doubted the reasons he had already.

"Shit." Donny's head hit the back of his chair. "I fuckin' knew it."

There was a moment of silence before the man said, "We can make this go away."

"You keep saying that," Donny said through clenched teeth, "but look what happened to that other guy. He's dead."

Loxley smiled, knowing they were speaking about Richard Thompson.

"That had nothing to do with this."

Donny glared at the tall man through narrow slits. "How can I be so sure you're telling the truth?"

"You have my word." The man shifted in his seat, touched his IV. "When's the last time you spoke with Stetson?"

"Not since he's been locked up." Donny dropped his tone to a whisper. "Why? You think he has something to do with this?"

The man shrugged. "He counted on you to have his back no matter what. Wouldn't be that difficult to arrange a visit and get him to agree to tell his side of the story."

"I'll have his back when he gets released. Besides, let's not forget that Stetson did that to himself." Donny leaned forward and touched his side, near his waist. "Look, I know I don't have much time, but I need you to get me everything she has on me before I leave town tomorrow night."

"Where are you going?"

"Don't worry about it. Get me what I ask and I'll make sure you get what you need." Donny eyed the man. "Just like you've always wanted."

"And if she makes it impossible for me to get what you want?"

Loxley lowered the magazine and turned his head to face his next victim. Donny flicked his gaze around the IV bar, barely glancing at Loxley. But that brief look was enough. Loxley knew Donny had no idea that he was nearly dead and nothing could save him now.

"Figure it out," Donny said to the man, ripping his IV from his arm. Donny Counts marched out of the building without saying another word.

Loxley watched Donny leave and turned to find his friend staring.

"Amazing stuff, huh?"

Loxley smiled. "Incredible."

CHAPTER TWENTY-SIX

AFTER SEVERAL GRUELING HOURS BENEATH THE LAMP, I WAS free to go. Lieutenant Kent Baker of the Denver Police Department, and longtime ally and someone I thought of as a friend, walked me to the door assuring me that my interrogation wasn't personal.

"But Samantha, this isn't over," he said in a serious tone. "And I'll need you to continue to cooperate until it is."

Baker was left over from the days of when my husband, Gavin, wore a badge and we were like family. Baker knew as well as I did that Gavin's legacy lived in both of us, and it was important to maintain that solid foundation. But what I couldn't say was how fractured I felt by the department's betrayal at what happened here today. I still didn't understand the alphanumeric key code, but I had my suspicions on who might have put my article in Thompson's hands.

I held his eyes for a moment before saying, "And by cooperating, you mean to hit pause on my own reporting?"

"Depends."

"On?"

"Whether you're with us or against us." Lieutenant Baker

didn't blink. "Chief Watts is more concerned with how the TV reporters will spin this than he is with whatever you decide to put in print."

I wasn't sure if I should take his words as a compliment or treat it as a slap to the face. But I knew what he was saying. TV had ratings to chase, where us paper reporters only had subscribers to maintain—which currently wasn't all that many readers.

"No matter what more gets said about Thompson," I tipped my head back and took one step forward, "there will be a shift in the public narrative. If I'm going to hold off on telling my side of what happened here today, the department is going to have to let me in on what you all know."

Lieutenant Baker's eyes narrowed. "We'll be in touch."

By the time I exited the station, it was evening and the temperature was falling. As I made my way to my car, I began catching up on missed phone messages. Mason was at work, Heather too. All was good on the home front, and it put a smile on my face knowing I hadn't been missed. Then the calls came from the girls.

I listened to the first message from Erin. "Sam, I'm meeting up with the girls at our spot. You should come. Call me."

There was a call from Susan. "Samantha, we're all at the Rio and it's just not the same without you. Take a break from whatever you're working on and come join us."

An hour later, Allison called. "Sam, where the hell are you? You're supposed to be buying tonight. Call me. I need to know you're alive."

I sent a group text confirming they hadn't left. They all responded at nearly the exact same time, getting me to laugh and releasing some of the day's tension from my chest. Sliding my key into the ignition, I thought how a drink and time spent with the three women who understood me best was the exact recipe I needed to decompress from the storm I just endured.

Fifteen minutes later I was stepping up to the bar and ordering a margarita before plopping my butt down in the booth next to Ali. She put her arm around me and I laid my head against her shoulder before guzzling half of my drink in an impressive, and somewhat embarrassing, manner, the girls watching with disbelief.

"My god, girlfriend, I can't wait to hear what's on your mind." Susan's jaw dangled as she stared.

I laughed and wiped my face with the back of my hand, feeling exhausted as soon at the alcohol seeped its way into my bloodstream.

"You look tired." Allison was the first to see the look of exhaustion pulling my face down. "And a bit beat up."

"Where did you disappear to?" Susan wrapped her lips around her own straw and asked.

I glanced to Erin who knew about my visit to the Thompson residence but, for whatever reason, had kept it a secret from the girls. "You wouldn't believe the afternoon I had." I summed up my visit to Thompson's house and what led to me having to take a trip downtown to answer some questions.

"The cops are investigating Thompson's death as a homicide?" Susan sounded surprised.

My brow twisted when I apologized for keeping my story a secret.

"You could have told me, you know?" Susan said, pressing her lips together in a thin line.

"I kept the lid on this one." I flicked my eyes to Erin. "Had to."

"Susan's already forgiven you," Allison assured me before rolling her eyes to Susan. "Haven't you?"

Susan leaned forward and propped herself up on both her

elbows. "I have this fear that I'm going to mistakenly find myself promoting another scam now."

It wasn't my intention for Susan to doubt her clients, but now it made sense why she seemed to be glaring at me from behind a curtain of dark lashes.

Allison took a carrot from the appetizer plate and snapped off a bite. "Don't worry, Sam. I got Susan's back on this one. We're planning to check out this new client of hers together, isn't that right?"

Susan nodded and smiled at Allison. Then she paused a second before asking me, "Did I inadvertently make Richard Thompson rich?"

I slid my hand across the table and draped it over hers. Her hands were warm and soft to the touch. Susan had organized enough fundraisers for Thompson to be concerned, but none of it mattered. "You didn't know. At the time, neither did I."

"What's in the past is in the past; don't beat yourself up." Allison nodded, speaking not only to Susan, but to all of us.

Erin was still stealing glances at me and I could tell by the look on her face that she was still waiting to hear me confirm if Thompson had been murdered or not. Without speaking, I looked her in the eye and confirmed her suspicions with a single head nod.

"You were right," she said lightly.

"Wait, what?" Susan glanced around the table. "Thompson *was* murdered?"

The three of us shushed her and told her to keep her voice down. Then I said, "I don't know what the police found, but the department just doesn't send four homicide detectives to a scene without reason."

"What does this mean for your story?" Susan asked.

"The story goes on." Allison flicked her gaze to me. "Right?"

"If Thompson was murdered, I need to learn what the police found and whether he was killed because of the dirt I uncovered on his charity foundation." I fixed my gaze on Erin. "And we need to know if LilJon was behind it, like he seemed to be suggesting."

Allison and Susan shared a look of concern and I knew I had opened up a huge can of questions that were soon to follow.

"Wait." Allison held up one hand. "Are you saying you know who the killer is?"

Erin took her eyes off of mine and flicked her gaze to Allison. "We might."

CHAPTER TWENTY-SEVEN

ERIN PULLED UP THE MESSAGE LilJon LEFT ON OUR message board and passed her smartphone around the table so that everyone could read what it said.

No one knew what to say or how to respond. It was creepy enough that Thompson might have been murdered, but now that it seemed like Erin and I were being watched by the man who could be his killer, the hair on my arms was permanently upright.

A minute passed in silence before the table fully erupted like a propane explosion. A dozen different theories and thoughts twisted around the booth in a dizzying array of possibility. Suddenly, it wasn't speculation that Thompson had been murdered, but truth, and everyone had an opinion as to why.

"Whoever wrote that was watching us work," I said.

"Are they still?" Susan fingered the necklace draped around her neck as she looked to the faces stationed around us.

"I can only assume they are," I muttered as I twirled the straw through my ice.

Susan looked me in the eye. "You're not a suspect, are you?"

"They certainly made me believe I was," I said, summing up the questions the detectives asked and how it was related to my story. "They found a printout of my story on Thompson's desk inside his home. It was postmarked *two* days before it went to print."

"This isn't good, Sam," Erin said. "Someone is setting you up."

Suddenly, I didn't feel so hot. Susan didn't like this, and neither did I. Anyone with access to my and Dawson's shared folders was on my list of potential suspects to be tracked down and interviewed, but that might not even yield any results.

My mind churned as I thought about how the paper got hacked—how Travis had his intern Brett working everyone's private computers, updating the security software. Then I turned to Allison and asked, "What do you know about key codes?"

Allison quirked an eyebrow. "Why do you ask?"

"A key code was found with my article on Thompson's desk." I shared more of the specifics, said I had seen it only for a moment, and everyone sat still waiting to see where Allison would take this next.

"Was the string of code alphanumeric?"

I nodded, producing a pen and jotting down the first few characters of the code. I couldn't remember past the sixth digit.

Allison glanced to my example. "Did it contain a QR code?"

"Not that I saw."

The table was silent as they listened to Ali and me volley back our questions and answers. Suspense built, buzzed in the air overhead, and I could see the spark in her eye the further down the path we traveled.

The crease between her eyebrows deepened. "Did the code happen to begin with a 1 or 5?"

Slowly, I nodded, pointing at my example. "One."

Allison licked her lips and cast her gaze to the table as she took a moment to gather her thoughts. When she was finished thinking it through, she asked me, "Sam, do you have a digital wallet?"

"Digital wallet?" I had no idea what she was referring to.

"Yes. A digital wallet refers to a cryptocurrency vault. Do you have one?"

"No. Is that what the key code is?"

"By what you're describing, it sounds like that's exactly what this is." Allison sat upright and explained, "There are two sets of key codes—one private, one public—and both are needed to transfer and pay with Bitcoin."

"When you asked about it beginning with 1 or 5, what did it matter?"

"Because that determines who is paying and who is receiving."

"And a 1 means what exactly?"

"That's the public key code, or, in other words, the code that receives money, kind of like their account number." Allison continued on, breaking things down as best she could when explaining QR codes and that most who use virtual currency elect not to go the paper wallet route like what it seemed the detectives had found on Thompson's desk. "That's highly unusual and certainly something to make note of. Whoever was setting this up should have used a seed phrase instead. Much safer."

I nodded, blood thrashing in my ears, now certain why I was called in for questioning. They were hung up on a digital wallet, something I knew nothing about.

"But why would this key code have been found with Sam's article?" Susan asked.

Allison lifted both her eyebrows. "Hate to say it, Sam, but it appears that someone was trying to make it look like you were the one blackmailing Thompson with your article and getting paid in Bitcoin."

CHAPTER TWENTY-EIGHT

"Donny, baby, you shouldn't have." Rose took Donny's face between her hands and pressed her lips against his.

"You're worth it." Donny's lips fluttered against her mouth as he pushed his fingers through her long cascading curls and deepened his kiss.

Rose moaned and giggled as she pulled away to glance once again at the diamond necklace Donny had just clasped around her neck. Her cheeks burned with color and her eyes lit up with love.

"I have more where that came from." Donny ironed his hand down her side, landing on the flare of her hip.

Rose smiled and gave him a look that said, *you shouldn't have*. Then she leaned in and swiped her tongue against his as Donny opened the front of her shirt and pulled it down her arms. Peppering kisses across her neck, Donny pushed Rose onto the couch and she wrapped her body around his. Soon they were naked and making love on the couch, Loxley missing out on all the action.

Busy responding to work emails on the monitor opposite

the love nest, Loxley caught himself unknowingly rubbing his arm where the IV had been placed earlier in the day.

He glanced down and ran his index finger over the bruised vein, feeling noticeably more alert since his impromptu health and wellness check with Donny Counts. "I should personally thank you," he said, turning to the monitor where Donny was just finishing up with Rose, "for introducing me to the hydration bar."

Loxley watched Rose slide out from beneath Donny and leave the couch first. Her breasts were small but firm and did nothing to entice Loxley to follow her to the master bath where he knew she was going.

"Enjoy it while it lasts," he whispered to Donny.

Not long after, Donny disappeared off screen and Loxley listened to their conversation as both of them showered. Ignoring most of what they said, Loxley busied himself with system maintenance checks and made sure everything was in order. Tonight was the night Loxley planned to kill Donny.

Little John, the cat, jumped into Loxley's lap and purred loudly. Loxley rubbed his ears and continued working. He hadn't originally planned to kill Donny today, but after what he heard at the hydration bar he knew he had little choice if he was going to do it before the opportunity passed. Loxley hurried home and immediately went to work.

Cracking into Donny's home security system, Loxley had eyes and ears in nearly every single room. When he lost track of them, he simply switched over to the camera on Donny's cellphone which usually gave him a nice visual of Donny's smug little face staring back at him.

Luckily, Loxley knew just how he was going to kill Donny and had done plenty of research beforehand to not only be sure he could complete the task, but confidently get away with it. The excitement built and he could feel the itch in the way his fingers moved over the controls.

A dark shadow moved across his upper right computer monitor.

Loxley tipped forward and squinted into the screen.

Donny was back in the living room and in particularly high spirits. Loxley checked to see Donny was wearing his insulin pump when Rose soon followed close behind. They were both wearing silk robes as they opened another bottle of white wine from the refrigerator. They toasted over plates of expensive looking seafood flown in from the coast and game meats from the mountains of Colorado. Donny was living the high life, a life drastically different from his poor upbringing. It was almost sad to know this American Dream would die a quick death. It had to be done.

The corners of Loxley's lips tugged as he grinned.

"You see here, Little John," Loxley pointed at Donny in the screen, "he is planning to disappear and take all the money he stole from his investors along with him."

Little John flicked his tail and softly meowed in response.

As Loxley stared at his target, he thought it amusing that he would never allow that to happen. He controlled Donny's future; the man's destiny rested solely with him.

"Of course, we won't allow that to happen," Loxley said to Little John.

Heat traveled down Loxley's spine and settled between his legs. The intense tingling feeling was back. Loxley knew that tonight was going to be a great night. One he would certainly never forget.

"You said there was another present for me?" Rose asked Donny. Donny nodded. "So where is it?"

Donny laughed into his wine glass before placing it on the center of the island counter between the platters of food. He moved to the edge of Loxley's screen, told Rose to turn her back, and Loxley watched Donny produce a letter-sized envelope from a drawer near the stove.

Rose covered her eyes, bouncing on her toes with excitement as she laughed.

Donny moved behind her, wrapping his arms around her small body. He pulled her against his chest and held out the envelope for her to take. "Go on, open it up," he murmured in her ear.

Rose twisted around, glanced at him once, and quickly opened up the envelope.

Loxley held his breath as he intently watched, not knowing himself what it was. He waited to hear Rose squeal with delight when suddenly she surprised him by saying to Donny, "What the fuck is this?"

"First class tickets."

"I can see that." Rose was pissed.

"Southeast Asia. It's where you said you always wanted to travel."

"One way, Donny?" Rose snapped.

Donny latched his hands onto her hips and tugged her against his pelvis. "Tropical blue waters and spicy Thai food forever."

Rose pushed him away. "I thought you said you were going to take care of it."

Loxley chuckled as if watching a comedy on YouTube.

"I did, baby." Donny chased after her. "I met with him today."

Rose snapped back and waved the tickets in front of his face. "Then why are we hiding in Thailand?"

"We're not hiding," Donny pleaded.

"Oh, no? What would you call it?"

"Retirement." Donny smiled.

"I don't know, Donny." Rose sighed.

Donny scooped her up in his arms and dipped his mouth over hers. "What don't you know?"

"It seems sudden."

Donny kissed her. "We have no choice. It's the way it has to be."

Loxley sat up straight, laced his fingers together, and extended his arms in front of him until his fingers cracked. Then he hunched forward, grinned, and went to work.

"It's time, Little John," Loxley said. His arousal was so hard it hurt. Throbbing against his zipper, Loxley begged for a release. He turned to the framed desk photo and blew a kiss to Samantha, then said, "Say your goodbyes Rose. And don't worry, you won't be going to Thailand alone."

CHAPTER TWENTY-NINE

IT WAS NEARLY TEN O'CLOCK BY THE TIME I ARRIVED HOME and was letting Cooper out to relieve himself. I stood on the front stoop watching him sniff around the two cottonwood trees in my neighbor's yard as I mentally began putting together a list of who might want to frame me. None of this made any sense, and there were too many potential suspects to even begin narrowing down my investigation.

Cooper trotted his way further up the sidewalk and finally lifted his back leg on his favorite pine.

That was how my day felt. Like I was the pine getting pissed on. Nothing seemed to shake itself free once I said goodbye to the girls. Erin asked if I wanted to come over and talk things out, but I didn't have it in me. I just needed to be alone and find answers to the questions I couldn't stop asking myself.

What was my article doing in Richard's house in the first place? What was whoever put it there hoping to achieve? It wasn't like they had stolen my story. I still had a copy. It was going to get printed regardless. So how did that explain the digital wallet? It made no sense.

When Cooper finished, he kicked up the grass and wiped his paws as he hurried back to the house. My head was pounding, my eyes blurry with exhaustion.

Thompson's death had only brought on more headache. It didn't take me long to circle back to the beginning of where this mess all started, with anyone who had access to my files.

I reached behind me and retrieved my cell from my back pocket. Scrolling through my list of contacts, I quickly found Travis Turner's number. It was only the IT office and useless this late at night. No one would be in until morning. I thought about calling Dawson, but again, I didn't have it in me to explain how I was questioned by the police. In the end, I just wanted to get to sleep and start fresh in the morning.

Cooper trudged up the house steps and turned to face the street when sitting next to me. I scratched his head and tipped my own back to stare into the orange glow overhead. There was a chill but nothing uncomfortable.

A pair of headlights turned onto our quiet street and I instantly thought it was Mason. I expected him home from work any minute. I watched the car park behind my Outback and, as soon as the lights flicked off, Cooper leaped from the stairs and bounded toward the driver's door. King stepped out and greeted Cooper before landing his gaze on mine.

He smiled, but my expression remained deadpan and uninviting. King made his way over to me regardless of my glare. "I was hoping I would find you awake."

"Not for much longer," I said.

King leaned in and kissed me on the cheek. I closed my eyes and inhaled his masculine scent, appreciating his bravery to drop work and treat me like his lady.

I rolled my eyes over to his. "I hope you're here to relay a message from Baker."

King's eyes hardened—the look of a seasoned professional with too many difficult years on the job. There was so much I wanted to ask him before I allowed him into the house, and I was still a little hot from him advising me not to call my attorney before the inquisition began.

"Can I come inside?" he asked.

"You have something you'd like to share first?" He had to earn his invite.

King gave a single nod of his head and followed me into the house where, together, we kicked off our shoes at the door before falling heavily into the couch. King spread his arms out over the back and I leaned against his chest, settling in for an honest conversation. Then he wrapped his big protective arms around me and instantly melted away my concerns. It didn't take long for me to close my eyes and listen to him breathe. Eventually, King broke the silence by saying, "Sam, I'm sorry for what you had to endure today. My hands were tied. There was nothing I could do to stop it."

I stared at the wall with round, tired eyes as I chose my next words carefully. "You said you had something you'd like to share with me?"

"I spoke with Leslie at the coroner's office." He paused. "Richard Thompson was drunk at the time of death."

"So that explains how he didn't get out."

"It's the best theory we have."

Squeezing his forearms, I felt his muscles twitch beneath the pressure. "The key code you found with my article is a Bitcoin paper wallet."

King's thumbs stopped stroking, letting me know they hadn't figured that out yet. Something about that made me smile. "Allison helped me figure it out," I said. "But you should know that it wasn't mine."

"I didn't think it was."

"And I don't know how my article made its way to Thompson's home office."

"I never suspected you did."

"But someone thought I did."

"Robbins and Zimmerman had to ask, Sam. You know the procedure."

All too well, I thought as I rehashed my day and started to get angry about it all over again. The fire in my belly was back and I was more determined than ever to find out how I managed to end up dead center in the hottest investigation in town.

"Please tell me that today wasn't designed to silence me," I murmured.

"What?" King tipped his head forward. "Is that why you think I asked you to the station?"

I mentioned what Baker said to me on my way out.

"The department isn't trying to stop you from doing your job."

I thought King's words over before I said, "There is something that I couldn't say to the other detectives." I felt King stiffen behind me. I gently unwrapped his arms and twisted around to face him so I could look him in his eyes when I told him about the message Erin and I found on our message board.

King sucked in his bottom lip, stood, and shoved a single hand through his hair. I knew he was pissed, feeling betrayed by my silence. We found ourselves in uncharted waters when having to navigate both our professions and our relationship.

"You couldn't have mentioned this to me earlier?" he asked.

"How could I when I was being treated like the department's primary suspect?"

King stared with a pinched expression like I had never seen.

"We think LilJon might be responsible."

King's cell phone rang before he could respond. He took the call in the kitchen and, without overhearing more than two sentences, I knew he was being called to a potential homicide.

"That was work." King pointed to his cellphone when he came back into the living room. "I need to go."

I stood there nodding with my arms folded and my hands tucked under my arms.

"We need to talk more about this message and who you think that paper wallet belongs to."

I nodded. "Just so long as it's a two-way street."

King gave me a look and I kissed him goodbye so he wouldn't forget who he was dealing with.

He slid on his shoes, opened the door, and left me to watch him drive away through the front window with Cooper by my side.

Without warning, the house lost power.

I glanced to the neighbors to make sure it wasn't just me standing in the dark. They were out too. When my cell phone started ringing, I stumbled through the pitch-black house and checked to see who was calling, thinking it might be King.

"Erin," I answered. "Is your power out?"

"No. Why?"

The lights flickered back on. "Never mind. It just came back on," I said, hearing my computer in the kitchen reboot. Making my way there, I watched with bewilderment as my computer came to life and the printer spit out a piece of paper with a block of text neatly etched on a single sheet.

"Listen, Sam," Erin said into my ear as I retrieved the printout and began reading what it said. My heart stopped as I finished, and the hairs on my neck raised with absolute fear. "Lil' Jon just sent another message."

CHAPTER THIRTY

JOEY GARCIA WAS UP BEFORE THE SUN, AS USUAL, AND BACK from his morning run by the time his wife, Cecelia, and their three-year-old daughter, Katie, were beginning their morning ritual of stories and oatmeal for breakfast.

Wiping the sweat from his brow, Joey entered the room and said, "Good morning."

His wife's lips barely broke a smile. He leaned in to kiss his bride and was stunned when she pulled away. "Not know, Joey."

Looking his wife in the eyes, Joey slowly retreated and felt her rejection stab his heart with the dull pain that seemed to only be getting worse. Nodding, he turned to their master bedroom and stripped the sports towel away from his neck, snapping it down to his side in a rare show of frustration.

Joey was convinced this was only a bump in the road and eventually it would pass. His marriage was solid, or so he thought. It wasn't like they hadn't experienced difficult times before, but this one was different. The entire house could feel the change in energy blowing in swiftly like the change of seasons.

Shedding his running clothes, Joey jumped into the shower knowing he was still madly in love with his college sweetheart. As he scrubbed the sweat off his skin, he thought about the relationship he had with Cecelia—both past and present—and still found himself smiling when thinking of her. It was a once and a lifetime type of love and he would do anything for her—and his daughter.

After the shower, he dressed for work—slacks, buttoned up collared shirt, and shined leather shoes—before entering the home office and firing up his laptop computer.

Joey dove into today's emails with the same enthusiasm as when he first started reporting. As a rookie journalist, he was out to prove himself as one of the best. Slowly, he climbed his way to the top and still held lofty goals for what he saw his career eventually becoming, but seven months ago everything changed, including the steam driving him forward.

Work seemed to be his only escape from the torments of his current life. The fact that his chosen industry was struggling to maintain a foothold in today's hypercompetitive world of print journalism only made Joey more anxious to know what came next.

He clicked away, knocking out one email after another, responding to dozens of sources he'd been in communication with when, suddenly, he stopped on one particular headline that gave him reason for pause.

A bubble closed around his head.

Joey stared at the screen, debating whether or not to open the email that had his palms sweating. His heart knocked against his ribs in a steady drum of nerves. Though he knew he needed to see what was inside, he feared that he might not like what he was about to learn.

He turned his head toward the door and thought about his wife, his daughter, and the life he wanted to give them.

Knowing he had little choice, he turned back to his computer and clicked the email open.

It was short and straight to the point. Though he didn't move, his heart beat faster as he wiped his face to ward back the pellets of perspiration he felt forming across the backs of his shoulders and over his brow.

Joey couldn't believe what he read.

Donny Counts was in the hospital.

The email didn't say how or when it happened, just that he was in critical condition. But that was enough information for Joey to know what he had to do next.

In a moment of panic, he closed his email browser and navigated to his work folders stored on the cloud. It took a minute to load but, as soon as it did, Joey entered his username and password only to receive an error. Joey entered his credentials again. Another error.

"Not now," Joey said to himself as he cleared his browser and tried again. When his access had been denied for a third time, Joey knew that something was wrong.

He leaned back in his chair with a perplexed look twisting his brow. Never one to fully trust computers with his most important files, Joey kept his work stored in several places, including an external hard drive. Unfortunately, what he was after today, he could only get on the cloud.

Pushing back from his desk, Joey stood and passed beneath his many journalism awards hanging on his walls, wondering what happened to his once prestigious career and at what point it started to go wrong. He could trace it back to seven months ago when he received the worst news of his life, but he was certain that there were signs even before that fateful day.

Joey opened up a cabinet file and retrieved a thumb drive and other important files before dropping them into his shoulder bag. Closing up his office, he made his way into the kitchen only to find another problem waiting.

Since he'd been gone, Cecelia now had Katie's medical bills fanned out across the kitchen table. Cecelia heard Joey enter the room and, without looking up at him, said, "They're threatening to take this to collections if we don't pay."

"Let insurance handle it."

Her tired eyes lifted to his. "No one wants to take responsibility. I'm on the phone with the insurance company and the hospital and both are making me feel like we're the victim."

Joey flicked his gaze to Katie. A small smile sprouted on his lips. Turning his attention back to his wife, he could see her holding back the tears that threatened to fall. Suddenly, he felt his gut writhe with feelings of guilt. Katie coughed and got Joey to look at her again. Their little girl didn't have the appetite she once did, and not long from now her hair would disappear and she would be skinnier than she already was. Her leukemia was affecting them all—forcing their backs against a wall and placing them in front of the carnage neither of them ever saw coming.

Joey turned back to Cecelia. "It will all work itself out."

Cecelia gave him a skeptical look.

"Have I ever let you down?" Joey stepped to his wife, cupped the back of her skull, and pressed his wet lips between her eyes.

Cecelia gripped his arm and whispered, "I love you with all my heart."

In that moment, Joey's throat closed and he wanted to cry. Instead, he headed out the door with the intention of surviving at least one more day.

CHAPTER THIRTY-ONE

IT CAME TO ME IN MY SLEEP AS MOST BIG REVELATIONS DID. I couldn't believe I hadn't thought of it before, but now I was certain I knew what type of killer we were dealing with.

After locking the doors and ensuring Mason got home from work safely, I put it all together. Now it was morning and I was once again going over the pieces to the puzzle spread across my kitchen table, making sure that it all still made sense.

And it did. I hadn't been dreaming.

In front of me were my notes on Richard Thompson along with the photos I had taken of his smart home technology system first mentioned by Matt Bales. The answers had been there all this time but until I received last night's letter from our mysterious LilJon, I hadn't been able to see it as clearly as I did now.

"That's how he did it," I said to myself, sipping my coffee nice and slow. "He hacked Thompson's house."

The roasted taste lingered on my tongue and my head was dizzy with disbelief. His name was Loxley, and the way he killed Thompson was genius. Without having to ever step foot inside his victim's house, there was no evidence linking him to the crime. Which had me questioning if he even knew about Thompson having my story, or if it was pure coincidence that it had been there at the time of his death. I didn't know. If it was coincidence, what else was at play, and who was behind that?

Without thought, I picked up the printed message Loxley had sent me just after the power went out last night. Reading it again, I was left with the same queasy feelings as I went to bed with.

Precious Bell, for we live in a time of insatiable greed, and if not checked, will give the green light for others to follow. I, for one, will not allow this to happen. I hope you won't either. Your loving admirer, Loxley.

I sat back and rubbed my face inside my hands. There was another coincidence that I needed to make sense of, and this one scared me to death. It was the timing of when the house lost power and when Loxley somehow wormed his way into my computer to personally "hand" deliver this note. It was too perfect to ignore. He knew that I was home, but did he also know that I was alone? And if my theory about how Thompson died was right, then I wouldn't put this past him either.

The tips of my fingers were cold as I sat there asking myself who Loxley was; if it was a he or she, even; and how close to my house were they when sending me this message?

Reaching for my cup, I slurped another hot sip of coffee, hoping to warm my shivering bones before putting my laptop directly in front of me. Over the next half-hour I scoured the web in search of news of another death similar to Thompson's. When I found nothing, I messaged King. He was quiet and never responded to my text so I turned to my police scanner, once again coming up empty. Could Loxley still be hunting his next victim? Or was this just his way of making me believe there was a next victim?

My stomach rolled and a sour taste swelled my tongue. There were too many unknowns to decide where I should start looking. I took Loxley's messages seriously and was worried this psycho killed somebody else or was gearing up to murder again. Who that was, I couldn't say. King's call last night could have been related, but he hadn't told me anything. What really had me creeped out was how Loxley seemed to involve me in whatever sick game he was playing.

Loxley was watching me and waiting to see how I would respond to his latest letter. I had to be careful I didn't fall into his trap. Still, there was no evidence to suggest Thompson had even been murdered, only Loxley's admission to guilt through a series of encrypted messages that read like a vigilante's poem to the world.

Why he chose me, I still didn't know. Nor did I like that he had. As I sat in my quiet little house waiting for my son to wake up, waves of paranoia moved up and down my body as I looked at everything electronic being a potential point of vulnerability.

Could he be listening to me now? I asked myself when staring at the new smart speaker I purchased because Mason thought it was cool. Was he monitoring my keystrokes to know what thoughts I was having when searching the web? These thoughts crippled my pursuit and I wondered if that, too, was by design to keep him at a safe distance.

Birds chirped outside my window and cars sputtered on a nearby street, but I heard nothing until Mason's bedroom door creaked open.

I saw my son getting ready for school, and I welcomed the distraction found in our morning routine. It was his last week before summer break and he was already mentally checked out. I couldn't blame him. It had been a long year with plenty of ups and downs and we were both ready for a new routine.

Five minutes later, and a quick scramble to figure out who Loxley's next victim might be, Mason skidded across the kitchen floor on his socks.

"Alexa," he spoke to the smart speaker, "should I go to school today?"

The smart speaker didn't respond.

"Hey, who unplugged this?" Mason asked me, holding up the cord.

"Sorry, honey, the power went out last night and I was worried a power surge might fry its insides." Mason gave me a funny look. It was a white lie, and I felt bad about it, but I didn't have the heart to tell him the real reason I decided to pull the plug.

Mason jammed the prongs into the outlet and fired it up. I listened to it boot up, wondering what excuse I could make to get rid of it without upsetting my son. I had none.

"Ah, shoot. Whatever," Mason said, not having the time to wait until the software loaded. "I'm running late as it is."

"Make the most of it, kid," I said, blowing him a kiss goodbye.

With his bookbag on his back, Mason flung the front door open just as Allison was climbing the steps. I watched through the glass as they shared a quick laugh, Mason giving her a fist bump before turning up the street.

"Door's open," I said when I heard Allison knock.

Allison found her way to the kitchen. "In case you ever find yourself doubting your ability to parent, just know you're doing an excellent job."

I smiled at my friend. "Thank you."

"No way I could have done as good a job alone like you did."

"But I'm not alone. I have you."

Allison smiled, then asked, "So, what's up buttercup? Why did you drag me out of bed so early?"

I pushed the chair across from me out from under the table with my foot and said, "You might want to sit down for this."

CHAPTER THIRTY-TWO

ALLISON WAS UNCHARACTERISTICALLY QUIET AS SHE READ the note I received from Loxley. "Is this who stole your article?" she asked when she finished and raised her eyes to mine.

"I don't know. Could be," I said. "I was hoping you'd be able to help figure that out."

Allison cast her gaze back down to the paper. "It seems like he wants to admit that he is the one behind the murder of Richard Thompson."

Bringing my elbows to the table, I agreed. "It's the second time he's hinted at wanting to own Thompson's death. He also promised in his first message there would be others to follow. It's like he wants people to think he did it."

"So, the question we need to ask ourselves is if he's only an attention seeker," Allison raised one eyebrow, "or the actual murderer."

"Exactly."

"And what do you believe?"

"I think he might actually be the one to have killed Thompson."

"Any others you know about?"

"Not that I know about."

Allison sucked back a deep breath that whistled on its way in, and was still pinching a corner of the paper in one hand when she said, "It's a strange way to take credit." She lifted her gaze. "*Loving admirer?*"

I nibbled on the inside of my cheek and shrugged. "I'm struggling to decide if he's a complete psychopath or a vigilante out to set the record straight."

Allison shook her head and blinked a couple of times before asking, "Anyone else know about this?"

"Only Erin."

Allison had a quizzical look on her face. "No other media outlets?"

"Nothing. I haven't heard from my editor about any other reporting, so I'm thinking I'm the only one he's communicating with."

"Which would explain why he's calling you *precious* and his *loving admirer.*"

My lip curled with disgust but I knew what Allison was thinking, because I was thinking it too. Loxley was coming out of hiding and beginning to let the outside world in. He wanted us to know he murdered Thompson, like the public would thank him for doing it. I was afraid of exactly that happening. We had a vigilante on our hands and it wouldn't be long before his story got picked up by others—perhaps even inspiring others to take up his cause.

Allison set the note down and I watched the crease between her eyes deepen. "Tell me again how you received this."

I rehashed the same story from a minute ago. "I know he hacked into my network; I just can't prove how exactly he did it."

"You're probably right, but let's take a look under the hood and see if we can't find any traces he might have left behind." Allison rubbed her hands together and motioned for me to give her my laptop. I turned my computer to her when she asked, "Is this a work computer?"

"No. Personal."

"But you mentioned there was a hack to the *Times* network, right?"

I nodded. "I learned about it yesterday, but no one knows when the breach actually happened. It could have been months ago."

We shared a knowing look. "Which could be the reason you were personally targeted, too."

"And might also explain how my story made its way to Thompson's home office."

Allison held my gaze and said, "Less logical things have happened."

Over the next several minutes, I watched Allison work. Her fingers moved swiftly across the keys, the air dancing with clicks and taps as she searched for vulnerability and points of access between the cracks in my computer security. Coming to an abrupt halt, Allison asked, "Have you noticed any unexpected redirects, popups, or unsolicited software installs?"

I thought about it for a moment before shaking my head no. "Nothing that I can recall. Everything seemed to be working as expected, it was just that one reboot after the power went out, and then my printer spat out that note."

The lines on Allison's forehead deepened. "Your computer seems to be running a tad slow from what I would expect, but nothing that makes me suspicious. Let me take a look at your security settings."

I dropped my chin into my hand, propping my head up with my arm, and mentioned how my bank and other accounts all seemed to be fine. Allison nodded as she worked, then, without warning, suddenly flicked her brown eyes up to me.

"What is it?" I asked, the crown of my head floating to the ceiling like a balloon.

"It appears that your antimalware software has been disabled."

I shook my head. "It wasn't me."

Allison pursed her lips and dug deeper in search of the cause. I moved around the table and dropped down in the seat next to her to see what exactly she was doing. I couldn't keep up. When she was working, she spoke an entirely different language.

"No doubt someone gained access to your system, but I can't prove it because there is no trace of it." She mentioned toggling on my antimalware and putting my security software through the most recent update. Then she said, "Whoever Loxley is, he's good."

Looking into her chestnut eyes, I asked, "How easy would it be to hack into someone's smart home technology?"

Allison stifled her laugh. "Incredibly easy."

"And to trip a stove or furnace through that same system?"

"As long as it's all connected, not difficult at all."

I reached for Loxley's notes and found myself staring at the words *insatiable greed*, wondering if Loxley was one person or two. "That's how he killed Thompson." I rolled my gaze to Allison. "Hacked the smart home system."

The color in Allison's face flushed. "If you're right, God help us all. From what I can see here, there would be no way to prove he murdered Thompson."

My front door slammed open and Susan came running through the house calling my name. "I'm in the kitchen," I said, hurrying to see what was wrong. "What's going on?"

"He's dead."

"Who's dead?" I reached for her arm, my heart fluttering in a sudden panic.

"That cryptocurrency founder, the one that's been all over the news." Susan rolled her wrist and looked to Allison for help in remembering his name.

"Donny Counts?" Allison said.

Susan snapped her fingers. "That's him. He died this morning."

CHAPTER THIRTY-THREE

LOXLEY BARELY SLEPT. HE WAS TOO ANXIOUS TO LAY beneath the covers for too long. All night he tossed, turned, and flicked through various news channels hoping Donny Counts's death would soon be reported. When nothing came, Loxley only grew more nervous, thinking maybe Donny didn't die after all.

Now, morning, his blood was still jittery with nerves as he paced through his apartment complex with the same feelings of euphoria often felt after a long distance sprint. But without Donny's death confirmed by local authorities, Loxley had no reason to celebrate.

He stopped near the couch, took the TV remote into his hand, and flicked on the television once more. The screen flickered in the dark room, casting shadows on the wall behind him, as he waited to feel some kind of vindication for what he had done.

It was a bold move the way he murdered Donny, but he should have known what was coming if he'd paid attention to the warning signs surrounding his nearly every move.

Leaving Josh Stetson behind to take the fall for their first scam was Donny's first mistake, and thinking he could get away with scamming the public again was his second. Unlucky for Donny, Loxley had been watching the entire time —waiting for the perfect opportunity to strike. He'd taken it too far. When Loxley learning of his planned—and sudden—departure, he had little choice but to kill him before he fled the country for good.

Loxley's grip tightened as he continued to stare at the television screen. Little John nudged against Loxley's calf. His cat's tail pointed straight up like an antenna as he purred and circled around Loxley's feet.

Crouching down low, Loxley scooped up his little furry friend and tucked him under one arm as he listened to the eight o'clock newscast, remaining hopeful that his hunt would finally get the attention it deserved.

One story after another, Loxley couldn't believe that there wasn't a single mention of Donny's death. What happened? How could this be? Donny had made headlines nearly daily, and now nothing? Something wasn't right, Loxley thought as he glared at the bright screen, considering his options.

Little John jumped from his arm and scurried into the kitchen. Loxley followed, feeding Little John from a can, before gathering a handful of fruit from the bowl for himself.

Shirtless and wearing only grey sweatpants, Loxley made himself a fruit smoothie with added protein powder as he did every morning of the week. Routine and ritual were the habits of success, and Loxley knew he was successful—a perfectionist that strived to not work harder, but smarter, than anybody else.

He paused and lifted his gaze, thinking once again about Donny.

Loxley retraced his steps a couple dozen times and still didn't know how it could be possible Donny survived the hack attack. His plan was ingenious—flawless—but nothing being reported left Loxley in a perpetual state of doubt. It was a new and uncomfortable feeling Loxley had rarely experienced before.

Keeping an ear on the television, Loxley found his way behind his computer and began scrolling through dozens of webpages as he sipped his smoothie. He typed Donny's name into the inquiry and then found what he'd been waiting for.

His shoulders relaxed as if a sudden weight had been lifted.

Breaking News. Cryptocurrency exchange founder, Donny Counts, dead at the age of 32.

Loxley folded his arms across his chest as he leaned back and smiled. Soon he found himself laughing at how absurdly easy this was for him. He now understood why the military used drones in combat zones. Killing your enemy from the deserts of Nevada was a hell of a lot easier than having to look them in their eyes when taking an enemy's life.

Loxley read on.

Donny died shortly after being admitted to the hospital. The cause was not yet being released to the public, but to Loxley's delight, there wasn't a single mention of foul play.

Perfect. Loxley grinned. *Fucking genius.*

Taking another man's life didn't affect Loxley like he thought it might. And he certainly wasn't worried about being caught. Not once had he stepped foot in either of his victims' homes, and yesterday was about the closest he ever ventured to Donny. But even that wasn't enough to cause suspicion if the cops did come asking questions. It had to be done. Just like Thompson, Donny was another disrupted line in the code that needed to be fixed to ensure the program of life continued uninterrupted and without flaw.

Finishing his smoothie, Loxley's mind was on anything but work. He liked this new game of his, and he planned to continue to play for as long as he could make a difference. But still, there was something missing that could make this game more fun—Sweet Samantha.

Closing the news article, he checked Samantha Bell's crime blog, surprised to find nothing on Donny Counts. He considered giving her another nudge toward Donny, but thought better of it. It wasn't the risk that made him hesitate, but that he wanted to toy with the girl who melted his heart and keep her wondering what might come next. That, too, was a game he liked playing.

With Donny out of the way, Loxley was itching to get on with his next hunt. Which got him thinking, was his next victim awake yet?

Within minutes, Loxley was scrolling through a dozen live video feeds when he caught movement in the far right corner of the screen. He stopped, zoomed, and stared.

"There you are." Loxley grinned. "Good morning."

The man was extremely wealthy and the face he put on for the public wasn't too different than what Loxley saw on both Richard and Donny. It was one of deceiving innocence and something that made Loxley sick to his stomach.

Loxley's next victim moved through his sprawling mansion, bickering at his help, mumbling different complaints both to himself and to others, as nothing seemed to bring him joy.

Though they lived side by side, he and Loxley moved in different worlds and played by different rules. Even now, as Loxley watched the asshole interact with his seemingly perfect wife, living his seemingly perfect life, Loxley knew the truth and it was time to send him a wakeup call to see if he was listening.

A surge of great energy traveled over Loxley's body. He felt invincible, like he could cancel out one wrong to make a thousand rights, and do it again and again without the faintest hint of remorse.

A small twitch between his legs let him know he was still alive, and when he felt the blood swell, he flicked his gaze to the photo of Samantha perched on top his desk. "One day, baby, we'll be doing this together."

CHAPTER THIRTY-FOUR

JOEY GARCIA HAD JUST ARRIVED TO ROSE MEDICAL Center when he heard on the radio that Donny Counts was dead. He felt his stomach drop with sudden disbelief and he parked in the first open space he came across. Turning up the volume, he sat still—frozen stiff in his seat with a gaping look planted on his face—as he listened to the complete report.

Flicking his gaze up into the hospital's windows, he couldn't believe what he was hearing. His stomach rolled with nausea. A part of him wanted to flee, to go back in time and have a redo on his year. Just one chance to get it right.

Rubbing his aching head, he stared up into the windows reflecting the soft light, framing a single cotton ball cloud lazily skirting across the blue sky above. Time seemed to stop for him as Joey struggled with deciding what to do next. His plans to solve all of his life's problems were unraveling as quickly as his daughter's health. Now he was more lost and confused than when his troubles first began.

Once the cloud left the window, Joey dropped his gaze to his dash. He wiped the dust off with his hand and flicked it onto the floor with defeat.

Since saying goodbye to Cecelia, Joey had hoped that Donny's initial report of being in critical condition wasn't true. It was wishful thinking, but that seemed to be all he had lately. And even those candles were nearly all gone. But Donny's sudden death explained why Joey didn't receive the payment promised to him. He hated reducing Donny's life to pure monetary terms, but Joey had been counting on those payments to reduce the stress he knew his wife was feeling, too.

Joey's head hit the back of the headrest as he sighed.

Worse was that he'd just met with Donny yesterday and didn't know what secrets could be traced back to him. There had been many, and he'd been so careful to remain discreet when keeping things as anonymous as possible. But now he couldn't be sure who knew what and what they would do about it if those secrets were ever discovered.

He closed his eyes, rubbed his face inside his hands, and groaned a little when trying to shake away his thoughts of despair. Never in his life had he felt so helpless. His thoughts drifted back to his wife and daughter—the only light remaining in his life that was worth fighting for.

Turning the key over in the ignition, Joey put the car in reverse and backed out of the space, leaving the hospital, to figure out how he would get himself out of the hole he had dug.

As he made his way across town, he regretted taking that meeting with Donny yesterday. If only he'd delayed it for just one more day, then maybe he could have had better luck at escaping the questions he knew were heading his way. But he hadn't, and now he was going to have to face the fact that he was probably one of the last people Donny ever spoke to in person. Because of that, his name would soon move up the list of suspects the police would want to interview.

"Christ, Garcia, you're smarter than this," Joey yelled as he punched the dash.

He hit rush hour traffic and the wall of cars slowing his pursuit only made him angrier. His body was on fire—an intense flame scorching his skin—as he squinted into the blinding sunlight hitting him square between the eyes from the rearview mirror.

Joey kept the radio off. He didn't need to hear any more of what was being said about Donny. He knew everything that he needed to know—and didn't want to know how he died. The less he knew the better, even if his editors would eventually tell him otherwise.

The earlier broadcast played on repeat inside his head. *Rushed to the hospital...Doctors unable to save him.* Again, Joey was asking himself how this could have happened.

He slammed his hand on the wheel and roared through clenched teeth.

His fingers trembled as fear took hold. Traffic barely moved as Joey reached across the console and retrieved his legal pad, needing to not forget a thought that just came to him. Biting off the pen cap, he jotted down a quick note for the article he knew he'd be asked to write. Then he grabbed his phone and made a call, but the person he was hoping to speak with didn't answer.

"C'mon, c'mon," he mumbled to the commuter traffic that surrounded him.

He drummed the steering wheel as he glanced in his mirrors. When no one was coming, he cranked the wheel hard to the right and hit the gas. Driving on the shoulder, he took the next exit, knowing he needed to get ahead of this story before it was too late.

Weaving his way through neighborhoods, he soon pulled onto the street where Donny Counts lived. Joey had been here once before—long before they began working together

—and hadn't forgotten the address. Surprised no TV vans were here, he parked across the street and waited a minute before stepping out. The tsunami was coming. He could feel it in his bones; he needed to act quickly before the first wave arrived.

He glanced to Donny's house. It looked dead inside. And though Joey didn't want to do it, he didn't have a choice. This was his future he was fighting for; everything was on the line.

Hurrying to the front door, he jabbed the doorbell repeatedly with his index finger until he heard the deadbolt click over. The door opened and he found himself staring into a sad, but beautiful, pair of green eyes. Her otherwise long black hair was tied up on her head in a messy bun. Joey assumed that she'd only just gotten home herself. He knew who she was, but had never been introduced.

"Are you Rose Wild?" he asked.

The dark bags beneath her oval eyes were heavy with grief and told of the night she'd endured.

"I'm—" Joey started to introduce himself.

"I know who you are."

Joey jerked his head back. Her tone was more aggressive than her appearance suggested and it caught Joey somewhat by surprise. "You do?"

Rose's eyes sharpened like daggers. "And I know why you're here."

Joey stared, not knowing what to say.

"He died, you asshole," Rose cried. "There is nothing else for you here."

"I'm sorry about Donny." Joey paused. "But he and I had an agreement."

Rose's jaw muscle bulged as her nostrils flared with heavy breaths of air. "Whatever agreement you made is no longer valid."

"What did he tell you?"

Rose reached into her back pocket and tossed a crumpled ball of paper between Joey's eyes.

"Go fuck yourself." She slammed the door in his face.

Joey stood still for a second with his eyes closed before turning to glance over his shoulder. No one was watching from the street or a neighbor's window. When he was certain only the birds had seen, he bent over and scooped up the ball of paper and hurried back to his car.

Once safely tucked behind the wheel and out of sight, he opened up the paper and recognized the key code printed on it immediately. He also knew how much trouble he was in.

"Shit," he whispered as he closed his eyes.

Just when he thought it couldn't get any worse, it had. Clenching his abs, he sped away from Donny Counts's house, promising to strike first before he went down in flames himself.

CHAPTER THIRTY-FIVE

Susan was still catching her breath when we locked eyes. I hadn't moved—my legs rooting firmly into the floor as my head spun around on the top of my shoulders. I still couldn't believe what Susan just shared. Had I been right about Loxley's message? It frightened me to think that I was.

"Sam, did you know him?" Allison asked me.

My eyes were open but I was lost inside my head as my thoughts traveled back to the Bitcoin paper wallet found with my article on Thompson's desk. I couldn't figure out how the two were related, but something told me they were.

"I knew of him," I said.

Feeling lightheaded, I needed to sit down. I moved to the table, leaned forward, and perched myself up on the points of my elbows. The blank wall in front of me allowed me to focus my thoughts without interruption.

Could Counts be the death Loxley was warning me about? It had to be. But what did Counts do to gain the attention of Loxley? It could have been his affiliation with Josh Stetson, but that was months ago and I hadn't heard of anything since. Counts must have done something else, but what?

When I rolled my neck, I caught Allison staring. The look on her face said she was stunned by the news as well. Donny Counts was someone she would have followed, as they were both making waves in the fast-paced world of technology.

"Sam," Allison cleared her throat as if trying to stay strong, "you know that's why he sent you the note."

I held her round eyes inside my own. We were too afraid to admit it, but even before Susan shared the news, I knew it was only a matter of time before the next death caught up with me.

"You weren't writing a story on him, were you?" Susan asked.

I blinked and rolled my gaze over to her. "No. Not currently," I said, giving the girls a quick summary of my coverage of Josh Stetson, his SIM swapping, and how I was warned to keep my eye on Counts, for he would be the next to fall.

Susan shifted her gaze to Allison. Then Allison asked, "Who told you to watch Counts?"

"I don't know his name." I tried to remember the details from that day, but it was thin.

"Could it have been this Loxley guy?" Allison jutted her chin toward the note from Loxley.

"Wait one second." Susan held her hands up and showed us her palms. "What note are you two talking about, and who the hell is Loxley?"

Allison beat me to it when we both reached for the note from Loxley. She handed it over to Susan, saying, "Sam's computer network was hacked last night and he sent this note through her personal printer."

I watched goosebumps prickle their way up Susan's arm as she lowered her eyes and began reading the note. When the room fell quiet, I found myself rubbing my own arms warm.

I didn't want to believe it was Loxley who told me to keep an eye on Counts after the Stetson sentencing. That would mean he had been watching me for nearly a year without me knowing.

My whole body rocked through a foundation-cracking tremor.

"Jesus, Sam." Susan shook her head and glanced at me. "*Loving admirer?*"

"He's bringing me into his fantasy world."

"You think?" Susan set the note back down on top of the kitchen table. "And you think he killed Donny?"

"It's possible."

"Maybe Richard Thompson, too." Allison caught Susan up to speed with everything we'd discussed before her arrival.

"But we're only making these assumptions by reading between the lines. There is no other evidence suggesting a homicide even occurred. For either of the victims."

"How did Donny Counts die?" Allison asked.

No one knew. I needed to get Erin on the phone. I stood and moved to the counter, diving my hand into my purse to retrieve my phone. Allison pulled my laptop around and immediately searched for more information on Counts's death. Word about his death seemed to be traveling slowly and when I asked Susan about how she heard, she said she had been talking on the phone with Benjamin early this morning.

"He was the one to tell me. Heard it from a colleague," Susan said.

"Isn't he in New England?" Allison asked.

Susan nodded.

"Did he get the job?" I asked, dialing Erin's number and pressing the phone to my ear.

Susan lowered her gaze and frowned. "Didn't ask."

Next thing I knew, Erin came flying through my front door. "Sam. You here?"

"In the kitchen," I called out.

"Oh, good, you're all here." Erin hit the brakes and locked eyes with me. "Our killer struck again."

"Donny Counts," the three of us said in unison.

Erin squished her eyebrows together. "Why didn't you call?"

I lifted my hand and showed her the phone I was still holding. "Just did."

"Oh. Well..." Erin bounced her gaze around the room. "What else have you all learned?"

Allison mentioned how she confirmed Samantha's network had been hacked, and Susan shared how she thought of Sam and the Bitcoin paper wallet as soon as she learned of Donny's death. We all understood Loxley's message wasn't a hoax, but we still needed to prove he was the one behind these sudden deaths.

Erin turned her eyes to me. "That's scary shit, Sam."

"I know."

Everyone started talking at once, their words worming their way into my subconscious. Next thing I knew, a twenty-ton epiphany was nearly knocking me to the floor. The digital key code wasn't a missed clue, it *was* the clue.

I sank deep into my thoughts, ignoring the chatter happening around me.

Was that even possible? Could Loxley—if he was the one to have killed Thompson—been able to put it in Thompson's possession knowing that it would eventually find its way to me? If that was true, then why did he want me to know who his next victim was? What else was I missing? Was he planning to kill again? My blood shook.

"Tell us what to do, Sam." Susan pushed her shoulders back and tipped her chin up. "We're here to help."

"First," I went to work, "we put together a list of hackers who are smart enough to pull this off, but also who might have past white collar criminal convictions."

"I'm on it, Sam," Allison said.

"And I'll help her." Susan stepped forward, reminding Allison, "We have that meeting with Damien Black later today anyway. Might as well make it a day."

Allison didn't object.

"Good," I said. "Erin, you find out how exactly Counts died. We need to confirm that these deaths are even the slightest bit related before we start spreading rumors."

"You got it." Erin nodded. "What will you do?"

"I'm heading into the newsroom. I'm sure Dawson will want me to cover Counts's story in some form or another."

Allison pushed my laptop away. "I've strengthened your firewall, Sam, so you should be good to go but," she rolled her eyes to my smart speaker perched like a tiny lighthouse on my countertop, "if I were you, I would make sure to keep that thing unplugged just in case he's listening."

CHAPTER THIRTY-SIX

PARKER COLLINS THOUGHT HIS HOUSE WAS NOTICEABLY cooler than it should have been. Fumbling with the thermostat, his head was tipped back as he cycled through the controls. Pushing his reading glasses further up the bridge of his nose, he grumbled, "I swear Maria keeps changing these settings."

"Don't be ridiculous," Parker's wife, Joan, said as she passed behind like a stiff cold wind.

"Then it must be you." Parker turned his head and glared at his wife. "Because it ain't me, babe."

Joan rolled her eyes with annoyance and disappeared into the master bathroom to finish getting ready.

Parker turned his attention back to the thermostat and chuckled. He enjoyed pushing his wife's buttons, teasing her with the same jokes and pranks he'd been telling her for the twenty-two years they'd been together. But this thermostat wasn't a prank, and Parker certainly didn't think it was funny that it wasn't working.

"Joan, honey, is there hot water?" he called out to his wife from the bedroom. Something must be wrong with the boiler, he thought as he listened to Joan turn on the faucet.

"It's hot," she called back.

"Then it must be the thermostat," Parker muttered as he turned back to face the device attached to the wall.

It was the latest in state of the art home technology. Despite it being pitched as intuitive, Parker thought it came with a steep learning curve—then again, maybe he was just too old for some of this stuff supposed to make their lives easier.

Joan passed behind him. "Just call John," she said.

Parker hemmed and hawed his way through the settings, too proud to ask for help. "I'll figure it out," he told her.

Joan stood and faced her husband as she pulled her left sleeve up to check the time. "In this lifetime, or the next?"

Parker swung his head and gave his wife a look above the rim of his glasses that said, *very funny*.

Joan smirked. Then her expression changed when she pointed to the front of the house. "There it goes again."

"The house is haunted," Parker said, finally happy that he'd set the temperature to his liking.

Joan hurried out of the bedroom and Parker finished getting ready. He quickly slung a tie over his neck and tied it. Then he slid his arms through a sports coat and met his wife near the kitchen. Joan was holding the phone in one hand and searching through her list of contacts when she said, "The garage door opened again without explanation."

"And you're calling who, Ghostbusters?"

Joan raised a sharp eyebrow. "Real funny, smartass. I'm calling John. Get him to come fix it. You want him to take a look at the boiler, too?"

Maria, their maid of the past three years, walked into the kitchen holding several cleaning tools and sprays in her arms.

Parker smiled and said, "Maria can keep an eye on it, can't you?"

"Certainly, Mr. Collins." Maria smiled.

"Whatever," Joan said. "We won't be here anyway."

They gathered their wallets and purse and left in Parker's BMW. After backing out of the drive, Parker stopped to make sure the garage door fully closed. It went down with ease, and once securely in place, he turned to Joan with a glint in his eye.

"See? Works just fine." Parker pointed toward the house.

Joan wasn't amused. "C'mon, I don't want to be late."

Parker drove at a leisurely pace as Joan played on her phone. His thoughts drifted to the wake they were on their way to attend for his acquaintance Richard Thompson and how Richard's death didn't hit him particularly hard. He wondered if he should be feeling sadder than he was, but what was this really about other than another excuse to bring people together to talk business.

"Lee needs us to be at Metro State no later than 12:30PM," Joan said, detailing out their schedule for the day.

Parker took his eyes off the road and glanced at Joan's phone. Not a second later, a car honked and tires squealed. Parker acted quickly and swerved before getting sideswiped by the oncoming car.

"Christ, Parker?" Joan's white knuckles clenched the dash. "What the hell were you thinking?"

Parker had both hands on the wheel. His eyes were wide open and his heart was pounding in his chest. "That was a close call," he said calmly.

Joan shook her head. "That's exactly why you shouldn't be driving."

"But I like driving," Parker shot back. "It gives me a sense of independence."

"We're better people than that. We can afford to hire a driver."

Parker ignored Joan and flipped on the radio. He could feel her glaring at him, making certain he remained in his lane.

"Donny Counts, dead at thirty-two," the radio news broadcaster said.

Joan rolled her eyes to Parker. "You don't expect me to go to his funeral, too?"

Parker ignored her comment and flipped the station to listen to some soft rock. Turning down the volume, he said, "We'll pay our respects to Richard's family and then be on our way."

Staring straight ahead, Joan said, "I don't like associating myself with someone accused of charity fraud."

This wasn't the first time Joan voiced her thoughts about some of the families in their circle of business associates. Parker was well aware of how she felt—especially about Richard Thompson. But his wife was good at putting on a face, and he expected nothing less from her today.

"And what didn't you like about Donny?" Parker inquired.

Joan turned her head and gave him a look. "Where should I start?"

Parker chuckled, put on his blinker, and took the next turn. "How did I get so lucky marrying you?"

CHAPTER THIRTY-SEVEN

KING AND ALVAREZ WERE STAKED OUTSIDE THE HOLY
Ghost Catholic Church just north of Civic Center Park in
lower downtown, making a list of faces and names of those
attending Richard Thompson's wake.

Alvarez belched and the smells of his breakfast quickly
filled the car. King glared and rolled down his window to let
fresh air inside.

They arrived early after pulling an all-nighter working a
homicide in Denver East. The victim was a fourteen-year-old
child, not much younger than Samantha's son Mason, and it
left King crying on the inside. The boy should have never
died, but thanks to a drive-by shooting at the hands of what
was probably a territorial dispute between rival gangs,
he did.

King bent over and rubbed the blood back into his
swollen ankles. His feet hurt from canvasing the neighborhood through the early morning—coming up with nothing
solid to go on—when Lieutenant sent them here to rest their
bones and give the appearance that they were treating
Richard's death as suspicious.

"If anyone asks, you're there to pay your respects to an honorable man in our community," Lieutenant had told them.

King didn't argue. He followed the command's lead. It was Alvarez who was having a difficult time accepting their assigned role.

"I can't listen to this again." Alvarez leaned forward, turned off the radio after another news cycle circled around about the death of Donny Counts.

"But he's being remembered as a man of great talent," King said sarcastically.

"Oh, yeah. And an infectious personality to go along with it," Alvarez scoffed.

"Don't forget," King leaned toward Alvarez and wagged his finger in the air between them, "Donny was proof that the American Dream is still possible."

Alvarez laughed and shook his head. "And here we are, front row seats to probably the biggest protest in town."

King read the picket signs that pounded the asphalt across the street and listened to the shouts for the Thompson family to give back the money Richard stole through his scam charity. Sectioned off by a handful of uniformed officers, Alvarez mumbled, "Just more of our city's tax dollars going to work for the rich and famous."

King let Alvarez's comment bounce around his head for a moment as he thought about the message Samantha said she received. *Thompson is the first of many more to come. If you don't believe me, just ask these two.* King knew that her article was the reason these people were here today, but what he really wanted to know was who the digital Bitcoin wallet belonged to.

"Where the hell is the media?" Alvarez twisted his spine and glanced through the back window. "Shouldn't they be here instead of us?"

"They'll come, I'm sure."

Alvarez looked at his partner. "Don't get me wrong. I can appreciate the need for working with the press when solving important cases, and I hope Samantha's right, but I still wish she would have waited to run Thompson's story. At least until the man was in the ground."

"Why? We're having so much fun here." The corners of King's eyes crinkled.

"You talk to Sam since her questioning?"

King nodded, watching a man over six feet circle around the protestors, taking their photograph. He wondered who he was—who he might work for. He didn't recognize the face, but made note of it in case he needed to come back and reference it later.

More of Thompson's friends and family arrived, moving in an endless stream from the paid parking on 19th and Welton. King watched as they filed themselves inside the holy cathedral.

"Any one of these assholes could have wanted him dead," Alvarez said. "I've read stories about these people and how they conduct their business. Ruthless, man. Manipulative and backstabbing." He shook his head. "I don't get how us sitting here is going to fool anyone into thinking we have a real reason to be here."

King took a sip of his cold coffee and told Alvarez about the key code.

Alvarez stared at King with narrowed eyes and parted lips. "Come again?"

King raised his brows. "Samantha figured it out. Bitcoin digital paper wallet."

"Well that certainly complicates the matter." Alvarez sighed. "I hope she learned of it after we had her in for questioning."

King assured him she did. "She only learned about the key code during her questioning." Now that they knew what the key code was, it was time for them to figure out who might have been trying to blackmail Thompson. "What we really need to be asking ourselves is who among these people are most likely to be using cryptocurrency?"

"Are you kidding?" Alvarez snorted a quick laugh. "Probably every single one of them."

King stared, thinking the same. Except, then there was the promise that more would follow, and Donny Counts—the King of Crypto—had died unexpectedly, just as things were starting to get interesting. "You know what I'm thinking? I'm thinking that Donny Counts's death might be related to Richard Thompson's."

Alvarez pushed himself up in his seat. "What other secrets did Samantha tell you?"

King was thinking about the first message Samantha received when he said, "I just don't believe in coincidence, is all."

Alvarez grinned, turned his head, and spotted Parker Collins and his wife walking hand-in-hand toward the entrance of the church. "Now there's a real man. You know he drives himself everywhere?"

"You read that, too?"

"In fact, I did."

King flicked his gaze to billionaire Parker Collins. *Real guy, my ass*, King thought.

"The only difference between him and me is the number of zeros tacked on to the end of his bank account." Alvarez nodded. "You know he donates a certain percentage of every sale to charity?"

King gave Alvarez a skeptical look. "You mean like Thompson?"

"Nah, man." Alvarez looked hurt. "This guy is different."

King was shaking his head when he received a call from

Lieutenant Baker. "LT, what's up?" King answered his cell. "We're still outside Holy Ghost. Not much to report."

"Good," Lieutenant said. "I need you across town. The station just received a call from Rose Wild, Donny Counts's girlfriend. I assume you've heard the news."

King said, "Can't get away from it, but why did she call the station? I thought I heard he passed at the hospital."

"He did." Lieutenant Baker's gravel voice lowered. "But she's claiming Donny was murdered."

CHAPTER THIRTY-EIGHT

MY BRAIN SCRAMBLED WITH QUESTIONS AS I DROVE TO THE office. Who was Loxley? Was he in Denver? Even in Colorado? Was the key code found on Thompson's desk as important as I thought? I was terrified by the possibility that there was a hacker out there who could seemingly control everything without ever being seen.

This story was made for movies. As I passed cubbyholes on my way to my own desk, I overheard snippets of a dozen conversations, nearly all of them name dropping either Counts or Thompson. It was the talk of the newsroom, but there was only one opinion I cared to hear.

Joey Garcia was sitting down, facing his computer monitor, when I knocked. He turned and gave me a small smile. "Hey, sorry Sam." He retrieved the sticky note I'd left for him yesterday. "I'm just seeing your note to call now."

I stepped inside his cubicle, waved off his not getting back to me as no big deal, and lowered my tailbone to the edge of his desk. Garcia didn't look himself. His eyes seemed to be sunken further into his skull than normal, and his face looked puffy and swollen. I knew he was going through a lot at home and could only imagine the stress he must be feeling.

"How is Katie doing?" I asked.

Garcia's eyelids drooped halfway over his pupils. "She's fine, for now."

I gave him the best smile I could as I thought about his little girl, feeling my own heart shatter. I remained hopeful, though it was a terribly sad story. We were all rooting for her, believing Katie would beat cancer. "If there is anything I can do to help—"

"I know. Thanks, Sam." Garcia glanced to his computer, his cursor blinking on his login. He stood and looked around like he was waiting for someone to arrive. "Where the hell is IT?"

"Can't log in?"

Garcia sighed. "I called IT but no one picked up." He turned his eyes to me. "Have you seen Travis?"

"Only yesterday," I said, telling him how Travis and his new intern were working on the system.

"New intern?" Garcia raised a single brow.

I nodded. "Brett Gallagher."

"Unpaid, I assume?"

I shrugged my shoulders, not knowing the details, and watched Garcia drop back into his chair and swivel around to face me. "Were they working on my computer?"

"I found them working on mine and know they were making their rounds."

"Can they even do that without our permission?"

"When the *Times* system is hacked," I folded my arms and nodded, "they can do what they want."

A worried looked crossed over Garcia's face. "Hacked?"

I told him as much as I knew about the update in security Travis was making sure everyone's computers had. "Apparently, someone clicked on something they shouldn't have."

Garcia glanced to his blinking cursor and sighed. "And just when I thought things couldn't get worse, now I have to deal with the possibility of someone accessing my work."

My brows squished. "Have any of your files gone missing?"

"I hope not, but without being able to log in it's impossible to know for sure."

"Hey, look, about the Thompson story, I didn't mean for my reporting to contradict everything you've ever reported about him."

Garcia waved it off. "It was a good story you wrote, even if it made me look like a schmuck." We both laughed. "But I wish you would have told me, Sam. I could have helped. Saved you time."

"Top secret." I held up three fingers and gave him the Girl Scout sign for promises kept. "Direct orders from the top."

Garcia chuckled and glanced at his watch. "Ah, shit. I should be attending Thompson's wake now. Instead, I have to follow orders from editorial and write up a piece on Donny Counts." He wiped a hand over his mouth. "Apparently he died last night."

"I heard."

"And because of how well my piece about Thompson went, I'm now unofficially the obituary writer around here."

I smiled. "Have you heard how he died?"

"Not the specifics, but something related to his diabetes." Garcia shrugged.

"Can you confirm it was an accident?"

Garcia shook his head. "Why do you ask? Don't hold out on me, Sam. If you know something about how he died, I need to know."

"It's just a hunch, maybe the strange timing of how he died so soon after Richard Thompson, but in all your reporting do you know of anyone who might want either of these two dead?"

"You hang out with too many cops." Garcia smirked.

I grinned along with him. No one but Dawson knew about my article being found inside Thompson's house, and until I understood what was going on, I planned on keeping it a secret.

Garcia tapped his space bar a couple of times. "All anyone ever wanted to hear was Counts's fast road to success."

I recalled Garcia's reporting and thought how his stories often made his subjects the celebrities of entrepreneurism. "What wasn't there to like? Tons of aspiring people looked to him for inspiration," I said.

Garcia rolled his eyes. "You know some people are saying he might not even be dead."

"And what about you?" I knitted my eyebrows. "Do you think he's dead?"

A glimmer of suspicion flashed over Garcia's dark eyes. "Don't go spreading rumors, but there are whispers suggesting his cryptocurrency exchange was nothing but a well-oiled Ponzi scheme." Garcia nodded, opened up his phone and navigated to his Twitter account. He turned the screen to me and said, "The mob against him is speaking out, and they aren't happy."

I immediately thought of Loxley, the messages I'd received, and how this could be the reason Loxley called for someone's death. I couldn't believe the uproar I was reading, but Garcia must have more than what he was showing me to suggest Donny might actually still be alive.

"Have you called the hospital? The morgue? Can we confirm that Donny Counts is even dead?"

Garcia dipped his chin and shook his head. "It's just what somebody on Twitter suggested. I'm sure Donny is dead as a doornail." Then he leaned forward and opened up his drawer. "Anyway, you think someone is knocking off the rich and famous, here's everything I have on both Counts and Thompson. Have at it. It should cover the last year of reporting, maybe more. I can't think of anything off the top of my head, but if someone did want either of them dead, you might find what you're looking for in here."

I took the thumb-drive into my hand, said thanks, and left Garcia's desk thinking a Ponzi scheme would be reason enough to want Counts dead. But was it Loxley who had killed him, if in fact, Counts really was dead? I didn't know, but I sure planned to find out.

CHAPTER THIRTY-NINE

THE SCENE OUTSIDE DONNY COUNTS HOUSE WAS strikingly similar to the one outside Thompson's wake. King approached cautiously as he kept one foot on the brake pedal while reading the picket signs being hoisted into the air from the opposite street curb from where he drove.

"Christ, what do you think is going on here?" Alvarez asked King.

King shrugged, his gut telling him that it had something to do with Thompson.

"Samantha write anything about Donny?"

"Not that I know of," King said softly. But it would certainly explain the protestors if she had.

Alvarez turned the radio on and scanned for more news about Donny that maybe they had missed. There was nothing new—no one reporting on the protestors or reasons why they were picketing outside a dead man's house.

"Coincidence?" Alvarez furrowed his brow. "Or is it just that everyone is pissed off these days?"

King pulled into the drive and parked near the front of the house. As soon as they opened up their car doors, the roar of an angry crowd filled the air. Tensing, King remained vigilant—deciding it safer to stay on his toes than to make a wrong assumption about something he knew little about.

Alvarez tugged on his sports coat and made his way toward the front door of the house. It seemed like the screams and shouts from the protestors were suddenly being directed at the two of them.

"Let's just get this over with so we can get back to solving the murders no one but us care about," Alvarez said as he looked to King.

King rang the doorbell, surprised there was no security beyond the technology he could feel watching them through the lenses of hidden cameras that were probably mounted on every corner of the house. King silently agreed with his partner—he also preferred working cases no one else gave a rat's ass about. He thought about the black child who was murdered last night and would much rather be seeking justice for him than being called out here where money controlled city resources.

The door opened. "Ms. Wild?"

One eye blinked between the crack in the door. "Yes."

"We're homicide detectives King and Alvarez with Denver PD." King held up his badge for Rose to see. He watched her check it for authenticity. "You wanted to speak with us about your boyfriend's death?"

Rose nodded her porcelain head and opened the door further. She was wearing a cranberry colored silk robe over her jeans and tee.

"Did you invite these protestors to the house?" Alvarez pointed over his shoulder.

Rose's ponytail swished across her shoulders as she shook her head. "They started showing up as soon as word spread about Donny's death."

"Let's talk about that. May we come inside?" King politely asked.

Rose signaled for them to enter.

Alvarez glanced over his shoulder one last time before shutting the door behind him. He was the last to enter. It was quiet inside and provided a nice buffer to the shouts that were certain to have unsettled the entire neighborhood. Disturbance calls were probably flooding dispatch as they spoke.

"Thanks for coming out so quickly," Rose said over her shoulder as she glided into the living room.

"We're sorry to hear about your boyfriend," King said, noting the towering ceilings and large windows that made him feel smaller than his six foot two frame.

"Fiancé." Rose held up her hand and pointed to the diamond ring that looked like it cost more than King's house. "Rumors are spreading that simply aren't true," she insisted.

"What rumors would those be?"

"Please. Have a seat." Rose pointed to the sectional sofa couch. Alvarez took the corner but King chose to remain standing. "People are saying my Donny wasn't who he said he was."

Alvarez flashed King a hard glance. King knew his partner was already feeling annoyed by the call, but the way Rose was speaking about her fiancé must have been killing Alvarez. King turned his gaze back to Rose, unable to decide if it was a look of anger or devastation that had her motivated to seek revenge for Donny's sudden death.

"I'm sorry," Alvarez said, turning his attention back to Rose, "but I was under the impression you called us here to investigate your fiancé's death."

King listened as he looked around the house. There were zero photographs of Rose and Donny. The walls consisted mostly of expensive paintings that were way above King's pay grade. But, more importantly, he didn't see any signs that a crime had been committed. The house was neat and orderly, lived in. Something wasn't adding up.

"You said you believed Donny was murdered." King locked eyes with Rose. "What makes you say that?"

Rose wet her lips before saying, "As you can imagine, not everyone liked Donny. Yes, despite what you may think, he had enemies." She nodded. "I know, hard to believe, right? But not everyone liked how quickly he made his money."

"And who are these enemies of Donny's?"

"Donny was being followed, watched, and investigated by several reporters."

King titled his head to the side. "Investigated for what?"

"For being a fraud."

"And was he?"

"Of course not. Donny was an honest person. But people have been wanting what Donny worked so hard to achieve since they first learned of his success. You see, part of Donny's success is because of the way the media treated him. But then, after he started making serious money, they turned on him."

"These reporters you said were following him, do you have names?"

Rose nodded. "It's a reporter from the *Colorado Times*."

Alvarez turned his head to King. King was still staring at Rose. He feared Rose was about to name-drop his girlfriend and wondered if Rose knew he was dating Samantha. King couldn't help but feel like Rose was playing some sort of sick game, but he kept his mind open, hoping that she would soon reveal some concrete information they could actually use.

"Can you tell us who that is?"

"I'd rather not." Rose twisted the engagement ring around her finger.

"Why is that?"

"I'm afraid." Her hand stopped moving. "Afraid of what they already know, and what they'll do to me to get what they want."

"Without a name, there really isn't much we can do for you, Ms. Wild."

Rose's spine straightened. She took a moment to gather her thoughts. Then she continued, "This is what I can say. The reporter who I'm referring to wanted Donny dead."

"And why would a reporter want your fiancé dead?"

"Because Donny refused to pay them, and since Donny didn't give into their demands, they wanted the money in Donny's exchange to forever be locked away."

King hid his hands inside his pants pockets and asked, "Are you saying this reporter from the *Times* blackmailed your fiancé?"

"That's exactly what I'm saying."

"I'm sorry," Alvarez shook his head, "but what money are you referring to?"

Rose explained the digital currency exchange Donny started and as King listened to Alvarez get caught up, he fumbled inside his pocket and took out the key code from Thompson's house to show to Rose.

"Is this a digital wallet that can be found on Donny's exchange?"

"That's a joke right?" Rose's laugh was small, cynical. "Donny's exchange moved money around daily using codes just like that."

King flipped the code around and looked at the string of text. "The funny thing about these digital wallets is that there is no name to identify who it belongs to."

"No, there's not." Rose grinned. "And that right there is why people are attracted to blockchain technologies. It's impossible to trace an identity back to that code." Rose held out her hand and asked, "May I have a look?"

King handed the paper over when Alvarez asked more about what happened before Donny was taken to the hospital. After staring at the key code for a lengthy pause, Rose lifted her eyes, and said, "It happened so quickly. At first I thought Donny was joking. Finally, I realized he wasn't and his confusion was real. Then he dropped to the ground over there," she pointed to the empty carpeted space, "and had a seizure." Rose dabbed at the corners of her eyes. "He never responded after that." She choked up. "He was barely alive when he arrived at the hospital."

"Forgive me, Ms. Wild, but I'm not seeing a crime," Alvarez said. By the look on Alvarez's face, King knew his partner was only hearing blame.

Rose gave him a hard look before leaving the room.

"Jesus, John, you couldn't have put it a little nicer?" King shook his head in disbelief. "The young woman is mourning."

Alvarez flipped his palms up and shrugged. "What? Do you see a crime in anything she has told us?"

"That's not my point." King's expression hardened.

A minute later Rose was back in the room holding a small electronic device in one hand. She handed it to King. King inspected it and asked, "What's this?"

"That is how Donny died."

Alvarez stood and requested to see it himself. "An insulin pump?"

"That's right." Rose crossed her arms and held her chin high. "Look into it. A crime has been committed. I'm sure of it. And when you get the chance, ask Joey Garcia at the *Times* if he recognizes that key code." Rose turned her narrow eyes on Alvarez. "Then come back here and tell me my Donny wasn't murdered."

CHAPTER FORTY

I PAUSED MID-STEP AND GLANCED ONCE MORE OVER MY shoulder in the direction of Garcia's desk with my head still spinning. He caught me looking on his way out and paused. "We should get a drink sometime. Just you and me."

"Sure," I said, watching Garcia smile and head to the exit.

I had never had a drink with him before, that I could recall, and never had seen him outside of work without his wife being there as well. The whole invitation seemed to be as odd as his behavior. I couldn't make sense of it.

Garcia appeared deflated, like he'd given up. It could have been Katie's health that was dragging him down, and I wouldn't blame him for that, but something had me questioning if there could be something else going on that had him feeling sunken.

As soon as I entered my own cubical, I set my bag on top of my desk and fired up my computer. It loaded without issue, and I immediately pushed in the thumb-drive Garcia gave me. As I waited for it to load, I thought about what he said about Counts running his exchange like a Ponzi scheme. It was the first I'd heard of it, but because Counts had a history with Josh Stetson, I didn't doubt it being possible. It certainly would fit the mold of what I already knew.

Several dozen folders populated my screen, each clearly labeled by sources names, dates, and headline stories. I dove into my work with zealous focus with the intention of learning who might be watching me.

Who wanted these two men dead? More importantly, who also wanted me to take the fall with them? Those were the two questions I kept asking myself as I began my search.

There was more here than just Counts and Thompson, but I went straight to digging into what Garcia had on Donny Counts first. Garcia had more information on him than I believed possible. Mostly good, boring details of Counts's rise to the top and the celebrity he became. But then I came across a folder for Donny's exchange.

I clicked it.

It opened.

But nothing was there.

I fell back into my chair and stared at the empty folder wondering what happened to the documents inside—if there ever were any. The noises coming from the desks around me soon disappeared as I drifted deeper into my thoughts. Garcia was one of the best, but maybe this empty folder was a mistake?

The key code flashed behind my eyelids as I thought about the paper wallet found with Thompson along with my story about him. Was that the clue to tell me that Counts was next to die?

Charity fraud.

A Ponzi scheme.

And Loxley's warning about people's insatiable greed.

It was all there, spinning around, slowly coming together to form a single bond.

Taking a pen between my fingers, I leaned forward and

began making notes, comparing the two victim's lives, trying to find a common denominator that could link them both to Loxley.

Over the next half-hour, one by one, I connected the dots.

Both men were extremely wealthy. Both had a reputation of giving back to their communities. There was a difference in age between the two, and a slightly different road to success, but, most striking of all, both appeared to be hypocrites. They spoke highly of themselves but lied to the people they said they were trying to help.

I thought about Loxley once again, asking myself how he could know so much.

I couldn't get his name out of my head. Was that what this was all about? Knocking these men off because they weren't who they said they were? There had to be more to it than just that, but what was it? Was Loxley jealous of their success? Did he know them personally?

My thoughts rolled around my head like marbles.

I swept my gaze away from my paper and watched as the room suddenly got brighter.

Then I had a thought.

Robin of Loxley.

"Robin Hood and Little John. That's it," I said to myself, lunging forward and typing up a quick internet search.

I couldn't believe I hadn't thought of this before. It was so ridiculously obvious I should be ashamed of myself. And I was. Because Robin Hood was a self-proclaimed vigilante fighting the rich and working for the poor, just like Loxley made me believe he was doing. Except the legend told a story of giving back to the poor. As far as I knew, Loxley hadn't given anything back.

I continued my search, looking for more insight into the legend of Robin Hood. Then I turned to Real Crime News's message board to see if Loxley, or LilJon, assuming they were the same person, had posted again. There was nothing, but I quickly got sucked down a rabbit hole that led me nowhere fast. Not wanting time to get away from me, I packed up my bag, deciding it was time I learned how Counts died and why.

I closed up shop, gathered my things, and stopped by Garcia's desk on my way out to return his thumb-drive. I got what I needed, and I was sure Garcia would happily let me borrow it again if I asked.

I found his cubicle empty but a flier on his messy desk for an event at Metropolitan State University caught my eye. I didn't mean to be nosy, but I walked closer to get a better look. The keynote speaker's name had been circled with Garcia's scribbled chicken scratch next to it. But what left me both frightened and confused was why Garcia had written my name next to Parker and Joan Collins' names. What was he up to? Why did he want to involve me?

CHAPTER FORTY-ONE

Loxley circled Parker Collins's parked BMW, raking the tips of his fingers over the white paint as he walked. He was amused that his next victim was paying his respects to Loxley's first. Nothing felt better than knowing the two of them were getting together for their last goodbye.

The gulls squawked overhead and everything around him disappeared. The protestors' shouts drifted off in the wind. The planes flying overhead didn't make a sound. His steps were slow and deliberate when suddenly the chorus inside erupted into a powerful and emotional song that raised the hairs on the back of his neck.

American Grace.

Loxley stopped and turned his head toward the church. Peering through the front, open doors, he thought how nice it would be to see the entire building ignite in a fan of hot flames.

A small, deep chuckle rumbled its way up his chest.

With the people he knew to be inside—wealthy people who had traded their souls to the devil himself—he wouldn't put it past divine intervention to do his job for him. But he knew better, knew that it was up to people like him to do God's work for Him. It was why he was placed on Earth—his calling from above.

A sharp smirk curled his lips.

It was a nice, dangerous thought to imagine the people inside burning, but not the type of activity he was interested in doing himself. Perhaps he'd get lucky and one of the protestors from the street would start the fire for him.

Loxley continued walking, circling Parker's vehicle. The stones crunching beneath the soles of his shoes, scraping over the asphalt below. Stopping near the front passenger window, he glanced around. When he was certain he was alone and no one was watching, he brought his hands to his brow and peered through the tinted glass window, peeking inside at the controls.

It was a 2019 BMW 7 series—one of two vehicles he knew Parker preferred to drive—and a model Loxley was familiar with. He'd never driven one himself, but he would have liked to someday. It was a luxury car—a noticeable one at that. A car that made a statement. He appreciated Parker's choice in wanting to drive a newer car—a vehicle with computer systems that controlled nearly every aspect of the car's engine. When it mattered, that was what Loxley was after—the computers.

"Greed kills!" a man yelled while thrusting his sign into the air.

Loxley backed away from the car and turned to stare at the approaching protestor. Loxley smiled, loving the drama. He couldn't have planned it any better himself, but it certainly added to the flair that would become Richard Thompson's final day above ground, and maybe Loxley's legacy too.

"Greed kills!" the man shouted again when locking eyes with Loxley.

How appropriate, Loxley thought, liking how he was just another face in the crowd of many. *Nothing suspicious here.*

Stuffing his hands inside his pants pockets, Loxley walked away with a grin spreading across his face. Heading back to where he parked, not more than fifty yards from Parker's car, he dipped inside his own vehicle and fired up his laptop.

Resting the computer on his thighs, he used his cellphone as a WiFi Hotspot. As he waited for a signal, he browsed the Twitter mob busy attacking Donny's and Richard's characters. It had exploded since the last time he'd checked, the rumor growing even larger.

"Donny Counts faked his own death?" Loxley laughed. "Wonderful." He smiled. "Absolutely wonderful."

There was nothing better than a conspiracy theory to keep the public occupied while he planned his next murder. Soon, his thoughts drifted to Samantha Bell and wondered why she seemed to have gone quiet after the letter he'd sent her last night.

A pang of loneliness stabbed his side. Pursing his lips, doubt fell over him. It was uncharacteristic of him to lose confidence, but when it came to Samantha, Loxley grew weak. She was his crutch, the one person he would do anything for. He hoped he hadn't scared her off. That wasn't his intention. He needed her to play along, to see him for who he truly was. He wasn't a monster. He was a crusader. And keeping track of his favorite reporter's thoughts and movements was one of his top priorities. All Loxley wanted was to be seen by her.

The internet signal connected and Loxley opened his software program and got to work.

He knew Samantha would be attempting to connect the dots, put the pieces of the puzzle together, but had he given enough of a clue to point her toward Parker Collins? He wasn't confident he had. Nothing had been written since the

Thompson story broke and that concerned Loxley. Maybe he should give her a push?

A twitch between his legs had him sucking in his bottom lip.

Surprised to find himself with an erection, Loxley was in heat. There was only one cure to get him to relax. He needed to draw blood, needed to bring Samantha into his world and feel her touch. If she didn't respond to last night's letter, he would have to find another way to get her attention. And he had just the idea to do it. But first, he had a job to complete.

Ignoring the intense and painful throb between his legs, Loxley's keystrokes were swift and precise as he wrote the code needed to crack into Parker's car's computer system, sending arbitrary diagnostics to the motherboard.

He lifted his head, fixed his eyes on the white BMW, and hit *enter*.

The tail lights came on with the engine.

Loxley played with the wipers and blinkers, laughing while he did, before killing the engine to Parker's car.

Swiveling his head on his shoulders, he looked around. No one suspected a thing—didn't think anything of the car starting all by itself. He might as well have been alone.

His erection had gone limp, but an intense and lasting warmth bloomed across his body.

He closed the lid on his computer and turned on his own car. Driving away from the church and Thompson's wake, he knew where the Collins' were heading next, and he planned to kill Parker there.

CHAPTER FORTY-TWO

RYAN DAWSON WAS ON HIS WAY IN AS I WAS ON MY WAY out. We greeted each other at the door and then he asked for me to follow him into his office. Together, we turned around and headed back inside, weaving our way across the newsroom floor. Once his office door was closed, he turned to face me and said, "Sam, tell me, did you speak with the police?"

My eyes glimmered. "I speak to Detective King daily."

Dawson didn't budge. He kept his eyes glued to mine. I could see he meant business.

"Yes. They found me at Richard Thompson's residence."

Dawson spoke like a true reporter, fast and furious, no fluff. "Did you find any evidence suggesting he was the one to have threatened you?"

"I wish I had gotten that far. Unfortunately, Mrs. Thompson got to me first." I told him how she accused me of killing her husband.

Dawson's arms were tightly folded as he stared at the floor, nodding his head. "Then it's true—the police are saying Richard was murdered?"

"They certainly made me believe they're at least exploring the possibility."

I summed up my afternoon getting drilled by the police, relaying the types of questions they asked and why. Dawson listened intently, not moving or asking follow-up questions until I was finished speaking. Then he said, "You should have called. And you should have been represented by the paper's attorney. You know better, Samantha."

I shook my head, feeling frustrated all over again. "Thompson had the story I wrote about him. It was dated two days before ever going to print. Who could have given it to him?"

Dawson inhaled a deep breath and I watched his eyelids click.

"It had to be someone in this office. Someone with access to our shared folder."

"You didn't keep it on a personal thumb-drive?"

"I know my personal copies weren't compromised. It had to come from the cloud." I kept hinting at it being that new intern, Skinny Tree Brett Gallagher, without saying his name, but Dawson didn't seem to catch on.

Dawson's eyebrows pulled together. He stared through narrowed, confused eyes. "And you're sure it was the final draft?"

"It doesn't matter. It was all there. Everything we reported on his scam charity." I rubbed the back of my neck. "But there was something else."

Dawson lifted his eyes.

"A key code for a Bitcoin account was also found with my story."

Dawson titled his head to one side. "What the hell for?"

"Still trying to figure it out, but it seems to me that whoever gave Thompson my story either sold it to him, or wanted it to look like I was the one attempting to blackmail him."

"I assume you told the police about this?"

I shook my head. "I didn't learn about the Bitcoin digital wallet until after my interview with the police. King knows what it is now, but at the time they were still trying to figure it out."

"Christ, Sam, I don't know what to say."

I raised both my eyebrows. "Brett Gallagher, I don't like him."

"Sam, unless you have incriminating evidence against Brett, let's keep names out of this. Okay?"

"You heard about Donny Counts?" Dawson said he had. "Then let's not forget how Brett was the one to have my notes on Donny open when he was only supposed to be updating my security software."

Dawson held my gaze for a second before edging around his desk and dropping into his chair. "Everything you've told me is truly concerning, and I'll talk with Travis, see what he has to say about this. We're still working to confirm what, if anything, was taken during the suspected hack, but maybe now we know."

"How long until we have an answer?"

"Hopefully by the end of this week."

"That's too long, Dawson. By then, everyone involved would have moved on."

Dawson raised one hand, making me pause. "Until we learn how a leak might have occurred, we keep this between us. Got it?"

I answered with a scowl.

Dawson raised an eyebrow and changed the subject. "We need a piece on Donny Counts."

"Did you assign Garcia the story?"

"He'll cover it. Just as he did with Richard Thompson.

What I need from you is to confirm whether or not he was legit or running an elaborate Ponzi scheme like some are suggesting."

"What other assignments you have Garcia working?" Dawson looked annoyed by my question. Before he could answer, I said, "Parker and Joan Collins? Is he writing a story about them?"

"Why do you ask?"

"Is he or isn't he?"

"Not that I know of," Dawson conceded.

I glanced at the clock and thought about mentioning Loxley and how he seemed to be channeling his message through me, but I decided against it. I couldn't afford loose lips to destroy the only leverage I currently held when protecting my reputation. I knew Dawson wasn't the mole, but maybe someone close to him was.

"I better get going," I said. "I need to figure out how my article found its way to Thompson's desk and if Donny's death was an accident like the police are suggesting, or something else entirely."

"You think he was murdered?"

I gave Dawson a look. "Don't you?"

CHAPTER FORTY-THREE

MY CAR HAD TROUBLE STARTING. IT WAS KNOWN TO misbehave when the weather was cold, but not this time of year when the days were warm. I felt my blood boil with frustration. It seemed nothing could go my way. Sure, my car was getting up there in age, and despite my regular oil changes I had to face the fact that I might need to find a new pair of wheels soon. Even if it meant taking a hit to my bleak savings.

I tried a second time. The engine clicked but nothing happened.

I fell back into my seat with a thump and whispered a curse before asking whoever might be listening for just a little bit of luck to come my way.

As I gave myself a minute to cool down, I relived my conversation with Dawson and couldn't stop thinking about Brett Gallagher.

Recalling my interaction with him, it was the way he acted as he invaded my privacy that had me distrustful of his true intention. He treated it like it was no big deal. As frustrating as it was, that Donny Counts was now dead left me suspicious.

I pulled my cellphone out of my tote and called Travis in IT.

"Turner here," he answered almost immediately.

"Travis, its Samantha Bell."

"Hey Samantha, what can I help you with?"

Sounds of the highway traveled through the line, and I suspected he was behind the wheel. "Are you not in the office?"

"Driving," he said, quickly telling me how his office line was re-routed to his cell. "I can do the same for you if you want?"

"No, that's all right," I said, thinking I received enough calls as it was. "Do you expect to be back soon? There is something I would like to speak to you about."

"Out of the office most of the day. Meetings," he grumbled. "I hope it's not an emergency. But if it is, Brett is in the office and I'm sure he would be able help with whatever you need."

"No, he's not there," I said. "I checked already."

"Huh."

I imagined Travis scratching his head. "Have you learned any more about who might have hacked us?"

"I'm not supposed to talk about it."

"Really? Who said?"

"Don't do this to me, Sam. I like working at the *Times*."

We all did, but that didn't mean we were all entitled to ride off into the sunset and retirement after a long, successful career with a failing paper.

"What's this really about?" he asked.

"Brett had one of my folders open yesterday. The folder that contained my notes on Donny Counts." Travis was quiet and when he didn't respond, I added, "You heard the news, right?"

"Wait, you're not suggesting—"

"I don't know what I'm suggesting, but what I do know is that I need a favor from you."

"I'm listening."

"I need you to keep this between us." I gripped my steering wheel with my free hand. "Can you give me your word?"

"As long as it's nothing illegal."

"I'm glad you think so highly of me," I teased.

"Sorry, Samantha, I just don't know what you're asking me to do."

I bit my lip and stared out over the sea of parked cars, their rooftops shimmering in the sunshine. "I was hoping you could confirm whether or not Brett has a Bitcoin account."

"For a second, you had me scared." Travis laughed. "And can I ask what this is about?"

"First confirm whether or not he does. Then I'll decide if I can tell you why."

"You drive a hard bargain, Mrs. Bell."

"How do you think I got this far in life?"

Travis laughed his way off the line and as soon as I ended my call with him, I turned the key and the engine finally rumbled to a quick start. "Yes!" I shouted, giddy with excitement.

Soon I was traveling toward Rose Medical Center, thinking about Garcia and the possible reasons why he might have scribbled my name next to Parker Collins's.

What did I have to do with Mr. and Mrs. Collins? I wasn't writing a story on them. Should I be? Or should I be asking Garcia who his favorite vigilante was? The whole train of thought seemed ridiculous. Garcia was a great reporter, someone you could trust. But still, there was something off that left me feeling incomplete.

I rolled to a stop at a light and turned my head to the left.

What the hell was he up to?

I thought about calling his wife, Cecelia, but instead called Erin.

"Sam, I'm at the hospital. No one is giving me access to Counts's report." Erin talked fast and was clearly frustrated by the hospital putting up barriers to her request. "They don't know who they're talking to."

"No they don't."

"But maybe the *Times* still carries enough clout for someone to listen to you?"

I told her I was five minutes out. Then I said, "I figured out the meaning of why our guy chose the name, Loxley."

"I'm listening."

"Who is the vigilante who steals from the rich and gives to the poor?"

"Robin Hood?"

I smiled. I knew Erin Tate was a smart cookie. "Robin of Loxley. Little John, second in command of the Merry Men."

"Listen to you."

"It makes sense, though, right?"

"But is he stealing from the rich and giving to the poor? From what I recall, Loxley has only suggested he might be behind our victims' deaths. He's said nothing about giving back."

I had come to the same conclusion, and still didn't have a clear answer to explain that missing piece of the puzzle. But it was the closest thing we had to explaining the name Loxley without knowing any other specifics about who exactly we were after.

"Have you been on Twitter recently?" I asked.

"You're referring to the rumors people are spreading about Counts running a Ponzi scheme?"

I said I was. "If this is true—"

"Then Loxley knew about it."

We were getting ahead of ourselves. First, we needed to

confirm Counts's death was something other than an unfortunate accident. Getting our hands on the hospital reports could give us the answers we needed.

Erin told me how she was monitoring the growing resentment toward both victims while she waited for me to arrive. "It's all very interesting, Sam. Just like our message board, what these men are accused of doing seems to have angered a lot of people."

Including me, I thought. "What else is being said about Counts?"

"Oh, they're pissed, Sam. People who used his exchange can't access their digital coins. Unless Counts left his passwords to someone close to him, the money will be stuck there forever."

Suddenly I felt sick to my stomach. Innocent bystanders were going to lose everything. Garcia's off-the-cuff comment about Counts faking his own death suddenly made a whole lot more sense. At the time, it sounded like a farfetched conspiracy theory. Now it could be Counts's way to keeping all that money for himself.

We needed to get our hands on the hospital reports—at the very least, a death certificate—before this thing really spiraled out of control.

Not more than five minutes later, I entered the hospital and found Erin still demanding to see Donny Counts's chart at the counter. She never gave up, and I knew she wouldn't. The nurse behind the desk recognized me. "Are you with her?" she asked me.

"I am," I said. "I'm sorry if she's caused you any trouble."

Erin glared, then turned back to the nurse. "I told you I wasn't lying."

"I'll show you the chart," the nurse said quietly when her colleagues weren't looking. "But only because I liked your last story. I was one of the many people who gave to Richard Thompson thinking we were doing good."

"I'm sorry," I told her.

The nurse's hard gaze softened, but only slightly. "This is all strictly off the record. My name won't be anywhere and you can't publish what I show you."

Her round eyes volleyed back and forth between me and Erin. "I promise."

Her knowing eyes held mine before she finally dipped down and opened a drawer. Donny Counts's file was thin, but conclusive. "He overdosed on his own insulin pump," the nurse said, after I read through the report.

"Has that ever happened before?" Erin asked the nurse, her hands planted flat on the countertop.

"First I heard of it." The nurse raised her brows. "But with technology, anything is possible."

CHAPTER FORTY-FOUR

"Benjamin is going to take the job, I just know it."
Susan's distant gaze traveled across the road and watched the
traffic start and stop at the light. "And what makes it so hard
is that I really like him."

Allison reached over and pressed her hand between her
friend's shoulders. "Does he know this?"

Susan shrugged without looking. "I assume he does."

"But you haven't told him?" Allison's brow was pinched
with concern for her friend.

Susan shook her head no, still staring at the traffic coming
and going. "I'm too afraid it might change things." She turned
and looked into Allison's chestnut eyes. "You know how
quickly things can go belly up once parameters have been
established."

"Telling the man you like him isn't a parameter, darling."

"No, maybe not. But defining our relationship would be.
And I don't want to scare him away by making things too
serious."

Allison's eyes crinkled as she smiled. "You're having fun."

"Like you wouldn't believe." Susan lifted her chin and

laughed. "And now I wonder if I waited too long to tell him how I really feel. If he takes this job, it's over."

"You wouldn't follow him?"

"To New England? And leave you and the girls behind?" Susan's brow furrowed. "No way."

Allison squeezed Susan's hand. "Your winters would certainly be colder."

"I'm not leaving Denver." Susan flicked her gaze up the sidewalk, looking again for Damien Black, hoping he'd show soon. "I love Colorado."

"Me, too, sister." Allison pushed up her sleeve and checked the time. Tapping her toes, she asked, "Are you sure this is the right place?"

Susan's eyes flashed with disbelief as she pointed to the sign above the door. "Do you know any other Backstage?"

"Then why don't we go inside? He can find us there."

"He told me to specifically meet him at the door." Susan peered through the glass window behind her. Her reflection stared back. Through it, she saw occasional dark shadows of movement drift across the floor. There were people inside but it wasn't Damien. They'd checked when they arrived, and now they were stuck waiting beneath the intense afternoon sun for someone they barely knew, wondering if he'd show at all.

"I don't get it, why would he do that?" Allison questioned.

"I don't know." Susan palmed her cellphone and checked to see if Damien messaged back. "He made it sound like he wanted everything inside to be a surprise."

Allison looked her friend in the eye and laughed.

"What's so funny?" Susan's tone hardened as if suddenly feeling offended.

"First, you're worried because he picks you up out of the blue and convinces you to meet him here. Now you're filled with doubts he'll even show by making you wait."

Susan crossed her arms, lowered her brow, and inched closer to Allison. "What's your point?"

Allison's gaze locked with Susan's. "My point is, you're falling into his hands like putty. And you know what else?"

"What?" Susan said through clenched teeth.

"I think you might like him."

"Don't be ridiculous." Susan turned her head away before Allison could see her cheeks bloom like red roses.

"I don't know." Allison's head swiveled on her neck as she looked around. "This place seems legit. I don't think there's anything you have to worry about."

After their rendezvous at Samantha's house early this morning, they'd spent the rest of their morning arranging their work schedules before making a list of potential hackers who could possibly be behind the mysterious intrusion to Samantha's home network.

"Maybe I should just call him and tell him today isn't a good time."

"He'll show." Allison assured her. "Relax, would you?"

Susan shifted her weight and sighed. "Aren't you worried about Sam?"

Allison's lips closed. "Yes, but Sam knows what she's doing."

"Her house was hacked. Someone is watching her. Who knows exactly what other stories she's investigating."

"Listen, I'm scared too, but this isn't anything new for her. She's seen it and done it before. Let's also not forget that she's dating a highly decorated detective who is more than capable of protecting the woman he loves."

Susan knew Allison was right. King wouldn't let anything happen to Samantha—unless he didn't know about what was happening. *Argh*. Susan felt more unsettled than before.

"Screw it, Mr. Black can meet us inside." Susan reached for the knob, swung the door open, and stepped inside.

Allison was a step behind. As soon as they entered, a half-dozen young eyes lifted to see who walked through the door. Many of the young men and women were busy working on a collection of different projects, many of which also required them to be on a personal computer.

"It's nice," Allison said, taking a deeper look after her first glance around.

Susan agreed, watching Allison begin interacting with the students. Allison spoke their language, was easy to relate to, and soon laughs were shared and high fives were given as Susan found herself in the front of the room looking at a poster pinned to the bulletin board.

"Ali," Susan called. "Come take a look at this."

Allison was all smiles as she made her way to the front of the room.

Susan jutted her jaw toward the poster. "Should I still be cautious?"

Allison tipped her head back and read what it said. Her eyes narrowed into tiny slits and Susan knew that Allison was thinking the same.

"Tell me I shouldn't have brought you along."

"This doesn't mean anything." Allison tossed her hitch hikers thumb over her shoulder and pointed it at the announcement for a hacker event coming up. Speaking in a hushed tone, she said, "It's a computer lab. These types of events happen all the time."

Susan raised her eyebrows and felt the tightness in her chest squeeze. Could it be that she wouldn't have thought much of it if hackers hadn't already been on her radar? Maybe. But it was enough of a coincidence to further convince her to get to know Damien Black before signing him on as a new client.

The door jangled behind them. A warm breeze swept across the floor and Susan turned to find Damien enter. His

dimples deepened above a strong jawline that had Susan smiling. Making his way across the room, he greeted several
students as he passed. They seemed happy to see him, and
Susan considered that a good sign.

"I'm sorry I'm late," he said to Susan, not once
mentioning anything about not waiting for him outside like
he requested. "Have you had some time to look around?"

"We have." Susan introduced Allison. Damien shook her
hand and Allison gave her elevator pitch into what she did for
a living. Susan knew they would hit it off, and they did.

"Is that right?" Damien exuded a warm glow.

"Great place you have here," Allison said enthusiastically.
"I wish I'd known about it before; I know of several kids
from my neighborhood it might have benefited."

"We're getting our name out," Damien said. "Slowly, but
surely."

"I couldn't help but notice the hacker event." Susan
turned to face the bulletin board. "Are you the one spon-
soring it?"

"Not me." Damien had his hands inside his pants pockets
when he stepped forward. "But I encourage all our students
to consider competing."

"Any of your students take you up on it?" Allison asked.

"Yes." Damien turned his head and peered down into Allison's eyes. "All the time."

Susan wanted to ask him about where she could get her
hands on a list of names, but was afraid it might open up too
many questions she wasn't sure she had the answers to.
Besides, it seemed like an invasive request for having only
met yesterday. But her mind was still on Samantha, and this
could be their ticket into learning who this mysterious hacker
they were all after might be.

"Hackers are the unsung heroes of our time," Damien

said, getting Susan's full attention. "Without them, we'd be worse off than we already are."

"Vigilantes of our time." Allison grinned.

Susan couldn't believe what she was hearing. Was Allison playing along or agreeing with him? Susan couldn't decide.

"Yes." Damien looked to Allison with a bit of surprise flashing over his handsome eyes. "I suppose they are."

"I've heard of these events." Allison flicked her gaze to Susan. "Hackers compete against one another to expose cracks in the code to software we all use nearly every single day."

"Exactly," Damien said. "And bounties are paid to the winners. It's cheaper for companies to pay the hackers than it is to be caught vulnerable and exposed to something that could result in something much worse and certainly more expensive."

Susan stood there quietly thinking about Richard Thompson and Samantha's theories on how he died. "I guess I know nothing about them," Susan admitted.

Damien's voice perked up. "Hackers receive a bad rap but, like anything, one bad actor will set the tone for everyone else who follows. But that's why Backstage exists. I want to change that stereotype and bring the underground above ground. Events like these keep the club members interested in a healthy and productive way."

Susan glanced one last time to the poster, deciding her doubts were nothing more than fears keeping her from thinking hackers could only be bad.

"Come." Damien motioned for them to follow. "Let me show you the lab."

Over the next half-hour Damien walked them through the different projects the lab had to offer. They spoke to students of various ages and learned about all things technology;

computer programming, engineering, robotics, drones, games, and A.I.—artificial intelligence.

"It's truly impressive," Allison said, grinning as she let her eyes drift across the room. "But I know how much all this equipment costs, and it's not cheap. How do you afford all of it?"

Damien rolled his eyes over to Susan. "Funding is always a challenge to keep things going, but that's where I was hoping you could help."

"I'm almost there, but first tell me how you select the students who are here?"

Damien explained how each student goes through a lengthy application and interview process before being accepted into the program. "As much as we would like to allow anybody to be part of our lab, we want only those who are most serious. Once they're accepted, it's free tuition until they take their skills out into the real world."

Allison was staring at Susan when she said, "What more do you need to know?"

"There is one more piece to the equation that might help you decide." Damien cleared his throat. "We don't have much time, and if we can't secure a large donation soon, Backstage will be forced to close."

"Oh, my God." Allison gasped.

"The lease is too high." Damien nodded, his voice going soft. "But what scares me most is, if these doors close, then where will these young men and women be? Their alternatives are grim, and the last thing I want for them is to turn to a life of crime."

CHAPTER FORTY-FIVE

"What she's suggesting is that the insulin pump malfunctioned." King turned his attention to his partner who was still twirling Donny's insulin pump inside his hand, shaking his head.

"Everything is connected," Alvarez said without looking up.

"What are you saying, that maybe it was hacked?"

Alvarez lifted his gaze, stared out over the dash, and shrugged. "Maybe. Donny was a computer guy and we live in a world where machines are more eager to learn than humans. It's why jobs are being outsourced to robots. It won't be long before we're half-robot, half-human."

King stopped listening halfway through his partner's rant. Looking through the glare in the windshield glass, King did think that maybe Alvarez was right about one thing. Perhaps, the device could have been hacked. "Rose did say that Donny had enemies."

"Yeah. But could a paper reporter pull off a murder like this?"

Alvarez sounded skeptical, and King was, too. The crowd was still marching across the street from Donny Counts's house, shouting obscenities toward Rose's front door. Something didn't seem right about this—even Rose's excuse for calling them seemed a bit farfetched.

"There is no crime scene here," King shook his head and said softly.

Slowly, his fingers curled into his palm until squeezing into a tight fist. He was feeling as frustrated with this assignment as he knew Alvarez was. Worse, he was still thinking of the boy who was shot dead in the streets last night, and how the case would turn cold, just like the previous gang-related murders, because the city cared more about the rich than the poor.

"You see that?" King pointed to a picket sign that caught his attention.

Alvarez squinted behind his dark sunglasses. "And why would that man think Thompson *and* Counts are thieves?"

"Maybe that was what Rose was referring to?"

"Journalists just don't go writing stories to slander people's reputations." Alvarez didn't understand how the news about Donny Counts had spread as quickly as a brush fire in the hottest part of August, but that was exactly what had happened.

"The media has done far worse." King rolled his eyes to his partner. "But clearly, both men are guilty in the people's eyes."

"You know what I'm thinking?" Alvarez flicked his gaze to his partner. "I'm thinking Rose has the most to gain from Donny's death." Alvarez knocked the center console with his knuckles and nodded.

"You don't believe anything she said about Joey Garcia?"

"Something tells me it's not 100% accurate."

King cranked the engine, put the car in gear, and set the wheels in motion. "Then I guess we'll just have to ask him ourselves."

CHAPTER FORTY-SIX

KING STEPPED OUT INTO A NEIGHBORHOOD NOT TOO different than his own. The afternoon sun hid behind a tall spruce as he took a moment to glance around and gain his bearings.

He couldn't recall having ever personally met Joey Garcia, but he knew who he was, knew his column in the *Times*. King found Rose's comments most interesting, but they were walking a thin line since Robbins and Zimmerman's decision to bring Samantha down to the station for questioning. He was sure the *Times* attorneys were aware of it by now. Approaching another one of their reporters started to make it look like harassment.

"Garcia covered Thompson's death; maybe he's working on telling Counts's too?" Alvarez suggested as they approached Garcia's front door.

"Wouldn't that be interesting?" King knocked.

"You want to take the lead, or should I?"

"I'll take it," King offered, thinking he had an easy way in by name-dropping Samantha if he had to. "It's important we get ourselves into Garcia's office without having to get a warrant."

Alvarez nodded just as the lock clicked over. A dark haired woman of about thirty-five answered. "Can I help you?"

"Mrs. Garcia?"

"Yes, that's me." Her eyes traveled between the two detectives. "I'm Cecelia."

King introduced themselves, showed her his badge. The lines on her face deepened with anxiety. "What's this about? Is my husband okay?"

King heard little *pitter-patter* sounds scampering across the floor. A cute three-year-old wedged her head between the door and her mother's leg. King smiled and she giggled and played shy. "He is," King said. "Is Joey home?"

Cecelia's eyes glistened with worry. "He's not."

"When do you expect him back?"

"Not until evening. He's a reporter at the *Times.*"

King shared a knowing look. He and Alvarez had debated taking their chances and finding him at the newsroom, but in the end it wasn't really Joey they were after, but the secrets they hoped Joey kept hidden in his home office away from curious eyes.

"If this is about a story he's working," Cecelia's hand was on her daughter's head, "I can call him and find out where he is."

A motorcycle with a loud muffler ripped past on the street behind. "Can we come inside?" King asked as soon as the noise was gone.

Cecelia wet her lips and nodded her head.

Stepping inside the modest sized house, Cecelia was quick to offer them something to drink which both men politely declined. The little girl kept stealing glances at King, and King made her giggle when making a funny face.

"Has your husband seemed himself these past couple of days?" Alvarez asked.

Cecelia motioned for them to take a seat at the dining room table. King sat and watched the little girl pick up a doll. She was still giggling at King when he heard Cecelia say, "Joey has been under tremendous stress lately."

"Any particular reason?"

"Personal finances and the stress of potentially losing his position at the paper." Cecelia rolled her gaze to her daughter. "Is Joey in any kind of trouble?"

"No. No." Alvarez shook his head. "We just saw his story on Richard Thompson and thought maybe he was also writing about Donny Counts."

"I've seen the news," Cecelia said without being prompted. "Heard the little bit Joey talked about it. But I don't recall him ever mentioning anything about Donny Counts."

"He's covered him in the past, though, right?"

"I believe so." Cecelia cast her gaze to the wedding band she was twisting around her finger. "I can't keep up anymore." She looked to her daughter. "Katie has leukemia, and it's taken my attention away from Joey." Her eyes were back on King. "Unfortunately, our relationship has suffered because of it."

King was staring at Katie, feeling his heart slowly chip away at the thought of her battle with cancer. "I'm sorry to hear."

"We're dealing with it." Cecelia sighed. "Praying every day that a miracle will be given."

Turning back to face Cecelia, King asked, "Does Joey have a home office?"

"In the back."

"Mind if we take a look around?"

Cecelia's eyes were strong but sad as she held King's gaze.

"Sure. It's the last door at the end of the hall on the right."

King nodded and stood. Cecelia didn't follow them as they made their way to the back of the house. The office door was closed but easy to open.

"Nicely done, partner," Alvarez said quietly into King's ear once they were inside Garcia's home office.

Each of them went to work. They divided up the room between them, opening drawers, searching files, and thumbing through papers left out on top. The computer was on but password protected. After ten minutes of quiet, Alvarez asked, "Anything?"

"Only chicken scratch notes on a legal pad." King swiveled around in the chair he was sitting in and pointed to the center of the page. "But look here, recognize any of these names?"

"Parker Collins, Ronald Hyland," Alvarez muttered, "and Donny Counts."

They shared a look. "No mention of Richard Thompson."

"Either he wasn't part of this, or these names came after he died."

Alvarez kneeled and searched the trash bin. Digging through crumpled paper and empty ink cartridges, he suddenly stopped when finding something they'd both seen before.

"Holy shit," he said.

King stole it from his partner's grip. It was the exact copy of Samantha's article that Robbins and Zimmerman found on Richard Thompson's desk. "Maybe Rose wasn't lying after all."

"So did Garcia try to blackmail Thompson with a Bitcoin account? Or is Garcia in cahoots with Rose and they're in on this together?"

King was still studying Samantha's article when he said, "I don't know, but I think I might know someone who might."

CHAPTER FORTY-SEVEN

TECHNOLOGY WAS DRIVING ME MAD. AN OVERDOSE AT THE hands of Donny Counts's insulin pump and, suddenly, I knew that my mysterious online friend wasn't lying. Loxley had killed Counts. I still couldn't explain how he'd done it, but I now understood what he was communicating through the messages he was sending me. But who was Loxley? Was he planning to strike again?

"This is unreal, Sam," Erin said, looking at me with disbelief filling her eyes.

"I know."

"But it certainly fits the pattern."

We dropped into my Outback, shut the door, and I immediately called Allison, wanting to know if this was even possible. She didn't answer so I left a message telling her where we were and to call as soon as she got this.

I started the engine, but only to crack the windows. The truth was, I didn't know where to go or what to do next. Was it even worth reporting on Donny's potential Ponzi scheme when really we should all be asking ourselves who killed him and why? My to-do list was growing by the minute. I could call Dawson and report what I found, or I could follow up with the reason Garcia had my name scribbled next to Parker Collins. Neither of the two appealed to me.

I turned to Erin. She was busy scrolling through our message board's online comments. "Nothing from our friend, LilJon, but this thing is blowing up."

I felt the pressure in my temples slowly move to the front of my skull. Taking a swig of water, I self-medicated with an Advil. There were more people coming out saying they too had been duped by either Thompson or Counts, a few of them by both, and now people were calling for me to publicly expose Counts like I had done to Thompson.

"If only these people knew what was really going on," I said.

"You can't blame them for asking," Erin said, turning her attention to me. "They're locked out of their investments. All they're requesting is for us to put pressure on Donny's exchange with hopes of getting their money released."

I wasn't sure I could do that even if I wanted to. My priority was simple, and I kept my focus on one person and one person only. I needed to learn who Loxley was, why he was doing what he was doing, and who he planned to kill next. Because until he was stopped, none of this other stuff mattered. Someone's life was in his crosshairs and something told me he wouldn't stop until all this uproar died down.

Reaching for my cellphone, I began making calls to other local reporters, including Nancy Jordan, curious to know what they were hearing.

"Oh, hey, Samantha," Nancy answered. I didn't waste anybody's time. After catching her up to speed, she said, "Funny you ask. Of course everyone wants to know how he died, but what I found most interesting was how Donny gave a speech at Denver University just two days ago."

"About what?" I asked, my thoughts suddenly drifting back to the event flier I saw on Garcia's desk.

"The usual spiel about how great a businessman he was. But, get this, apparently he pitched his service pretty hard this last time around and now people who attended the event are assuming that he did, knowing that he about to exit."

"Exit?"

"Yeah, he was planning to skip town but died the night before."

"Where was he going?"

"Two one way tickets to Bangkok, Thailand."

"Who was the other ticket for?"

"His girlfriend, Rose Wild."

My mind drifted to Garcia's comment about doubting Donny was even dead. Garcia made me believe someone else had said it to him, but now I wondered if Garcia wasn't being completely honest with me. Then Nancy dropped even bigger news into my ear that I couldn't believe.

"And I'm still working to confirm this rumor, but there are lots of whispers about a possible vigilante who might be responsible for not only the death of Donny Counts, but also Richard Thompson."

"A vigilante?" I tried to sound surprised.

"It's big, Sam. Even if we don't know this guy's name, ratings are going to shoot through the roof. You just wait and see."

I rolled my eyes. TV reporters were always after one thing —hitting their audience hard with the juiciest story possible first, and fact-checking second. When I ended the call with Nancy, Erin asked for a summary.

"You don't think Loxley is also reaching out to other reporters, do you?" she asked.

"I don't see why not," I said, still waiting to hear back from Allison when I got a call from King.

"Hi, honey." I smiled, tried to sound upbeat.

So much had happened since we last talked, I didn't know where to begin. I needed to tell him about my latest message from Loxley and how Allison believed he hacked my home network about the same time Donny Counts was possibly being targeted.

"Sam, you available to meet?"

"Yeah. I'm at Rose Medical Center," I said, hearing a small tap on my window. I jumped when I saw King. "You can't do that to me," I said through the cracked window.

"Hey, King." Erin leaned across the seat to greet him.

King greeted Erin through the window. As soon as I looked in his eyes, I knew something wasn't right. It was the same grave expression that kept my lungs from exhaling, and the same one I'd seen him wear when it seemed like the world was about to end.

"Can I speak to you in private?"

I felt like a school girl being called into the principal's office. I told Erin to hang tight. Once I stepped out, I spotted Alvarez leaning against their sedan across the way. "How did you know where to find me? You're not tracking my phone, are you?"

King didn't take the bait. Instead, he reached behind and pulled a copy of my Thompson article from his back pocket. "You know where we found this?"

"It's not the same one you discovered at Thompson's house?" I asked, staring at my piece.

King shook his head. "Joey Garcia had it in *his* office."

It felt like I was standing on a bed of coals. Slowly, the flames tickled my calves as the heat climbed up my legs. I wasn't sure if I was mad because of possibly being betrayed by one of my own, or if it was because the police were once again harassing a reporter.

"You had a warrant?" I asked. There was a lot more King wasn't telling me.

"You're not mad?"

"At him or you?" I peeked through the back window and saw Erin trying to pretend to ignore us.

"Didn't need a warrant," King said. "His wife let us inside."

"But why were you there?" I asked. What King was suggesting Garcia did, wasn't the man I knew him to be.

My mind scrambled back to my conversation with Garcia just hours earlier and how something felt off. *Was this why he asked to have that drink?*

King caught me up with how he was assigned to look into Donny Counts's death.

"You're investigating a homicide?"

Nothing was said, no confirmation, just silence. King kept his mouth shut and it only drove me closer to the brink of war.

When asked, I told him I had heard about Donny's death, but downplayed much of what I already knew. Two could play at this game, I thought to myself as I stared him down. Then I mentioned, "The reason I came to the hospital at all was because of a tip I received from Garcia."

King cocked his head to the side. "And what exactly did Garcia say?"

"That Donny's death was related to his diabetes." King mumbled something about needing to get his hands on the official hospital report for his own records when I said, "Garcia doubted Donny was even dead."

I paused and let that sink in for a moment. King stopped breathing.

"Garcia suggested Donny was taking his money and skipping town before everyone learned his exchange was a fraud." I told King about how I was tasked to confirm whether or not Counts's exchange was a Ponzi scheme or not. He barely reacted, but I saw it in his eyes. He knew it, too. "And early reports suggest that it might be true."

I could see that King was shuffling through his own thoughts when he finally told me to follow him to his car. "There is something else you need to see."

We walked. Alvarez nodded as I approached, but that was as far as his greeting went. It was clear he was only here because of King. With me still looking like a possible suspect, I didn't see him warming up to me anytime soon.

King asked if I had met, known, or spoken with Rose Wild recently. That was twice now that I had heard her name being mentioned, and I couldn't wait to see what King wanted to show me.

"I haven't," I said, wondering if I should speak with her before she jetted off to Southeast Asia.

King nodded to Alvarez and I watched as John opened the back seat to their sedan, dipped down low, and came up a second later holding an insulin pump. He handed it off to King. "You know what this is?" he asked me.

"I think so."

"It's Donny Counts's insulin pump."

"Why do you have it?" I asked, thinking about the hospital report I'd seen.

"Rose Wild gave it to us. Said that this is how Donny was killed."

I could feel the warmth spread across the small of my back. "Can I look at it?"

King didn't see why not. He'd already sealed it away inside a clear plastic evidence bag for safe keeping. I took it between my fingers and stared at it, thinking about Loxley.

The hospital report had already given me a good glimpse into what happened, but I needed to open up King to gain better insight into what he knew. "The hospital said the same thing. The device malfunctioned."

King shook his head. "Sorry, let me rephrase that. Rose suggested someone took control of it and purposely *killed* her fiancé."

My heart started beating faster. I couldn't make eye contact with King.

King must have seen my face go pale because he asked, "Is Rose right?"

"I don't know," I said in my smallest voice. Then I told him how it fit my running theory that a hacker was behind both Thompson's and Counts's murders.

"The messages you've been receiving?"

I nodded. "He hacked into my home network last night right after you let."

"Christ, Sam." His face was a mix between anger and agony. "How long were you going to keep that from me?"

I shrugged. "It's all happening so fast."

King shoved his fingers through his hair.

"He signed his name on the last letter he sent." King spun around and stared into my wet eyes. "He's calling himself Loxley."

Alvarez took a step forward and shared a glance with his partner. Then I told them both what Loxley wrote, his fight against greed, and my theory of how he chose his name.

"A vigilante?" Alvarez quirked a single brow.

"Appears so."

"And if he hacked Counts's insulin pump, my money is on him being behind Thompson's death, too," I said, holding up the pump and explaining the intricacies of how a smart home system could be taken over remotely.

King inhaled a single breath of air and started his profile assessment of Loxley. "Young white male. Single." He ticked each one off as he counted them on his fingers. "Degree in computer science."

"Know anyone who fits the profile?" I asked both detectives.

"I do," a voice said from behind.

The three of us turned to look.

Allison hustled over with Susan struggling to catch up as she trotted along in her high heels. Waving her hand through the air, Allison called out, "Sam, I know someone who fits that description, and I can also tell you where to find him."

CHAPTER FORTY-EIGHT

"DAMIEN BLACK ISN'T THE HACKER." SUSAN FOLDED HER arms and glared.

Allison planted one hand on her cocked-out hip and stared right back. "That's not what I said. What I said was, he fits the profile."

"Stop," I said, stepping between them. "We don't have time to listen to you two bicker. Now, tell us, who is Damien Black?"

"Susan's new client," Allison said happily as she bounced her gaze around the circle, nodding her round head. "We had a meeting with him today to check out his program. You remember?" Allison rolled her gaze to me. "Susan brought me along to make sure she wasn't going to get Thompsoned again."

"Thompsoned?" Erin asked, joining the rendezvous by King's car.

"Yeah—duped into helping someone raising a shit load of money only to later learn it was a complete fraud."

"I see," I said, recalling the conversation we had earlier

today. The asphalt below my feet spun as I tried to keep up. "And now you think he fits the profile of Loxley?"

Allison's eyebrows squished. "Is that who we're talking about?"

I answered with a single look. King rubbed the nape of his neck. I knew he was losing patience.

"Wait, Samantha," King's gentle hand closed around my arm, "who else knows about Loxley?"

"Only us," I said.

"Shit, I'm sorry, Sam. I thought he knew?" Allison's gaze went distant.

Susan intervened and quickly told us who Damien Black was and why Allison said he fit the profile. I listened carefully and Susan painted a clear picture that I now understood.

"And he teaches computer science where?" King asked.

"Backstage. It's a non-profit on the north side of the city. But Damien Black is certainly not Loxley. I can guarantee you that."

"She says that because he asked her out." Allison smirked.

"And, like I told him, I'm off the market."

"Unless Benjamin decides he'd rather work in New England than have you."

Susan's neck craned. "I *am* work, honey."

"Christ," Alvarez muttered as he stepped away. "I can't listen to this anymore."

"Please, stop." I was growing just as frustrated as Alvarez. I didn't know what had happened or why they were down each other's necks, but now was not the time to fight. "People are dying and, for all we know, Loxley is watching us right now."

Everyone paused and glanced over their shoulders as if suddenly feeling hidden eyes in the shadows.

"All I'm saying is that he fits the profile." Allison bounced her gaze to me, then to the detectives.

I watched King check the time as I worked to bring everyone back to the table. "Let me take a moment to remind everyone that we're all pressed for time." When I made sure everyone understood, I turned to Allison and said, "King needs your help."

Allison lifted her head and grinned. "I didn't realize that was why you called."

It was, but it wasn't. Still holding Donny's insulin pump inside my hand, I held it up and said, "Is it possible to hack an insulin pump?"

Allison reached out to take it for herself. I watched her read the evidence bag, then she swept her gaze up and asked, "Whose is it?"

"Donny Counts," I said before King could stop me. He broke eye contact, rubbed a hand over his mouth, and turned his back. Alvarez didn't know what to do about the free-flowing information being shared between police, reporters, and civilians.

Allison swept her gaze to Erin. "And you think it was Loxley?"

"I do."

Allison swung her gaze to King. "It's quite easy, actually."

King twisted his spine and stared over his right shoulder.

Allison kept her eyes fixed on King for a moment before continuing. "A hacker can take control through the tiny radio transmitters here." Allison pointed to a corner of the pump. "Wireless commandeering, is what I like to call it."

"Cute," I said.

Allison thanked me before adding, "It's there to allow patients and doctors to adjust their functions. Generally, one would need to be nearby and know the serial number to get the device to respond. But based on what I've seen on Samantha's computer and knowing how good this guy is, I'd guess he wrote his own software and found a way to bypass the chain of command."

King's lips parted. "Unbelievable."

"Which is exactly what Loxley would want you to think," Allison said in all seriousness. "It's what makes his strategy so successful. He can attack without ever stepping foot inside the victim's house."

"Like Richard Thompson?" I prompted her, knowing King was listening.

"Exactly."

The air stilled, and everyone was silent. I let Allison's words sink into my brain, thinking about the hospital report I'd read and how it put Allison's words into perspective.

"How do you know so much about insulin pumps?" Susan inquired. I was glad she asked. I had a feeling we were all wondering the same thing.

Allison rolled her neck and looked Susan in the eye. "My cousin Sheri has one, but it didn't occur to me just how vulnerable it made someone until now."

It felt like my head was inside a vice being squeezed like a melon. Anyone using any type of technology were sitting ducks, and now I was beginning to think that Garcia's comment about Counts still being alive was nothing more than a diversion tactic to get me to turn my head the other way. There was no denying I felt betrayed by one of my own, and it stung bad, but was he also the owner of the digital wallet? I didn't want to believe it was true.

"Was an insulin delivery denied or was there an overdose?" Allison asked.

I blinked and came out of my thoughts. "Overdose."

Allison looked King in the eye. "Officially, my professional opinion is whoever killed him did so by wirelessly issuing a fatal dose." She paused and stared. "Counts had no chance of surviving."

I looked into the heavy gaze of King's eyes. King knew the city had a spree killer on its hands, one like Denver had never seen before, and catching him would be as difficult as proving these men were targeted and murdered by a ruthless killer. Nothing was scarier than this, I thought.

"So, if their suspect is a hacker," I spoke for King when speaking to Allison, "how does one go about finding him or her?"

"Chasing a hacker is like chasing a ghost," Allison said with an even tone. "They see you, but you don't see them."

"Then I guess we're lucky they're talking with Sam." King flicked his gaze over to me.

I swallowed the lump in my throat. *Yeah, lucky me,* I thought.

"Hold on. Wait just one second." Susan stepped forward with excitement flashing in her eyes. "I have an idea on how we can find this hacker, and it's easier than we might think."

CHAPTER FORTY-NINE

JOEY GARCIA STOPPED JUST SHY OF THE ENTRANCE TO THE Wells Fargo bank on W. 38th Avenue in Sunnyside to answer the call coming in from his wife.

"Cecelia, baby, is everything all right?" Garcia asked, knowing it wasn't like her to be calling this early in the day unless something was wrong.

"No, Joey, you're so far from being okay."

Garcia stepped to the side, grinned at a customer passing by, and turned to face the street. With a flexed stomach, he asked, "What happened?" *What did I do this time?* Cecelia spoke fast and was straight to the point. He couldn't believe what she was telling him. "And you let them inside without a warrant?"

"What's this about Joey? And don't lie to me because they weren't exactly tight-lipped when sharing their concerns about what you might be up to."

Joey tipped his head back, closed his eyes, and sighed. *She let the fucking cops inside their house.* His body was on fire as he let his thoughts scramble to understand. "What did they say?"

"Joey, they were here in connection to a homicide."

Cecelia paused. "Why do they want to ask you about a murder?"

Joey clenched his fist and bit his tongue. He thought about telling her a lie, saying that he was helping Samantha Bell cover the crime desk. But Cecelia could sleuth her way to learning the truth before Joey had time to cover his own tail. Inside, he was furious but he couldn't worry his wife—couldn't lead her to believe he might actually be closer to the murders than he knew was possible. Joey had one foot in his own grave and he needed to act quick before he, too, ended up dead.

"You're not in trouble, are you?" Cecelia's voice cracked and Joey knew she was on the verge of tears.

"No. Of course not," Joey said in his most reassuring voice, then dropped his chin to his chest and pinched the bridge of his nose. "It's just work. You know how it can be sometimes."

"I let them go into your office."

Joey gritted his teeth and stood there feeling like he was rocking on a boat about to sink. He tried to recall how he'd left his office, what the detectives might have found.

"Did they take anything with them?"

"I didn't ask, and frankly don't really care."

This can't be happening, he kept repeating to himself.

Then he reminded himself that it was impossible to trace his account back to him.

Suddenly, his eyes flew wide open. He stopped breathing and his heart stopped. In that split second, he felt the sky falling. Joey remembered something that he knew would bring him down. He couldn't believe that he didn't shred the evidence before leaving the house.

"What did they say when they left?"

"To call when you got home." Cecelia gave him the name and number of both detectives.

Joey promised to sort this out—he had it handled. Then he said, "I love you."

Silence hung on the line as Joey waited to hear her reciprocate the words he desperately needed to hear. Instead, the line clicked dead without Cecelia telling him she loved him too.

Joey squeezed his cellphone so tight he heard the plastic casing crack. Cursing into thin air, Joey felt like he was walking the edge of a cliff about to topple over and lose everything he ever loved.

He took a minute to calm down before sliding his cellphone into his back pocket. Then he entered the bank and was soon escorted to the private room that accessed his safety deposit box. Once alone, he took out his key, slid it into the lock, and opened it up.

Joey was smart enough to know his luck would soon run out. It was time to go nuclear.

He had no choice. What he was about to do had to be done. Not only for him, but his family. It wasn't personal. Only a matter of survival.

One by one, Joey pulled the folders of notes and stories he had been saving as a last resort. It was the information that he was sure would give him the severance needed to pay off his daughter's medical bills with hopefully enough left over to step into a self-imposed retirement. One questioned remained; who should he present it to first? That depended on who he thought the highest bidder may be.

He thought about the drink he asked to have with Samantha, and he thought that maybe he'd start by talking to her.

CHAPTER FIFTY

An hour later, Loxley parked his car in the Metropolitan State University student lot and found his way into the auditorium where the panel discussion was already in progress. He lingered in the back, gauging the crowd and its tone before turning his eyes to the stage. There sat a row of panelists, all invited here to discuss the importance of having a higher calling.

If only it didn't relate to business, then maybe it would be something Loxley could relate to. Instead, Loxley closed off his ears, not willing to listen to the same pack of lies he'd once believed himself. But that was long ago, and he was older and wiser now. Still, among the hundreds of young minds here today, one would see through the bullshit and share the same enlightened thoughts as Loxley now knew to be true.

Lowering his brow, Loxley scanned the rows, flitting between the various faces before finding his target.

"Not on the panel? Of course you're not," Loxley said under his breath, grinning at his clever wits. "How could I be so naïve?"

He was right again, knowing Parker Collins would be here. Part of Loxley wanted to know how Thompson's wake went, if his goodbye was satisfying or just a hindrance to a very busy schedule.

Parker was sitting in the front row—a paper coffee cup in one hand—as he watched his wife, Joan, move across the stage while discussing the importance of pursuing a path greater than just profit.

Shifting his gaze between Parker and Joan, Loxley listened to Joan's words very carefully. This was the reason he was here —the reason he chose them to die next. Like those who'd come before them, Loxley had done his research and knew that the Collins' business activities told a much different tale than the one he was hearing now.

Joan was a great spokeswoman, so much so that soon she had Loxley questioning if maybe she wasn't aware of the truth to Parker's boardroom decisions. Could it be possible? Would he keep that from her?

An ache in Loxley's jaw deepened as he stared at the back of Parker's grey-haired head.

Parker didn't even have the nerve to sell his own lie. What a coward, Loxley thought. He should be up there, the two-faced liar. But living a lie and telling a lie were two completely different tasks. It was always easier to live the lie than to keep up with it. That was why Loxley was convinced Joan was on stage and not Parker. She didn't know.

A flashbulb ignited and lit up the stage.

A photojournalist kneeled near the front and snapped a couple more photos.

Loxley watched intently as the photographer retreated back to his seat. There, he joined the dozen or so other journalists who'd come to cover the event.

Loxley rolled his neck, suddenly hating the predicament he found himself in. He hadn't expected to spare Joan's life, but the more Joan convinced him she knew nothing of her husband's lies, the more certain Loxley grew that he had to only kill her husband.

"It's your lucky day, Mrs. Collins," Loxley muttered to himself.

But how to get Parker alone? Loxley knew they'd come here together. This wasn't going to be easy, but nothing Loxley couldn't handle with a little foresight.

"Thank you," Joan said into the mic. Applause filled the room and Loxley began clapping to blend in with the others.

Keeping an eye on Parker, Loxley watched him stand. He clapped loudly for his wife, pointing at her as the media and cameras rushed him like a pack of wild dogs. They took his photo, asked him questions that should have been directed at Joan, and treated him like a celebrity who had just spent the last thirty minutes speaking.

Loxley clenched a fist and found himself turning his attention to Joan who was now being congratulated by her colleagues on the stage. He grinned, thankful someone recognized her smarts.

Lowering his hands to his sides, Loxley thought about the benefits of leaking Parker's secret to a member of media here today. After a minute of mulling it over, he decided against it. They wouldn't do the story justice. It deserved to be told in its entirety and with enough passion to make a splash. And Loxley knew of only one person who had the talent to do just that.

The woman sitting in the row in front of him was busy scrolling her social media page when Loxley leaned forward and asked to borrow her phone. "Mine must have fallen out on the bus ride here," he lied.

The woman eyed him, then smiled. "Sure, no problem."

"Thank you." Loxley pressed his palms together and

bowed. "My girlfriend is probably wondering what happened to me."

Falling back into his seat, Loxley quickly wrote out a text message to Samantha. Once it sent, he handed the phone back to the woman and began making his way to the front of the auditorium.

He needed to look Parker in his eyes, see the evil that was hiding behind those colorful irises of his, make sure Parker saw him and knew who he was. How close could he get? Would Parker recognize him? It was a risk worth taking. Soon, he would be gone.

Loxley moved slowly and deliberately down the steps, stalking his prey like a leopard.

His heart beat faster with each step.

Parker shook one last hand and turned toward the stairs.

Then, suddenly, Loxley stopped.

He stared and felt his pulse race the closer Parker got to him. He was coming straight for Loxley. And when Parker lifted his chin and locked eyes, Loxley held his breath and watched Parker give him a knowing smile before patting Loxley on his shoulder as he passed.

Blowing out a hot, stale breath, Loxley touched the spot where Parker's hand had landed. It crackled with static electricity. It never occurred to him that his victim would touch him only minutes before he planned to kill him. Then he turned on a heel and watched Parker exit the auditorium.

He swallowed down his surprise, licked his lips, and looked around the room. No one else was paying any attention to him. Alone, like always, he hurried up the steps, picked up his pace through the halls, and stiff-armed the exit hoping Parker hadn't gotten away.

It didn't take long for Loxley to catch sight of Parker's Q-tip hair weaving through the parking lot. He hurried to catch up, needed to get to his own car himself. This was perfect.

Parker was alone, just as Loxley needed him to be. Just when his feeling of excitement was beginning to take hold, Loxley spotted a familiar face heading straight for Parker. This, he never saw coming.

Quickly, he hid behind a red Ford pickup truck and watched through the window glass.

The reporter called out to Parker. Parker stopped. Loxley watched as they met—not shaking hands—and when the reporter presented Parker with a thick folder, Loxley knew that he may have very well struck gold.

CHAPTER FIFTY-ONE

"AND YOU SAW THIS WHERE?" KING DIRECTED HIS ANGER at Susan.

For a split second, I saw Susan take a step back in complete surprise. It was a side of King she had never seen before. I hadn't seen much of it either. But I knew he meant no harm, and it certainly wasn't meant to be personal. He had his badge clipped on his belt and his gun strapped beneath his arm. For him, this was only work. King was on duty, canvassing for information.

"Backstage. Damien Black's lab." Susan spoke confidently before looking in Allison's direction. "We were just there." She turned back to King and narrowed her eyes. "Didn't you hear anything we said?"

Damien's name kept coming up and I made note of it. I'd given them instruction to put together a list of hackers, but I didn't expect this.

Allison played peacekeeper when she held up her hand like a white flag waving through the air demanding a cease-fire. "Backstage keeps young adults out of trouble and is putting them on the straight and narrow. They may know how to hack, but I doubt they have the skill like what we're witnessing here," she said, pointing to the insulin pump.

I listened and agreed, trusting Allison's assessment. But it didn't come without personal doubts. Just because a man was trained to kill in the field of battle didn't mean that the skill couldn't be applied off the battlefield.

"This was what Sam tasked us to find." Allison was now staring at me. "And guess what? We found it."

King turned his head and gave me a look of disbelief.

"When is this hacker event?" I asked when all eyes were on me.

"Doesn't matter," King said. "We can request a list of participants and work from there."

"Before we go throwing our youth up against a wall and frisking them for information, let's not forget that these types of events happen all the time," Allison said.

"You have a better idea?" Alvarez openly asked.

"Backstage is doing these kids a service. If its doors close like Damien says they might, then what?" Susan raised her brows, flitting her gaze around the circle. "He's already afraid some will turn to crime."

"More reason to get our hands on the list of students," King said.

If they haven't already, I thought. The more I heard, the more I was ready to jump in my own car and ask Damien some questions myself. "I'll do it," I said. "I'll get the list."

King snapped his neck and glared. "No you won't."

"Don't tell me you expect me to just forget about this and sit on my hands?"

"That's exactly what I expect you to do." King made it clear there wasn't room for debate. "Go back to work. All of you."

"No way; we're involved. You need us," Allison said, pointing to the insulin device, subtly reminding King how she informed him about how it worked. "An attack on one is an attack on all."

"Christ almighty," Alvarez grumbled as he left the circle.

"This isn't negotiable," King said, requesting to speak to me alone.

I felt the girls staring as King led me to the back of his car. He knew I was the ring leader, the instigator, and he might be right. But this was my investigation as much as it was his.

"Sam, you have to stay away from this case."

King's hands were rooted into his hips, his pupils tiny pinpricks of anger. "I can't call them off," I said, pointing at my group of women. "We're too deep and know too much."

"It's dangerous."

I knew what he was saying, appreciated the concern, but there wasn't any way I could stop now. "This is personal, Alex. Not only for me, but them, too. There's no way any of us can back out now."

King stared at my friends, his brow furrowed with thoughts. He inched forward and lowered his voice. "Look, Sam, I appreciate the knowledge your friends bring to the table, but police work needs to go through the proper channels, especially if we're going to see this thing through to a conviction."

We didn't even have the suspect's name. "What are you saying? You want me to get an inside scoop on Damien?"

"No. I want to know more about what you mentioned to me earlier." King paused. "Was Donny really running his exchange like a Ponzi scheme?"

"I don't have any evidence to prove it." All I had was enough doubt to make me question it. "Look," I said, "I'll get them to back off Damien long enough for you to pay him a visit, but I'm going to need something from you."

King's face tightened. "And what would that be?"

"Tell me everything you know. And don't hold back. Like you said, my life could be in danger."

King scrubbed a hand over his face and gave me a look that said he couldn't. "You know it's too risky to speak too much about an ongoing investigation."

I folded my arms across my chest and stared. I knew the spiel. Heard it a million times before. Stories could spin out of control, contaminate jury pools, and all but destroy everything everyone worked so hard to get. But I was different. He could trust me. He just needed to be reminded of who I was.

I reached for his hand. He didn't push me away—didn't resist. Our touches were featherlight but they crackled with electricity hot enough to start a fire. Soon, King had his fingers threaded through mine when he squeezed my hand. In that split second, I watched his gaze soften. King disappeared and Alex surfaced.

"You know I'd do anything to protect you and Mason," he said.

"I know," I murmured as I squeezed his hand and told him I loved him with my eyes. "So, tell me. What do you know? I've already shared everything I know. This has to be a two-way street, otherwise it won't work."

King looked to the girls to make sure no one was listening. He rolled his shoulders back and I watched him transform back into the strong detective he was. When the air was clear, he said in a soft voice, "When we spoke with Rose, she said to ask Garcia about the Bitcoin key code. She said he would recognize it."

"Was it his?"

King shrugged. "But Rose made it clear she thought Garcia might be the one behind Counts's murder."

"Shit," I breathed before King followed up with another juicy detail.

"We don't know the details, but it appeared that maybe Garcia had, or was trying to, blackmail Donny."

I swallowed past my constricting throat. "That's why you were at Garcia's house?"

"Yeah."

My blood pressure dropped and I was still not any closer to learning who might be threatening me, but the evidence we had strongly suggested Garcia. If it was him, why was he doing this to me? Was it even possible he had the knowledge to do what he was doing? None of this made sense, but it was the best information we had.

"You should put eyes on Rose Wild," I said. "My sources are telling me she and Donny had one-way tickets for Thailand, leaving today."

King's eyes popped like I had just revealed the numbers to last night's jackpot winning. He snapped his fingers and shouted to Alvarez just as my cell phone started to ring. I plugged my ear and answered. "Dawson, what's up?"

"Garcia just called your desk."

I froze.

"Said he was looking for you."

"Well, that's great because I'm looking for him." I turned and watched Alvarez jump behind the steering wheel. "What did he say?"

"Just that he needed to speak with you ASAP. It sounded urgent, Sam. Which is why I'm calling. Everything all right?"

I assumed it had something to do with Donny Counts. Did Garcia know that I was at the hospital? Did he know what King found at his home? My pulse ticked hard and fast as I grew more defensive with every breath. Then Dawson dropped another surprise.

"What's this about Parker Collins being a fraud? Did you uncover that while investigating Donny's exchange?"

My eyebrows squished. "I'm still working on the Ponzi

scheme story," I said. "I haven't confirmed anything yet." I stared at my toes, not knowing what the hell Dawson was talking about.

"I'm just repeating what you wrote in the email you sent me fifteen minutes ago."

"I didn't send an email."

"Really?" I heard Dawson tapping away at his computer. "Because it came from your account."

The sky swirled above as I thought about how Travis left Brett alone, free to roam staff computers, and wondered how, if at all, it related to Garcia looking for me now.

Suddenly, all the evidence, all the facts, came crashing to the forefront of my brain like a tidal wave and I was overwhelmed by the influx of information.

"You said Parker Collins?"

"Yeah," Dawson said.

This was Loxley. I was sure of it, and Dawson confirmed it. He was telling me who he was going to kill next.

"Does that mean something to you?"

I wished it didn't, but I knew it did.

CHAPTER FIFTY-TWO

In a panic, I rushed to Erin. "I just got a tip from Dawson."

Her eyes widened a fraction as she looked toward King. It was clear she'd heard everything he said about needing to get to Rose Wild before she possibly escaped.

"Loxley is going after Parker Collins next."

"How do you know this?" she asked.

"Dawson received an email for me, an email I *didn't* send." I could see her planning our next move as I explained what was inside the email to make me think Collins was next on Loxley's list.

"Sam, I don't know who that is. Should I?"

Parker Collins hadn't been on my immediate radar either, and I certainly didn't know the crimes he was being accused of. But I caught Erin up to speed with what little I did know.

"He's a business mogul who has his hands in dozens of projects around the world. But I've never written a story about him and I'm not completely sure why Loxley is targeting him, just that he fits the pattern of the others and I can't take any risks by *not* acting."

Erin didn't argue but I could see the doubt creeping up her spine. "But if you don't know what he did, how can we be sure Loxley is even targeting anybody?"

It was a valid concern, one I didn't have an answer for. At least when it came to Richard Thompson, I'd known. Thanks to my history with Josh Stetson, Donny Counts made sense, too. But Parker Collins? He was on an island all by himself.

Erin was staring into my eyes as if debating whether he was worth the risk or not.

"What do we have to lose?" I said, almost immediately realizing we had everything to lose, including our reputations if we got this wrong. Parker Collins would destroy us. But if I was right, I could potentially save his life.

"Do you even know where to find Collins?"

"Believe it or not, I think I do," I said, mentioning the flier for a business leader's impact entrepreneurship summit at MSU. "Garcia had my name chicken scratched next to Collins's. I should have seen it then—"

"Is Garcia Loxley?"

My answer caught in my throat. I didn't want to believe he was, but I didn't have enough evidence to cross him off my list of suspects either. "If so, we'll see him there."

"And if he's not, how will we even know who to look for?"

My mind scrambled to think how Parker might be killed. Up until now, Loxley had chosen ingenious methods. Without getting in his mind, we were left to only guess.

King stared from a distance as we debated our options. Susan was chatting with Alvarez while Allison was staring into her phone's screen. Soon, King found his way over to me.

I briefed him on the email, following up with, "Parker Collins, is he on your radar?"

King's thoughts swirled in his pupils. "No, but I recently came across his name," he said, telling me about the notes he found at Garcia's house.

"Garcia had what?" I snapped.

"A list." King mentioned who was on it. I couldn't believe it. "I just assumed they were either stories or sources he was working."

I rubbed my temples to little relief. If I doubted Garcia's involvement before, the case against him was now growing so substantial it was hard to think it could be anybody else.

"That's it. We have to go," I said, leaping forward.

King grabbed my arm and pulled me back. My hair cascaded over my eyes. "Where, Sam? Where are you going? What exactly are you going to do?"

"Don't you see it?"

"One name, Sam. That's all. Everyone else on that list is only a guess."

I didn't want to admit it, but I knew it was true. But Garcia also had my Thompson story in his home office, and Rose said Garcia would know the key code to the Bitcoin account found with Richard Thompson.

I looked to Allison. She'd had her head buried in her phone for the last ten minutes when she suddenly snapped her head up and shouted, "I found something."

Everyone stopped what they were doing and turned to stare.

Allison held her phone into the air. "Damien Black was a convicted hacker."

King's expression pinched. Alvarez asked for directions to Backstage. And everyone's next move seemed to be lining up for them.

"I knew I was right to have my suspicions about him," Susan said.

Was Garcia working with Damien Black? No, it didn't make sense. I needed to get to MSU and track down Collins with hopes of finding Garcia there before anything bad happened to either one of them.

I caught King staring. "Damien is about to lose his lab. If you ask me, that's motive for targeting the people he despises. He has the resources and know-how to do it without getting caught."

"But is he our guy?" Erin asked openly to the group.

We couldn't take any chances. Not with what Allison just learned about Damien Black.

Without discussing it any further, everyone jumped into action at once.

Alvarez already had the engine rumbling when he called out to King, telling him to jump in.

King opened the car door and pointed at me. "Stay behind, Sam. I'm serious. Don't go doing police work. I'll call in for a uniformed officer to look out for Parker Collins."

"No way. We're in this together," I argued, waving Erin to my car. With King speeding away, I hit the gas as soon as Erin was buckled into her seat and we squealed out of the parking lot with no time to spare. I had to get to Parker Collins first and stop the evil I thought was coming for him.

CHAPTER FIFTY-THREE

I DROVE MY CAR LIKE IT WAS STOLEN AS WE RACED ACROSS town. Weaving through traffic, I accelerated through the knots of cars, listening to my engine whine. I cranked the wheel when having to make tight turns and heard the tires squeal as they skidded over the asphalt.

There was no time to stop. We couldn't afford to be late or get this wrong.

I kept my grip tight on the wheel and my foot heavy on the gas.

Erin hung on as if her life depended on it. Once she settled into the crazy rollercoaster ride I'd put us on, she asked, "So who is Loxley? Joey Garcia or Damien Black?"

I'd been asking myself the same question. "If Damien is Loxley, it could be the reason he picked Susan up out of the blue."

Erin said she'd been thinking the same thing. "Maybe as a way to get closer to you."

I flicked my gaze to her. Our eyes met and locked for a second as the thought settled in my gut. It was a frightening thought, but also one that would explain how Loxley seemed to know so much about me.

Neither of us had mentioned any of this on our blog or on Erin's podcast. Somehow, Loxley still knew—writing to me as if we were friends fighting a common enemy.

A wave of chills moved beneath my collar. I was hot. I was cold. Mostly, I was just pissed.

Erin had her doubts, too, and expressed them to me. "Loxley is smarter than that."

"Than what?" I asked.

"For it to be Damien. It's too obvious a choice."

"Hiding in plain sight? Asking Susan out? Working his way into our tight circle?" I could have kept going but Erin got my point. Damien and Garcia were all we had and I couldn't stop thinking about the hacker event. I needed to know more, see a list of competitors—stop the madness.

As I honked at the car in front of me drifting into my lane, my thoughts swung back to King.

I appreciated him sharing what he knew, but I didn't like him telling me to back down. And I certainly didn't like that King found my Thompson article in Garcia's house. But what bothered me most was Garcia's list of targets or possible targets. Donny Counts was already dead and it appeared that Parker Collins was likely next. I had my bets on Ronald Hyland's life coming into Loxley's crosshairs soon.

We needed to warn Collins. We had to throw a wrench in Loxley's plans. But the longer it took us to get to MSU, the more I doubted we'd make it time.

I hoped I was right about Collins—if he lived—but was also afraid of what I might be walking in to.

Did Loxley want me to figure this out? If so, why? What would he do to me if I stayed away? What would he do to me if I got too close to the truth?

The tips of my fingers tingled and I wrung out my hands

as I kept glancing at the clock. Suddenly, my rearview mirror flashed a red and blue with emergency vehicle lights creeping up on me fast. The vehicles behind me pulled off the side, and so did I.

Erin twisted around in her seat and we both watched as the first police cruiser flew past us. It was quickly followed by an ambulance. Something told me we had the same destination in mind.

I punched the gas and quickly caught up with the ambulance.

"What are you doing, Sam?"

Knowing I was breaking the law, I said, "Hitching a ride."

"You think it's going to the university?"

"We'll take it as far as we can," I said. "I hope I'm wrong."

Moments later, black smoke was visibly billowing into the air. Silence filled the air when the ambulance killed the siren and hit the brakes, EMS rushing out to help anyone lucky enough to survive the car crash.

I tipped forward in my seat and stared at the dark Toyota RAV4 smoking out its front, but it was the white BMW 7 series that stopped my heart. I pulled off to the side and said, "That could certainly be Parker Collins's car." Erin raised a brow. "Only someone with money can drive a brand-new Beemer like that."

Next thing I knew, Erin kicked her door open and took off running. I was quick to follow, chasing after her. The front of the RAV4 was smashed and billowing a thick smoke, threatening to explode. A woman had been pulled from the seat and was now being led to safety by a couple civilians. She was bleeding from the nose but appeared to be fine.

I flicked my gaze to the BMW. Three men worked to pull an unconscious man from the front seat. There was blood everywhere and I couldn't immediately tell if I was looking at Parker Collins.

"Is it him?" Erin clamped her hand on my shoulder and pushed up on her toes.

"It's him," I said, catching a glimpse of his face. His body was limp and he was unconscious. I swiveled my head around thinking Loxley might be here, watching to see if I came. Then, as if on cue, I felt my phone hum with an incoming text message. One glance at my screen and I knew it was him. Loxley. He was here. And he was watching me.

CHAPTER FIFTY-FOUR

IT DIDN'T TAKE LONG FOR THE SCENE TO GET CHAOTIC with EMS and fire crews dashing in and out of the crash. Everything seemed to get louder—the water spraying from the fire hose, the shouts for assistance, even the rumbling of cars passing by. Soon, the fire was out and I kept looking for Loxley.

There were too many faces, too many distractions to hide behind. But my gut told me to keep looking. Then Erin surprised me by saying, "I'm going in."

She took off running before I could stop her.

"Miss, did you see what happened here?" a uniformed officer asked me without seeming to notice Erin sprinting toward Collins's car.

"No," I said, looking to see if he recognized me. "I arrived after the crash."

Then a man stepped forward from the group behind me. "I saw that same BMW nearly collide with another car about three blocks back. I thought the driver was drunk."

The officer turned his head and asked, "And did you see what happened here?"

"No," the man said. "But I'm certain it's the same car." He pointed to an emblem near the rear tail light and the officer pulled him off to the side to make an official statement.

I spun around, pressing a hand to my forehead.

Loxley's message was still bouncing around my head.

Men of power are robbing us of our riches as you stand around and do nothing. The rich are getting richer and the poor are getting poorer. I am here to put a stop to it. No longer will I allow their lies to justify their means. But I cannot do it alone. I need your help. When will you recognize that?

Just as I was asking myself where he could be, I looked up and found the eye of a traffic camera staring down on me. Could he be watching from there? I darted my gaze to several people recording from their cell phones. Or was he watching from those? With Loxley, he could be anywhere.

I stepped out of the way when the tow truck arrived. Collins was being loaded into an ambulance and I prayed he would survive to tell the tale of what happened.

"Sam," I heard Erin call from twenty yards out as she stood behind Collins's car. "Come take a look at this," she said, waving me over.

With the officer standing with his back to me, I hurdled over the obstacles in front of me and pushed my way through the line, curious to know what Erin had found.

"Stay down, they won't like us being here," Erin said. "But I had to look for myself, and I'm glad I did."

We were crouched down low next to Collins' crumpled car, thumbing through a packet of notes and transcripts neatly packaged together. They were addressed to Collins and, ironically, also all about him.

"It's dirt," Erin said.

I saw it too. Every story and fact a negative piece to Parker Collins's life. "Is there a key code here?" I asked, splitting up the papers into two piles.

Erin took half and quickly filed through each paper. "Nothing here."

My breath caught in my chest when I suddenly stopped my search.

"What is it?" Erin asked, taking her eyes off her pile and casting them to mine.

My heart was beating loud and fast as I read through the threat that had my name on it. I handed it to Erin.

Her eyes moved across the sheet of paper as she read it aloud. "I suggest you think long and hard about what this means, because all this could quickly go to Samantha Bell." Erin swept her gaze up to mine. "This has Joey Garcia's name written all over it."

As much as I didn't want to believe it, I had to come to terms with the fact that Garcia might have been attempting to blackmail Collins. Did that also mean he could have black-mailed Richard Thompson? Could Rose Wild actually be telling the truth?

"Sam, do you recognize any of this?" Erin fanned out the papers in each of her hands. "Was this a past story you were working?"

I thought about the event at MSU and Collins's name on Garcia's desk. I had a better idea now what was happening here, and I knew this was him. But could I prove it?

I gathered the papers and placed them back into the neatly packaged folder before lifting my shirt and stuffing it into my waist. "C'mon. Let's not discuss this here."

As soon as we stood, a fireman started yelling at us. "Hey! It's not safe to be back there."

Without hesitating, I reached into my back pocket and produced my press badge. "Samantha Bell with the *Colorado Times*."

"And you can join the others in the bullpen over there."

He pointed to the first of the news vans, its crews already reporting.

We headed back to my car. There was nothing else for us here. On the way, I called King. "Have you found Damien Black?"

"We're just pulling into his place now."

King must have heard the commotion swirling around me, and when he asked, I said, "Parker Collins was in a car accident."

King was silent for a brief pause. "Is he injured?"

"From what I could see, yes." But I already knew his chances of making it were slim. I was still in a state of shock, none of what just happened sinking in yet. King asked how and I told him what I knew. "I don't know if this was Loxley or just a freak accident," I told him. But that was Loxley's MO. Murders made to look like unfortunate accidents.

"Wait there," King said. "I'm turning around."

I swung my head and glanced at the scene, now dying down. "Don't bother. It's over." King didn't protest, and I told him to speak with Damien as originally planned. "Maybe gain insight into whether he was behind this accident or not."

"Stay safe, Sam."

"You too."

As soon as I ended my call with King, I dialed Joey Garcia's cell hoping he could explain the list King found on his desk and why Parker Collins had a pile of dirt that seemed to have come from Garcia's desk.

CHAPTER FIFTY-FIVE

Joey Garcia was driving when he felt his cellphone vibrate.

He touched his breast pocket where the device rang. He was curious to know who was calling, but decided not to answer. Having only met Parker Collins less than thirty minutes ago, he was afraid that it might be him calling to tell him he'd changed his mind.

Joey shifted his weight, kept changing the stations on the radio. No matter what he did to take his mind off of the risk he he'd taken, nothing could settle the nerves popping like electricity over his entire body.

He glanced in his mirrors, drove no faster than the posted speed limit, and kept thinking that maybe this time it would work.

Joey just needed to get as far from MSU as quickly as possible before anyone knew he'd been there. This was it, his last effort at getting the money he needed, before throwing in the towel. It had to work. He was out of options

His phone dinged with a voicemail.

Unable to take the suspense any longer, Joey pulled his

phone from his breast pocket, swiped his thumb over the screen, and hit play on his voicemail.

Brake lights shined in front of him and Joey slowed his car to a complete stop just as he heard a Detective John Alvarez say he had some questions for Joey and needed him to call him back. He recognized the detective's name. It was one of the two Cecelia said dropped by their house earlier.

Joey swiped the back of his hand over his forehead, wiping the pellets of sweat off his brow. He was nervous and experiencing paranoid thoughts that made him think everyone was watching—knew his secrets and what he had done.

Needing to get back to the newsroom and have his face be seen, traffic was at a standstill.

Suddenly, the sound of sirens sent his heart into a flutter.

Joey killed the radio, cracked his window, and listened to the wails get closer. Soon, the emergency lights of a police car appeared in the rearview mirror and Joey worried that maybe Collins entrapped him and called the cops. That's what he would have done. But Joey didn't want it to end like this.

He tightened his grip on the steering wheel and held his breath as he thought of the crimes he could be charged with if caught. Extortion and bribery were at the top of the list, maybe a few others as well.

His stomach rolled. He didn't feel so hot.

The flashing lights got closer and all Joey could think was how the police were probably watching him since their visit to his house. It would make sense. This was his window of opportunity, perhaps his last chance ever at getting the money he knew his family needed. Now he was worried he'd taken it too far.

Joey pulled to the side of the road. He felt his chest strangle his heart. Closing his eyes, he said a quick prayer. When he heard the police car zoom past without ever slowing down, he snapped his eyes wide open and began to laugh.

He needed to relax. Everything would be just fine.

Shaking off his nerves, he turned the radio back on. He drummed to the music, not caring that traffic was inching its way forward at a snail's pace. Several minutes passed before traffic was funneled to a single lane, and that was when Joey saw the accident ahead.

He sat forward and stared through his windshield. Even from here, he recognized Parker's white BMW crunched in a heaping pile of bent metal. Bile rose in his throat and he quickly swallowed it down. He might have made some foolish decisions, but he wasn't stupid.

Another extortion and another *death*? Was that what was happening here?

He didn't want to believe Collins was dead. Even if he wasn't, Joey knew that this couldn't be coincidence. First Richard Thompson, then Donny Counts, and then this? If he wasn't scared before, he was terrified now.

Someone was watching him. Someone knew his secret.

But who? And how long did he have before he was next?

Joey kept his wheels straight, continuing to follow the car in front of him as he silently debated which was worse; the fact that the police had already been in his house, or that each person he had attempted to extort for money has now dead—or an attempt had at least been made on their life.

He gripped his chest and felt his heart slow to a stop.

Joey knew he looked guilty. Not only did he not have the money for a high-profile criminal defense lawyer, he also knew the police could make a strong case against him.

Joey Garcia was doomed.

Slowly, he rolled past the scene of the accident. Now he was certain that was Parker Collins's car. He thought about stopping, trying to collect all he had just given to Collins in a

last-ditch effort to hide the evidence. But even in his despera-
tion he knew it was too late. All he could hope for was that
those documents would somehow make their way to the
salvage yard along with the totaled vehicle.

When he locked eyes with none other than Samantha
Bell, he almost caused another accident. He was too slow to
react. She'd seen him.

Shit. Now an eyewitness. How could he explain his way
out of this one?

But when his cellphone rang, and he saw that it was
Samantha calling, he knew that maybe he couldn't.

CHAPTER FIFTY-SIX

"I KNEW THAT NAME SOUNDED FAMILIAR," ALVAREZ grumbled into his phone's screen.

King kept one hand on the steering wheel and leaned over to see what he had found. They were parked outside Backstage, planning their visit.

"Damien Black, one of America's most wanted computer criminals." Alvarez was reading from the department's database. "Convicted of stealing corporate secrets, he was sentenced to five years in prison, plea bargained down, and was released after having only served sixteen months, the judge allowing him to finish his sentence out under strict supervision."

"So how is he now Managing Director of this place?" King pointed at the entrance to Backstage.

Alvarez swept his gaze up and stared over the car's dash. "Must be part of his parole agreement."

King flicked his eyebrows, thinking it wasn't completely unheard of. "Come to think of it," he said, "I've read stories of computer hackers who, after prosecution, later go into consulting and public speaking, teaching others about computer security."

"It appears Mr. Black may have done the same."

The detectives exited the vehicle and were feeling unqualified with the questions they knew they needed to be asking when they entered Backstage. The computer lab had a college campus feel to it as King noticed a couple students busy working on a robotics project.

"Can you get it to do whatever you want?" King asked the two young men as he approached.

"It can't quite do everything we ask, but watch this." The young man held a control in his hand and made the robot do a backflip in the air. They didn't seem too concerned with having a new face inside their walls, and King took it as a positive sign.

King clapped, clearly captivated. Then he asked about Backstage. As the students explained what it was and why they were here, King grew impressed by the program. "Is your instructor here now?"

"Damien is out."

"Damien Black?"

"The one and only."

No one knew where Damien was or when he would be back. The two students said they hadn't seen him today. As King listened to what they said, his thoughts drifted to Samantha's news about Parker Collins.

King thanked the young men, encouraged them to keep up the good work, and turned his curious gaze to the young woman working alone behind a large computer monitor. Her hair was tied up in a messy bun, a heavy set of headphones wrapped around her ears. She flicked her gaze up to King, smiled, and went on working.

Alvarez was standing at the corkboard in the front of the

room when King joined him. "Anyone besides Damien teaching these kids?"

"I didn't get that impression." King stepped forward, taking particular interest in the event flier they had heard so much about. "A bounty?"

Alvarez wagged his head. "Far cheaper than the alternative of having your complete system held for ransom."

King knew little about the underworld of computer hacking. He turned to the young men and asked, "Are you two planning to compete in this event?"

One of the boys pointed to the woman. "She is."

"What am I?" The woman removed her headphones and hung them around her neck.

"Competing in the hack event."

"Oh, yeah." The woman's neck craned. "Damien encouraged all of us to join."

"Mind telling us what exactly it is?"

The woman jumped to her feet and skipped to the front of the room. She explained the different events, the types of challenges presented. "Damien has been working with me personally, preparing me with the best skills to win. And, this year, the crown cup is mine. I can feel it."

"Who won last year?" Alvarez asked, not sure if this event was annual or a first of its kind.

"Some kid from California." The woman made an angry face, then burst out laughing. "Nah, I'm only kidding. I'm happy for him, but Backstage should have won."

"And if you win, you get to keep the prize money?"

"Yeah, but I've already promised Damien I would donate it back to Backstage." Her eyes stared at the flier, a serious look falling over her face. "We need this win bad. Backstage will close if we lose."

"A lot's riding on your shoulders then?" King said.

The woman nodded. "I've been training day and night for this event. I'm ready."

"What's your name?" Alvarez asked.

"Marion," she said proudly. "But my hacker name is Maid Marion."

The detectives shared a look.

"Damien nicknamed me that." When asked, she added, "Because he said I'm beautiful, confident, and sincere."

"Damien nicknamed you that?" King automatically thought of Sam's theory, the name Loxley, and how she believed they were chasing a computer hacker vigilante who thought of himself as a modern-day Robin Hood.

"That's right." The girl's head bounced on her shoulders.

Suddenly, King's cellphone rang. He answered the call from Lieutenant Baker. "What's this about sending a patrol car to Rose Wild's house?" LT asked.

"I received information that she might be planning to leave town." King explained the flight risk and how she might be a suspect—or at least a valuable witness—to Donny Counts's investigation. "Has she been located?"

"We have eyes on her now, but not without repercussion." King asked for an explanation. "Rose Wild is threatening a lawsuit against the department for harassment."

King pinched his eyebrows. "LT, she was the one to request our help."

"Apparently she's had a change of heart."

Alvarez had one ear on King's conversation, the other on Marion who was still talking his ear off, when King turned his back on them. "Don't believe it, LT. As soon as we have our backs turned, she might disappear."

"Your source better be good, because Chief Watts is already on my ass about these protestors popping up around town. There's another one growing outside MSU chanting for Parker Collins's head."

King mentioned the car accident. Lieutenant Baker hadn't heard.

"Did he die?" LT asked.

"It doesn't sound good," King said.

"Let's hope he makes it. If not, that would be the third rich man in as many days to die, and we're still without an arrest," Baker muttered into the phone. When King didn't respond, Baker asked, "What else do you know that I don't? And why does it feel like we have a vigilante on our hands?"

King turned and looked into Maid Marion's sparkling eyes. "Because, sir, I believe we do."

CHAPTER FIFTY-SEVEN

THE HOT DRY AIR WAS SILENT AS RONALD HYLAND LINED up his putt. He was shooting for birdie when he tapped his putter gently against the golf ball that had his business logo imprinted on it.

Ronald held still, ignoring the dark shadow of cloud splashing across the green, as he watched his ball travel up the slope, then take a sharp curve toward the cup. The ball picked up speed and hit the opposite edge with enough force to nearly send it flying out of the cup. An aggressive ping filled the silent air before miraculously falling into the hole.

Grinning, Ronald took a step back and pointed his putter at his opponent. "Now, that, my friend, is how it's done."

Damien Black tucked his club beneath one arm and clapped. "Nice shot. But you got lucky."

"A man makes his own luck," Hyland said. "But I suppose you already know that, seeing as you're here today."

Damien grinned. "We use what resources we have available to us."

"And that is why I'm going to make you a deal." Hyland

handed his club to his caddie and loosened the glove he was wearing on one hand. A glimmer of hope flashed in Damien's eyes. "If your next drive goes further than mine, I'll agree to give you the money you asked for."

With raised eyebrows, Damien looked over both shoulders. No one was around. It was just the two of them and their young caddies. "Without any witnesses, I'll have to get this in writing."

Hyland chuckled. "My word isn't good enough?"

Damien was steadfast with his lack of a response.

"And here I thought I was the greedy one."

"Greed comes in all shapes and sizes," Damien whispered close to Hyland's ear. Then he asked, "What's the catch?"

"Catch?" Hyland tucked his chin, looking offended. "Why does there have to be a catch?"

Damien angled his head and said, "With you, there is always a catch."

Hyland held Damien's gaze for a moment before flinging his arm around the back of Damien's shoulders. Together they walked, meandering down the cart path, stepping over the shadows of the towering blue spruces on their way to the next hole. Their caddies followed no closer than twenty-five yards behind, and were just out of earshot when Hyland said, "Tell me, Damien, what happens if you're able to raise the money elsewhere first?"

Damien eyed Hyland suspiciously. "You know about my meeting with Susan Young?"

Hyland gave him a knowing look. "Like you, I have also done my research. But tell me, who was that black woman she brought along with her?"

Damien's mind churned when deciding how much he was willing to share. Working with Hyland was a game of cards—nothing could be revealed without risking it all. "Allison

Doyle. Very intelligent, and knows software technologies extremely well."

Hyland tipped his head back and stared. Damien watched as Hyland's pupils narrowed. "Should we be worried?" Hyland asked.

Damien turned his head and gazed the length of the fairway when thinking about Hyland's health. He felt confident in his ability to persuade anybody into doing anything he needed, but he didn't know how much Hyland already knew. That worried him. Suddenly, shouts came from the woods behind.

Hyland's assistant seemed to have come out of nowhere.

Waving his arms frantically over his head, he shouted for Hyland.

"What is it? For Christ sake, get a hold of yourself," Hyland ordered the younger man. "You're making a scene."

Catching his breath, Hyland's assistant swallowed his excitement and said, "It's Parker Collins." He flicked his eyes to Damien. "He's dead."

Hyland rolled his neck over his shoulder and glared at Damien.

Damien felt his chest squeeze.

"How?" Hyland asked his assistant. His assistant said it was a car accident. "Was he alone or was Joan also with him?" Hyland inquired, pressing his palm flat against his skipping heart.

"Alone, sir."

"Very well, thank you." Hyland's assistant scurried off over the bluff.

Damien kept calm, acting like this news didn't bother him. But as Hyland strode closer to him, he held his breath and waited for the volcano to erupt.

"Let's try this again," Hyland said sharply. "Should I be

concerned with these deaths somehow finding their way to me?"

Damien swallowed a single breath. "Everything I've been able to gather tells me no."

"Good," Hyland said, lining up for his shot. "Let's keep it that way."

CHAPTER FIFTY-EIGHT

KING ARRIVED BY THE TIME WE WERE BEING TOLD TO GO home. I wasn't sure how much longer we could just sit here without being towed ourselves. By now I was beginning to doubt what happened to Collins could even be possible. But I knew it had to be Loxley because of the timing of his message to me.

"The car was hacked. It had to have been," I was saying to Allison over the phone.

"It's possible," Allison said, her words encouraging.

How Loxley did it was beyond comprehension. We were working through the possibilities when I suggested he messed with the traffic lights.

"I'm thinking that sounds far too difficult. He would have had to time Collins's movement perfectly." Allison reminded me of how precise Loxley's execution would have had to be. "It would be far easier to attack the car itself."

"But is there a way we could prove it?" I asked.

"Not unless you can get me access to the system computer logs."

The tips of my fingers were digging into my forehead when I thought about how Loxley could be doing this from anywhere in the world. He didn't need to be near, only needed to have access to Collins's vehicle's computers. A part of me just wanted to ask Allison to hack it herself—crack the safe and bust into the black box that would tell us everything. But it was too risky now that the cops knew we were chasing a hacker. There had to be another way.

Allison asked what King found on Damien. "He just arrived," I said, watching King canvas the scene. His strides were long, his jawline strong, and I handed my phone off to Erin and opened my door. "Keep Ali on the line," I said. "I'm going to talk with King."

I stepped out of the car and walked beneath the partly clouded sky. King badged a fellow officer, and I watched them talk as I made my way over to him. Time slowed as I flitted my gaze across the scene, thinking about what we had to work with and how hopeless I felt at ever being able to find Loxley. It seemed impossible, but I had to stay positive.

My call with Garcia didn't help either. He delayed having a drink with me and I knew something was up. I still didn't have an answer to what that might be, but it only made him guiltier in my eyes. Him driving by Parker's accident didn't help matters, but he didn't tell me where he was going. Worse, I couldn't confront him over the phone with the question I needed to ask. It had to be subtle when I asked him how my article ended up in his home office—if he was the one to give it to Thompson.

When King's eyes landed on mine, I smiled.

I heard him call out to his fellow officers to treat the area as a crime scene, to comb the place for evidence. There was mild confusion what exactly they were looking for, but they followed his orders regardless. Then he waved me over and said, "Damien wasn't at his lab and no one knew where he was."

I tucked my hair behind my ear. "If you can't prove this was a crime, LT will put you on nightshift."

"I'm already halfway there." The corners of his eyes crinkled with his smile. "But I'm not going to take any risks either."

"Can I show you something?"

His smile vanished.

"But first, let me make it clear that I can't give you what I'm about to show you."

"I'll be the judge of that."

I reached behind my back and pulled out the folder Erin found in Collins's car. Handing it over to King, I watched him file through the papers. He was a quick study and recognized the significance right away.

"Where did you get this?"

"Inside Parker Collins's vehicle."

King sighed. "Garcia give it to him?"

I assumed as much. We discussed Allison's theories, understanding that Collins's car may have been hacked, but we didn't know by who. Garcia's name was all over it, but Damien had the skills. Could they be were working together? It was a conclusion we could agree on.

"I need these," King said, holding up the packet. "They're evidence."

The moment he held them up, I snatched it out of his hands. "You can have it after I'm finished."

"Finished?" King growled. "Sam, if you take those, it's obstruction of justice."

"I need to see Garcia's face when I show it to him."

"I've just declared it a crime scene."

My eyes bounced inside of his. I wasn't about to back down.

King flicked his gaze to the people working behind me. Then he lowered his voice to a whisper, saying, "Give them to me as soon as you're done."

I thanked him, appreciating his decision to let me hang onto them a while longer, knowing he was putting his credibility—perhaps even his job—on the line for me. But Loxley was smart, clever, and it scared me to know we couldn't stop him. At least I had enough to hopefully scare Garcia into telling me what he knew.

"So, without knowing Damien's whereabouts, where do you go from here?" I asked.

King peered down when lowering his voice. "According to one of his students, Damien has everything on the line with this hacker event."

"Susan and Allison said the same," I said.

"If they take the prize money, it will keep his lab open for at least another year."

"And if they don't win?"

"Tough to say." King shook his head. "But, get this, the woman who told us this, she said Damien called her Maid Marion."

I didn't blink. My entire body froze. *Did I hear him right?*
Loxley.

Little John.

And now Maid Marion.

"Did you know Damien has a past conviction?" King asked.

I shook my head no.

"Convicted of stealing corporate secrets via computer hacking."

The world around me spun and the contrails of light made me nearly topple over. Suddenly, Damien had the motive and know-how to thrust himself into the Number One suspect slot. With eyes on Rose, we couldn't afford to lose him.

But there was only one problem. I also had to learn what Garcia knew before he disappeared, too.

Then I had an idea. "You want to get Damien first?" King nodded. "I think I know what might get his attention."

CHAPTER FIFTY-NINE

JOEY GARCIA TURNED OFF THE NEWS RADIO AND PARKED IN a dark corner on the same street as his house. With his hand up by his mouth, he silently stared toward the address in which he began his life with Cecelia nearly a decade ago.

The window was cracked open and a robin chirped from a nearby tree branch.

At one time, this was his dream. Everything he ever wanted. All that he needed could be found in that tiny house. Love. Encouragement. Dreams and lofty aspirations. Now, as he stared at that same house that once seemed so bright, he felt only nerves of uncertainty. Joey was afraid of what was waiting for him inside.

He checked his mirrors, wondering if he was being followed. Were the cops still watching the house, waiting for him to come home? He was deathly afraid of an ambush.

Seeing Parker Collins's accident left him shaken. With so much uncertainty, he feared he could be next. He was as guilty as the people he extorted for money. But who was doing this, and why? Joey didn't know.

The walls were closing in. Time was running out.

He had so many regrets. His predicament was his own fault. He knew better than anybody. Joey made bad choices, decisions that he would have never otherwise made had it not been for Katie's diagnosis. But a man's choices were dictated by circumstance, and his was particularly bleak.

After several minutes of watching a quiet street, Joey exited his vehicle and marched toward his house thinking of his wife, Cecelia. With each step, a memory of his past flashed behind his eyes. He visualized the woman he fell in love with—the woman he was still madly in love with—and how he would do anything to keep the love alive.

That was his biggest regret. It wasn't fair of him to neglect the importance of his marriage. It meant everything to him. It was all he had. His world. Now he was risking throwing everything away, and for what? To have someone else cover the cost of his own life? His father—may he rest in peace—would be so ashamed of the man he'd become.

Joey stopped just shy of the front door. He gulped down a couple breaths of air, rubbed his face awake, and put on a face that he hoped Cecelia could believe in—something to fill her with certainty.

Slowly, he turned the knob and quickly jerked his head back.

Cecelia was there waiting as soon as he opened the door. They stared in an awkward moment of silence as neither of them moved. He could see the sharp look she was giving him and it made him sick all over again. He loved her more than anything—knew she was the only one for him—but could he dull the knives now cutting his heart?

"Why would the police be looking for you?" Cecelia's words cracked the still air like a whip.

Joey's eyelids clicked, startled by her tone. The buzz of

agitation moved up his spine and he felt every muscle fiber in his entire body flex. "You should have never let them inside the house without a warrant."

"Joey," Cecelia scowled, "they're investigating a homicide."

Joey knew what his wife was suggesting.

"Did you kill somebody?"

His eyes widened with a hot flare of insult. Without warning, Joey stormed across the floor, gripped his wife's mouth between his fingers and clamped down hard. Growling through clenched teeth, he said, "Do you not know me at all?"

Fear flashed over Cecelia's soft brown eyes. Soon, Joey saw tears pool in the corners.

In that split second, Garcia's chest hollowed and he didn't know the man he suddenly was. He released his grip, snapped his hand down to his side, and stepped back. Cecelia breathed heavily, holding her chin high, refusing to be intimidated by the man who'd sworn to protect her into eternity.

A small noise had Joey snapping his neck toward the sound.

An intense sharp pain filled his chest as he felt his heart shatter once again. His daughter stood clenching her blanky, about to burst into tears herself. Saddened to see his little girl witness what he had just done to her mother, he hurried across the living room floor and scooped her up into his arms.

Katie wailed into the air, tears streaming down her rosy cheeks. "Let me go, Daddy. Stop. You're scaring me," she cried.

Cecelia flew across the room and yanked Katie out of Joey's arms. "I think it's best if you leave." Cecelia shielded their daughter from Joey.

Joey stared and felt his throat constricting as if a noose had closed off his windpipe. He was too afraid to ask for clarification, but assumed what she meant. He'd taken it too far, scared his little girl, lost control of his actions. There was no taking back the damage he'd caused—what was done was done.

Flares of hot breath shot through his nostrils.

His angered heart thrashed in his ears.

This was his house—she can leave if she wants, he thought to himself. I Instead, he said, "I'll be gone after I collect some things from the office."

Cecelia said nothing. Only held on to Katie as tightly as her muscles allowed.

An electric buzz of agitation heated Joey's body. Without a word, he turned to his office, needing to remove himself from the equation before his daughter only remembered him as the bad man who assaulted Mommy.

As Joey marched down the hall and into his office, he wanted to punch a wall, wail, and blame the world for dealing him a bad hand. Instead, he closed the door softly and slumped in his chair, hiding himself behind his desk.

Staring at the half empty bottle of whiskey perched on top of a nearby shelf, Joey thought about wrapping his lips around it and drinking his problems away. No he regretted not taking Samantha up on her offer to get the drink he'd proposed this morning. But even that was too risky after seeing her at the scene of the crash. He was still confused why she didn't mention seeing him, so maybe she hadn't? Even if she hadn't seen him drive by, it was better to believe she did. Staying paranoid would help him survive and, God knew, he would take any advantage he could get.

The bottle tempted Joey again. The amber liquid shined and glowed as it called out to him.

Joey licked his lips and wondered if Samantha knew what he was up to. Was that why she asked what he knew about

Thompson and Counts? Clenching his jaw, his adrenaline was high. Joey doubted his every move—even the decision of whether or not to have a simple drink.

Taking his eyes off the bottle, he cast his gaze to his desk.

It was easy to imagine suit-wearing detectives rummaging through his things. A free-for-all. Joey assumed they knew about him and Counts, and soon Collins too. He knew there was no account information here, but the list of clients he extorted was gone, along with the Thompson article he knew was taken from the trash.

The detectives were building a case.

Firing up his desktop computer, it loaded. As soon as it did, a message from an unknown sender pinged Joey's profile.

Joey's brow pinched as he hovered his finger over his mouse, thinking it might be from Samantha.

With nothing left to lose, he clicked the message tab and opened it up.

A twenty-four-hour time clock popped up in the center of his screen.

The crease between his brows deepened with sudden confusion. He didn't know what it was or what it meant, but as he scrolled further down the page, the color drained off his face.

I've been watching your every move. You can run, but you can't hide. I know what you've done. Don't deny it because I have proof. You have two choices; confess publicly, telling the world of your crimes (preferably through the Times), or pay the ultimate sacrifice. And by that, you know what I mean.

Joey looked to see who it was from, but there was no signature. His computer dinged when an email hit his inbox. Again, it came from an unknown sender. He opened it regardless of his fears of clicking on a wrong link. The pixels of an image populated his screen and, with it, another message. "I'll give you exactly 24 hours to decide. After that, I'll have no choice but to tell the world what you've been doing."

Now Joey knew he was being watched. The image he was staring at was proof of that.

Afraid, he retrieved his Glock 17 from the locked desk drawer and dialed Samantha Bell's cellphone.

CHAPTER SIXTY

KING AND I MADE A PLAN TO RECONVENE LATER TONIGHT. So, two hours after I witnessed Collins's car get loaded up and towed away, I dropped Erin at her house and headed across town, steeling myself to confront my colleague. I couldn't believe he called requesting to meet. He sounded better than the last time I spoke to him, and that was a good sign. But Garcia still had an edge to his voice that kept me vigilant. I was starting to doubt who I could and couldn't trust.

As soon as I parked outside Garcia's house, Susan called me back. I got straight to it. "So, will you do it?"

"I can't believe you're asking me to be your pawn." Susan was clearly upset.

"We don't know where he is. Since he asked you out, he clearly has a thing for you."

"But he could be dangerous." Susan sighed. "Besides, I'm still with Benjamin. He won't like me going out with another man while he's away. You know how that would look?"

"Have you already told Damien no?" I pressed.

"Sam, listen to yourself. What you're asking me to do is ridiculous."

"He's invited you into his life, sought you out, and you're the only one who has been given the inside tour of his operation."

"Allison, too. She was with me at Backstage," Susan reminded me. "Why don't you ask her?"

I paused, the silence hanging on the line for far too long. I was losing steam and the art of persuasion had me feeling exhausted. I wasn't sure I had the patience to keep things civil; I just wanted to find Damien Black, preferably tonight.

"There is another way, you know." Susan's voice sang with absolute certainty. "An easier way."

The tone in Susan's voice had me believing I didn't have to sell her on anything. Maybe she had a better idea—an idea she could go along with. "I'm open to whatever," I said.

"He wants to hire me."

When she didn't add anything more, I asked, "But?"

"But... I still don't know if I want to do it."

"Then just pretend," I said.

Susan understood that three people may have died at the hands of Damien Black, and I understood her fears. If Damien was Loxley like we thought he might be, and he discovered what we were trying to do to entrap him, what would he do to Susan? I wasn't sure Susan was cut out for that kind of battle—I wasn't sure I was either.

"Let me sleep on it," she said and, reluctantly, I agreed. It was the best answer I could have hoped for after dropping the bomb of Damien Black's possible guilt. Then she told me to stay safe and I told her to do the same before the line disconnected.

Losing daylight, I gathered my tote and phone and knocked on Garcia's front door, thinking I still had a chance at solving this tonight. Less than a minute passed before I heard the lock click over.

A pair of brown eyes peeked through the crack. "Samantha?"

Cecelia was surprised to see me. We knew each other but weren't exactly friends. She seemed to be surprised at my arrival.

An awkward silence hung between us and I didn't know how to break the ice, so I simply asked, "Is Joey home?"

Her gaze fell off my face. "You just missed him."

My brows pulled together in confusion. Had I misunderstood Garcia? I could have sworn he asked me to meet him here. Then Cecelia gave me the once over—a judgmental glint in her eye that suggested maybe I was here for something other than work.

"Do you know where he went?" I asked.

Cecelia was always friendly, but the shimmer of uncertainty grew wider in her sideways glance. It had been a long time since we last saw each other, and I knew the challenges Katie was having. Beyond that, I had no idea how much or how little she knew about me. Did she know I was a widow?

"Can I ask what you two are meeting about?" Cecelia sharpened her gaze when roaming my face for answers.

When I put myself in her shoes, seeing couldn't take offense at her question. The late evening request, the fact that we hadn't done this kind of thing before. I glanced down my front, happy for once to be looking as disheveled as I did, as haggard as I felt. I laughed. "Oh, no," I said. "It's a story I'm working, about people Garcia worked with in the past."

Cecelia was slow to nod, and did so only skeptically. But it didn't take her long to come around after I asked about Katie.

"It's not looking good." She invited me inside, and I followed close behind.

Joey's house was both modest and domestic, exactly how I imagined it would be. Katie was asleep upstairs and Cecelia didn't seem too interested in speaking much about her. So I let it go. Then Cecelia stopped and turned to me. "Can I ask you something?"

I smiled. "Of course."

"How is my husband's behavior at work?"

I searched her eyes for meaning. "Professional."

She let a tiny laugh escape. "I meant his mood."

This was a good sign, I thought. She was worried about him. But it was the first hint that something was off. Something bigger was going on—something I suspected too. I found myself staring at her wedding band when I told her, "He hasn't seemed himself."

"Any guesses as to why?"

I shared my assumptions: the increased workload and the potential of getting laid off. I told her nothing of what I recently learned, and stood with my spine ramrod straight as I wondered if she would mention King's visit here earlier.

Cecelia sighed again. "Joey has been afraid of losing his job," she admitted.

She told me to sit, offered me tea, and over the next half-hour we indulged in girl talk. It felt good to finally get to know her, even with the constant reminders of the resentful feelings I was having toward her husband. Soon, Cecelia brought our conversation back to Joey's work and, not wanting to miss an opportunity, I asked if she knew whether or not her husband had a Bitcoin account.

"I don't think so, but ever since Katie's diagnoses, Joey has been trying to do anything he can to help pay the bills."

Cecelia mentioned their struggles with health insurance, the cost of Katie's care, and how Joey wasn't making nearly enough to afford their seemingly simple life. I couldn't know the full extent of it, how bad it truly was, but I could feel her worries of having to live in a constant state of unknown.

"I don't know what to do," Cecelia said, dropping her gaze

to her wedding band. "It's not like Joey has the time to take on a second job."

I leaned forward and reached for her hand. "I might be able to help," I said, telling Cecelia about Susan. Cecelia was aware of her company since the school shooting several months back. "I'm sure she would donate her time for Katie."

Cecelia was open to the idea. I wondered how much emotional support she had because she suddenly opened up to me by saying, "I don't blame Joey for what he's done. He's been under a lot of pressure."

"What did he do?" I pressed, my interest suddenly piqued.

"He's just blowing off steam," she glanced a heavy gaze to the front door and touched her cheek, "but I expect him to be home soon. He wouldn't leave me, would he?"

Cecelia seemed delirious and I wanted to attribute her odd comment to exhaustion. But I didn't know where it came from. I told her Garcia wouldn't dare leave her, but I had no idea if that was true.

By the time I was finished with my tea, it was getting late. On my way out the door, I told Cecelia to give me a call when Joey came back home.

With a shell-shocked look still printed on her face, she promised she would. That was the best I could have hoped for. I left with a heavy heart, knowing it was time for me to go home and work on my own relationship with King.

CHAPTER SIXTY-ONE

I was concerned for Garcia, but mostly I was worried about how his behavior was affecting his family. Katie needed his strength now more than ever, and so did Cecelia. It was clear to me that Cecelia was hiding the pieces that had already been chiseled off of her, and that killed me to see.

But then I remembered the missing files on Donny's exchange from Garcia's past research. I still didn't want to believe he was using the work he did at the *Times* to blackmail these people who were dead. But that was exactly what it seemed like was happening, and it still didn't make any sense to me.

Was Garcia Loxley? Or was Loxley choosing his targets through Garcia's research? Was that the reason the paper was hacked?

The house was particularly dark when I curbed my vehicle and glanced through the front windows. I looked for Cooper who was usually the first to put his nose against the glass, wagging his tail, welcoming me home. But even he was absent, sending my mind into a spiral of what-ifs.

Slowly, I exited the car and looked up and down the block. It was a quiet evening, and I relaxed when spotting King's car parked adjacent to mine.

With him here, I was safe.

A minute later, I stepped through the front door and found King playing video games with Mason in a dark house. I never could get a hold of Garcia again, which concerned me. I didn't know what he was up to, and not knowing drove me insane. I was afraid of his vulnerability—of his expressed fear—how he was choosing to handle the increased stress. But watching King and Mason joke and laugh quickly stripped away my own day's troubles and the sight made me smile. I flipped on the light.

"Hey," Mason argued.

"Hey to you." I smiled.

King fixed his eyes on me and winked.

I smiled, impressed with King's ability to disguise his workday—the difficult one I knew he'd had—and make the world seem brighter than it was. Especially that he could do it all so effortlessly in front of my son. It was something I wished I had myself but, more than anything, I was glad to finally be home.

King set his control down and came to me.

I took him by his hand and led him to the back, just needing to be held. His big arms wrapped around me, his thick lips pressing against my forehead. I nuzzled my face deep into his chest and closed my eyes. We stood like that for what felt like forever—frozen in time, without a single worry to make us doubt our decisions. Just as my mind cleared, freeing it from all its chaotic thoughts, King asked, "If the *Times* never reported on these people, would they still be alive?"

I opened my eyes and my breath caught in my throat.

How was it that he seemed to always know what was on my mind? The same fear had crossed my mind as I drove back from Cecelia's. I was feeling personally responsible— that, once again, somehow my investigation, my reporting, was the reason a sick bastard was choosing his victims. I told King that, trusting him fully to listen, knowing he'd understand what it was I was grappling with.

"What Thompson did was wrong, but he didn't deserve to die, and neither did anyone else," I said.

"Don't beat yourself up, Sam." He palmed my skull and tugged gently on my hair. "You know this isn't your fault. It's not just your reporting I was referring to. It's others at the paper, too."

It still didn't make me feel any better. Worse, I knew it was going to happen before it did. "I saw a flier on Garcia's desk in the newsroom this morning about the event at MSU. He had my name scribbled next to Parker Collins. But I didn't go, and, well... look at what happened."

King was quiet for a minute as he mulled over his words. "It's easy to know what to do in retrospect."

We both had been down this road before. Our track record spoke for us. We couldn't catch them all, even if we had all the resources made available to us. But I still wanted to believe we could.

"But the clues had been there and I had missed them both," I said, telling King about the mysterious email sent to Dawson about Parker Collins being a fraud. The call had come too late.

"The department spoke with Joan Collins."

I peeled my cheek off his chest, tipped my head back, and asked, "What did she say?"

"It was her, not her husband, giving today's keynote."

My thoughts churned. Loxley spared the women and seemed to only care for men. Was Loxley a woman who had a grudge against men? Or was Loxley a man like we'd been thinking all along who was jealous of what these other men had?

"Joan also said she and her husband were at Thompson's wake this morning."

I thought how ironic that was. Did that have any influence on how Loxley chose his next victim?

"But, get this," King raised both his eyebrows, "strange things were happening at their house that couldn't be explained."

"Like what?"

King couldn't believe it when he heard it, but it sounded similar to what happened with Thompson. "Like the thermostat not working properly, and a garage door that kept going up and down by itself."

"Did she report it?"

"Not to the police, and she didn't suspect anything wrong with Parker's car when they drove it to Metro State, either."

It had to be Loxley. But why test the home, only to have Collins die in a car crash? Did he know the police were figuring out his puzzle? Or was this a clue for me to follow?

Stepping away from King, I moved to the kitchen sink and gazed out the window into the neighbor's yard. I stood there for a minute thinking about the list King found in Garcia's office. I wondered if Ronald Hyland was preparing any upcoming speeches.

"That's it," I said, turning on a heel. "It has to be."

"What?"

I cleared the kitchen table, retrieved my notes from my tote, and flipped the lid to my laptop. King hovered over my shoulder as I worked. I gave him insight into what I was thinking. "Collins was at the event with his wife earlier today, and Counts was part of a panel at DU earlier in the week."

"Okay." King nodded. "What about Thompson?"

My eyes lit up. "Thompson just did a big charity event that received expanded news coverage. His face was everywhere in the hours leading up to his death."

King remembered. I wasn't aware of Thompson being part of a panel discussion like the others, but two out of three? My hypothesis didn't come without its flaws, but it was the best we had.

King scrubbed his hands over his face. "We'll check it out. Along with Damien."

I told him about Susan needing the night to think things over before making her decision to flush Damien out. Then I turned to my notes, realizing that Garcia knew more about each of these victims than I did. Did he cover the events these people spoke at? I didn't know.

I told King about my visit with Garcia's wife as I looked up Ronald Hyland's contact information. Hyland was also on the list from Garcia's office, and that concerned me. "We should at least warn him," I said, speaking about Hyland.

King gave me a skeptical look. I knew what he was thinking. Hyland had a reputation for resenting journalists. Since I was one, it wasn't going to be easy getting through his thick skull. But I had to try. I knew I would never be able to forgive myself if I was right and Hyland was Loxley's next target.

My cell phone rang.

I checked the caller ID. It was Garcia's home number. I quickly answered. "Is Joey home? Did he come back?" I asked Cecelia.

"He's not here." Cecelia sounded frantic. "But he took his gun with him."

My vision blurred as I felt my blood pressure drop. Gun? Joey had a gun?

"I don't know why I went looking, but I'm glad I did. I found his gun drawer empty."

"Have you tried calling him?"

"His cell goes straight to voicemail. Sam, what am I going to do? Is my Joey going to hurt somebody?"

My lips parted but no words came out. I hoped he wouldn't, but it seemed like he might.

CHAPTER SIXTY-TWO

THE VOLUME WAS TURNED DOWN AS LOXLEY SAT QUIETLY behind the wheel. The engine was off, his face hidden by a dark splash of shadow from a thick tree branch above. He listened to the news, waiting for details to emerge that someone was getting close to figuring out it was him behind these deaths. Instead, they only talked about Parker Collins's contribution to the world and how much he would be missed.

Loxley stroked the point of his chin between his fingers, knowing the only reason Parker Collins's name was mentioned at all was because of his extreme wealth. Any other man and the news would have found another story to tell. But not him. That was part of the resentment Loxley felt needed correcting.

"Of course he will be missed," Loxley muttered to himself. "That's the point."

He was particularly tense and trying to put the upsetting information out of his mind when he noticed his finger had moved off the trigger guard and had curled around the trigger itself.

Loxley glanced down to his lap and stared at the metallic glint of the gun's muzzle. It was tempting to forgo the discreet nature of hacking and instead choose to use a bullet. Though easy, guns were messy and they involved little skill. Anybody could pull a trigger. Not everyone could hack their way into a clever murder.

He lifted the weapon and moved it into the light. Studying it for what it was, Loxley never liked guns much but he understood their necessity in the world. Like most tools, there was a time and a place. This might be the time and place to switch tactics.

Placing the gun safely back onto his lap, Loxley looked to his computer propped up on a plastic filing box on the passenger seat next to him. The video feed was clear as the night and his erection stiffened every time Samantha's face was perfectly framed in the lens.

Loxley took note of her tired eyes, wished he could be the one to rub the tension out of her neck. He listened to her words, internalizing and getting to the root of what she was saying. Only when she was responding to a text or checking her emails on her phone did he have a clear view of her beautiful face, as he had hacked into her cell phone camera and was now with her every step of the way.

Samantha stared directly into his eyes. He held her gaze and felt the flutters tickle his insides. This was his most difficult breach yet, but he'd managed—never giving up—and Loxley was thrilled by the thought of them always being together.

Sweeping his eyes off the computer, he stared at Samantha's front door.

He had followed her here she spoke for a lengthy time with Cecelia.

The radio caught his attention. He turned up the volume,

but only a notch. Tilting his head, he listened. Finally, someone was asking why the public shifted their anger off Thompson and Counts and over to Collins.

No one knew Parker's crimes, and that disappointed Loxley. But they soon would. Loxley blamed his lack of preparation and the fact that Parker's death happened far too quickly to allow the leaks of the man's crimes against society to build an initial buzz. But time was of the essence. Due to a change in circumstance, tactics and procedures were forced to change as well.

Which explained the gun, Loxley thought, once again staring at the piece.

He just couldn't decide which was of greater importance; Ronald Hyland or Joey Garcia.

Both men, Loxley wanted to kill. But which of the two would move his cause forward faster? And how could he turn the angered public on an award-winning journalist they trusted?

Planning... Loxley needed more time to plan. He needed to get this right. It was a delicate balance of choosing worthwhile victims and not getting caught. Loxley played the game well, enjoyed what he did immensely. But could he kill the man who fed him his first few targets? If he did, where would he get his leads once he was gone?

Everything changed when Loxley saw Joey Garcia blackmail Parker Collins in the parking lot of Metro State. He knew Garcia was a liar, but now understood why. How long had Garcia been extorting his subjects in exchange for favorable press coverage? Loxley could only imagine it was for as long as the coverage had been good. This was why Loxley had to take out Garcia. What he did was just as bad as what the other men died for doing. But with Donny Counts's cryptocurrency exchange down, how was Garcia going to request anonymous payments now? Loxley chuckled softly.

It didn't take Loxley long to uncover Garcia's Bitcoin account. But what really ground on Loxley's nerves was how Garcia purposely stood Samantha up.

Loxley needed them together, needed Samantha to see Garcia for the hypocrite he was. Even more than that, Loxley needed to manipulate the situation and control the narrative. I If he didn't, things were certainly going to spiral out of control.

Loxley turned his attention back to his computer screen and stared, waiting for Samantha to show her face again. Wrinkling his brow, he refused to leave her alone. She needed his protection because Samantha didn't know the danger that was coming for her.

Then, as if hearing her name being called, Samantha stepped into the kitchen window and showed her face.

Loxley felt his chest relax. Even from half a block away, he was close enough to reach out and touch the woman he loved. Her bangs framed her delicate eyes. There was a radiant glow highlighting her cheeks that had Loxley's blood pumping fast. His erection was painfully hard now, his heart fluttering against his ribs like tiny butterfly wings that tickled his insides. Leaning back, he unzipped his pants and took his shaft in his hand. He stopped just before he was about to begin stroking.

Detective King stepped behind Samantha, wrapped her up inside his arms, and nuzzled his face into her neck. She leaned into him, closed her eyes, and smiled.

A pang of jealously stabbed Loxley's side. Next thing he knew, he was holding his limp dick inside his cold hand as he watched the two tongue kiss. Loxley knew that something had to be done about Alex King if Samantha was ever going to see him.

"Endless obstacles; so many ways the code could be written," Loxley whispered to himself as he zipped up his pants and started the car. "But I'll find a way. When there's a will, there's always a way."

CHAPTER SIXTY-THREE

As soon as I opened my eyes, my mind went immediately to Damien Black. I couldn't stop thinking about what King said about Damien being not only an award-winning hacker, but a convicted felon as well. Was he our guy? Maybe.

My thoughts churned over, bouncing between Black and Garcia before I finally flopped onto my side and flipped my legs around, dropping my feet to the floor. I padded across the carpet, making a turn to the toilet, before heading into the kitchen. Once at the table, I opened my laptop and began browsing articles covering Damien Black's trial from five years ago.

It could have been me covering his trial, but it didn't work out that way. Back then, the paper was financially stable. We had more than enough journalists to cover the same stories we now reported on with only a third of the staff. I remembered hearing bits and pieces of the case but, until now, none of the details sank in.

I read more about Damien's corporate espionage. I began thinking about what Erin found in Collins's car. I'd spent the better part of last night studying the dirt we found in the neatly packaged folder on Parker Collins's business. Whoever put it together made a pretty convincing case that his social entrepreneurship was nothing more than a marketing gimmick to fatten his personal wallet.

Greed. It was quickly becoming the number one killer.

Leaning back, I paused to stare at the text glowing on my screen.

Corporate espionage and uncovering dirt on someone's business and personal life was the same, but different. What I wasn't sure of was whether I could put the two events in the same pile as Loxley.

I still believed that Damien could be Loxley, and that Garcia could be working with him, maybe as a side hustle to pay Katie's medical bills. But was Damien still on parole? Who had the skills to complement Garcia's if Damien wasn't Loxley?

His protégé, Maid Marion, was first to come to mind. But now I questioned if I was right about Loxley also being LilJon, or if he, too, was another person entirely.

I reached for my cellphone and checked if Susan responded to my request to help track down Damien. I had a burning desire to go knock on Backstage's door myself but needed to give King time to conduct his work. Besides, I still felt awful about trying to twist Susan's arm into accepting Damien's offer to take her out. She was clever enough to produce the same results by keeping their relationship strictly business, and I failed to even have considered it. I just wanted to know if Damien's name should be crossed off my list of suspects or not.

There was nothing from Susan. I placed my phone next to my keyboard and went back to reading.

Would anyone know if Damien was up to his old tricks again? Even under the supervision of a parole officer, would they be savvy enough to recognize his secret identity—if he had one? I doubted the city could afford to assign such a skill to someone like him, and besides, I was reminded of what Allison said about how good Loxley was. I'd experienced it myself. The fact that even King didn't have a solid suspect in the case was proof of just how good this individual was.

I heard Cooper's nails clacking their way into the kitchen. He rested his big head on my thigh and demanded an ear scratch.

"Who do you think Loxley is, boy? Black or Garcia?"

Cooper raised a single eyebrow and licked his chops as he headed to his empty food bowl. My stomach grumbled as well. I fed him first, then I made myself some buttered toast before heading into the living room where I turned on the TV and flipped to the news.

Nancy Jordan's story about the mystery vigilante was still the talk of the hour. I thought how she got exactly what it was she was after—perhaps even better than she could have imagined herself. Prime Time quickly turned into, All The Time. Not only did the story last the night, but momentum seemed to be growing.

I stood with my arms crossed and shaking my head, knowing Nancy was singlehandedly jeopardizing this entire case with this one story quickly spinning out of control. Worse, I feared it might spawn hoaxers who would confuse us even more.

Then I heard something even more surprising—something even worse than hoaxers.

The story of an unknown vigilante on a killing spree not only stoked fear, but it also opened the doors for many to come out in support of what it was Loxley was doing. Overnight, Loxley had become a nameless, faceless celebrity with a growing fan base cheering him on. Maybe Loxley wouldn't hide because of the publicity, but rather be inspired by it.

I felt new wrinkles formed as I listened to one concerned citizen say, "These people were criminals. They stole from me, you, and anyone else they thought they could manipulate by using their power and wealth to influence. Whoever this guy is that's killing these people, he's doing us all a great service. We should be grateful."

Disgusted, I flipped the channel.

Another man was being interviewed. He was armed and on the hunt to stop the vigilante himself. He didn't care that there was physical description, name, or anything to go on to know who it was. He just wanted to get in the fight.

I sighed and wondered how much time we had before the ones chasing Loxley became the victims themselves. A quick scroll through the news stations told me they, too, were piggybacking off of Nancy's story. It was the talk of the town.

My phone rang and I hurried into the kitchen to answer it. "Hello."

"Samantha Bell?"

"Yes, this is she." I didn't recognize the deep baritone.

"Mrs. Bell, my name is Chuck Morgan from the hospital morgue."

"What can I do for you Chuck?" It was never a good sign to get a call from the morgue. At least I knew Mason safe.

"I was returning your message about Parker Collins. I'm afraid he didn't make it."

The air stilled as I was instantly transported to the scene of yesterday's crash. I could still smell the scent of burning oil, the shouts of the fireman rushing to contain the scene. Inside, I'd known Parker wouldn't make it. But it was nice to have confirmation. "Okay, thanks for getting back to me."

"I'm sorry for your loss."

As soon as I was off the phone with Chuck, my phone lit up with another call. This time it was Cecelia Garcia.

"Have you heard from Joey?" Cecelia asked me. "He never came home last night."

I could hear the stress in her weak voice. "No, nothing," I said.

"It isn't like him to disappear without telling someone."

"Have you tried calling the newsroom?"

"He's not picking up. No one has seen or heard from him since yesterday." Cecelia was afraid Joey reached his tipping point and was about to do something crazy. Her words were scaring me into believing she could be right and Joey might actually do something we'd all regret.

"Maybe he got caught up in a story; you know how crazy our jobs can get some time," I tried to reason, but even I didn't believe the lies I was telling.

"There is something I didn't tell you last night," Cecelia said, acting as if she hadn't listened to a word I said. "Before you arrived, Joey and I had a fight."

My brow wrinkled as I searched for what response I could give. "What was it about?"

Cecelia paused, the phone's static popping in my ear. Then she said, "Two detectives came by the house yesterday, said they were investigating a homicide and wanted to speak with Joey."

"Did they?" I played coy, already knowing the details King shared.

"He wasn't home," Cecelia said, telling me how she allowed the officers to search his office without his permission. "Joey was furious I had done that without a warrant, but what was I to do?" Cecelia wasn't looking for a response. "He assaulted me last night... in front of Katie."

I tipped my head up and felt my eyes widen a fraction. Now her behavior last night was beginning to make sense, and so was her obvious concern for what Joey might be planning to do. But assault? Did I not know the man I'd worked with all these years? It seemed like I didn't.

"This is all my fault."

"Don't blame yourself, Cecelia."

"You don't understand. I told him to leave."

"Joey wouldn't harm anyone," I said, suddenly not sure that was true. "Maybe he took his gun as a needed precaution."

"I don't think so. He's going to hurt someone, Samantha. I can feel it in my bones. I'm afraid it might be those same detectives who came to the house that he's after."

"What makes you say that?"

"Because they took something I know Joey didn't want them to see."

CHAPTER SIXTY-FOUR

"Alex, it's me again. I really need to speak with you. It's about Joey Garcia. Call me back as soon as you get this." It was the second message I'd left with King in the last half-hour. I didn't know where he was or why he wasn't picking up, but I didn't like not hearing from him after what Cecelia told me.

I gripped my phone in my hand, exited my vehicle, and headed into the newsroom with a stitched side jabbing me with worry.

Garcia knew we were on to him, knew the detectives were at his place. I was afraid we were backing him into a corner where he'd have no choice but to fight.

Not too long ago, I would have never thought he'd be capable of doing such horrendous things. Cecelia did a good job convincing me otherwise. I just hoped King would call me back so I could give him a heads up.

I headed straight for Garcia's desk and wasn't surprised to find it empty. His computer was on, but no one was around. I dipped into his cubbyhole and pressed my palm into his seat cushion. It was warm. Someone was here, but was it him? I stood and looked above the walls without any luck in spotting him. Then, as soon as I turned around, I collided into Travis Turner.

Papers dropped to the floor and Travis took a step back, quick to apologize. "I'm so sorry," he said. "My head was in what I was reading."

"No." I kneeled and helped gather what he'd dropped. "It was my fault," I said, trying to see what had his attention.

Travis looked over his shoulder before guiding me back inside the walls where we hid near Garcia's computer. In a hushed tone he said, "I looked into Brett Gallagher like you asked."

I'd completely forgotten about my request. So much had happened since. "And?"

Travis nodded slowly.

My eyes did a double-take. "He has a Bitcoin account?"

"I confirmed it." Travis grinned. "Don't ask me how, but I did."

I couldn't believe it. Skinny Tree Brett Gallagher had a Bitcoin account confusing me more than ever. Just when everything was convincing me Garcia was the one to have blackmailed Richard Thompson, possibly the other victims too, now I learned this. But if Garcia wasn't blackmailing them, then what was he doing with the stories we found in Parker Collins's car?

"Are you going to tell me what this is about or what?" Travis's eyes glimmered with hope.

I stared into his curious eyes, remembering my promise to tell him why I wanted to know about Brett's possible use of cryptocurrency. If I could match the key code found on Thompson's desk to Gallagher, then we'd be one step closer to our perpetrator. "I can't say." I stood and made a turn to the exit. "Not right now."

"Samantha," Travis grabbed my arm and swung me around, "that wasn't our agreement. You said—"

"I know what I said." I cast my gaze to his hand still pinching my arm. When he let go, I said, "I need to speak with Brett. Why don't you come with me?"

Travis broke eye contact and let out a heavy sigh. "He's not here, Samantha. A no-show."

"What? Did he call in sick?"

Travis shrugged. "Last I heard from him was yesterday. Thing is, I found Joey Garcia's cell on a sticky note on Brett's desk." Travis turned his head and glanced to Joey's desk. "That was the reason I was here. I was hoping to speak with Garcia myself, see if he was still in need of my department's services."

I raised a single eyebrow. There was something Travis wasn't telling me. I knew he had been on Garcia's computer only minutes before I arrived. My bullshit detector was sounding the alarm, and when I asked him about it, his face reddened with guilt. Now I knew something was up.

"Travis, I can see it on your face," I said in a harsh, whispered tone. "Why were you really coming to speak with Garcia?"

He held my eyes and cleared his throat. "I found something."

I folded my arms and angled my chin. "Found what?"

"I shouldn't be telling you this." He scrubbed a hand over his face. Then he inhaled a deep breath and said, "Keep this between us, but Garcia might have been selling favorable press coverage to the very people his stories glorified."

"Names, Travis. I need names."

I watched his eyelids droop over his irises just as he said, "You know the names."

My head floated back as the names of Richard Thompson, Donny Counts, and Parker Collins rang in my ear. Could the files Erin found in Collins's car yesterday be what Travis was talking about? It certainly seemed likely.

"I stumbled upon it this morning while finishing out the last of the system updates. I shouldn't have read the email, it was none of my business, but I thought it was work related and was curious to see what Joey was asking Brett."

"What did you find, Travis?"

"Evidence proving what Garcia was doing." Travis jutted his jaw to Garcia's desk. "He had it on his computer. All the files... all the dirt."

"But if Garcia was the one extorting these people for money, why did Brett have the Bitcoin account?"

"Your guess is as good as mine."

My heart knocked against my ribs steadily. Brett was suddenly at the top of my list of possible suspects when I started thinking about how someone hacked my email telling Dawson about Parker Collins also being a fraud. Could it have been Brett and Garcia working together?

"Interesting," Travis said after I told him about it. "I should probably take a look on your computer."

Trading Garcia's desk for mine, Travis asked me if I'd heard about the vigilante the TV news stations couldn't stop reporting. "I thought maybe you would have picked up the story yourself," he said.

"I'm not interested in sensational news," I said, dropping into my chair and swiveling it around to my computer.

"Fair enough, but do you think it's true?"

After logging in, I asked if he found anything mentioning Parker Collins. I was hoping Travis would have found the information I needed to confirm that Garcia did in fact give the files to Collins just moments before he died. Travis hadn't, so I redirected our conversation back to how my email might have been hacked.

"It's quite easy, actually, and may not have been hacked

through this computer specifically," Travis said, reminding me that my email account ran separately from my laptop and phone.

"Are you any closer to learning who might have hacked the paper?" I asked, getting out of his way so he could check my account.

He locked eyes and pretended to zip his lips shut.

"Why can't you talk about it?" I snapped, thinking that with what I knew it had to have been Loxley.

Travis rolled his gaze toward upper management's doors. Then he inhaled a deep breath and murmured, "Because no one wants to hear what I have to say."

CHAPTER SIXTY-FIVE

"I'll believe you," I told Travis. "Tell me, what is it?"

Travis's fingers typed furiously as he clicked his way through my account, opening and closing different browsers while reading the script code behind the scene, telling him what my computer was doing and why.

I set my hand on his shoulder and he stopped. "You can trust me."

Travis turned his head and stared at my hand on his shoulder for a long pause before sweeping his glistening eyes up to mine. "It's too risky for me to tell you here."

"Then let's go to your office."

Travis held my eyes inside of his and shook his head.

I knew whatever it was he was keeping from me had to be big. The suspense was killing me.

"Even there isn't safe," he said, reaching behind himself to retrieve his wallet. I watched him open it up and pull out a single business card. Flipping it around, he bit off the pen cap with his teeth and jotted down his personal cell. Handing it to me, he said, "I'll call you later today from this number."

I took the card between my fingers and studied the digits.

Travis stood and said, "I couldn't find a breach in this computer but, like I said, email hacks can be tricky to locate as they can happen from anywhere."

"What should I do?"

Travis looked me directly in the eyes and said, "Tell the story you were told to write."

I stared into his crinkled eyes thinking it an odd thing for him to say. Then I thanked him for taking a look under the hood before he exited my cubicle. Shoving his card into my front pocket, I needed to speak with my editor.

As soon as Dawson caught sight of me, he called me into his office. "What was that about?" he asked the moment I entered.

I shut the door behind me and summed up how Travis was looking into who might have sent the email to Dawson yesterday about Parker Collins's supposed fraud.

"Is it true?" Dawson asked.

I still didn't know. Then Dawson asked about the possible Ponzi scheme Donny Counts was being accused of running and where I was with that story. "No time to investigate," I said, thinking Garcia already had all the information I needed but was keeping it a secret from everyone, including editorial.

Dawson's expression pinched and I could see it in his eyes. He was losing patience with me, as I'd given him nothing since my Thompson story.

How long had Garcia been sitting on the information? Would his sources even reveal to me what they knew if Garcia threatened to extort them, too? Garcia not only abandoned the ethics we swore to abide by as journalists, but he threw the entire paper under the bus by risking each of our reputations with what he was doing. I was so angry with him. I wanted to bring it up with Dawson but didn't know how without making it seem like I was stabbing a colleague in the back.

"Have you been following this vigilante story circulating TV news?" Dawson asked, quick to mention the public outcry that followed.

"Total bullshit," I said.

Dawson's eyebrows flicked as he tucked his chin and grinned. Then he looked me in the eye and said, "I need something, Sam."

"The story is already out there. There is nothing more I can say that hasn't been said on social media already."

He threaded his fingers together and placed his hands on top of his desk. "You sound like you've given up."

I felt like I had. Loxley was killing me softly.

Dawson frowned. "Have you heard any more from Loxley?"

"No." I shook my head. "He's been quiet." It wasn't the complete truth, but I knew the angle Dawson was fishing for. Even if I had it, I wasn't sure I would have been willing to reveal my cards for the sake of selling papers. The more Loxley played with me, the less I wanted to be part of anything he did.

"I'm running out of options." Dawson rolled his eyes to the left and sighed.

My body temperature spiked as I needed to tell Dawson about Garcia—what I spoke to Cecelia about and what Travis just revealed to me as well. Except Dawson beat me to the punch.

"IT found something that might explain Garcia's behavior," he said.

"I heard," I muttered softly, wondering how much Dawson already knew. Without him asking, I told him about what I knew the detectives found in Garcia's house—my Thompson story and the list of people Garcia may have been extorting. Dawson couldn't believe what I was telling him, but wasn't all that surprised, considering what Travis found on Garcia's computer.

"What's going to happen to him?" I asked, thinking about his family.

"If it's true?"

I nodded.

"He'll first be put on suspension until a thorough investigation can prove he was selling favorable coverage. Then he'll be fired while we're left to clean up his mess."

I shifted in my seat, unable to get comfortable. The crease between Dawson's eyebrows deepened as he eyed me with enough suspicion to get me to blush.

"You haven't heard from him, have you?"

I shook my head no. "But his wife is looking for him, too."

Dawson paused to stare and I finally got around to mentioning my visit to his house without saying anything about Garcia taking his gun with him. I didn't want Dawson to put the newsroom on lockdown. I was still confident Garcia would show up—peacefully. "Does Cecelia know about this list of victims?"

"I didn't ask, didn't tell. She has her hands full with Katie." Dawson frowned and nodded. It was a devastatingly sad story and I was starting to believe no matter what happened next, we might have already lost Garcia forever.

Breaking the silent air, my cell phone rang. It was Susan. "Can you hang on?" I asked Susan when I took the call. "I'm in the middle of something."

Susan agreed to wait, and I headed for the door, saying, "Ronald Hyland was on that list, and I'm off to track him down if you need me."

"Ronald Hyland?" Dawson acted surprised.

"Yeah. I thought you knew?" My eyebrows pinched. "Does that mean something to you?"

Dawson only knew about the targets who'd died. No one mentioned Hyland's name to him, and I wondered why that was. "It certainly does mean something to me." Dawson stood and rubbed the back of his neck. "It's his company whose security software Travis Turner just installed on all our computers."

My head felt like a helium balloon floating off into space. Did I hear him right? Did Dawson not know that Ronald Hyland hated journalists? He was a sworn enemy to the truth. Who could have made such a mistake?

"You know he hates journalists, right?" I said.

"It's the best security software there is." Dawson lifted his wrist and checked the time. "Shit. I'm late for a meeting." He grabbed his phone from this desk and hurried out the door. "If you hear anything about what we just discussed, call me."

I nodded and put my phone to my ear. "Sorry, Susan, what's up?"

"I'll do it."

"You'll meet with Damien?"

"I'm heading over there now."

"Keep cool. Act yourself."

"Girl, you know I'm the smooth operator."

My lips tugged at the corners. Then it was back to business. "If he is who we think he might be, he'll smell fear a mile away."

"Don't worry, Sam. I've got this." Susan seemed rather upbeat compared to last night. I wondered what changed her opinion. When I asked her about it, her tone dropped like an anchor. "Benjamin called this morning. He's going to take the job at Dartmouth."

CHAPTER SIXTY-SIX

I DROVE DOWNTOWN WITHOUT PAYING ATTENTION TO what I was doing. I was sorry for Susan and what her relationship with Benjamin now meant, but all I could concentrate on was how Ronald Hyland's cyber security software was installed on the *Times'* computers and if that was the reason why his name had been added to Garcia's list.

I watched the same dark SUV follow me from the newsroom. It stayed just far enough back to be suspicious. Keeping one eye on its location, I kept driving toward Ronald Hyland's downtown office.

Did Garcia know something that we would learn later? The skeptical part of me kept asking if Hyland could then use that same software as a portal into our system to learn what news was being reported. With how much I knew he hated journalists, and with what we did for a living, I wouldn't pass him up to at least consider it a possibility.

I ground my molars just thinking about having to confront Ronald Hyland myself. He was the last person I wanted to speak with today, but I couldn't afford not to visit, either.

Flicking my gaze to the rearview mirror, I watched the
SUV continue to follow me onto Blake Street. A minute later,
I dipped into a parking garage and waited for it to pass. At
the gate I stared into my mirror's reflection, holding my
breath—my heart knocking against my sternum—until finally
the vehicle passed without ever stopping. I wondered if it had
missed my turn, or if in fact I was only being paranoid. Either
way, I wasn't quick to write it off as being nothing.

Who it was and why it was following me, I had no clue. I
didn't even know anybody who drove a vehicle of that make
or model, let alone something remotely similar.

After taking the ticket from the kiosk, I circled my way
down the concrete bunker until finally finding an open space.
Gathering my things, I slung my tote over my shoulder and
exited my vehicle, heading to the elevator.

The garage was spectacularly clean, fresh smelling, with
expensive cars filling the rows. It was a nice first impression
of what I was getting myself into. I just hoped Ronald Hyland
was here, and that he would be willing to listen to what I had
to say without putting up too much of a fight.

After a quick and lonely ride up to the lobby floor, I
stepped out of the elevator car to a cathedral ceiling with
pink granite walls beautifully polished to shine as bright as a
mirror.

I made my way to the building directory and located the
floor for Hyland Software Securities, then turned back
around and headed for the elevator. Another quick ride up in
the car and I had entered into a world of its own.

The emblem of the company was prominently displayed
on the wall behind reception like a world championship
trophy. It made a bold statement and set the tone for what
was to surely come my way. Though the floor was quiet,
elegant, and open, I was quick to note the casual way the
employees dressed.

Collared shirts were left untucked, and jeans were acceptable attire. But besides the grand first impression of a small tech company making a big splash in Denver, Colorado, one thought kept circling back to the front of my mind; everyone in this office could potentially have the same knowledge Loxley also possessed. That kept my mind swimming in possibility as dozens of eyes floated past me.

Time slowed as I approached the front desk with a smile. I thought about what I was going to say, how I would react if asked to leave. All my prepared answers were waiting on the tip of my tongue when I said, "Hi, I was hoping to speak with Ronald Hyland. Is he in?"

"Do you have an appointment?" the middle-aged receptionist with dyed blonde hair kindly asked, eyeing me like she knew who I was.

"I'm afraid I don't."

"Aren't you—"

I nodded and showed my press badge. "Samantha Bell with the *Times*."

She snapped her fingers and smiled. "Yes. Samantha Bell. Of course." She turned to her computer and clicked away at her mouse. "Mr. Hyland's first available opening isn't for another two and half months."

I flashed her a silent questioning look. "Really? I have to wait over two months just to speak with him?"

She locked eyes and grinned. "I'll pencil you in if you'd like?"

I caught sight of a security camera mounted to the ceiling and assumed I was being watched. But by whom, I didn't know. Leaning forward, I dropped my voice and said, "It really is important that I speak with him today."

"I'm sorry. It's the best I can do."

"Is he here now?" My head swiveled around as I searched for Hyland's office. Then I heard voices echoing off the walls when suddenly Ronald Hyland emerged, walking with one of his employees.

I glared at the receptionist. When I turned back around, Ronald strode straight for me.

He was an intimidatingly tall man, with shoulders broad enough to be a linebacker. His grin was as sharp as his eyes and I would be lying if I said I wasn't frightened of him. But I steeled my nerves and stepped toward him, forgoing any type of introduction. He knew who I was. Now he needed to know why I was here. "I need to speak with you in private," I said.

Hyland flicked his gaze to reception. "Did you make an appointment at the front desk?"

"Mr. Hyland, I'm so sorry for the interruption." The receptionist was now standing, her round puppy dog eyes begging to be forgiven for my sudden, and rude, intrusion.

Hyland held up his hand, motioned for her to sit back down and relax. She did. Then he rolled his gaze back to me. "I'm afraid my schedule is tight, Mrs. Bell." He lifted his wrist and tapped his timepiece with his opposite index finger. "I really must be on my way."

"It will only take a minute and is completely off the record."

"I would certainly hope so." He chuckled. "Even a minute is something I don't have. Now, if you'll please excuse me."

I stepped in front of him and tipped my head back further, making a final stance with hopes of getting his attention. "You're going to want to hear what I have to say."

Speaking softly, he tucked his chin. "I know why you're here, but I'm nothing like those other men." His eyes narrowed with each word slithering off his tongue. "You can dig all you'd like, but I promise you you'll only be wasting your time."

Now I wondered if maybe I *should* be taking a closer look.

Maybe Garcia had already been here, extorting him with real dirt that could highlight the misery Hyland lived in. I wished I knew what it was, because Hyland seemed awfully defensive without knowing exactly why I was here.

"It's not what you think it is," I said.

"You want to help?" His eyebrows raised high on his head.

"I do."

"You can start by leaving."

It all happened so fast. Hyland reaching for his chest, his shortness of breath as he landed a heavy hand on my shoulder to keep from falling face first into the hard floor. I widened my stance in order to carry his load. With his face only inches away from mine, I watched as his color faded and waited for him to topple over in front of me.

"Mr. Hyland, are you all right?" the receptionist called out.

Hyland closed his eyes, nodded slowly. He caught his breath and stood upright again, the color starting to come back to his face. He was once again towering over me, acting like nothing happened at all. I stood speechless as I stared at his chest, wondering if he just had a heart attack.

"What you're after, Mrs. Bell, is a product of your imagination. It doesn't exist."

My eyes clicked up to his. I didn't know what the heck he was talking about or what the hell just happened. I was only concerned with learning why Garcia had his name on the same list as the people who were now dead.

I asked, "Even if your life is in danger?"

"I'm in good hands, Mrs. Bell." Hyland ironed down his tie with the flat of his hand. "Now, if you'll excuse me, I really must be going."

CHAPTER SIXTY-SEVEN

SUSAN SAT IN THE FRONT DRIVER SIDE OF HER VEHICLE staring at her own reflection in the rearview mirror. Her eyes were perfectly framed in the rectangular glass as she flipped her bangs and fluffed her hair in preparation for her meeting with Damien Black.

Though she was nervous to be meeting with the man Sam considered her number one suspect, there was also a gaping hole in her heart that needed to be patched. Benjamin's news, though not surprising, was nothing short of disappointing. But life went on and Susan knew that she couldn't let her sadness show, especially now when she already felt so vulnerable.

"You knew this was coming," she whispered to herself as she applied a new layer of lipstick. "You might not know why now, but trust that there is reason behind this pain."

It was how Benjamin decided to break the news that really bothered her. He mentioned nothing of what would become of their relationship, or if Susan would even consider moving across country with him. That was what stung most, because Susan wanted to believe she meant more to him than being so easily forgotten.

It was too good to be true, she thought. They were both married to their careers. She knew it at the start of their relationship, and it wasn't fair of her to ask him to do something she wouldn't do herself. Over the course of the last few months, they'd had fun, and it was those memories Susan decided to hang on to. It was a lot lighter than having to carry the heavy bag of resentment.

Deciding she looked professionally stunning, Susan took one last breath before exiting her car. With her clutch and phone in one hand, the sun beat down overhead. She rounded the corner of the brick building that was home to Backstage with her heels clacking loud and proud over the concrete as if to announce her arrival. She reached for the door handle and was greeted with a stiff air-conditioned breeze.

Slowly, Susan strode through the remarkably quiet computer lab, looking around at the many empty desks, wondering where everyone was. Did she get the time wrong? Had Damien misspoken when they talked on the phone?

Samantha had mentally prepared Susan for her meeting with Damien, but Samantha's concern did make her feel uneasy. Damien Black had secrets and they were deep enough to make Susan anxious to know more about his true intention. But where was Damien? Did he know that his secrets had been uncovered?

Susan continued to browse, wiggling a computer mouse to a live computer. The screen came alive and her heart leapt into her throat when she heard a sound behind her. Damien stepped out from the back workroom, surprising her with a playful grin tugging at the corners of his lips.

"Oh, my God." Susan had her hand on her heart, feeling it pound against the tips of her fingers. "You scared me."

Damien was casual in his approach. His hands were

stuffed into his pants pockets, his chin tucked into his chest. Susan watched his dimples deepen with a sharp grin. There was a suspicious glint in his eye that made her think he was up to something he shouldn't be.

"I wasn't sure you were going to show." His voice was as soft as a whisper.

Susan's thoughts were everywhere. She did her best to hide them from him. "I've given what you said some thought," she said, happy to know Damien wasn't hiding like Samantha thought he might be.

Damien stopped a short breath away and peered down into her eyes as he murmured, "About Backstage or my offer to take you out?"

Susan smiled despite her muscles quivering in a tender ball of nerves. "Both."

Soft murmurs of people talking came from the back, comforting Susan, knowing she wasn't alone. "I'm sorry, I didn't realize you had students here." She pointed to the workroom, shifting the conversation to more neutral territory.

Damien's head floated up toward the ceiling. "A few of us are just waiting to put Marion through some drills to prepare her for the event."

"Ah... I see."

"Though we're not sure where she is—" Damien's words were cut short when the front door jangled opened. Both Damien and Susan turned to the front. "Speak of the devil, there she is now."

As soon as Marion's eyes landed on Susan, she hit the brakes. Susan watched her mouth open, then quickly shut. Biting her cheek, Marion's shoulders tensed as if deciding whether or not she should say anything in front of Susan. Susan knew the young, anxious look now lining the young woman's face. It wasn't long ago she was the same age, struggling with the transition between student life and beginning a career. But something was clearly bothering Marion and Susan wanted to ask what it was, be her support, but knew it wasn't her place.

Marion swung her gaze to Damien. "Can I speak with you?"

Damien pinched his eyebrows. "Everything all right?"

Marion shook her head no, her eyes glistening with fear. "I just need to talk to you about... that *thing*."

Damien said he would be in in a minute and for her to wait before speaking about it to anybody else. Susan listened, more curious than ever to know what exactly they were referring to. But she couldn't ask. Then Marion flicked her gaze at Susan, quickly ducked her head and diverted her gaze. Susan gave Damien a questioning look as soon as Marion shuffled into the work room.

Damien was staring at the floor lost in thought. He remained like that for a long pause, then suddenly snapped out of it. "Feel free to join us if you'd like."

"I can't stay long," Susan said.

"Then I guess I shouldn't bother asking you to lunch?"

Susan looked into his soft gaze with questions swirling. She wanted to say yes, to get to know him better, feeling in her gut that he wasn't the man she originally thought he was. A face like his was harmless. Wasn't it?

Susan asked, "Do you have a place we can talk in private?"

Damien nodded, pointing Susan toward his office. "Give me a moment to see what is bothering Marion."

Susan tucked her hair behind her ear and smiled. "Of course."

Damien reached out and touched her elbow, his eyes saying thank you.

Susan headed toward the office and looked over her shoulder when reaching the door. She watched Damien disappear into the workroom, and all Susan could think about was how he was a convicted hacker who'd spent time in prison.

She didn't want to believe he was Loxley, but she couldn't stop thinking about what he said yesterday. *Hackers are the unsung heroes of our time.* Why would he say that? Could it only have been a coincidence?

Susan floated across the floor, browsing the artwork hanging on the walls, and stopped at the bookshelf near the window. Damien had many intriguing titles, many of them non-fiction and science related, but none of them the one title she was hoping to find; Robin Hood. It was a small glimpse into learning the man he was. Satisfied with what she found, Susan circled back around to his desk.

It was incredibly well organized. Neatly stacked papers in perfect rows and not a single particle of dust could be seen.

Susan inched closer with a bloom of heat spreading across her chest.

She glanced to the door, listened to see if she could locate Damien. When she was certain she still had a minute alone, she stepped to the desk ledge and moved a printout to the side with her painted nail.

Her eyes rounded a fraction wider.

Underneath was Ronald Hyland's business card, a sticky note attached to that. Susan picked it up and flipped it around, and read:

Ronald Hyland meeting 4PM.

The Colorado Times.

Det. Alex King.

Feeling her pulse spike, Susan quickly opened her clutch and retrieved her phone. Unlocking the screen, she hurried to snap a quick photo to send to Samantha.

Damien snuck up on her without warning. "Find everything you need?"

Susan's fingers fumbled her phone and her pulse ticked

fast in her neck. She stood frozen and bright eyed, hoping Damien didn't notice her spying. But she was quick on her toes and deflected the attention away from what he was really asking—*what are you doing at my desk?*—to the device she'd just picked up.

"Is this a pacemaker?" she asked.

Damien took his gaze off hers and swung it to the small oval device. "It is."

"Interesting piece of art to have on your desk." Susan arched a brow and gave him her best smile. "Don't you think?"

Damien laughed and moved to stand opposite Susan. "It's part of Marion's training."

"A pacemaker?"

Damien opened his palm and Susan dropped it into his hand by the wire attached. "It's important we prepare her to be able to hack anything the judges present her with." Damien stared at the pacemaker, stroking the pad of his thumb over the device. "Phone lines, home security software, smart speakers." He lifted his eyes to Susan. "Even pacemakers."

"The more I learn of this event, the more concerned I am."

Damien laughed softly. "It's to expose the vulnerabilities so engineers can patch the code." Susan remembered that from yesterday. "Truth is, each new medical device brought to market is extremely vulnerable. Pacemakers like this can easily be commandeered by someone who knows what they are doing."

"And why would anyone want to hijack a pacemaker?"

"Control."

Susan watched Damien's pupils shrink to tiny pin-pricks. She felt a stone form in her throat. "To control someone with a pacemaker?"

"Exactly. They do it by placing malware into the device and then... anything is possible."

"Even death?"

"Most certainly death." Damien hid the device away in his pants pocket. "But, not to worry. Only the best can override the security measures currently in place on the all the latest medical devices." Damien stopped when noticing Susan's face go pale. "Everything all right?"

Susan bit the edge of her lip when deciding how best to ask him. "Why didn't you mention your criminal conviction to me?"

An awkward silence came between them.

"It was only a matter of time before I found out."

"You're right." Damien nodded. "I should have told you sooner. But I wanted to create a good first impression. I was thinking only of Backstage's future."

Susan looked around the office. "Are you even allowed to be teaching this stuff?"

"It's part of my parole agreement." Damien mentioned the strict supervision he received, and the reporting he was required to do.

"To teach young people how to hack?"

"Look, I know how it seems."

"You might be closely watched, but are your students?"

Damien stayed calm when he said, "Is this about what's been being said in the news?"

"Yeah, a little bit I guess."

"I'm not him." Damien assured her with a smile.

Susan wanted to believe him. But since learning about Richard Thompson, her confidence hadn't been what it was. "But you can see why others might think you are."

"What I did was wrong; I'll be the first to admit that." Damien held her gaze inside his eyes. "I'm not the man I used to be. I've turned my life around. A lot has changed since those days, even opportunities for hackers to make a great living doing what they we do best."

Marion popped her head into the office, a stiff perfumed wind following her. "I cracked it, boss. Come take a look. I'll even show you how to do it if you're nice."

Damien smiled and congratulated Marion on her efforts. "I'll be there in a minute."

Marion stared at Susan before spinning back toward the workroom, leaving with the same enthusiasm and energy as she came in with.

Damien swung his attention back to Susan. As soon as their eyes met, Susan said, "But can your students differentiate between good and bad?"

"I believe with the proper mentorship, yeah, they can."

"What you are teaching them is tremendously powerful."

"And I understand the responsibility that comes with it."

"But how well do you know your students?"

Damien rested his tailbone on the edge of his desk and crossed his arms. "None of them are behind what the news is suggesting is happening, Susan."

"How can you be so sure?"

Suddenly, Damien's cellphone vibrated in his pocket. He read the message. "Come with me to lunch. Let me introduce you to someone who might convince you that I'm worth taking a chance on."

"Who?"

"It will be a surprise." Damien stood and offered Susan his hand. "You just have to trust me."

CHAPTER SIXTY-EIGHT

KING SPUN THE STEERING WHEEL TO THE RIGHT AND EASED his foot off the brake as he completed the turn. His eyes were glued to the rearview mirror, his stomach flexed as he anxiously waited to see if the same black SUV that he believed was following them would do the same.

Alvarez was leaning forward and staring in the side mirror. "There it is. Definitely following us."

King didn't react. He remained calm and continued driving at the pace of traffic. "Can you get the plates?"

Alvarez twisted in his seat. Squinting through the back window, he shook his head. "Too far. But it's a black Ford Explorer."

"We shouldn't slow down."

"No. Keep him back." Alvarez kept shifting his eyes between the side mirror and swiveling his head around to look behind them. "Who do you think it is?"

King had a suspect in mind the moment he was sure they were being followed. He summed up what Cecelia Garcia told Samantha last night. Alvarez questioned why King hadn't told him until now. King expected a phone call, not for Garcia to track them down.

"I don't know." Alvarez scrubbed his hand over his chin. "The vehicle looks too expensive for a journalist."

That, King could agree on. But if not Joey Garcia, then who was following them?

"Call it in." King unclipped the radio from the dash and handed it to Alvarez. "See if we can get a patrol car to pick it up."

King's thoughts churned as he listened to Alvarez communicate with dispatch. When he turned left, so did the SUV. Squinting into the mirror, he knew they couldn't make their next stop without first losing the tail. But when did they pick it up? Was it before or after their last home visit? King swore it was after they met with Rose Wild, but it could have been when leaving Mrs. Thompson's. Mostly he was asking himself what, if anything, it had to do with what they just learned.

Alvarez palmed the radio and relayed what King had already heard come through the radio. "A patrol unit is in the area. Should pick him up any minute."

The detectives' morning had been busy. First, they spoke with Mrs. Thompson, who was still not happy with Samantha's article in the *Times*. Their next visit, with Rose, didn't prove any better. She was still angry for basically being under house arrest without ever being charged with a crime.

"Thailand was Donny's idea," Rose explained. *"I would never go there without him."*

But Rose had to stay, and King didn't blame either of the women for not being particularly thrilled to see him come to visit again. Their grief was only escalated by the perpetual news cycle. They doubted that the police were any closer to catching the SOB who was responsible.

"My husband may have been murdered, and I have to find out

about it through the evening news," Mrs. Thompson snapped at one point during their conversation.

Her words were still ringing in King's ears. He'd put up with the abuse, hoping they would reveal the secrets to what it was he was after. His patience eventually paid off as both women told him Damien Black had recently been in contact with their partners prior to their deaths.

Alvarez turned to King and asked, "Any chance it might be Damien Black?"

It had crossed King's mind. "Both Wild and Thompson said Black was seeking funding from their partners, yet no one gave him any money. Why?"

Alvarez was staring in the mirror when he responded, "Because they were keeping their money for themselves."

That could be, King thought. They knew what Thompson and Counts were being accused of, but what King couldn't shake was how it also gave Black motive to kill them. To make matters worse, they were about to sit down with Joan Collins, hoping the third interview of the day was the charm. But, first, they had to lose this tail.

"Where did it go?" Alvarez spun in his seat.

King checked his mirrors, his eyes searching. He'd taken his attention away from the SUV for one second and it disappeared. "Did you see a patrol car?"

"I didn't see shit," Alvarez said.

King slowed the car to a stop and parked alongside the curb. They waited, searching, wondering if the SUV would pass.

After several minutes of nothing, Alvarez said, "We weren't making that up, were we?"

"No," King said. "It was definitely tailing us."

Alvarez jumped back on the radio, relaying to dispatch an update to the situation. King palmed his cellphone and cursed. He'd missed another call from Sam. Hitting the call back button, he pressed the phone to his ear.

Samantha answered in a panic. "Alex, baby, are you all right?"

"I'm fine. What's wrong?"

Samantha summed up her phone call with Cecelia earlier in the morning.

"What vehicle does Garcia drive?" King flicked his gaze to his partner. "It's not a black Ford Explorer, is it?"

"You had one following you, too?"

"Who is it?"

"It's not Garcia, but we must be close to discovering who the hell Loxley is because it feels like I'm being watched."

King said Garcia hadn't been located, then asked, "Did you meet with Ronald Hyland?"

"Went about as well I expected." When King asked when she was followed, Samantha said on her way to the meeting. "Security escorted me out of the building before I had a chance to tell Hyland his name was on the same list as the others."

"Guess who visited at least two of our victims before they died." King paused, but only for a second. "Damien Black."

"Shit."

"What is it?"

"Susan is with him now."

"Sam," King sighed, "You have to tether yourself to her. It's important we don't tip off Damien that we're on to him. If we do, he'll do whatever it takes to survive. And I mean, *whatever* it takes."

CHAPTER SIXTY-NINE

ALVAREZ WAS SPEAKING TO KING WHEN HE ASKED, "Should we pick him up?"

King couldn't decide. Damien seemed like the likely suspect but couldn't be certain. There wasn't enough conclusive evidence to nail him to the wall. At least not yet.

Alvarez prompted, "What do you want to do?"

"Nothing yet." King put the car in gear and drove. "We take our chances."

King assured Sam that it was a good thing Susan was with Damien Black. It meant they had eyes on him while they worked to close the circle of guilt surrounding him. He understood Samantha's fears, but a hostage situation seemed unlikely and King was willing to roll the dice and take his chances.

By the time he and Alvarez arrived to the Collins' house, the street was quiet but Joan was home. She opened the door, letting a sudden release of damp air escape the closed-up house. King could smell the tears of sadness he knew she had been crying, could see it in her bloodshot eyes.

"Sorry, to bother you Mrs. Collins—"

"I've already spoken to your colleagues, Detectives Robbins and Zimmerman," Joan said with lips as flat as her eyes.

"We're aware, Mrs. Collins."

"Then why are you here?"

King answered her with a look that said, *you really want to do this here?*

Her eyes flicked between them, then she stepped to the side and opened the front door further as she motioned for them to enter with a single head nod.

Her depression could be felt—a heavy air that made it difficult to breathe. Like summer in the Carolinas. Based on the papers scattered across the dining room table, and the notes King stole a peek at, Joan was already busy arranging her husband's funeral.

Joan stopped in the middle of the room and turned with clasped hands held down at her waist. "With the second set of homicide detectives coming to my house since my husband's death, I can't help but wonder if Parker was murdered."

Despite the theory King and Sam had discussed yesterday, they had no further evidence to suggest Parker's car crash was anything other than an unfortunate accident.

"I'll take your lack of a response as a yes." Joan moved to the dining room table and sat at the far end. Swinging one leg over the other, she continued, "I'll also assume the reason you're here is because of what the news is reporting."

King gave no indication of his thoughts on the vigilante or how irresponsible it was of Nancy Jordan to be instigating such hysteria. Instead, he swung the pendulum toward the questions he needed answers to with hopes of finding his way to Damien Black next. "When you were at Metro State yesterday, did you see anything out of the ordinary?"

"What constitutes ordinary?"

"Did your husband meet with anybody? Did you see him speak with anyone that might have upset him?"

"I saw Parker speaking with the reporter, Joey Garcia, after the event."

Alvarez jotted notes down on a pocket-sized pad while King asked the questions.

King asked, "Did that surprise you?"

"Not initially."

King tilted his head and arched a single eyebrow. "But later?"

Joan bobbed her head in tiny nods. "Joey covered my husband and our business before in the *Times*. But yesterday was different."

"How so?"

"I saw Joey arrive late, and he was without a pen, notepad, or even a recorder. All he had was an envelope tucked under his arm."

"Any idea what was inside the envelope?" King asked, already assuming it was what Samantha pulled from the wreckage.

Joan shook her head no.

"Did he speak to you?"

"That was what was also strange. No, he didn't. But I saw him confront my husband."

"And you don't know what they talked about?"

Joan cast her gaze to her diamond wedding ring and shook her head. "Parker was... gone before I had the chance to ask. That was the last I saw him and nothing was recovered from impound. I can only assume that whatever was inside that envelope, Joey kept for himself."

She dabbed at the corners of her eyes and the detectives gave her a moment's pause before asking, "Do you recognize this man?"

Joan took the picture of Damien Black from King's hand and studied it. "I know Mr. Black. Why do you ask?"

"In what capacity do you know him?"

Joan handed the glossy image back to King. "Mr. Black has been seeking funding for his non-profit computer science project, Backstage. He's come to us several times in the last few months, hoping to convince us to write a check to help keep his doors open."

"Did he convince you?"

"Despite what you may have heard about me, I'm a tough sell." Joan mentioned Damien Black's prior conviction as her reason for not trusting him. "We have a reputation to uphold. I can't let our shareholders question our personal decisions."

King found her statement to be completely ironic, considering the dirt he knew Sam had found in her husband's car yesterday afternoon. Joan's next statement nearly made his heart stop.

"Perhaps you might be better off speaking with Ronald Hyland."

King's eyes narrowed. "Ronald Hyland?"

Joan nodded.

"Why him?"

Joan perked up. "You know who he is, right?"

"I do," King said.

"Good. Because I saw him with Mr. Black at the country club this morning. They've been together there quite a bit lately, actually. Surprising, considering Ronald Hyland's health." Joan frowned. "The man had a pacemaker implanted a year ago and, honestly, I thought he'd never pick up a club again. Perhaps he'll be the lucky one to give Damien the money he's after." Joan glanced to her watch as she stood. "Anything else before I go?"

King glanced to Alvarez. "That will be all for now," Alvarez said.

Joan walked the men to the door. "You'd tell me if my husband was murdered, wouldn't you?"

King looked her directly in the eyes, thinking how Ronald Hyland was the last name on the list found in Joey Garcia's home office. "Of course."

CHAPTER SEVENTY

SUSAN'S BODY ACHED AS SHE SAT STIFF IN HER SEAT, waiting for Damien Black to tell her where they were going. From the moment the wheels started spinning, Damien went quiet. It only heightened Susan's awareness of the dangers she might be getting herself involved in, but by the look on Damien's face, something was clearly on his mind.

Glancing at him out of the corner of her eye, Susan could see Damien's thoughts swirling behind dark eyes. With one hand on the wheel, Damien drove without hurry. He was so deep inside his head, Susan didn't think he'd hear anything she said.

Turning to her window, Susan watched the world go by. The radio was off as they bumped along to an undisclosed location to meet with a person whose name couldn't be revealed.

Susan's lips went dry. She didn't like the idea of surprises with all the talk of a vigilante on the loose. Feeling her bundle of nerves only ball up tighter inside her stomach, Susan had to let Samantha know of their change of plans.

Keeping Damien in her peripheral, Susan unclasped her

clutch and removed her phone. She wasn't surprised Damien didn't react. Without wasting a second, Susan tapped at the screen with her thumbs.

With DB now. Going to lunch. Don't know where. Oh, and I found this...

Susan attached the photo she took of Ronald Hyland's business card, along with the notes Damien had jotted down. If anything, she hoped Samantha would know what they meant. Then she added, *also a pacema—*

Attacking like a shark shooting out from the deep abyss, Damien's hand landed on Susan's, cutting her off before she could finish typing. Susan startled with surprise. His fingers closed around her phone. With her thumb near the send button, she tapped the screen just before Damien stole her phone away from her.

"Excuse me?" Her lips parted.

The corners of Damien's glimmering eyes crinkled. "I need you here." He held up her phone. "Not here."

"I was here," she spun her index finger around in a circle, indicating her presence in the car, "until you disappeared."

Damien chuckled. "But you're not present when your attention is on your device."

She sighed and flashed him a look of disbelief. Only a second ago, she was a ghost to him. Now she was at fault for ignoring him? What was this guy's deal?

"Damien, please. I have a business to run."

Still driving, he asked, "When's the last time you unplugged?"

Forever ago, Susan thought. "I'm a small business owner, I can't afford that luxury. Now, can I please have my phone back?"

Damien shook his head no. "Today, you do have that luxury." He stuffed her phone inside his left breast pocket, making it clear the conversation was over.

Susan couldn't make up her mind about him. One second he was hot, the next he was cold. Worse, she swam in perpetual doubt when having to remind herself that Damien could potentially be the murdering psychopath everyone was chasing.

Susan said, "Then at least tell me where you're taking me."

Damien turned his head and grinned. "To lunch."

"Yes. You've said that already." Susan was growing frustrated. "Does this place have a name?"

Damien said, "It's a place I'm sure you'd like."

"How do you know what I like?"

The vehicle slowed to a stop when approaching a red light. Angling his body toward hers, he reached up and tucked a loose strand of hair behind her ear. Susan's heart fluttered inside her belly the moment her breath hitched. His touch was gentle. That was perhaps what scared her most. There was too much unknown to trust who this guy really was and what his underlying intentions were.

"I know that you like seafood over steak. Prefer lattes to espressos. Most of all, I know you'll never say no to Mexican food."

Susan was breathless as she stared into his gaze. "How do you know so much about me?"

The light clicked to green. Damien continued to stare. "There is a lot I know about you."

The car honked behind them. Damien eased off the brake, applied pressure to the accelerator.

"You've done your research."

Damien flicked his gaze to her. "I like to know what I'm getting myself into."

Susan raised her eyebrows. "And so do I."

"I'm still not telling you where we're going."

Turning her head away, Susan knew exactly where in the city they were. The sun was shining bright between scattered cloud cover, and everything was fine except for what she didn't know about the man she was with. That kept her on an uncomfortable edge.

Ever since meeting him, Damien had a stalkerish ability to be everywhere. He seemed to know what to say and how to phrase it to get the response he needed. But knowing her personal likes and dislikes was a new line he had crossed. Susan didn't like feeling so exposed. It wasn't information that could just be pulled from an About page on her website. He knew details to personal likings that only her friends knew. How did he learn so much about her? Why did he act like it wouldn't scare her?

Susan slowly turned her head and glanced at his breast pocket. Damien's narrowing eyes were flickering between the mirrors. He was watching something—perhaps making sure they weren't being followed. Susan needed to get her phone back but didn't know how. She still couldn't believe he had taken it—the one thing that she had to defend herself with.

When they arrived to Maya's Cantina, Damien said, "It's no Rio Grande, but I'm hoping you'll enjoy the food nonetheless."

Susan's palms were sweating with nerves when suddenly Damien slammed on the brakes, tires squealing. Susan's seatbelt caught, digging into her chest when she palmed the dash as she braced herself against the sudden impact tossing her body forward. They had nearly collided directly into the front end of a shiny new Ford Explorer that was now staring them down.

Damien tipped forward, leaned over the wheel, and said to the driver of the other vehicle, "Well, you going to move or what?"

Susan stared into the vehicle but couldn't see through the intense glare reflecting in the glass. "I think he wants you to move first."

Damien grumbled a few choice words. They were both surprised when they saw the passenger door swing open. A man with a high-powered camera lens stepped out and immediately began snapping pictures of her and Damien.

"Oh, you got to be kidding me." Damien rolled down his window and started yelling at the man to stop.

The man's arms were covered in tattoos, his black shirt tight against his chest. "You Damien Black?" he asked, still snapping pictures as he approached Damien's door.

Damien's eyebrows were pulled together in a perfect V. "Who wants to know?"

Hiding behind his camera, the shutter kept clicking. "It's him," he called out to the black SUV.

Susan didn't have a good feeling about this. "Let's just leave."

Damien shouted through his window, "What's this about?"

"The vigilante who's come to Denver." The man lowered his camera just a bit. "It's you, isn't it?"

"Why would you think that?"

"Because you teach people how to hack."

Susan had a sudden loss of appetite. Wishing she had her cellphone, she tapped Damien on his arm, watching with her heart knocking in her chest as the driver of the SUV stepped out.

Damien put the car in reverse but found himself boxed in as another mid-sized car sat behind him waiting to park. They were trapped.

Susan locked her door and said a quick prayer. The driver strode toward them, hiding beneath a baseball cap and mirrored sunglasses. Susan swore he was staring at her. Suddenly, he shifted direction and went straight to Damien's window.

They stared at each other for a long pause before the

stranger said, "I know who you are and what you're planning to do next." The man glanced to Susan. Susan couldn't see his eyes, but his glare could be felt. Susan's limbs were shaking as she gulped down a couple of breaths and remained quiet. The man turned back to Damien. "I also know he's paid you lots of money to protect him. But his time is up. You just wait and see."

"I don't know what you're talking about," Damien responded.

A small smirk curled the corners of the stranger's lips. "I thought you might say that." He pushed a tiny square of folded paper through Damien's window. Damien pinched it between his fingers and continued staring at his own reflection in the stranger's sunglasses. "Now, if you'll excuse me, I have to get out of someone's way."

Susan watched the two men load up into the Explorer and back away in the same direction they had come from, disappearing behind the restaurant. Damien was staring at the note when she asked, "What was that about?"

Damien's face was pale as a ghost. He unlocked his phone and made a call. Susan heard the line click over. Damien said into the phone, "There's been a change of plans. We need to meet now."

CHAPTER SEVENTY-ONE

I HADN'T HEARD BACK FROM SUSAN. HER PHONE KEPT going to voicemail each time I called. Something wasn't right. I regretted my decision to use her to draw out Damien Black's location.

"Susan. It's me again. Call me back," I left in another voicemail. "I want to ask you about the images you just sent me."

My stomach was hard as a rock the moment I killed the call. I went back to staring at the photo Susan sent, trying to decipher her message that seemed to have gotten cut off.

...also pacema

I swept my gaze up and stared ahead while I tried to guess what it was she was trying to tell me. My windows were cracked, but the inside of my car was heating up the longer I sat without running the engine.

Her sudden disappearance sparked dozens of visualizations about what Damien might be doing to her now. I didn't want to think about any one of them, but the thoughts wouldn't stop. I wished it was me with him—it *should* have been me. It was impossible not to assume Damien had caught her taking this photo—sending this message—and learning we were on to him.

I dropped my gaze back to the image. The note seemed personal and I wondered how Susan managed to get it without Damien seeing. She was taking so many risks. I hoped they weren't all in vain.

Then it hit me.

Pacemaker.

Was that what she was trying to tell me? That Damien was working on hacking a pacemaker? If he was our guy, whose was it? And why did Damien care? I immediately thought back to my visit with Ronald Hyland. It had to be him. Perhaps that was why I thought he had a heart attack right in front of me. His heart was failing him and his pacemaker gave his heart the jolt it needed to stay ticking.

But there was still something else that I couldn't ignore.

Damien Black having Ronald Hyland's business card was one thing, but having King's name on that same note was troublesome. Especially with Cecelia Garcia saying Joey could be targeting the detectives who took something from him. It was clear both King and Hyland were likely targets, but who would Loxley go after first?

I needed to make sure King saw this.

I fired off a quick text message and he called me back almost immediately.

"Did you look at the image I just sent you?" I asked.

"Where did it come from?"

"Susan sent it." Everyone was a possible target. No one was safe. But I reminded King how I was convinced Hyland was next to die. He saw it, too.

"Have you spoken to Susan? Is she still with Damien?" He was traveling the same single conclusive path as I was.

It was rare for King to sound panicked, but in that moment I could hear his heart racing. I didn't know—didn't know anything except for what I just sent. "I can only assume she is," I said.

"Christ, he's going to kill Hyland," King muttered into a static filled line. Then he told me about his visit with Joan and how Damien was seen with Hyland this morning.

"What time was that?" I asked. King gave me an approximate time. It was before my own visit to Hyland's offices. If Damien was planning to kill Hyland, why didn't he do it then? Or did he try when I was with Hyland at his office and failed? Then King let me in on the reason he was panicked.

"Ronald Hyland recently had a pacemaker installed." King instantly confirmed my assumption about what I thought Susan was trying to tell me. "If Loxley is planning to kill him, that's how he's going to do it."

I shared the last half of Susan's message, the part that got caught off. If King had any doubts before, he didn't now.

"Sam, we need to learn where they are."

"Susan isn't answering. I've called a dozen times. She went silent after she sent me that photo."

King didn't say it, but I knew he was afraid of what might happen to Susan. "Keep trying," he said. "If we can let Black know that he's of interest to us, then maybe we can get Susan out of there before anything happens to her."

Suddenly, Hyland's Tesla appeared at the parking garage exit. His driver was behind the steering wheel, but I could see Ronald's silhouette in the back seat.

I turned the key and listened to my engine's belts whine. Following Hyland, I said, "There is a way I might be able to stop this."

CHAPTER SEVENTY-TWO

THERE WAS ONLY ONE THING ON SUSAN'S MIND AS DAMIEN led her into the upscale restaurant in south Denver by her arm. She had to get her phone back, and do it soon.

Keeping stride with Damien, Susan noticed he was playing with the pacemaker still hidden in his pants pocket. Everything seemed to be spiraling out of control, and Susan swore she was at ground zero of whatever was about to happen.

"Who are we meeting here?" Susan asked the moment Damien reached for the door.

Based on the sudden change of plans and Damien's earlier phone call, they were likely not meeting who he'd originally planned. Either way, nerves were high and tensions were tight.

"You'll see soon enough," Damien said under his breath.

A group of three exited the restaurant as they entered. Susan studied her surroundings. There was a handful of white-collar business professionals eating at the bar, a dozen others scattered around various tables amongst the socializers and afternoon crowd lingering in a cool environment to escape the afternoon heat.

"Mr. Black," the hostess said cheerily. "Right this way."

Susan didn't react to how the hostess seemed to have been expecting him, but the fact that she never once glanced or acknowledged Susan's presence only made her even more nervous than before.

Damien never shared what was on the note that was given to him by the driver they'd nearly collided with in the Maya Cantina's parking lot. Was it paparazzi? A freelance journalist wanting to get in on the vigilante hype? Susan didn't know. The entire situation was odd, and her nerves were still crackling with enough electricity to light up the darkened room they now meandered their way through.

The hostess led them to a private room in the back. "Your guest should be arriving momentarily."

Susan was hugging her body when she stared in Damien's direction. "What are we doing here?" she asked as soon as it was just the two of them. "I thought you wanted to take me to lunch. This seems like something else entirely."

Damien paced back and forth on the opposite side of the long rectangular table. Susan watched as he kept glancing toward the entrance before finally falling into a chair somewhere in the middle. He filled a glass with the pitcher of ice water and proceeded to chug it until the last drop. Damien was still rocking back and forth on the balls of his feet when Susan heard her phone hum.

Without looking at her, Damien pulled her phone out from his breast pocket and glanced at the screen. Susan waited for a reaction—some kind of facial expression to let her know who was calling—except Damien gave her nothing. He tipped his head back, closing his eyes as he inhaled a deep breath of air.

With a beating heart, Susan stared at her phone, planning

how she could take it back without him noticing. It seemed like an impossible task, one in which she needed to complete.

Quietly, she floated to where he was sitting and gently gripped his shoulders. Beginning to massage out the tension, she asked, "Why are you so tight?"

Damien dropped his chin to his chest and groaned.

"You're not the vigilante." Susan wasn't sure what to believe, still thinking that if it wasn't Damien who was killing these people, then perhaps it was his student Marion. "The media spins stories to increase ratings. Trust me, I know. This will eventually blow over."

Damien lifted his head and turned his gaze to meet with hers. Susan's breath caught in her throat. "It's too late," he said.

Susan's thumbs stopped pressing into his muscle tissue. "Too late for what?"

Damien's eyelids went half-mast as he gently shook his head. Suddenly, Damien's eyes clicked wide open and Susan felt his body stiffen as he stared toward the door. She turned to see what he was staring at and immediately recognized the titan of cyber security, Ronald Hyland.

Susan's lips parted as they both watched Hyland make his way to the back room.

It couldn't be coincidence, Susan thought. The note. His business card. The reason Damien couldn't tell her who they were meeting with. But did Damien really expect Susan to have Hyland convince her to trust him enough to take him on as a client?

Susan removed her damp hands from Damien's shoulders. He stood, and she took a single step back.

Ronald Hyland was unbuttoning his sport coat when he entered the private room. He barely noticed Susan, instead focusing his energies on Damien. They gripped hands with a tight squeeze. With a tiny wag of his head, Hyland motioned for Damien to follow him to the other side of the room so they could talk in private.

Susan stood quietly with her hands clasped over her stomach, trying not to look in their direction when she heard Hyland whisper, "What is she doing here?"

Susan didn't know what to do. It was obvious Hyland knew who she was, but how? She stared at the table, wanting to steal her phone while keeping an ear on their conversation. They whispered in hushed tones, making it impossible for Susan to hear what was being said. When she thought no one was looking, she lunged her hand forward, swiping her phone off the table and taking it back into her possession.

Hiding it behind her clutch, her heartrate shot through the roof when Damien called out, "Susan, what do you think you're doing?"

Slowly, she rolled her eyes to Damien. Had he seen her? Her pulse ticked hard and fast as both men were now staring at her. She licked her dry lips, murmured, "I was just looking to freshen up in the powder room."

Damien stared without blinking, as did Hyland. Susan held her breath, hoping Damien believed her lie. Seconds froze as her vision tunneled. Then Damien pointed across the room. "The ladies' room is that way."

Susan released the breath she was holding and forced herself to smile. Hurrying down the hallway, she pushed open the ladies' room door and closed herself into an empty stall. It was just her in the bathroom when she checked her phone, noticing all the missed calls. She immediately called Samantha.

"Did you get my message?" Susan said as soon as Samantha answered.

"Where are you? Are you all right? I've been trying to call." Sam's words came flying at her as fast as bullets. Susan heard a car door shut on Samantha's line and told her where she was. The sound of feet running over concrete filled Susan's ears.

"Is he with you now?" Sam asked.

"Black is meeting with Hyland. I don't know what's going on, Sam, but something isn't right." Susan mentioned Damien's strange behavior, including how he stole her phone. "I need to get out of here."

"You're in luck."

Susan paused and looked up.

"I'm outside. Coming to you now."

Susan rose off the toilet where she was sitting on the lid. "You're *here*?"

"I followed Hyland. I was hoping he would lead me to you. Listen, I don't have time to explain, but Hyland is in danger."

"That's what I was trying to say." Susan mentioned what happened in the previous parking lot. "Damien is going to do something, isn't he?"

"Just stay where you are and tell me about the pacemaker."

"Oh, good. You figured it out." Susan explained, but it didn't make sense until Sam completed the puzzle. "That's how he's going to kill him?"

"Maybe." There was more rustling through the phone line. "I'm inside. Where are you?"

Susan told her about the private room in the back. Suddenly, Susan heard shouts coming from Damien's direction. "Oh, shit, it's happening."

"Stay where you are."

The shouts increased and it sounded like a chair may have been knocked over.

"I'm going out. I have to see what's going on."

Susan dropped the call and rushed through the hallway, swinging her body back inside the private room. She yelped when seeing Ronald Hyland lying completely flat on his back. Covering her mouth with her trembling hand, she watched as Damien ripped open Hyland's collared shirt. *He did it. The bastard actually killed him.*

"Damien?"

Damien's head spun around as soon as he heard Susan's meek voice. "Don't just stand there, call for help, dammit."

Susan turned to face the door just as Samantha entered the room. They both shared a look, then Susan began to cry.

Samantha snapped her neck to Damien. "What did you do?"

"Nothing. He fainted." Damien had Hyland stripped down to his bare chest. "Something is wrong with his pacemaker."

Samantha ran across the room, skidding in next to Damien on her knees. "How did you know about—"

Damien was checking Hyland's pulse when he said, "Because I was the one he hired to engineer the software to prevent it from ever getting hacked."

CHAPTER SEVENTY-THREE

I couldn't believe it. It happened so fast. Susan was still ghost white and pacing the room like a vulture circling overhead when I repeated what I just told King. "Damien Black isn't Loxley."

King asked, "How can you be so sure?"

I turned and looked over my shoulder. The EMTs that arrived shortly after Susan called 911 were wheeling Hyland's body out of the restaurant on a stretcher. "Because Hyland is dead. It happened right in front of me."

The line went silent and, for a second, I thought I had lost my connection with King. Then he asked, "Was it his pacemaker?"

I told King everything, spilling my guts with raw emotion pouring out of me. I shared my thoughts, even those that still hadn't yet gelled. Even why I followed Hyland here, and that Damien was meeting with Hyland to help convince Susan to take him on as a new client. King listened without interruption, all the way until I told him Hyland's pacemaker had malfunctioned.

"It's no accident, Sam."

A part of us all suspected it wasn't. Loxley had killed Hyland just as he did the others. Even Damien couldn't believe someone was able to override the security protection he wrote himself. But, again, we had nothing to prove what we believed was happening was actually true.

"Wait, back up." King needed to be caught up. "Hyland hired Damien?"

King wanted to know everything I knew, and after I explained my side of the story, I shared that Hyland had hired Damien to write the software to protect his pacemaker from being hacked. "Hyland suspected he was on the list—"

"Why would he think that?"

I didn't have an answer, but I could assume it had something to do with Nancy Jordan's vigilante story. King groaned. I could imagine his skeptical eyes crinkling as he tried to make sense of the mess.

I said, "All I know is that we had it wrong."

"Lieutenant Baker is still going to want us to get a statement from Damien."

I flicked my gaze across the room. Damien was rubbing his hand in circles between Susan's shoulder blades, whispering something into her ear. She was shaken up, but I knew she would get through this. We all would.

"I don't think he'll have issue answering your questions," I said, thinking back to what Damien said about them coming face-to-face with a disguised man driving a black Ford Explorer—the same make and model that seemed to be following us all.

"There's only one problem," King said. "If Damien isn't who we thought he was, then who the hell is Loxley?"

A text buzzed the line. I pulled my phone away from my ear and glanced at the screen. My heart skipped a beat. This couldn't be coincidence.

Let's have that drink. What do you say?

With a pinched expression, I brushed my lips against the microphone piece and said, "Someone who drives a black Ford Explorer."

"Not helpful."

"Listen," I steeled my nerves as I prepared myself for the final showdown with the one person who managed to allude all of us, "Garcia just messaged me."

"Just now?" King's voice raised a notch higher.

"He wants to meet." I told King where.

"I'm not far. I'll meet you there. But, Sam—"

"I know. He's dangerous," I said, thinking about the man I thought I knew but didn't.

"Please, don't do anything until I arrive."

I didn't make any promises. Ending my call, I spun around. As soon as Susan met my eye, she asked, "What is it?"

I flitted my eyes around the room, wanting to look at anything but her. My mind swirled as I wondered if, and how, Loxley was choosing to watch us now—and if Garcia really could be him. The timing he chose to message me was remarkable. It was enough to make me think he was the man we were all after.

After I shared my plans with Susan, she called out to Damien. "Show Samantha the note that driver of the Ford Explorer gave you."

Suddenly, I was lightheaded. *Note? What note?* Why was I just learning about this now?

Damien hurried across the floor, unfolding the small square of paper as he walked. Handing it to me, I read what it said. Sweeping my gaze up, I looked Damien in the eyes.

"I don't know what it means." He raised both of his eyebrows. "Do you?"

The poetic text I read flashed behind my eyelids. "I do now."

CHAPTER SEVENTY-FOUR

"I DON'T KNOW, SAM."

Susan didn't know if it was Joey Garcia who gave them this note. I explained what he looked like again.

She responded, "I heard you the first time. He hid his face. I don't know what he looked like."

I pinched my lips, extremely focused on solving this problem before another victim was claimed. Ronald Hyland was the last name on the list King took from Garcia. We were now out of clues. What was Loxley's plan? Who would he target next? I feared he would disappear before getting caught and we would lose him forever.

Still looking me in the eye, Susan said, "Honestly, Sam. I don't know who this man was."

It didn't matter. I was losing time. Garcia texted and told me to find him at the Motel 6 on W. 49th Ave. and Federal Blvd. I knew exactly where it was. I passed the sign every time I was heading West on I-70. It was just north of Lakeside and I knew I could be there in less than ten minutes if traffic was good.

"I've got to go."

Susan grabbed my arm before I could get too far. She asked, "Do you want company?"

I shifted my gaze to Damien talking with restaurant management on the opposite side of the room. "You okay staying behind with him?"

Susan's brow wrinkled. "Should I be?"

I gave Damien one last assessment. "I think so."

"Doesn't matter, Allison and Erin are on their way." Susan ran a hand over her head.

"Take a table near the front," I said, gripping her hand. "Make sure an employee knows you're there."

She nodded. "I'll be fine. Go, meet with Garcia."

I leaned in and we hugged—told each other to be safe. I turned toward the exit and bounded toward the door.

"And don't do anything stupid, Sam," Susan called after me. "I want you to catch Loxley—whoever this asshole is— but I want you to come home in one piece, too."

"Don't worry." I smiled, backpedaling my way out of the private room. "I've got this."

Then I was off to have that drink with my colleague with hopes of putting an end to this madness. Despite what I told Susan, I was afraid. But I wasn't going alone. King was meeting me there. So, with a white knuckled grip on the wheel, I made my way across town, reciting the note the mysterious driver gave to Damien. It read more like a poem, but was as creepy as everything else I received from Loxley. It had to be him.

You'll find me at Motel 6 where rooms are rented cheap.

I didn't want to have to kill these men, but their greed made it hard for me to sleep.

Now is my last stand before I'm buried six feet deep.

It was impossible not to think of Garcia's struggles, his wife's worries, and what language Loxley chose to use when communicating with me. But still, I didn't want to believe he was actually behind these murders.

Pellets of sweat formed on my brow as I retreated deep inside my head.

I was excited and nervous, a flutter of mixed emotions rolling in thick waves through my entire body. I'd been waiting to confront Garcia ever since King found my Thompson article in his trash bin, and now it was about to happen. I thought about what I would say, what I would do if he reacted violently. Soon, the ache from a clenched jaw spread to my ears as I pulled into the motel parking lot. I slowed my wheels as I circled around looking for a black Ford Explorer. I didn't see it anywhere, but I did find Garcia's red Camry.

Suddenly, it hit home what was happening. It didn't seem real.

I parked on the opposite side of the building and edged the wall until coming to the door that housed Garcia. It was on ground level. As I felt my shirt sticking to my sweaty chest, I listened to the sound of the highway humming along not far away. I looked for King, hoping he'd arrive soon. It was just me and the fate that waited for me behind this closed door. Nothing was more frightening.

My breath was shallow and I had my shoulders pressed so deep into the cool concrete wall, I thought we might just become one. But I wanted to make sure to stay out of sight. I stood like that for what felt like forever, then I heard the sounds of sirens wailing off in the distance. I crossed my fingers it was King. My heart lunged, and my entire body flinched, when I heard the single pop of a gunshot, now ringing loud in my ears.

It came from Garcia's room, only feet from where I was standing.

As soon as I knew I was okay, my eyes flew open and I

lunged for Garcia's doorknob. The door opened with ease and it slammed into the back wall with a loud crash. I rushed inside to see what happened.

Blurry contrails filled my vision as I frantically looked to the bed, then the bathroom, before coming to an abrupt stop. Then everything stilled.

Slowly, I padded across the floor, heading in the direction of where I could see legs sticking out from behind the bed.

Garcia's body was sprawled out across the floor between the wall and the Queen-sized bed, still neatly made. A Glock 17 lay next to him; a single gunshot to his head had his eyes left open and looking like white marbles. It wasn't worth checking to see if he was still alive. I knew he wasn't.

"Why, Joey? Why did you do this?" I took my eyes off the blood and called 911 to report it. I didn't know what I said to dispatch. All I could think about was his family, and how he left Katie and Cecelia behind.

As soon as I was off the phone, I searched the room for clues. I was hoping Joey left a note, telling us why he decided to end his life here, now, after asking me to meet him.

He wanted me to find him. It wasn't until I stepped up to his opened laptop perched on the small table near the window that I figured it out.

The curser blinked at the end of an opened Word document.

Tipping forward, I read his note where he confessed to extortion while blaming the rich for failing Katie. One sentence stuck out in particular.

They wrote the policies that erased human dignity and turned life into a piece of data that could be categorized into profit and loss.

It made me cry. There was a lot of truth to what he said. But he still didn't have to end his fight like this.

"It didn't have to be this way." I turned my head and spoke directly to Joey.

There were other options he could have taken. But when I got to the part about naming each victim—Richard Thompson, Donny Counts, Parker Collins, and Ronald Hyland—I knew with Joey dead, it was game over.

I heard a police cruiser arrive, their sirens quieting to silence, quickly followed by the sounds of heavy boots hitting the pavement as they ran to the door. When I felt their cool breeze swirling into the room, I turned with tears in my eyes and stared at Alex.

He flicked his gaze to Garcia's legs sticking out from behind the bed, then back to me. "Sam, are you all right?"

"I heard it." My lips opened and shut as I struggled to find the words to describe what I witnessed. "When he shot himself," I pointed with my right hand, "I was just on the other side of that wall."

King stepped into the room, took me by the hand, and led me outside. Alvarez took over the room and assessed Joey's body. I was babbling through blubbered tears, telling King about the note Joey left, confessing to his crime.

King took my face between his hands and stroked my wet cheeks with the pads of his thumbs. "I'm just glad you're okay."

But I was so far from being okay. This one was going stay with me for a long time. "I was waiting for you to arrive when Joey decided life wasn't worth living."

King's broad shoulders drooped. "It could have been so much worse."

It wasn't long before the entire squad arrived. Lieutenant Baker was on scene soon after King. King took me from the small motel room and sat me on the curb in a safe spot so he could brief his superior on what happened.

I sat on the curb, hanging my head between the shoulders, feeling dozens of eyes looking at me like I was the victim. Footsteps approached but I didn't look up until an arm brushed against my body as someone sat. I lifted my head and was surprised to see Travis Turner sitting next to me.

He stared ahead at the chaos swirling around us before asking, "What happened here?"

His eyes sparkled in the sunshine like fire. "Garcia, he——" But before I could say he shot himself, I asked, "What are you doing here?"

Travis inhaled a deep breath, palmed his cellphone, and said, "I received a strange text from Garcia." He turned his phone around to show me the same poem Damien received. "Told me to meet him here."

I asked, "Why?"

Travis rested his elbows on his knees when he flicked his gaze between the boots shuffling past us. Then he turned his head and stared at the open door to where the detectives were now working. Lines of confusion deepened with each second that ticked by. Then he softly said, "I don't know."

I told Travis about Joey's suicide note—how he confessed to the crime of extortion. Travis didn't show any expression, and I attributed it to the same amount of confusion as I was also feeling.

"It doesn't seem like Joey."

"It's absolutely bonkers," I said.

A perplexed look twisted Travis's face. He stood and offered me his hand. "I need to show you something."

My thoughts froze as I stared into his eyes, asking myself, *what now?*

Travis pulled me to my feet and led me to his car. Opening the driver's side, he retrieved an envelope, cracked the seal, and showed me what was inside. "Read it," he said.

I took it between my fingers and read each page. "Is this who hacked the paper?"

"It seems like Joey might have had the same theory as I

did." Travis flashed a knowing look. "I got most of that information from his personal files."

Joey knew? Why didn't he say anything? I dropped my gaze back to the report and sorted through the data suggesting a conspiracy that was both far-fetched, *and* plausible. I said, "But I was just with Damien Black."

"Excellent." Travis sprang into action, sliding over the hood of his car, and opened the driver's door. "Then you'll know where we can find him."

CHAPTER SEVENTY-FIVE

TRAVIS WAS SPEEDING OUT OF THE MOTEL 6 PARKING LOT faster than I had time to text King.

This might not be over. I just learned something about Damien Black. Loxley might still be alive.

I swept my gaze up, watching the contrails of color fly past us as Travis floored it onto I-70 heading east. He was telling me that Hyland's name kept coming up when he was trying to learn who hacked the paper. My nerves were frayed. It took everything I had to focus on what he was saying because all I could think was how absolutely insane this was to be chasing Damien like we had the authority to make an arrest.

"I followed the clues Garcia left and it led me down this rabbit hole." Travis kept flicking his gaze between me and the highway as he filled the gaps to his story. "That's when a second name kept showing itself."

We locked eyes when I said, "Damien Black."

A knowing glimmer flashed in Travis's eyes. "So I did some research and learned who he was."

"A world-class hacker."

"And one who had a history of stealing corporate secrets."

I knew it. It'd had Damien in my sights early on but lost confidence without the evidence to suggest he could actually be the man sending me messages. But, even worse, was that I left Susan with him.

I wanted to tell King everything I was hearing, but there was no time. He was taking care of the scene at Garcia's suicide. It was all surreal—almost unbelievable.

Still holding the report, I asked Travis, "Was the paper the only company Damien hacked?"

"It's the only company I had access to." He dropped his right hand and gripped the gear shift. "Maybe, but probably not. I'm sure there are others."

What Travis was accusing Damien and Hyland of running was a genius scheme unlike anything I had ever heard of. And they nearly got away with it, too.

The only hole in this theory was that Garcia admitted in his note to killing Thompson, Counts, Collins, and Hyland. Everything suggested Damien would have been the murderer.

I saw what happened in the back of that restaurant, even looked Damien in his eyes. What I saw was fear—so much so that I believed it to be his true feeling. Now I was questioning if that was real or if it was just one hell of an act.

Flipping through the report for a third time, I asked, "Who told you to install Hyland's cyber security software on our computers?"

"I knew it was a good program before I was told to install it," Travis said. "Not more than a week before I learned our system had been breached, a sales rep from Hyland's office came to me pitching the latest version of their software."

"Coincidence?"

"Couldn't be." Travis shook his head. "I refused their offer, said that our systems were doing just fine."

"And you think Damien hacked the paper after they didn't close the sale?"

"I've yet to figure that part out, or nail down an exact time when the hack occurred, but now I'd say it seems likely that's what happened."

I pulled my hair back and hooked it around my ear. It was one hell of a business model if proved to be true. Damien exposed the vulnerability and Hyland provided the solution to solve it. They each cashed out and Travis had the details laid out with the evidence to back it up. I wondered how many other companies, small businesses, or even government institutions they conned. And that Susan was right to be cautious of Damien Black from the very beginning.

"Get off on Colorado," I said, telling Travis where to go. I was leading him back to the restaurant, but I knew our chances of finding Damien still there were slim.

By the time we arrived, Travis let me out near the front. I hurried inside and was quickly told what I already knew. Everyone who was here before was now gone. The staff was busy cleaning up and forgetting what happened earlier. I could smell the preparations being made for the soon-to-be dinner rush.

Pulling my phone out from my back pocket, I called Susan.

"Sam, you all right?"

"Joey's dead."

"Jesus, I can't take it anymore," she cried.

"Any chance you're with Damien?"

"No. Why? What's going on?"

"I'll explain later."

"Sam, I don't like your tone. What's really going on?"

I turned around and exited the building. "I'm with Travis, from work, but it appears we may have been fooled by Damien."

"What do you mean, fooled?"

Travis was staring through the open passenger side window, looking at me like he was listening. "I'll explain later. I was just hoping you knew where Damien went."

Susan didn't know where he'd gone, but I doubted he would have gone back to Backstage. He was probably on his way to the airport, jetting off to some faraway place.

"Any luck?" Travis asked as soon as I was buckled in my seat.

I shook my head no and shoved my fingers through my hair. What were we going to do? I said, "He's got to know that his secrets are out." My head wouldn't stop shaking with disbelief. "This is such a bad idea," I said, picking up the report again. "We need to hand this case over to the authorities and let them decide what to do."

Travis looked me in the eye and said, "I have a better idea."

I gave him a sideways glance.

"Let's hack the hacker."

My eyebrows squished. "You can't be serious."

Travis shrugged. "If he's on the run, it's our only chance to get him before he's gone."

We had nothing left to lose. I'd given everything I had. I had to at least let Travis try to catch this bastard.

"All right. Let's do it," I said.

CHAPTER SEVENTY-SIX

TEN MINUTES LATER, WE ARRIVED TO A DUPLEX IN A QUIET neighborhood on the north side of the city. I stared out my window the entire drive, feeling my adrenaline spike waning. My day was quickly catching up to me, exhaustion settling into my bones. But I couldn't let Damien disappear. If he did, I knew he would go underground and never surface again.

Travis opened his door and I asked, "Is this your place?"

Travis nodded and stared at the closed garage we parked in front of. "It's not much but it's home."

The yard was well-kept, and I could see a raised bed garden along the side of the house—a nice early season sprout taking off. I kicked my door open and stepped out, thinking how unreal today really was. There hadn't been one, but two deaths already, and just the thought of another made me want to vomit up what little food I had inside.

Travis held the front door open for me. "I have my computers set up in the kitchen."

I entered the dark house, pausing a moment by the door to allow my eyes time to adjust. There was an odd odor I couldn't place. I would do anything to ensure that no one else died today, but with each minute that passed we were losing precious time that only filled me with doubt.

Travis headed straight for the table where he had two laptops already open and running. Tapping away, I floated close behind, checking my phone as I went.

There was still nothing from King, but then I noticed I was also without service. I fell into the wooden chair opposite Travis. Restarting my phone, I asked, "How are you going to hack him?"

Without taking his eyes off of his work, Travis said, "I'm hoping I can use his cell phone number." He paused and locked eyes with me. Then, as if reading my mind, he added, "I found it on Backstage's website. I'll use that to track his location."

Once my phone was powered on, I still didn't have any bars. "You have service?"

Travis fingered his cellphone, resting near the right side of the keyboard. "Huh. Nothing."

I clicked my tongue and gazed out the window.

"If I can get inside his phone, I'm hoping he's dumb enough to have installed Hyland's own security app. With that, I should be able to triangulate his approximate location."

As Travis spoke, I couldn't help but think of Allison. The only difference between them was that Allison spoke a language I could actually understand. I just nodded along, trusting he knew what he was talking about.

I angled back to the table and suddenly felt my foot accidently tap Travis's beneath the table. Then, acting as if that was some kind of invitation, Travis slid his foot up my calf.

My eyes widened a fraction as I froze, hoping he was joking. Slowly, I lifted my gaze and found him staring with a glint in his eye that had me scrambling to figure out how to tell him no.

"Travis—" Things quickly got awkward.

"I'm sorry." He shook his head. "You're right. I shouldn't have done that."

Feeling extremely uncomfortable, I asked, "Is there a bathroom I can use?"

Travis was slow when pointing to the back. "Yeah, it's just around the corner."

Taking my things with me, I locked myself inside the small room, turned on the faucet, and splashed my face with cold water. I needed to cool off—wash away my sudden anger. It was a mistake. Nothing more. But how could he have gotten so distracted when I hadn't even made an invitation to flirt?

Gripping the sink ledge, I stared at my reflection and reminded myself to stay focused.

After drying my face, I opened up the medicine cabinet and began peeking around out of sheer curiosity. There were a couple toothbrushes, first-aid stuff, deodorant, and a comb. I picked up the comb and gave it a closer look. There were strands of hair attached that were much darker than Travis's dirty blonde.

Maybe a girlfriend, I thought, placing the comb back where I'd found it. I didn't know what I was looking for or why I did it, but I popped the top on the clothes hamper and gingerly pulled out one shirt after another.

There was a scent I recognized, but it wasn't Travis's. The clothes seemed to be much too big for a man his size. I closed the lid and stood there with a racing heart. Thinking back to when we arrived, I didn't remember seeing any photos of people, and the duplex seemed only half lived in.

Did he just move here? Or was he a minimalist who didn't own any stuff? I couldn't explain it, but something felt off.

Turning to the door, I pressed my ear against the wood and listened. It was quiet. Gently, I exited the bathroom and tip-toed my way across the floor until I reached what I assumed to be the garage door. Holding my breath, I turned the knob and cracked the door open.

That's when I saw it.

A black Ford Explorer.

The same vehicle that had been following all of us.

With my blood thrashing in my ears, I wondered whose house we were really at, because it certainly didn't appear to be Travis's. Feeling my adrenaline kick in again, I knew I needed to escape without being seen. But my phone was dead and the house was much too small to slip out the backdoor without being noticed.

The hairs on my neck stiffened the moment I felt the cool breeze of someone breathing down my neck.

I froze—my entire body went stiff.

I slowly turned around and flinched as Travis swiped his hand through the air before stabbing me in the neck with something sharp.

My eyes popped wide and I crumbled to the floor like dead weight, watching my world go black. Then everything went cold, and I was out.

CHAPTER SEVENTY-SEVEN

AFTER BRIEFING THE UPPER BRASS ON WHAT HAPPENED, Lieutenant Baker wanted to get an official statement from Samantha. She was first on the scene, and the only witness to hear what happened. If Garcia was Loxley, the department needed to close out the case properly before moving on.

King exited the motel room, promising to get Samantha's statement, and headed back to where he'd left his girlfriend sitting on the curb minutes ago. King's stride shortened as he approached. He looked around with a furrowed brow, wondering where she disappeared off to now. The spot was empty, As King looked around, he could only hope Sam was seeking shelter in the shade and didn't follow a scent that would take her in a new direction.

Shoving his fingers through his hair, King muttered, "Where did you go, Sam?"

King could feel it in his gut. Samantha had left without telling him why or where she was going. He knew her well enough that it must have been something enticing to get her to leave so quickly.

"Hey," King stopped a uniformed officer lingering in the

area, "there was a woman sitting here a minute ago." He pointed to the curb. "Have you seen her?"

When the officer looked confused, King gave a description of Samantha. Again, the officer shook his head. "Sorry," he said. "Haven't seen anyone sitting on the curb."

King gritted his teeth. "Ask around. Go find her. She's our only witness to what happened here."

The officer nodded and marched off to do what he was told.

King straightened his spine, held his hand above his brow to shield the sun from his eyes, and began searching for Samantha's car. If she was here, her car would be, too. Not having any luck finding it, he began weaving his way through the parking lot. After clearing the front, he made his way to the back of the building. There, Samantha's Subaru Outback was parked near the chain link fence. But there still wasn't any sign of Sam.

King jogged to the car and lifted the door handle. It was still locked. He peeked inside through the glass and saw her purse sitting on the front seat. Now King was beginning to worry. She would never leave her purse behind unless she left in a blind panic.

Reaching behind his back, he retrieved his cell phone and was about to hit dial on Sam's number when he noticed she'd already messaged him. The crease between his eyebrows deepened as he turned his back to the sun beating down overhead. Reading her message, heat rose behind his eyelids.

Damien Black?

He twisted his spine and glared at the motel building behind him.

The sky spun overhead as King tried to make sense of what Samantha was trying to tell him. He'd read the note Garcia left behind. It read like a suicide note, but was it?

They had been treating it as such, but should they not be? Now he was more confused than ever.

Pounding the green button on his phone, King called Samantha.

It went straight to voicemail.

"Sam, I just got your message." King started making his way to the front of the building. "Where are you? What information are you going on? This is a serious allegation. Call me back as soon as you get this."

As soon as King lowered his phone from his ear, Alvarez was waving him in with his arm. "King, you've got to come see this."

Picking up his pace, King asked his partner, "What is it?"

Alvarez was already heading in the direction of the motel room when he said, "You've got to see it to believe it."

Stepping back into the room, King wiped the sweat off his forehead and watched as a team of technicians worked on Joey's body.

"They found this in his hand when they flipped over his body." Alvarez lifted up the evidence bag and handed it over to King.

King pinched the bag at its corner and moved into the light. He read the scribbled words.

Brett Gallagher knows the truth.

King asked, "What the hell does that mean?"

"We're thinking it has something to do with a message one of the investigators found on his computer."

King turned and looked over his shoulder. The investigator was still searching through Joey's laptop. King walked over and peered over the man's shoulder, asking himself who Brett Gallagher was. A clock was ticking down, almost to zero, but it was the message flashing across the screen that caught King's attention.

"Who sent it?" he asked.

"No idea. I'll have to send it to the lab for further research."

King rubbed the back of his neck, thinking that something wasn't lining up here.

"Any ideas?" Alvarez asked.

King shook his head as he took a step back.

"Where's Samantha?" Alvarez cast his gaze through the door, squinting into the bright light. "Get her inside, have her take a look at this."

King turned to Alvarez and said under his breath, "Sam's not here."

Alvarez's eyes flashed with surprise. "Where did she go?"

King shrugged. "I don't know."

Alvarez scratched his jaw as he walked to the door. King nudged him outside and said to follow him. Leading him away from others, King told him about Sam maybe having gone after Damien Black again.

"But—" Alvarez pointed to the motel room where Joey's body was being loaded up on a gurney.

"I know." King wet his lips. "I don't know the details, but what if she's right?"

Alvarez locked eyes with King. "You read Garcia's suicide note. He admitted it was him."

"He never specified he murdered these men, only that he was sorry for extorting each of the named victims."

With both hands on his hips, Alvarez rolled his eyes toward the motel room. After a pause, he asked, "Who the hell is Brett Gallagher?"

King didn't know, but now he was starting to think Garcia may have been coerced into divulging something he wanted to keep a secret. Clearly, whatever it was was worth taking his own life over.

Alvarez asked, "What are you thinking?"

"That whoever is behind that timer ticking down on

Garcia's laptop must also be the computer whiz who's killing these powerful men."

Alvarez's chest rose as he sighed. Then the officer King asked to help find Sam interrupted. "Detective, the woman you were asking about—"

"Did you find her?"

The officer shook his head. "But was told she left with a man. Six foot. Sandy blonde hair."

"And the vehicle they left in?" King assumed they took off in a car. "Did anyone see that?"

"Toyota 4Runner. Seen leaving about fifteen minutes ago."

King glanced at his watch. He knew they had an impossible lead on him. "Anyone get the plates?"

The officer frowned and diverted his eyes.

King thanked the officer and hurried to his car with Alvarez one step behind. Someone took Sam. King needed to learn who and why. Falling into the front seat of his sedan, King thought about who Sam was with before she responded to Garcia's text. Then he called Susan Young.

"Is Samantha with you?" he asked as soon as she answered.

"No, why? What's going on? I just talked to her."

"You did? Do you know what she was doing?"

"She's looking for Damien Black."

King cursed Sam for not telling him where she was going. "Did she say who she was with?"

"Travis from work. I think he's IT or something."

Susan didn't have a last name or a phone number, but King didn't need it. He had resources that could find the information he needed.

"What's going on? What kind of trouble is she in now?"

King couldn't get distracted by his own fears. "If you happen to speak to her, just tell her to call me."

CHAPTER SEVENTY-EIGHT

WITHIN MINUTES, KING HAD TRAVIS TURNER'S HOME address and the entire force was on the lookout for both Travis's vehicle, *and* Damien Black. This time, King wasn't taking any chances. Loxley had targeted Samantha from the beginning. Now he couldn't stop thinking that he'd finally gotten to her.

The tires squealed as King slammed on his brakes. Parking outside Travis's apartment building, the detectives kicked their doors open and hit the ground running. They knew what they were up against—knew time was against them.

Bounding up the stairwell, they stiff-armed their way onto the fourth floor and hurried down the hallway before taking position at Travis's front door.

Gripping his department issued Glock in one hand, King looked Alvarez in the eye and his partner nodded, giving King the go-ahead to knock.

"Travis Turner. It's the police." King's knuckles rapped on the door. "Open up."

King held his breath and listened. It was quiet inside. He pounded on the door again. "Denver Police. Open up, Travis."

Alvarez's finger brushed the trigger guard as he stared at the door knob, waiting for it to turn. Suddenly, the sound of cautious footsteps approached the door. Slowly, the knob turned and as soon as the door cracked open, King shoved a shoulder into the door, knocking the man behind it to the floor.

"Get on the ground," King shouted. "Put your hands behind your head."

"What the fuck?" the man protested, lacing his fingers behind his head as he lay flat on his stomach. "I didn't do anything."

King holstered his weapon and took the man's tattooed wrist behind his back, binding his hands together with a zip-tie. Once the threat was eliminated and the scene was secure, King asked, "You Travis Turner?"

"What?" The man's eyes locked on King's "I'm not Travis."

Alvarez said, "Let's see some ID."

The man's brow furrowed as he jutted his chin across the room. "My wallet is on the desk."

King watched as his partner approached the elaborate set of computer monitors towering over a long glass-topped desk. There were four monitors in total, each of them on, different images populating each screen. Empty Red Bull cans littered the work area. Alvarez immediately recognized the two faces in the photos nearby and didn't like what he saw.

"King, you got to come take a look at this."

King told the man to stay put or risk getting shot and made his way to the workstation. Edging the desk, he stared into the eyes of both Susan Young and Damien Black, together, inside a car. Alvarez found the wallet, removed the identification card, and shook his head when handing it to King.

Pinching the corners of the card, King said, "Aaron Martinez."

"See, I told you I wasn't Travis Turner."

"Then what are you doing here?"

"I'm house sitting for Travis while he's gone."

King handed the card back and headed into the back bedrooms to conduct a thorough sweep of the place. The first room had only a futon with sheets, tossed like someone had been sleeping on it, and cardboard boxes stacked to the ceiling. The smell of a kitty litter box was coming from somewhere near the closet. King checked that but found nothing inside. The second room King stepped into had something far more interesting.

After sweeping the closet, he moved to the dresser and stared into the eyes of his girlfriend. Then he flicked his gaze to the next framed photograph. Again, Samantha's bright eyes were gleaming. It was a shrine worshiping Samantha Bell, and next to her framed photographs were cut-out articles she had written—even her latest one on Richard Thompson.

King squeezed his hand into a fist and flexed his muscles.

Damien Black wasn't Loxley. It was Travis Turner.

As soon as he joined up with his partner, he heard Alvarez ask Aaron, "Did you take these photos?"

"Why? You like them?" Aaron grinned.

King's eyes narrowed. "You don't even know who they're of, do you?"

"Just trying to cash in on the hype, brother."

"Hype?" King's nostrils flared. "Do you know how much trouble you're in?"

"Travis swore to me he could get me a shot of the vigilante. Said I could make an easy grand. And he did. Earlier today, I captured those images."

King couldn't believe what he was hearing. Travis had orchestrated it all. Treated this like a game and played his cards well. But he wouldn't get away with it. King swore to himself he'd kill him if given the chance.

Alvarez was staring at King when King said, "This asshole is lying." He mentioned the shrine in the bedroom. Alvarez pinched his lips and stood frozen in the headlights. "Travis is Loxley and this scumbag is covering for him while he makes his getaway."

"What? That's not true." Aaron protested, suddenly looking confused. "What are you talking about? And who the hell is Loxley?"

King marched straight up to Aaron, gripped him by the collar, and threw him up against the wall. Breathing down his neck, King bared his fangs when saying, "You better start talking before I really lose my temper."

"Yeah. Anything." Aaron nodded his head vigorously. "I'll tell you anything you want to know."

"You can start by telling us where Travis said he was going."

"I don't know, man," Aaron cried. King tilted his head and shoved his knuckles deeper into Aaron's chest. "I swear. He just gave me access to his equipment as long as I took care of his cat."

Suddenly, Alvarez's cell phone rang.

"You better not be lying." King dropped Aaron to the floor. He stepped to the couch and caught sight of the cat. Scooping it into his arms, he read the cat's name imprinted on the gold collar. "Little John, of course." King shook his head in disbelief.

"Call came in," Alvarez said once he was off his phone. "Someone reported a suspicious male-female couple entering the house of Brett Gallagher."

King dropped the cat to the floor and flipped his head around.

"It sounds like it's Travis and Sam."

King turned to Aaron. "It's your lucky day, punk."

"You can't arrest me." Aaron kicked and screamed as King pulled him up to his feet.

"I'm not arresting you."

"Then where are you taking me?"

"Outside."

"But my things—"

"Are now part of our investigation."

CHAPTER SEVENTY-NINE

I FELT GROGGY, MY BODY HEAVY WITH SEDATIVE, AS I WOKE up. My eyelids felt glued shut, but not as weighed down as the bags beneath them that draped like hammocks. I struggled to keep my eyes open. I didn't know how long I had been out.

As soon as my lids clicked open, they quickly snapped shut again. Over and over it went, as I lay strapped to the bed, suspended in time.

I wasn't sure how long it went on like that, but by the time I had the strength to lift my head, I realized the predicament I was in.

"Shit," I whispered as my head hit the pillow.

"I bet you're thirsty."

Travis's voice caused me to tense. When I opened my eyes, I flinched at the sight of his hand coming straight for my brow. With nowhere to turn, he brushed my sweat-drowned bangs out of my eyes. I sucked on my tongue that tasted like a dried-out sponge. Smacking my lips together, my body screamed for liquid. I was dehydrated and drugged.

"Yes, you are," Travis said, petting me like a dog.

He smiled and stared, then reached to the nightstand,

retrieving an unopened bottle of water. I watched him twist off the cap and drop a straw through the mouthpiece before bringing it to my lips. It took all my strength just to hold my head up, but as soon as I sucked back the first gulp of cold water, I knew it was worth the pain.

"There you go, sweetheart." Travis tipped the bottle to make the suction easier. "That will make you feel better."

I finished half the bottle before spitting out the straw and gasping for air. A cool wave chilled my body and prickled my exposed skin. Suddenly, reality hit me. Travis had stripped me out of my clothes and had me tied to his bed in only my underwear.

I asked, "Where are my clothes?"

Travis hovered over me, following the movement of his finger as it grazed over the top of my underwear. Breathing harder, I watched as his erection grew, pressing against his zipper. Anticipating his desire, I thrashed against my restraints, unable to fight them off.

"No use in trying to break free." Travis's voice was as light as his finger strokes now circling my navel. "It will only hurt you."

I bucked my hips and blinked the fog out of my vision. "Travis, what do you think you're going to do?"

He bent over and pressed his wet lips against my stomach. I felt his tongue swipe against my skin. Then he murmured, "I've been waiting for this day when I could finally touch you."

My body was cold. I was scared. No one knew where I was, and only Susan knew I was with Travis. I started regretting my decision to go after Damien. Now I was sure that was Travis's plan all along—to create the perfect diversion in order to kidnap me.

I squeezed my eyes shut and opened them wide. I could feel my sense of awareness coming back—the strength in my arms flexing and releasing, battling for survival. "I should have known you were Loxley."

"That's just it." Travis grinned. "Everyone should have known, but no one was listening."

He touched my breast and I squirmed beneath his heavy palm. The front of his pants pitched taller and I was afraid of what he was planning to do with me now that he had me awake.

"You're an amazing journalist," he hooked my hair behind my ear, "but you failed to read between the lines."

I recalled the events that led us here. The more he spoke, the more sense it made. Then I remembered what I found in the bathroom—what I saw in the garage. "Where are we?" I asked.

Travis's hand ironed over the flat of my stomach as he leaned back to reveal the one secret that made me scream.

"Oh, no," I cried. "You killed him, too?"

Travis draped his torso over my pelvis and lay on top of me. His warm, solid flesh made me squirm. Looking me in the eye, he shrugged. "I suppose I did."

Skinny Tree Brett Gallagher was slumped in the arm chair in the corner of the room, his head hanging back, looking like he had been propped up just so I could see the monster Travis was. If he wanted me to be scared, it worked. I knew if I didn't go along with his master plan, I would be next to die.

Without thinking, my entire body went into a fit as I thrashed against the leather restraints, snapping against the bedframe, trying to break myself free.

Travis watched and laughed. "You're a fighter, Samantha." He clapped his hands. "That's why I chose you."

After a minute of giving it my all with nothing to show for it, I finally gave up. "Chose me for what?"

Travis's voice raised with delight. "To tell my story."

I couldn't look him in the eye. Didn't want to. "I didn't tell your story," I said to the wall.

"No, you're right. You didn't." He sounded disappointed. Then he sighed, "But you will."

I couldn't stop glancing at Brett. I felt guilty for blaming him for something I now knew Travis was responsible for. It wasn't fair. I was ashamed with jumping to conclusions before getting all the facts.

Travis saw me staring. "Brett was too smart for his own good."

Our eyes met. "And that's why you killed him?"

A spark caught his eye. "You didn't like him either."

"But not enough to want him dead."

Travis crawled his way up my body until I could smell his breath on my face. Turning away, he palmed my cheek and forced me to look into his crazed eyes. "God, you're so beautiful."

I thrashed my neck back and forth, shaking his hand off my face. It worked, but only for a second. He came back harder than before, pinching my mouth between his fingers as he shoved his tongue into my mouth. The taste of energy drink had me spitting him out as quickly as I could. Now I knew this wasn't going to end well.

Travis rolled off the bed, laughing, and grabbed his crotch as he moved to stand next to Brett. He fisted Brett's hair, held his head up, and laughed.

Inside, I began to cry. I couldn't take it anymore.

"He should have just kept quiet about what he found." Travis looked at Brett as he spoke. "But he didn't."

Soon, anger replaced my feelings of sadness. "What are you talking about?"

Travis stepped to the bed, ran the backs of his nails up the middle of my foot, causing my toes to curl. I regretted it the moment it happened because I knew what he'd say next.

"Do you do that when you orgasm, too?"

Ignoring his comment, I asked, "What did Brett find?"

The bed sank beneath Travis's weight. He kept touching random parts of my body that made me squirm, no matter how hard I tried to resist. He was playing with me—as he had done all along, even before he had me nearly naked in his bed.

"Brett came to me and said he discovered who hacked the paper."

"It was you. He beat you at your own game."

Travis turned and looked at Brett. "If you consider that winning, then I guess he did." He laughed.

I thought back to the night I thought I was being framed for Richard Thompson's murder. The gunshot that took Garcia's life was still ringing in my ears, and I remembered the chase Loxley put us on when trying to learn who was behind these killings. It stung to know I missed the clues. All this time, Travis hid in plain sight and made me trust him.

I said, "Brett knew the truth."

"Only about the paper. But even that was too much to risk. I could feel the walls closing in around me."

"Why did you do it?"

Travis dropped his head and chuckled. "People were happy that I was killing these greedy bastards."

"It doesn't make it right."

"You know," Travis looked at me with glimmering eyes, "it was your Richard Thompson article that made me realize something had to be done."

He must have hacked my computer to learn about Thompson. "He would have gone to court. Justice would have been served."

Travis was staring at his hand running up and down my thigh. "I never thought I'd enjoy killing as much as I did." He looked me in the eye, his pupils tiny pinpricks of sin. "You should have seen Richard's face when I told him why I was killing him."

I spat, "You disgust me."

"The world and its children couldn't afford to have a few bad men destroy it for the billions of others." Travis was still staring when he said, "But Richard Thompson threatened you, and I wasn't going to stand for it."

I was afraid how long he'd been watching me, reading my emails, probably monitoring my phone calls. What else did he know about me? How deep did it go?

"But then I learned what Garcia was doing to extort Richard for money. And, well, ironically, I was given an opportunity I just couldn't pass up after discovering Richard wasn't Garcia's only client."

"Garcia gave you an opportunity? I don't understand," I said.

Travis smiled. "He was my way out. With him extorting millionaires and billionaires, all I had to do was make sure he would take the blame if things started to get out of control."

I scrolled through Garcia's suicide note inside my head. Suddenly, even that came into clarity with what Travis was saying happened. Garcia killed himself not because he killed those people himself, but because he extorted them for money and was about to get caught.

"Your story should have been front page," Travis said. "Not his. You were the much better pick." Travis scooted up the bed and petted my hair. "What you were forced to endure because of what Garcia did, you must have been so scared."

Not as scared as I was now, I thought. "But you said Brett had a Bitcoin account."

Travis swung his legs over the side and was removing his pants when he said, "And he did. Just not one connected to any of this."

Travis tossed his pants to the floor, removed his shirt, and crawled into bed, snuggling up beside me. I trembled when he started peppering kisses across my body and squeezing my breasts inside his hand.

"Travis, stop."

He picked his head up. "All I ever wanted was for you to see me."

"I see you."

"No, Precious. You don't. And that, my dear, is the problem." He stared at my face as he wedged his fingers under the elastic waistband of my underwear.

I swallowed a single breath and kept asking him to stop. He only seemed to be inspired by my pleas. Soon, my underwear was pulled down past my knees. He positioned himself over me and I turned my neck, retreating someplace deep inside my mind, not wanting to remember what was about to happen.

Travis kissed me and told me how much he loved me. But I couldn't move, couldn't escape what was about to happen to me. Then, as if having my prayers answered, I heard the front door to the duplex crash open.

Travis startled at the sound and fell off the bed.

"Help!" I screamed, before Travis muffled my calls with his hand.

I heard boots clearing the bedroom across the hall, marching closer with each second that passed. I wiggled my jaw and was finally able to close my teeth into Travis's calloused flesh. A painful growl ripped through the air and I started screaming again for someone to come save me.

Next thing I knew, the SWAT team was surrounding the bed and shouting for Travis to get down on the floor and show his hands. I closed my eyes, not caring that I was naked. I could breathe again.

A sheet was quickly draped over my body and I opened my eyes.

"Are you all right?" an officer asked.

I nodded.

The officer unbound my limbs and I sat up in bed as soon as I was free. Wrapping the sheet around my shoulders, I covered myself up and watched Travis get handcuffed and escorted out of the house.

I was next to leave.

The officer who saved me kept me steady on my feet as I stared into the crimson and blue emergency lights flickering across the sky. News vans were already on scene, and so was Dawson.

"I'll take it from here," King said, running up to my side, looping his thick arm around my waist.

I hung off his familiar shoulder as he walked me to the waiting ambulance. Once inside the bus, I apologized for leaving the motel without telling him where I was going. But all he cared to know was that I hadn't been hurt.

"No," I said. "You got here just in time."

King wrapped his arms around me and gave me the biggest hug of our lives. We both knew I was lucky to have escaped.

"Sam," I heard my name being called out. "Holy shit." Erin hit the brakes and immediately did a once over. I was a sad looking sight, but I didn't care. Not now that I was surrounded by the ones I loved. "I came as soon as I heard it over the scanner," she said.

"You're late," I teased.

Erin frowned, and I knew she felt bad for not being there to protect me.

"But we got him." My smile hit my eyes. "We got Loxley."

Erin hugged me. "Thank God it's over."

CHAPTER EIGHTY

Six weeks later...

Erin's home office was silent except for the persistent clicking of her computer mouse. The clock was approaching 6PM but it felt closer to midnight. We'd been working nonstop in the weeks since Travis was arrested, feeling like it was our personal duty to settle the anger boiling over between the city's different socioeconomic classes.

"That should finish it," Erin said as she fell back into her high-backed leather chair.

"Good work." We shared a smile—a sense of satisfaction falling over us. With our last episode now edited, all that was left was releasing it to our anxiously awaiting listeners.

"I need a beer." Erin stood and headed toward the kitchen. "You want one?"

I shook my head no and rubbed the exhaustion from my eyes. "King is taking me to dinner."

"C'mon. Celebrate with me."

I gave her a look and finally agreed. We deserved this. "Okay."

Erin smacked her palms together and smiled. "That's my girl."

I called after her. "Just one though."

Erin said something about it being impossible to only have one drink as I tipped forward to collect my notes about Loxley spread out on Erin's desk.

Everything was laid out like an outline to a novel. The details to what happened, when, and who was involved. Having to relive our investigation was both healing and eye-opening. With each new episode we released weekly, I listened to Erin tell the story as if I hadn't experienced it firsthand. It was interesting, and bone-quaking frightening. A picture of Ronald Hyland made me think how lucky he was to make it out alive.

Travis had deceived Garcia into thinking Hyland was someone he wasn't. Even I was fooled into believing Damien Black and Ronald Hyland were orchestrating a scheme to have the *Times* purchase Hyland's security software for surveillance purposes. But now we knew it was all designed to turn our heads in the opposite direction Travis was moving.

The same happened to Aaron Martinez, but fortunately the police were already onto Travis. After the investigation was wrapped up and all the evidence had been collected, no charges were ever filed against Aaron. All he left behind was the poem that nudged me closer to Travis and nearly got me killed.

My cellphone vibrated with an incoming call. I screened it to see who was calling. "This is Damien Black's office," I teased.

Susan responded, "Not funny, Sam."

"No?"

"No." Susan sighed and I knew that her one date with him would be her last. Then she said, "Damien is a sweet man, and he got what he was after with Marion taking first at the event, but we're just not a good fit."

I understood, but I wondered if it was really just a matter of bad timing. Susan never spoke about it much, but I assumed she was still recovering from Benjamin's move to New England.

"What about a marathon?" she said.

A few weeks after Joey Garcia's private funeral, Cecelia surprised me with a phone call asking me if Susan was still interested in hosting a fundraiser to help pay for Katie's medical costs. Of course I knew Susan would help, and now we were both deciding on an event that would create the biggest splash.

"A marathon sounds great."

"The buzz would be phenomenal. And we don't have to limit ourselves to only having it be about Katie."

I imagined what it would be like—could see thousands of runners pounding their feet into the pavement as they raced down Colfax. I liked the idea, and something told me that Cecelia would also prefer her daughter not to be the face of the event, but there was something I was still confused about.

"Isn't there a marathon coming up?"

"Yes."

"Then does it make sense to do another?"

"I'm working on permits now," Susan said with a cheer, "and we might be able to have this happen soon."

Now I knew there was more to her plan. "How soon?"

"Like, within the week."

The same time as the other one. I felt the crown of my head pull to the ceiling. "You can organize an event that quick?"

"Don't be mad, but I've been discussing this with city officials for the last couple of weeks."

She didn't have to tell me why. I already knew the reason. We'd done everything we could to keep Garcia's extortion quiet, and Susan—as well as the rest of us—were crossing our fingers that his secret would follow him to the grave. It appeared they had, and it was now time to move forward.

"I know who the organizers are personally, and I've talked them into letting us join them."

"And they're cool with this?"

"Thrilled."

"Then I'll let Cecelia know."

"This is going to be phenomenal, Sam."

"With you at the helm," I smiled, "I have no doubt."

As soon as I was off the phone, I thought about Garcia's empty cubicle at the *Times*. We were out another reporter. I wasn't sure we'd ever have another business correspondent again—let alone an IT team that wasn't outsourced to some frat boy straight out of college.

"Here you are, my lady."

Erin handed me an opened bottle and fell into her chair. I closed my eyes and took a pull from the microbrew, letting the fizz bubble and pop on my tongue, before swallowing it down. It relaxed and eased the tension I'd been holding between my shoulders.

"It still doesn't feel real," I said, opening my eyes.

Erin held my gaze, nodding. "I know."

I flicked my gaze to my phone. "How can we ever trust our devices ever again?"

"We can't."

We sipped our beers in silence, letting our thoughts churn over inside our heads until they hardened like concrete. It was a sad but true reality we lived in. Our computers were the best—*and* worst—things that ever happened to us. I kept wondering if I could have done something differently that would have prevented any of this from happening. I wasn't sure I could have, but it did seem my Thompson article was what started it all.

"I should have never published my story on Thompson."

Erin's expression hardened. "Don't do this to yourself."

If Skinny Tree Brett Gallagher never discovered Garcia was the one to have used my story to blackmail Richard Thompson, would he have also never found Garcia's other crimes? And would that have been enough to prevent Travis from choosing his targets?

I finished my beer and set the empty on the desk. Erin asked me if I changed my mind in wanting another. I shook my head no just as I heard a knock on her front door.

I made my way to the front of the house and opened the door for King. I latched onto him, loving how his strong hands clamped onto my waist. Standing on my toes, I peered into his glistening eyes and kissed him. He kissed me back, and I knew tonight would be special.

"Drinking already?" he asked.

"Celebrating."

"Would you like one?" Erin was holding our empties as she passed behind us.

"Hmm... I think I would." King closed the door behind him, smiled, and threaded his fingers through mine as he led me into the kitchen.

The three of us sat at the kitchen table, sharing stories over drinks, when Erin's doorbell rang. She glanced at the clock. "Are you expecting anyone?" she asked me.

I shook my head no.

"I wonder who this can be," Erin said as she went to answer the door.

I reached for King's hand. "Mason is having a friend over tonight and my sister said she can stay with them. I could stay the night at your place, if you want?"

King got that fiery look in his eye that said he couldn't wait to have me all to himself. "My place, huh?"

My eyes crinkled at the corners. "Or you can always send me home after you wine and dine me."

King leaned closer and pressed his lips softly against mine. My body lit on fire as the buzz of electricity tingled up and down my spine. "I'd love to take you home."

My lips parted and just as King pressed his tongue against mine, Erin let out a scream.

We ran to see what the commotion was. Erin was stomping her foot hard against the porch as she danced around in a circle screaming, "Fire! Fire! Fire!"

King rushed to her side, quickly putting out the paper bag with a single stomp of his shoe. I stared in disbelief as the burnt bag smoldered beneath their shoes. But all I could see was a note pinned to Erin's front door. Taking it between my hands, I felt the tips of my fingers go cold.

"Punk kids think they can get away with this behavior just —" Erin stopped when she saw me reading the note. "What's that?" she asked.

I flicked my gaze up to King. "Were you followed here?"

"Why do you ask?"

"Sam, what are you reading?" Erin lifted her foot and shook off the embers. "Was that left on my door?"

My heart was knocking against my chest as I nodded. Looking Erin in the eye, I said, "I don't think it was meant for you."

Her brow furrowed. "Then who is it for?"

I flicked my gaze to King. "Him."

King took the note into his hand and read the words still scrolling across the front of my mind.

Erin asked, "What's it say?"

King clenched his jaw and turned to face the street. I watched as his head swiveled back and forth as he looked to see who might have left this message for him. But I knew whoever did it was long gone. *But would they come back?*

"What'd it say?" Erin whispered into my ear.

With pale cheeks, I muttered, "You haven't forgotten about me, have you? Of course you have. Burn in hell, pig."

Tap here and read the next story in the series, BURN IN BELL. You won't want to miss this chilling mystery thriller that will have you hanging onto your seat as you race to the dramatic suspense-filled ending.

A WORD FROM JEREMY

Thank you for reading BELL TO PAY. If you enjoyed the book and would like to see more Samantha Bell crime thrillers, **please consider leaving a review on Amazon**. Even a few words would be appreciated and will help persuade what book I will write for you next.

AFTERWORD

One of the things I love best about writing these mystery thrillers is the opportunity to connect with my readers. It means the world to me that you read my book, but hearing from you is second to none. Your words inspire me to keep creating memorable stories you can't wait to tell your friends about. No matter how you choose to reach out - whether through email, on Facebook, or through an Amazon review - I thank you for taking the time to help spread the word about my books. I couldn't do this without YOU. So, please, keep sending me notes of encouragement and words of wisdom and, in return, I'll continue giving you the best stories I can tell.

ABOUT THE AUTHOR

Waldron lives in Vermont with his wife and two children.

Receive updates, exclusive content, and **new book release announcements** by signing up to his newsletter at: www.JeremyWaldron.com

Follow him @jeremywaldronauthor

facebook.com/jeremywaldronauthor

instagram.com/jeremywaldronauthor

bookbub.com/profile/83284054